At fifteen, Margaret entered the firm of Madame Rosa's: Fashionable Dressmakers.

Her mother had hysterics and was drunk for three days. Thereafter she invented a story that Margaret went daily to be an unpaid companion to a rich old lady, an illusion which Margaret saw no point in denying if it kept her mother happy.

Within three years, Madame Rosa, who knew a good thing when she saw it, released her from her apprenticeship and made her third assistant with a wage of fifteen shillings a week and twopence in the pound on her sales. Triumphantly she put her red hair up and made herself a smart black showroom dress. Life had begun . . .

JOSEPHINE EDGAR

Margaret Normanby

GRAFTON BOOKS

A Division of the Collins Publishing Group

LONDON GLASGOW
TORONTO SYDNEY AUCKLAND

Grafton Books
A Division of the Collins Publishing Group
8 Grafton Street, London W1X 3LA

Published by Grafton Books 1986
Reprinted 1986, 1987

First published in Great Britain by
Judy Piatkus (Publishers) Limited 1983

Copyright © 1983 by Josephine Edgar

ISBN 0-586-06657-8

Printed and bound in Great Britain by
Collins, Glasgow

Set in Times

PROLOGUE

The Ball at Danesfell Abbey

By the time she could walk, Florence Jagger had accepted the power of her own spectacular beauty. The image in her mirror confirmed it, as did the adoration in her parents' eyes.

Thomas and Sarah Jagger were in their early forties when she was born and like the legendary parents in fairy tales had come to give up all hope of a family when they were blessed with this radiant baby on whom they could lavish their affection and spend their considerable wealth.

Nothing was too good for her. When she was eight Thomas bought ten acres of fertile land high above the town of Thornsby, on the edge of the moors, and began to build the fine house of Cliffs Edge and lay out the orchards and gardens. The comfortable old Master's House at the gateway of his Britannia Mills was not good enough for his treasured little daughter.

As Florence grew, the adoration spread to friends and servants, passers-by, and even the rough factory women who worked for her father and their pale, ragged children, would stop, and smile and their faces would light up with wistful pleasure when they saw Tom Jagger's 'gradely little lass'.

The little girl developed a queenly manner and a winning, wheedling charm. She was finicky and delicate, she shrank from dirt and ugliness or anything coarse or ugly, cried prettily when she could not get her own way and, occasionally, went into despairing tantrums over nothing at all, which the doctor put down to her delicate constitution.

5

It was a relief when the splendid new house was finished and they could move out of the noisy, dirty, industrial town into the big white stucco house, set among lawns and orchards, conservatories and shrubberies, with extensive stables for the new pair of horses that would draw the fine new carriage.

From an adorable baby Florence grew into an exquisite little girl. At fourteen, amid many heart-searchings, she was sent to an exclusive finishing school in Scarborough to correct her Northern accent, to learn to dance and play the piano adequately and to speak a little French, but chiefly to meet and make friends among the rich and sometimes aristocratic girls who could afford to go there.

At school the other girls fell in love with her and vied jealously for her friendship. The mistress spoiled and petted her and she was never punished, and everyone cried when at sixteen she left to be launched into local society.

Mr and Mrs Jagger entertained lavishly for her and were entertained in return. Young men called with posies, and at parties and picnics gazed with longing and sang romantic ballads of lifelong devotion. At the balls she attended throughout the county she was besieged by them as they begged for dances. In their eyes she saw the familiar devotion which she had come to regard as her due. She was not tempted by their fervent proposals – they were mostly the sons of rich local tradesmen and manufacturers, and Florence was looking for a fairy prince.

No one even suggested that age, poverty, pain or disappointment could touch her. If anything she really wanted was denied her, wheedling, tantrums and tears soon defeated Tom Jagger and her mother. Her one great talent was producing herself and she had developed an extravagant but exquisite taste in clothes to enhance her fragile loveliness.

If there was one ominous sign it was the fits of deep despair at trivial disappointments. This was put down to her sensitive temperament, and she was at once consoled with presents, a little rest in bed, trips to fashionable spas or smart watering resorts for that most efficacious of remedies, a change of air. The only books she read were foolish romances about high-born heroines who married into the peerage.

Hers was not the placid sweetness, beloved in the novels, of the type that develops into the gentle wife and loving mother. Nor had she the proud, carved beauty that retains its structure into old age. It was the emphemeral quality of the rose. A silken, pink-flushed skin, blue eyes almost too large for her delicious little face, golden-brown lashes that lifted and fluttered and in seconds could be spangled by reproachful tears. Her hair was fair, silky and fine. Although she was only medium height, her hands and feet were small, her waist an incredible twenty inches, and her neck long, like the stem of a delicate flower. She was the archetypal mid-Victorian beauty.

The love she inspired in men was not immediately sexual – it was a desire to shelter and protect her. No rough hand must touch her, no coarse word be spoken in her presence. And, tragically, she believed all this from the day she was born until the night of her wedding to Richard Normanby. Life's basic reality came into her room that night and brought a shock from which she never recovered.

Florence met Richard at a great ball at Danesfell Abbey which his father, Sir Wykeham Normanby, and his wife gave to the gentry, the tenants of their estate and the municipal dignitaries and rich businessfolk of

Thornsby town, so that the Jagger family were automatically invited.

This was a political occasion. The ball was to introduce Richard as prospective candidate for the constituency. Sir Wykeham had held the seat himself for many years, but the frequent and tiring journeys to and from Westminster were becoming too much for him, and the dwindling resources of his heritage demanded his continual presence at home, so he had decided at the next election his elder son Richard should stand in his stead.

The Normanbys were rigidly opposed to Parliamentary reform. Or, indeed, anything that might interfere with their hereditary rights.

Sir Wykeham hoped the responsibility would keep Richard out of mischief. He was by no means a sober, upright, young man suitable to become a Member of Parliament, but he *was* local, of a fine old family and should understand the local problems. And he had an irresistible, scapegrace appeal for both men and women. A handsome fellow, a fine rider to hounds, popular in local society and cutting a great dash in London.

The day preceding the ball, Florence was in such a state of excitement her mother had sent her to bed for the afternoon with the curtains drawn, and a cup of warm milk laced with brandy to settle her. It did not. She lay awake, vibrant with anticipation. This was a real ball – not a dull, municipal affair. She would, of course, be the most beautiful girl there. Her dress, made in Leeds from a Worth design and of French imported silks, had cost enough to keep a working family for a year. She did not doubt that she would be the centre of all eyes – and she was right.

At last it was time to dress. She stood in her fine cambric chemise and long ankle-length pantaloons edged with French lace, a tightly-laced blue satin corset rigidly

8

compressing her tiny waist. Her stockings were white silk, her satin dancing-pumps rose-pink. Jany Leck, her stumpy, dwarfish little maid, assisted by a downstairs girl, lifted the tape-and-whalebone crinoline frame over her head; then the white muslin petticoat edged with lace; then the rose-coloured taffeta underskirt with lace-edged flounces, and finally the dress skirt of pale pink rose satin masked with white silk gauze, looped with clusters of artificial wild roses. The pointed bodice went on like a jacket, framing her white shoulders with gauze and rose clusters, invisibly crosshooked in front, and button-looped to the skirt, the join hidden by a sash of azure-coloured satin. Small blue bows held back the bunches of curls from her forehead, with a spray of single blossoms fastening those on her neck. Fine white kid gloves were drawn up to her elbows. In one hand she held a bouquet of roses and stephanotis in a silver holder. On her wrist was a pearl-embroidered reticule containing a lace handkerchief and a crystal flask of smelling salts. She was ready.

The two servants, who had been dressing her for two hours, were flushed with triumph.

'Eh, Miss Flo,' said the young housemaid, 'You're a reight picture. Fit to eat you are, fer sure.'

Tiny Jane Leck, whom Mrs Jagger had brought from the Foundlings to wait on Florence, was speechless with pleasure. She had pressed every frill and goffered every piece of lace. Tears of delight ran down her shiny little moon-face to see her darling looking so beautiful.

Florence ran downstairs to the drawing-room, her pupils so distended with excitement that her pale blue eyes looked almost black. Her heart was fluttering, her pulse racing, her small breasts rising and falling rapidly beneath the tight bodice. Every mirror in the hall as she passed flashed back a picture of an angelic, rosy girl.

Tom Jagger, beaming but uncomfortable in his expensive new evening suit, was waiting for her. Her mother, still a handsome woman, wore brilliant blue taffeta and a blue-and-yellow paradise plume encircling her black hair.

Since Florence had returned from her exclusive boarding school she had seen her parents through different eyes. She loved them dearly, of course. But she wished their accents were more refined and that her father lived on an income like a gentleman and did not work every day down at the mills. She wished her mother would not wear such brilliant colours and that neither of them would praise her so volubly in public. There was no need – it was *so* vulgar and everyone could see, just by looking at her, how lovely she was.

Mrs Jagger mopped her eyes – she could never believe that she and Tom had produced this blossom of a girl.

'Flo, love, there won't be a lass in the whole county to hold a candle to you.'

'Thank you, Mama. Do I look nice, Papa? Am I pretty?'

His ruddy face was full of pride. He put his arm about her and she leaned away so that not even a curl should be disarrayed by his clumsiness.

'My love,' he said, and kissed her. He took a jeweller's case from his pocket. Inside was a necklace of rose-diamonds, the small jewelled flowers set in invisible springs so that they quivered and glittered at her every movement. It was a piece she had coveted for weeks.

'Oh, Papa! How lovely.' A shadow of doubt crossed her face. 'Am I old enough for diamonds? But this is so dainty – not one of those great heavy pieces.' He fastened it round her neck and stood back.

'It looks grand. It cost a pretty penny too. Stones of the first water, t'chap said. Nothing's too good for my little princess, I told him. There won't be many lasses there tonight wi' such a piece.'

'Do you think Mr Richard Normanby will dance with me?'

'O' course he will,' said Tom staunchly. 'If you were at Marlborough House or Buckingham Palace I reckon the Prince of Wales hisself would want every dance wi' you, and all the Dukes and Earls lining up beside him.'

Florence's eyes sparkled, and she waltzed round the room, watching herself in the mirrors.

'One day I'll marry, and be a great lady, and drive in the Park in London in my carriage and pair, and all the people will stop and say how pretty I am.'

Mrs Jagger frowned, mistrusting the dark brilliance of her daughter's eyes – knowing how quickly this wild elation could turn to depression and tears.

'Now, calm down, love. Put your cloak on. Don't get worked up, and don't go on at her, Tom, or when she gets to Danesfell she'll be fit for nothing.'

So Florence was wrapped in her white velvet cloak, quilted inside with silk and the hood lined with white fur. In the waiting carriage there were footwarmers, and muffs with hot-water bottles inside, and warm rugs to tuck about their knees. Outside the night was dank and misty, but the carriage was safe and warm and the evening ahead pregnant with undreamed of triumphs.

Sir Wykeham stood at the foot of the great staircase with his wife and his two sons. George, in his new scarlet uniform a plain, sandy boy, sensible like his mother, and Richard, a being from another world, as different from the local beaux as a racehorse is different from a rough hill pony. The cut of his perfect evening suit moulded smoothly to his slender shoulders, the gleaming perfection of his linen, the dark coppery curls combed fashionably over his forehead, his lean, tanned, mischievous face and the true Normanby eyes, violet-blue, smudged in with black lashes inherited from some Irish ancestor, sent every Thornsby girl yearning and dreaming. Particularly Florence.

He saw her at once. His eyes never left her as she moved slowly up the reception line with her parents until at last he took her hand and importunately asked for the first dance, the Grand Parade. Would she honour him by opening the ball with him?

Inside the great ballroom, candle and firelight glittered on gilt and crystal. It was heavy with the scent of the banked up flowers and the faint, acrid smell of new cloth as the men in their tight evening clothes began to sweat a little in the heat.

Young Henry Grimshaw stood with his father waiting for Florence to enter the ballroom, and when she did, between her mother and father, his eyes never left her.

Henry was stocky compared to Richard Normanby, broad-shouldered, narrow-waisted like a young fighting bull, broad-browed and flaxen-haired, with luminous light-grey eyes and a straight-lipped mouth which did not easily smile. He neither felt nor looked relaxed in his ill-made, old-fashioned evening clothes, nor in the company about him. He was happier on the rag stone sets of the Calder Beck Mills than in a ballroom.

He had known Florence when she was a child still living in the Masters' House at Britannia Mills, which were separated from his father's factory at Calder Beck by half-a-mile of open land belonging to Sir Wykeham Normanby. It was called the Water Meadows and the little Calder Beck still flowed unpolluted through grey granite outcrops, and there were willows and alders, and in the spring wild flowers. Henry still lived with his father and his sister, Millicent, at the Master's House at Calder Beck Mills.

Both Dyson Grimshaw and Tom Jagger wanted to buy the Water Meadows. They were rivals in business and there was no friendship between them. Henry's meetings with Florence had been stolen and secret, a strange, halcyon interlude of boyish love.

He had been a rough-clad lad, neglected by a sick mother and a penny-pinching bully of a father. His school holidays were spent working in the Mill, hauling the piece trolleys and sweeping up with the other lads. Dyson believed in his son working his way up from the factory floor.

Henry agreed with that. To co-ordinate raw materials, machines, men, money and power into a working whole was wonderful, what was called management, and that was what he wanted to do. What he could not stand were the vicious blows when he was too small to protect himself, the deprecatory baiting, the mocking of his hard-earned education and his dreams of a better life. Worst of all the mean tyranny towards his mother and sister.

But at the break for snap, the bread and jam and cold tea which the boys took at mid-morning, he would get through a hole in the wall into the Water Meadows and spend the half-hour wandering, or studying; and there, one day he found the ten-year-old Florence sitting on a wall looking down at him.

'Lift me down, boy,' she had commanded and he had obeyed. It was like holding a bird, she was so light and fragile. She smelled like a flower garden. The silk of her dress caught on his work-roughened hands.

The only girls he knew were the rough mill children and his glowering, stage-struck, handsome little sister, Millicent. This shining fair child was like a vision in her pale blue muslin and starched, frilled pinafore. She wore little white kid boots. She was so clean. Her curls shook like golden bells at every toss of her head. Her eyes were so big and so blue.

Florence simply accepted him as another devoted slave as he carried her over the stream, picked flowers for her, caught a fish and helped her to ride the pit ponies, falling in with her fantasies when she played the Royal Princess.

Then Mrs Jagger found out and she was whisked indignantly away, and shortly afterwards the Jaggers moved to Cliffs Edge five miles out of the town, high up on the moors.

Sometimes Henry would glimpse her riding with her mother in Tom Jagger's fine new carriage, and she would smile vaguely and he told himself that she remembered. And now, here she was, a grown-up girl in a dress like an upturned rose, more beautiful than ever, and half-remembered lines of poetry went through his head at the sight of her. *'I dare thee but to breathe upon my love.'* *'She is my lady, oh, she is my love. Oh, that she knew she were.'* The room seemed to darken, and then blaze with light, until Dyson Grimshaw, who had never read a line of poetry in his life, poked him in the ribs and nodded meaningfully across the floor.

Thomas Jagger, ruddy-complexioned and silver-haired, more like a moorland farmer than a successful mill-owner, returned the nod distantly. He disliked Dyson, considering him mean-spirited and, or so he had heard, cruel to his family. But he liked young Henry very well.

A bugle-call sounded, signalling the Grand Parade, and people began to move out on to the floor and line up with their partners. Richard was still receiving the latecoming guests.

'Get over there and ask Jagger's lass to dance with thee,' ordered Dyson.

'I'd rather not, Dad.'

14

'"I'd rather not, Dad",' He mimicked his son's more refined accents. 'Think you're not good enough?'

'Maybe.'

'It's not what you'd reither do – it's what I tell you to do. Jagger is the warmest man in the valley and that lass of his is a good match. Get over there and ask her to dance, or God love me when we get back home I'll tek a belt to you as I did when thou wast a bairn.'

'That was a great while ago,' said Henry drily. It was some years since his father had beaten him. But he flexed his broad shoulders and, his hands sweating in his tight white gloves, his heart bursting with anxiety, set off across the floor towards Florence and her parents, feeling like a great country bumpkin in his thick, local-made suit with its old-fashioned knee-breeches. She looked to him so ethereal that a breath of wind might blow her away. The thought of touching her made him dizzy.

'Miss Jagger . . . Florence,' he bowed, 'do you remember me?'

A faint puzzlement and then sudden enlightenment.

'Oh, *Henry Grimshaw!* Yes, of course.' Her smile was automatic. She was looking over his shoulder for Richard Normanby. If he did not come she would die. She had refused a dozen other young men. 'It's such a long time ago. I didn't know you danced.'

'I've learned a lot of things since the old valley days.'

A frown, light as a butterfly's shadow, darkened her face.

'Oh, don't talk to me about those days. That awful house at the Mill. The noise! The smells! Those dreadful men swearing and shouting at the horses. I declare I could not ask a friend to tea I was so ashamed!'

'But don't you remember the Water Meadows?' he persisted. 'When I used to scramble through the hole and lift you down from your wall? When we rode the blind

15

pit ponies they brought there to rest? And the fish in the beck? Remember when I caught a trout? Before you went away to school?'

But she was not listening. She was thinking of Richard. How handsome he was. How charming his deep, drawling, slightly arrogant voice. The flowers in her silver holder shook in her hands, tears trembled on her long lashes. He *must* come.

'Won't you dance with me, Florence?'

She could not stand with her parents and not dance. She must have a partner even if it were only awkward Henry Grimshaw in his thick ugly suit and ridiculous knee-breeches.

He offered his arm, and she put her white gloved hand out tentatively, but in that moment Richard Normanby pushed through the crowd to her side, snatching up her hand before it could rest on Henry's arm, smiling his apologies.

'I couldn't get away – but I told them to hold the Parade for us. You didn't think I was not coming? I'm not sure that I'm so keen on going into politics – it would be a dreadful bore if it kept me from seeing you.'

She was all smiles again.

Henry said assertively. 'Miss Jagger was about to dance with me.'

Richard turned and stared at him blankly.

'Who the devil is this?' he demanded.

'This is young Henry Grimshaw,' Mr Jagger said hurriedly, 'Mr Dyson's son from Calder Beck.'

'Indeed. Then he had better go back to Calder Beck.'

Characteristically Richard forgot the impression of kindly interest he was supposed to make on the local people. He looked at the thickset boy with his thatch of yellow hair and allowed his glance to slide mockingly over the old-fashioned, local-made clothes.

'My dear fellow,' he said smoothly, 'you must be mistaken. Miss Florence is promised to me – besides, she could not possibly take the floor with a fellow wearing those unspeakable breeches.'

There was a faint ripple of laughter from the people in ear-shot. Henry went bright red and strode back across the room.

Signalling to the orchestra Richard led Florence to the head of the Parade, bowed with smiling grace and her huge skirt billowed about her as she curtseyed, and then they were off round the ballroom, hand-in-hand, in the pretty mazurka-like change of step, smiling delightedly into each other's eyes.

Henry took refuge in the conservatory. One day he swore he would wipe the insolent smile from Richard's handsome face. He was not yet twenty, and he had no money of his own. Dyson paid him no wages, grudgingly giving him pocket-money in return for hard and devoted work. He was sick of it.

Sometimes he felt like one of the boilers that drove the steam engine at the mill – close the cocks and it would burst. He felt that he too would split open one day through sheer frustration and blow into smithereens.

He broke out into bitter laughter at himself. It beat cock-fighting as his father often said. For nineteen years he had put up with blows, insults and unpaid hard work, and now a pair of badly-cut breeches, for Dyson had refused to pay out for a decent suit, had brought him to rebellion.

That arrogant fop, young Normanby, had picked on his most sensitive point – his provincialism. And also, in spite of his excellent education, his lack of cultivated manners. He had been made to look a fool by someone he regarded as an idle, well-bred idiot and he bitterly

17

resented it. If his father would not pay him sufficiently then it was time he went out and worked for himself.

Dyson was by the buffet eating his way through the menu and enjoying the champagne.

He gestured to the food and said, 'Eat thy fill, lad. Tha doesn't get vittles like this every day. It's all for nowt.'

'Thank you, no.'

'I want you to speak to Sir Wykeham for me,' said Dyson slyly, 'Tell him I'll vote for that young wretch of his if he'll let me have t'Water Meadows at my price.'

'You'll have to speak to him yourself,' said Henry, 'I'm going now.'

'You're not going until I say.'

Richard and Florence swayed past them in a waltz, her skirts swirling in a rosy whirlpool, her lips parted, her eyes bright with delight. She smiled as she passed but she did not know at whom she smiled.

Dyson grinned shrewdly.

'Nay, never fear.' He sneered, 'The Normanbys won't buy a mare out of Jagger's stable. They'll want breeding as well as brass. They're gentry.'

'I'm going, Father. I'll walk home. Goodnight.'

As Henry crossed the hall he saw Thomas Jagger talking to a group of Thornsby businessmen. He went across to him.

'I'm going now, Sir.'

'I don't blame you, lad,' said Thomas. 'My feet are killing me. But Florence will dance until dawn, like as not.'

'Can you spare me a moment, Sir?'

They moved away to a quiet corner.

'Mr Jagger, my father is planning to speak to Sir Wykeham about the Water Meadows tonight. He had already made an offer.'

Thomas looked startled. He had always liked him, but disloyalty was something he could not understand.

'It's all right,' said Thomas, guessing his thoughts. 'I'm leaving Dad.'

'When?'

'Right now. I'll clear out of the house tomorrow.'

'Aye, well, he's been a bad father, and he's known to be a bad master. What wilt tha do?'

'Management. I know the trade floor up. I've had the schooling for the paperwork, and I've done all ours since I left the Clothmakers School. I know all that goes on in the sheds. I know the costing and the suppliers, and I can handle the men. Father would not let me handle the buying and marketing, and that's what I want to learn, because that's the first part of management.'

'Wilt tha come to me?' said Thomas impulsively. 'I could do with some honest help. Someone I could trust.'

Henry's face lit with delight.

'It was what I was hoping you would say. You're more progressive at Britannia. Do you really mean it, Sir?'

'That I do.' Thomas himself was a little shaken. His offer had been made on the impulse, thinking Dyson Grimshaw was a fool to let such a likely son leave him.

'I'm free now. I've no contract with Father, and he's paid me no wages. He drew a long breath, glanced down at his offending clothes, and said bitterly, 'Lad's pocket-money.' He seemed to have grown in stature during the last few minutes. 'I'll tell him tomorrow, and come to see you.'

They shook hands on it. Then Henry said, 'I'd put that offer into Sir Wykeham tonight – Dad could have raised his bid months ago! It'll be a grand property for whoever gets it.'

'Right.' They shook hands again. Thomas wished he had such a son to help him.

Henry walked home, still spinning dreams. He would work his heart out at Britannia. He would become Thomas's right-hand man – he would get to know Florence better and try to please her. Ultimately she would recognize the worth of his love and realize that all he wanted was to take every care from her and cherish her for the rest of their days.

But in the Spring of the following year she became engaged to Richard Normanby, and for a few days Henry thought he would have to leave Britannia and go away – emigrate perhaps. But if he had lived on dreams of Florence he also had ambitions for Britannia Mills and the Water Meadows where the foundations were already being laid for a large, modern mill. If it was successful, and there was no reason to believe otherwise, Thomas would have to offer him a directorship – or a partnership – because he was beginning to rely on his judgement more and more. So he stayed. But he was grateful that he did not see Florence – she was now moving in high county society, and was rarely seen in Thornsby.

One morning in the September of that year Florence called unexpectedly at the mill. Henry had living premises on the first floor of the Master's House, and the ground floor was given over to the offices. He was just completing his morning inspection of the plant when a clerk came running to tell him that Miss Jagger was in the office asking to see her father.

'But Mr Jagger always goes to the Exchange on Wednesday.'

'Aye, so I said. She said she'd forgotten, and asked to see you.'

Henry drew in a deep breath and struggled to compose himself. 'I'll come at once,' he said.

He followed the clerk, straightening his coat, glancing nervously at his reflection in the glass of the office door.

It was nearly a year since he had seen her. The clerks had all stopped work and were staring as though an angel had dropped from heaven. The dreary office was filled by her presence, her fair slenderness enhanced by the rich wine-coloured velvet of her dress and fur-collared pelisse. The air smelled of lilies of the valley. Her big, pale blue eyes gazed at him smilingly, and her glistening curls were framed by the white flowers lining her bonnet. He felt the old, sick, hopeless longing, and wished she had not come.

Florence was taken aback by his changed appearance, trying to relate this grave, well-dressed young business-man with the shabby boy she had once played with, and the ill-dressed, thickset hobbledehoy at the ball.

'Oh, Henry, how nice you look!'

The three clerks ducked behind their desks to hide their grins. Henry frowned, two fierce lines between his brows.

'Richard will call for me in half-an-hour. Oh, dear,' she looked quite lost, 'it was so important that I should see Papa today.'

'But didn't you see your father this morning?'

'No. I have been staying at Danesfell Abbey for the races. There is a house-party. So we thought that as Richard had to come in to town I would drop in and talk with Papa while he went on to see his agent about all these boring old election matters . . .'

It was scarcely the way for the candidate's future wife to speak. Henry hurriedly ushered her into her father's private office. When she pulled off her gloves he saw the half-hoop of fine diamonds on her finger.

'May I offer you my best wishes,' he said stiffly. He

21

was damned if he was going to congratulate her on catching that popinjay Richard Normanby.

'Oh, thank you.' She looked at the ring. 'It's nice, isn't it? There are lots of jewels in the family and I shall have them all one day.'

There was a brief silence.

'Can I get you a dish of tea? My housekeeper will make it.'

'Oh, no thank you. Nothing. Unless . . .'

'Yes?'

'Perhaps a glass of Madeira? A tiny drop? It is so cold driving.'

Henry was surprised. A young lady taking wine at this hour?

'I'm afraid we only have spirits.' Mr Jagger kept glasses and a small supply of drink for customers. 'Or, wait a minute – there is some port . . .'

'Just the tiniest drop, then.'

He poured her a glass but took none himself. There was a good fire burning, and she sat next to it sipping thoughtfully. He was conscious of a change in her. A shadow, almost imperceptible like the blight on a flower. A trifle paler? A harsher line beneath the pretty cheeks? He felt it, and it made him long to protect her.

'Can I help you, Florence?'

A tiny drop of port clung to her curved pink upper lip and disconcertingly the sight of it filled him with desire.

'I wonder . . .' she said slowly, and to his distress her blue eyes suddenly swam with tears.

'Oh, Florence, please – don't cry,' he was distracted.

'I'm in such a pet,' she said pathetically, 'Papa is so mean to Richard and me.' She brightened, finished her port and held out the glass imperatively so that Henry refilled it without thinking. 'But he does take heed of what you say. He's forever saying how clever you are,

22

and boring – I mean entertaining Mama and I with your great plans. Perhaps he would listen to you?'

'Well, if you will tell me what you want me to say I will speak to him. Although I am sure Mr Jagger could not be mean to you.'

'Well,' she raised her hands hidden in her little ermine muff and gazed at him over it. It was one of her pretty tricks. Richard swore that she would rake in votes like Autumn leaves.

'Well, Sir Wykeham has very generously let us have a small house, Fellside House. I expect you know it.' Henry's brows rose. The small house must have at least ten bedrooms and twenty acres of ground. 'It will do us very well when we are in Thornsby, but when Richard is a Member of Parliament we shall need a place near Westminster, and besides,' she gave a mischievous little smile, 'he loves London life, and I am *longing* to live in London – well, for half the year at least – so we want Papa to advance us some money towards a London house. Now – some friends of Richard's have a dear little house in Suffolk street, Mayfair, nothing splendid, but a good address, and they will let it to us very favourably, all furnished, and we can take over the present servants – only six, well seven with my Lecky – and Richard's friends, Lord and Lady Derring speak very well of them. The house is only two hundred a year. The owners . . .'

'I gather Lord Derring is not the owner?'

'No. He has it on lease. He is going to live abroad for a while so we can take up the remainder of his tenancy. But the owners insist on Bank Guarantees. We are not asking Papa for any more money, you see, only a guarantee . . .'

'More?' He questioned, 'More money?'

She was affronted. 'Papa has already concluded the marriage settlement, of course.'

23

The essential Yorkshireman broke through etiquette.

'How much?' asked Henry bluntly.

'Twenty thousand pounds.'

'Good God!' It was a fortune, even for so prosperous a man as Thomas Jagger. 'The capital is secured to you?'

'Oh, *no*! The Normanby lawyers would not consider it. The marriage settlements into the family are never secured to the bride. There have been terrible scenes about it, and I am quite worn out. At one time Papa said he would withdraw his consent, and then the wedding would have had to be postponed until I was of age, and if that had happened I really would have died, and I was so ill, Papa finally agreed. But he was not happy about it.'

Henry thought this very likely. Richard could spend all his wife's marriage portion and she could do nothing about it. His dismay showed in his face.

'They are a very great family,' she faltered, 'and Richard said he couldn't wait so long . . .'

Henry tried to be firm. She was so endearing. Such a child. 'But you must be sensible, Florence. You must think of your father's interests too. Ultimately they will be yours.'

'Ultimately?'

'When you inherit his wealth.'

'Oh, that! That's *years* away. Papa will live for ages and I want my house now.' She put her small hand on his arm. 'Please, Henry, don't be mean and sanctimonious like Papa. I just can't spend all my life here. I must have some fun. I long to go into London society. Richard knows all the great people – he has actually met the Prince of Wales. It's only a small thing to ask for.'

Henry began to understand why his employer had been so irritable and preoccupied of late and had left so much of the business in his hands, neglecting his real interests while battling with the Normanby lawyers.

'How long would the tenancy be? How long would your father have to guarantee the rent?'

'Five years. By then we hope to afford something better.'

'I will tell your father that you came and why.' His broad young face with its high carved nose and jutting Grimshaw jaw was grave. 'But I cannot give him advice on so personal a matter.'

'But Papa is a very rich man – everyone says so.'

'That's as maybe. But his capital is to a great extent tied up in his business.'

'But if you own things you can raise money on them. *Richard* says so. On Cliffs Edge – it's an ugly place, anyhow, and will be too big for them when I have left. Or on a bit of the factory. The Water Meadows, for instance.'

It was the last straw – that Richard Normanby should imagine they would raise money for him on the Water Meadows, that new, wonderful project, not yet completed.

'I could not advise Mr Jagger to mortgage the Water Meadows. We . . .' in his excitement he forgot he was only an employee, 'We will be in production this time next year. It will be the most modern manufacturing business in the valley – the whole of the West Riding perhaps.'

'Oh, why is everyone so horrid to me.' The tears began to run again. 'I'm sure I am never nasty to anyone, and we have always been friends, Henry . . .'

'And still are, I hope. I'm sorry, Florence,' he said gently, 'but the settlement your father has made on you is more than generous. You will be rich. Fellside House will be, I presume, rent free.' The evasive fall of her gold-tipped lashes told him this was true. 'You could easily afford the rent of the London house: perhaps you could let it for the months you will be up here . . .'

'You are just like Papa!' She rose in a huff, her face bright with anger. 'Why are businessmen such prigs! How can we let it when we will be coming and going? And the rent is not all. There will be an establishment to keep up. Servants, a London carriage and pair, expenses for entertaining, clothes, travelling . . . all sorts of things. You and Papa have always lived here, and you can't think anything can be different.' Her nose went up and her mouth set stubbornly. 'I can see you'll be no help. I'll speak to Papa myself.'

She swept towards the door but Henry reached it before her.

'Florence,' he said hesitantly, 'I – I hold you in great regard. I will always be your friend and help you as much as I can . . .'

'Well, then,' she began eagerly.

'*No!* Your father is my employer, he has been fair and honest with me as I must be with him if I am to serve his interests. What you ask does not. But please think of me as your friend.'

'Pooh,' Florence shrugged her exasperation, looking so pretty, rosy from the heat of the fire and the two glasses of port, that he longed to take her in his arms, 'Oh, fiddlesticks! What a useless friend. What a boring prig! You can't really care for me at all.'

A clerk came in to say Mr Normanby was waiting outside and would she please come at once. Henry followed her into the street. A splendid new chaise and pair of matching bays stood waiting, a groom at their head. Richard, resplendent in a long, elegant overcoat with a single cape, and a tall grey hat, was in the driver's seat.

'Come along, dearest,' he called. 'We shall be late for

lunch. They want to leave for the course at half-past twelve.'

Henry lifted Florence up beside him, tucking the carriage rug over her knees, blushing at the glimpse of the pretty legs her tilting crinoline exposed. She gave him a half-cross, half-smiling glance, angry, but not willing to let him off the hook, as always at her most endearing when she had driven anyone to exasperation.

'Thanks, Grimshaw,' called Richard, and as Henry stood back and the groom released the bridle and leaped up behind, he tossed a gold half-sovereign down to him. Henry went scarlet at the insult. But for Florence he would have been up on the chaise and dragged him on the pavement. As it was, he stood fuming, watching the chaise clatter off over the cobbles, Richard shouting to other drivers to make way.

The colour of Henry's face faded to white. He stood motionless. A grubby urchin pulled at his elbow – one of the boys employed about the yard to sweep up after the heavy dray horses.

'Dost tha not want this then, Mister?' he asked, holding up the half-sovereign.

'*No!*' shouted Henry. He turned away and immediately swung back again, bringing two silver coins out of his pocket. 'Here – we'll make an exchange. It will buy you as much.'

He put the half-sovereign in his waistcoat pocket. He would have it pierced and fastened to his watch-chain. He needed no reminder of his love for Florence, but every time he looked at the small gold coin it would remind him how Richard Normanby had gratuitously insulted him, and that somehow, he would get his revenge.

Chapter One

When Henry Grimshaw first set eyes on Margaret Normanby she was five and he was in his twenty-sixth year.

His mind was too occupied with anxiety and emotion to take much notice of a small child but he had an impression of red hair and aggressive blue eyes which regarded him with the utmost suspicion. He did not realize that to her he was just another of those horrible men who were always worrying her Mama and Papa about money. It was at this time she had begun to think that money was the most important thing in the world and the lack of it the most humiliating.

Henry had not seen Florence since her wedding. On that day he had stood at the back of the crowd outside the Parish Church and seen her leaning on Richard's arm wearing the Normanby diamond coronet to hold her veil, with well-born little girls strewing the ground before her with petals.

Onlookers smiled and sighed at the beauty of the radiant young couple. The Normanby diamonds had been lent by the Bank which was holding them as security against loans which Sir Wykeham had incurred in paying off Richard's gambling debts, but neither Henry, nor Florence, nor Mr Jagger – or, indeed, anyone but the Bank and Sir Wykeham knew about this.

Shortly after their wedding the young Normanbys left Fellside House and went to live permanently in London. A year after that Sir Wykeham was killed in a fall from his horse, a blown hack which should never have been put at a fence, the last in his once well-filled stable. His wife, learning the full extent of his financial troubles wondered if it had been suicide, for he had always been such a fine horseman.

Richard, who at once gave up all pretence of a Parliamentary career, was now the baronet. He inherited Danesfell Abbey, a great country house and a large estate, all of which had already been ruined by bad management and his own appalling extravagance. But he had a title and his credit was still good. He and Florence, after a brief spell of mourning (she looked exquisite in black) continued their spectacular attack on London society. They moved on the fringe of the Marlborough House set, for which they were a little too young and not quite solid enough financially. HRH's high gambling days were behind him and he cultivated city gentlemen who knew about Stock Exchange tips, not youthful high-flyers.

Undeterred, the Normanbys never missed a smart race meeting, and Richard belonged to the most exclusive clubs where the play was high. They travelled to Paris, Marienbad, Baden-Baden and Biarritz in the wake of the Court, where Richard's gambling and his wife's beautiful clothes caused considerable interest. They were the handsomest and most popular young couple in English society, and were thought to have inherited considerable wealth.

It was Henry Grimshaw's first visit to the capital. When the train slowed down, hissing gently to a standstill at the great terminus, he put on his square-crowned hat and his fine tweed overcoat, took down his case, and stepped forth trying to look at ease. He looked older than his years, for the past few years at Britannia and Water Meadows had been full of anxiety which increased daily as he discovered that Thomas Jagger, now a dying man, had been bleeding his fine business of capital as Sir Wykeham Normanby had bled Danesfell.

It was mid-morning and the dirty yellow mists were vanishing beneath the wintry sunshine. London seemed vast, noisy, crowded and confusing and smelled of soot and horse-droppings. He took a hackney carriage from the rank outside the station and told the driver to take him to Suffolk Street, Mayfair, where Sir Richard and Lady Normanby lived.

When he arrived he was immediately conscious that the small, elegant mansion had an air of neglect in comparison to the properties around it. He was about to raise the knocker when the door opened sharply and he found himself looking straight into the eyes of Sir Richard Normanby.

Richard was now thirty-five, a little heavier and more dissipated than Henry remembered. But he was still a very handsome man. In his fur-collared greatcoat, a shining top hat set at an angle on his curling chestnut hair, he possessed the unassailable confidence of privilege and birth.

Henry, who never thought beyond quality and cleanliness so far as appearances were concerned, immediately became conscious of his lack of style: his square-crowned hat, his serviceable tweeds and strong leather boots.

'Devil take it,' said Richard. 'Who the deuce are you? I am expecting Lord Allyson. Not a blasted dun, are you? Because if you are you'd better wait until I get back from the races.'

Then before Henry could speak Richard recognized him.

'Of course, it's Grimshaw, old man Jagger's chap. My wife told me you were expected. Let's hope you've brought some good news, because we only hear disaster from Danesfell since my father died.'

Henry, who knew, like everyone in Thornsby, of the waste and neglect at Danesfell did not reply.

31

There was a clatter of hooves and a high-wheeled carriage driven by a sporting-looking young gentleman, sparks flying from the feet of his horse, pulled up alongside.

'Here's my friend,' said Richard. 'You haven't any tips, have you? Some of those Yorkshire stables produce some decent horseflesh.'

'I'm afraid I know very little about racehorses.'

'Damned stupid of me to expect you to,' said Richard airily. He ran down the steps, then turned and asked, 'How's that pretty sister of yours?'

'Millicent?' Henry was startled. 'What do you know of her?'

'What all Thornsby knows. That she ran off to be an actress. Did she succeed? Or did she end up on the streets like most of 'em do?'

'She has been very successful. She is playing the lead in the comedy at the New Royalty Theatre,' said Henry furiously, and immediately cursed himself for a fool.

'Really,' Richard drawled. He was putting on his long, warm gloves lined with fur against the winter cold. 'I'll have to take my wife to see her one evening. Coming, Allyson. Good day to you, Grimshaw.'

Henry fingered the gold coin on his watch-chain. For a moment he had thought that Richard was about to repeat his insult of seven years ago. He turned again to the door and knocked.

A servant appeared. A very short little woman, almost a midget, with a high, shining forehead, a button nose and eyes like gooseberries. She was neat and clean, her apron spotless, a frilled cap on her sparse, scraped-back hair, and when she spoke he knew she was from the West Riding.

'You'll be Mr Grimshaw from Mrs Jagger?' she said.

'Yes. Is Lady Normanby in?'

'Aye. Will you come up then?'

He followed her into the hall. She seemed the only servant in the house.

She led him up the stairs into a room on the first floor where he was immediately transported into the sort of shell-like cosiness which Florence always created about herself.

A pale pink room with charming gildings, a bright fire in the grate, a bowl of white violets, expensive bric-a-brac and silver-framed photographs. Florence was reclining on a chaise-longue propped up on lace-edged pillows.

His heart nearly stopped at the sight of her. A lace and satin day gown, a cap of lace and ribbons on her golden curls, her little feet thrust into pink and silver slippers, one hanging seductively from bare toes.

He stood in the doorway speechless, feeling enormous in this doll-like, overpoweringly feminine room. She stretched out a hand, and when he took it, she felt him tremble and smiled.

'Henry! Henry Grimshaw! My old playfellow and dear Papa's right-hand man. Do sit down, Henry. It is so good of you to come.'

He lowered himself on to a small, gilt, satin-upholstered chair.

'I had Mama's letter saying you were coming, and I do hope you will explain what all this fuss is about? Papa is always out of sorts in the winter. I tell him he should go abroad. Nice – or even Egypt. But he won't listen – he won't leave that silly old factory.'

Henry put his hat down carefully on the floor beside his chair. Florence saw the boy had become a powerfully-built, good-looking young man. Unpolished and provincial perhaps, but still adoring her in the old transparent way. He should not prove too difficult.

'Now, you do look quite cross. Let me get you some

tea – or perhaps a glass of Madeira? And a biscuit? Lovely. It is what I usually have at this time.' She rang the bell and the little servant appeared. 'Lecky, get some Madeira wine for Mr Grimshaw – he will take a glass with me.'

Lecky hesitated, and an ugly sharpness crept into Florence's gushing manner. 'Well? Do as you're told. Do you want to follow the other riff-raff into the streets?'

Lecky went off and returned with a silver tray, glasses and a decanter of Madeira and a dish of macaroons.

'Only one glass now, Miss Flo,' she warned, 'Think on what t'doctor said.'

As she went out Florence's hand shook so much that the decanter clattered on the glass rim.

'Please, allow me,' said Henry. He took it from her and poured the wine.

'Those old servants! They become too familiar. After all these years she never remembers to say "My Lady". Always "Miss Flo" – as though I was still at school.'

'She has been with you long?'

'Too long. Mama took her out of the Foundlings. She is devoted to me, of course, but she can be very tiresome.'

'You have not been well, Lady Normanby?'

'Please call me Florence. I'm well enough. One gets tired – at the end of the season. I shall be glad to get away to France. People are beginning to go down to the South now. It is becoming quite the thing.'

'But you must go to your mother in Yorkshire. She needs you.'

'But what can I do? I am not strong. She knows that.'

'I promised her I would persuade you to travel back with me.'

'It is impossible. We are engaged in the country this weekend. I must see my dressmaker before we go abroad. I cannot leave London. And this weekend Lady Maberley has a house-party to which I am committed. It is believed that the Royals will be there.'

'Lady Margaret Normanby has also asked me to persuade you and Sir Richard to come. It is not only your father's affairs, but your mother-in-law needs help at Danesfell.'

'But there is an *agent* to look after Danesfell, and *you* are responsible for Papa's affairs.' Her lips began to quiver. 'Why is it we are fated to be served by incompetents? Of course we should love to come up North and have a house-party for the shooting or for Christmas. But things are so expensive. I keep writing to Papa and explaining, but now he does not even answer.'

Henry closed his eyes. It was like battering one's head against a wall. Or something soft and woolly on which he could make no impression.

For the past two years he had battled with Tom Jagger, only meeting with evasions until the old man had suffered a slight apoplexy and Henry at last had access to the private ledgers and learned the truth: that money had poured out of the business into Suffolk Street. The besotted old man had paid and paid until his private investments were exhausted, and had then used the company capital, robbing himself for Florence.

'Florence!' Henry almost shouted. She shrank back, and he lowered his voice. '*There is no more money!* Your father is confused and almost speechless. Your mother has power of attorney and she must not permit any further withdrawal of capital. God knows there is little enough left.'

'But Papa is rich,' she reiterated. 'He said I should never want.'

'He has been robbing himself to give you money.'

'But there is Danesfell. The rents and the mine.'

'Sir Richard has mortgaged Danesfell to the hilt and

the mines were closed before Sir Wykeham's death. They are unworkable.'

Florence began to cry, and to pour herself another glass of Madeira.

'Richard says that is all nonsense. There is so much land. We shall just sell more land.'

'You haven't any land . . .' he gave up. 'Danesfell is not my business. My business is Britainnia and Water Meadow Mills. They are your inheritance and I must try to save them for you. Your father has no more money – what happened to your marriage portion? That was twenty thousand pounds!'

She looked at him like a frightened child, and went back helplessly to the old refrain.

'But Papa promised me I should never want. Where is his money? You are his manager. Have you robbed us as everyone robs us?'

'Now listen – I shall have to try and borrow money to keep the firm going. For the first time since your father inherited Britannia our credit is bad. We will not be able to pay our debts next quarter. We need money for raw materials, for the worker's wages, and plant maintenance. We have already had to stop work at Water Meadows and lay off the hands. Your father is facing bankruptcy. They will have to sell Cliffs Edge.'

'Oh, oh, oh . . .' she wailed. 'I cannot bear it! I won't listen.'

Henry could not stand her terror. He knelt beside her and put his arms round her, and she wept against his shoulder, saying she did not understand at all.

'I would give my life to help you,' he said, 'but it's not so easy as that. We could close down and sell, but that would be a tragedy. Given time and borrowing money I can keep it going so that you and your mother could be comfortable and safe. Come home or you may never see

36

your father alive again.' This brought another helpless wave of distress. 'There, my darling. You are such a child. You should never have such anxieties, but unless I can borrow and we can retrench, your father will be bankrupt by the Spring. Please listen and try to help.'

The trembling pink lips, the long, soft lashes, dark with tears, were very near. He kissed her with passionate tenderness.

Outrage and distaste flared in her eyes, and he felt the horrified recoil of her thin body. He was filled with self-disgust. That he should force himself on her. He stumbled foolishly to his feet.

'Forgive me, Florence. I did not mean to do that. It is just that I still love you so much.'

There was a knock on the door and Lecky appeared, bonnetted and shawled and holding two small girls by their hands. He had forgotten that Florence and Richard had children. Twin girls born nine months after their wedding. He had always thought of Florence as a child herself.

She dried her eyes, had another glass of wine, and held out her arms to them.

'Goodness, is it time for your walk? It is so late, and Lecky must be back in time to help me dress, for Lady Maberley is calling to take me driving before lunching with her. These are my little girls, Mr Grimshaw.'

One of the children was ravishingly pretty, like a beautiful French doll, with Richard's red-gold curls and violet-blue eyes. The other was thin, pale and freckled, with thick-fringed bright blue eyes like her grandfather Jagger in his youth. Under their menacing gaze Henry ran his finger round his collar, feeling, uncomfortably, that nothing escaped her.

The pretty one ran to her mother, posing as though she already knew the effect of her beauty.

'This is Charmian,' said Florence proudly, 'who is going to be the loveliest debutante in London one day.'

'And who is this?' Henry asked distractedly.

'That is Margaret. My little plain Jane. Oh, dear, what a face. Are you sulking, Maggy?'

'No, I'm waiting.' She squinted up at the pale blue feather drooping from her velvet bonnet. The two children were dressed alike in the height of fashion. Blue velvet coats with white fur collars, and white buttoned gaiters, and the be-ribboned, feathered bonnets. Charmian looked like a French doll, Margaret like a little clown.

'I hate this stoopid hat!' Margaret said beligerently, and she fixed Henry with a look of fierce accusation. 'And I hates men who make my Mama cry!'

There was a painful silence, Henry was defeated and he knew it. He picked up his hat and case and left the room. Behind the closed door he heard Florence's burst of laughter, and heard her say, 'Why, Maggy, what a fierce little champion you are. I declare you really sent that odious man packing.'

But he did not see Margaret's quick, authoritative glance at Leeky, who at once picked up the tray and the Madeira decanter and took them out of the room.

Florence's good temper vanished. She and Margaret stared at each other, the child feeling the agonizing pain within her, as though she was being forced into an adulthood she could not bear. But Florence's eyes fell first.

She leaned back on her pillows, petting Charmian, winding her red-gold ringlets round her fingers, and feeding her with macaroons.

Margaret sighed with relief. There was not going to be a scene. She thrust her gloved hands behind her back to hide their trembling, and was relieved when Lecky came back to take them for their walk. Florence kissed Charmian goodbye with an exaggerated show of affection, but did not glance at Margaret, nor speak to her.

They walked towards Green Park in the Autumn sunshine, Charmian skipping ahead, Margaret walking silent by Lecky's side. The nice thing about Lecky was that although she was grown-up she was not so much taller than Margaret herself. She glanced at the set little face beneath the ridiculous feathered bonnet and took her hand.

'Now then, don't you fret, love. Your Ma doesn't mean to be unkind.'

'I don't care if she does,' said Margaret stubbornly, 'She knows she should not take Madeira – or not so much. She knows it makes her sick and silly. I won, though, didn't I?'

'Aye, I reckon,' said Lecky, 'Any road, she didn't make me bring it back. Happen you're the only one of us that does win.'

'You can't catch me, Maggy,' called Charmian, ahead, and Margaret's face lit up and she made a magic, instantaneous transition back into childhood.

'Oh, can't I?' she shouted. 'Well you just watch!' And she raced like a deer after her sister, catching her in a few strides, squeezing and tickling her plump little body until she squealed with laughter.

Chapter Two

Mr Levisohn of Levisohn and Groves in the City took to the earnest young man from Yorkshire at once – he had seen so much duplicity that he recognized integrity instantly. He had the facts before him and felt that Henry was fighting a lost cause.

'You had no idea what Mr Jagger was doing over the past years?'

'No idea at all. I ran the factory. I had no access to the private ledgers or to the banking – not until he was stricken with apoplexy.'

'And what do you propose to do, Mr Grimshaw?'

'If I can borrow the money, Sir, I can take on staff and get the Water Meadow Mill working again. It contains the very latest machinery. We would double production, turn a larger profit. You can see,' he pointed to the papers on Mr Levisohn's desk, 'that the firm was doing extremely well. It's just that we have no capital.'

'The cupboard was bare when you opened it, like with Mother Hubbard,' Mr Levisohn said, humorously. 'And where do you come into all this?'

'I can prevent bankruptcy and closure. I can ensure that Mrs Jagger and her daughter, Lady Normanby, are adquately provided for . . .'

'Lady Normanby? The wife of Sir Richard Normanby?'

'You know him?'

'Yes.'

'You have done business with him?'

'With Sir Richard Normanby? My dear young sir, do I look weak in the head? He has offered me a worked-out mine and a large estate already mortgaged up to the hilt as security. He has no profession and no income. If you can't keep the firm going, what will happen then?'

'Then the firm will have to be sold to pay our debts. It is a good business. It will fetch a good price. When everything is paid there should be money to invest for Mrs Jagger and her daughter.'

'Surely this would be the best way?'

'I do not think so.' He hesitated. 'I do not trust Mrs Jagger's ability to invest wisely.'

'Hm. You mean it might go after the rest?'

'To Lady Normanby – and thence to her husband, and then over the gaming tables and into the bookies' pockets!' Henry burst out, uncontrollably.

'Quite. Mr Grimshaw, I believe Mr Dyson Grimshaw, who owns adjacent property to Britannia, is your father.'

This knowledge of his background startled him. Mr Levisohn obviously left nothing to chance.

'Yes.'

'If Mr Jagger's business is put up for sale, won't it be expedient for your father to buy?'

'Yes, of course.'

'Well?'

'I quarrelled with my father,' Henry said, self-consciously, 'and Mr Jagger has been very kind to me. He has been foolish, but he has not been himself. I must try to save him.'

'*And* pretty Lady Normanby?'

Henry felt his ears burn and cursed himself for a transparent fool.

'As I understand it, whether the firm continues or closes is entirely in Mrs Jagger's hands,' said Mr Levisohn. 'I will advance you money if you can raise the security. Your father might help you?'

41

'He would. But it would look as though I were putting Tom Jagger's business in his hands. And I would be.'

'Quite,' said Mr Levisohn again. 'I cannot help you unless I have an absolute guarantee that Mrs Jagger will not sell.'

'She will give that, I'm sure,' said Henry, eagerly. 'I shall speak to her as soon as I return to Thornsby.'

'Keep me informed.' Mr Levisohn rose and extended his hand. 'If things go against you and your father buys, I shall be happy to do business with him – that is, with you.'

Henry gave a short angry laugh.

'It would not be necessary then, Sir,' he said. 'My father has a fortune – he has never spent an unnecessary penny on himself, or anyone else, in his whole life.'

His sister Millicent was waiting for him in the foyer of the great hotel built at the London terminus of St Pancras. A fantastic building, arched, towered and turreted like one of the mad King Ludwig's Bavarian castles. She was a striking girl, three years his junior, dark and vibrant, with cloudy black hair and brilliant brown eyes. She was like their mother, who had died young, her eager, loving temperament crushed by Dyson's harshness.

Millicent had already abandoned the tyranny of the crinoline. Why should a woman go about in a draped parrot's cage, she asked, just because the Queen, the Empress Eugenie and Monsieur Worth were devoted to it? She wore an elegant coat of dark blue velvet in the latest princess style and a dashing little toque of Russian sable, with a tippet and muff of the same fur. They had been expensive, but she regarded them as an investment – she had been told the Americans appreciated richness and style. Well, she had style – and she was in pursuit of

42

riches. She looked at Henry's tired face and the grooved lines of anxiety round his mouth and beckoned the waiter.

'A bottle of champagne, please – cold. And quickly. We will have it here before we go in to dinner.'

Henry's spirits lifted and he smiled as they raised their glasses. Milly had acquired a great deal of sophistication. She had been touring England and working in the West End while he had slaved in Thomas Jagger's business. Like the Normanbys she made him feel provincial and dull.

'This is goodbye for a long while, Henry. I don't know when I shall return.'

'My best wishes for your success. May you become a great actress!'

She smiled. He had been horrified when she had run off to join a third-rate touring company when she had been only sixteen.

'We'll see. I've come a long way. I've got a good part in a good play, and I'll be successful and popular. And one day I'll meet a man I like who wants to marry me and can also afford me.'

'You're very choosy.'

'I'm independent. Not many women are. I can afford to be choosy and I'm young enough to wait.' She said, abruptly, 'Tell me about the Normanbys.'

'What is there to tell?' Henry said, unhappily. 'They haven't a penny and have no intention of altering their way of life. He gambles and whores, I'm told, but I honestly believe she still loves him.'

Millicent gave an odd little smile.

'He is an attractive man,' she said.

'He asked after you today,' he said, suspiciously. 'Has he been after you, Milly?'

'I know him,' she said ambiguously, 'but I'm not one of his whores, if that is what you are suggesting, Henry.'

'No, of course not, Milly,' he said, horrified. 'I know you're not like that.'

'Dear Henry,' she said gently, 'my dearest brother, you know very little about me.'

He had been very kind. Sending her money in the early days which he could not really afford, although he had hated the idea of her being on the stage. She put her hand on his affectionately.

'How one can suffer over attractive fools! Florence is a fool, and her father must have been a worse fool not to know Dick Normanby could not be trusted. Those people are only for pleasure. Like this wine,' she lifted her glass, 'the fizz, the colour, the tingle of excitement. That's all there is to them. Enjoy them and forget them. That's the only way.'

'Well, you're right,' he said, grudgingly. 'He's still a grand-looking fellow, even if I hate his guts.'

'And so are you, Henry,' she teased, 'if you weren't so serious and worthy, and learned to enjoy life.'

'What time have I ever had for that?' he said.

They enjoyed their meal, Henry admiring her knowledge of food and wine, her beauty and style and lovely voice. There was no trace of the North in her deep modulated accent.

She walked with him to his compartment and kissed him goodbye, and both of them felt near to tears. Within the month she would have left for New York.

In the cab on her way back to the quiet, respectable, hotel where she lived she thought of Richard Normanby, and of herself at sixteen, playing bit parts in a scruffy company at a starvation wage.

Richard had walked through the stage door into her life and taken possession of her. Her untried young body had flared with desire beneath his practised love-making.

44

She had been the envy of the other girls in the cast. She was not to worry, he adored her.

When the company came to London he would take a place for them to be together – so she waited, and he did not return. And the other girls began to snigger as all the predictable sordid discoveries followed: the terrifying pregnancy, terminated in a dingy backroom in Drury Lane, where she lay bleeding and semi-conscious with gin, given to dull the pain by the harridan who had manhandled her child away.

Then she had read he had married Florence Jagger in a great expensive wedding at Danesfell Abbey. She had not seen him since. A married man with two children. A smart man-about-town with a reputation as a gambler and womaniser.

Miss Emilia de la Cartier was not sixteen-year-old Milly Grimshaw. She had met a hundred such mashers in the past few years. But the memory of pleasure, of pain and betrayal lingered beneath her indifference. And Dick Normanby was still a very handsome man.

It was Richard who finally persuaded Florence to go North and see her parents. She must persuade her mother to sell the business. What on earth did they want with woollen mills? They needed cash. And why trust that brute Henry Grimshaw, who would get everything into his hands if her father was so ill? If she and her mother sold, they could pay off their debts.

'And should we then have servants again, Dick, and a carriage?'

'Of course, my pet.' He had kissed her – she smelled of lily of the valley and brandy. 'We shall be set up again, and by all accounts your father is not long for this world, and so everything will come to you.'

'But there is Mama, Richard. She can't live with us in London. I mean it wouldn't be the thing at all.'

Richard burst out laughing, imagining introducing mother-in-law to the Marlborough House set, renowned for its beautiful, witty, sophisticated women.

So, on a cold December day, the twins drove with their parents in hackney to catch the train to Leeds. They were followed by another carriage carrying their luggage and Jany Leck, huddled in her bonnet and shawl.

The twins knew that their Mama did not wish to leave London, but they were bursting with excitement. They had only been North once, when their Grandfather Normanby had died. But Lecky had regaled them with stories of Cliffs Edge, the beautiful house where Grandmama and Grandpapa Jagger lived, and the great mills which wove cloth and apparently spun money, too, like the tale of Rumpelstiltskin, and Mama told them about Danesfell with its splendid furniture, lovely gardens, stables full of horses and acres of land.

Margaret, a logical child, had come to the conclusion that money was the most important thing in the world, as it was the only thing that made her parents happy. She could not understand how her Papa 'lost' money and thought he must be very careless. But she hated Suffolk Street, especially now there were no lessons, as they could no longer afford Mademoiselle. At least Cliffs Edge and Danesfell would be a change.

She was glad Papa was not going. She did not like him. She hated the scenes when he swore and Mama cried and men knocked on the door for money that they had not got. Perhaps Grandpapa Jagger would spin them some – in the train she fell asleep and dreamed of sacks full of spun gold.

Richard watched them go with a sigh of relief. He had not much faith in Florence being able to arrange their finances satisfactorily, but he was sick of her tantrums and tears, and frigid horror of anything but the light change of sex, which he found tedious in a grown woman.

The responsibilities of marriage slid northwards with the train, and he set his hat at a carefree angle and planned his first day of freedom. The afternoon was set aside for a card game at Allyson's, but this evening he thought he might go to the New Royalty and renew his acquaintanceship with little Milly Grimshaw. The thought of that thin, white, childish body, the cloudy dark hair and gypsy eyes aflame with passion, came back to him.

He would never have left her, but one of the girls in the company had warned him she was pregnant, and he wanted no trouble then. He had just become engaged to Florence, and old Thomas Jagger had finally capitulated about the marriage settlement which he had wanted to secure to Florence in invested income, not capital. It had only been Florence's despairing hysterics which had persuaded him.

Richard had not wanted anything to stand in the way of the wedding, because then Flo's rose-petal beauty had captivated him and it was important to secure Jagger's twenty thousand pounds. But all that was years ago. It was said girls always remembered their first man. He would certainly go and see Milly.

He was in the green room after the play at the New Royalty Theatre. Milly came in late, already dressed for the street. He had not expected the poise, the confidence or the elegance. She greeted several acquaintances, she smiled and accepted compliments, and gentlemen kissed her hand. She did not appear to notice him, which amused him.

She wanted him to pursue her? Well, he was willing. Flowers and sighs and gifts to heal the past humiliation? She went off to supper with two men, both rich and important: one in Parliament, the other a famous doctor. So! She was flying high. It did not even dent his vanity.

As she left the green room she turned unexpectedly and gave him a long, slow glance, which sent his pulses beating. If Florence at twenty-six was still a spoiled child, Milly Grimshaw at twenty-four was a magnificent woman. A half-sovereign to the stage doorkeeper gave him her address, and next day he sent round a bouquet of roses, which gesture he repeated every day for the next two weeks, making no attempt to meet her.

Then he sent with the flowers a pendant of rose diamonds which he had pilfered some time before from Florence's jewel-case with the intention of selling, and a passionate letter saying he had tried to be patient and hoped to receive some sign from her.

Did she really mean she did not want to see him again? He could only accept it from her own lips. He would call for her after the play the following evening – would she do him the honour of taking supper with him? He felt sure she would not refuse.

The stage doorman looked at him expressionlessly when he asked for her and said Miss de la Cartier was not in the theatre and her understudy had gone on for her tonight.

'Is she ill? Is she at home?'

'No, Sir. She's off to America. The new young lady has taken over the part.'

'She's *what*?'

'She's gone to New York, Sir. Had an offer there. Sailed yesterday. Will your name be Sir Richard Normanby, Sir?'

He found a small flat packet and handed it to Richard. It was the rose diamond pendant. There was a message. '*Thank you for the loan of the diamonds*,' Milly wrote in a fine clear copperplate hand. '*I enjoyed wearing them*

48

last night at my farewell supper. Everyone admired them enormously.'

'The bitch!' he said.

'What was that, Sir?'

'Was it a big affair – this farewell party?'

'Oh yes, Sir. All the toffs. A private room at the Cri.'

He put the diamonds in his pocket, and wondered how many people knew, and how many knowing smiles he would encounter in fashionable London.

It was pitch dark and very cold when Florence and the children arrived at Thornsby on the local train from Leeds and were met by Mr Henry Grimshaw. The two small girls were reeling with weariness, clinging to Lecky's hands, while the porters unloaded their trunks. Charmian was tearful, but Margaret became instantly awake and watchful. Her mother's white, exhausted face took on the cold little look Margaret knew only too well, and when she saw the cab waiting in the station approach the child held her breath. She hoped Mama was *not* going to start screaming – *not* here, *not* out in the street where everyone could see!

'A hackney!' Florence said, shrilly. 'Why hasn't Papa sent his carriage?'

'He no longer has one,' said Henry, patiently. 'It was the first thing that had to go.' He handed her in and picked up Charmian. 'Come along, children. It won't be long now . . .' He set Charmian on the seat by her mother, and turned to Margaret.

'It's all right, I can get in,' she said, 'I'm not a baby.' And stepped up quickly into the carriage. Henry prepared to follow.

'I don't want you to ride with me,' Florence said with venomous dislike. 'I don't want to talk with you.'

'Just as you wish,' he said. 'I'll go in the other cab with Miss Leck and the luggage.'

Lecky's face was like a small, pale moon in the far corner of the carriage. He sat down opposite her. She looked out at the passing town, cobbled and wet, with market debris blowing under the gas-lamps, black-faced miners clattering from the day shift.

'It's not changed,' she said. Then, 'You don't want to take on at her. Things have been hard. She still thinks her Dad will find the money.'

'There isn't any.'

'She won't believe that. Fairy tales. Life's a fairy tale for her. When it goes wrong she can't stand it.'

'And then she drinks?'

She gave him a haunted glance. 'Aye. Allus has. Nips. That and the drops. I'm to blame, too. I was nowt but fifteen when I came to her, and when she asked for it I didn't know it were bad. The doctor said she had a delicate temperament. Mustn't be upset. We were all as bad, her father and mother and me. Spoiled her daft.'

'You're getting no wages?'

She gave a grunt of derision. 'Wages? I've had no wages since I came with them to London. I've had my clothes and keep and a roof over my head. I saved a bit when I was at Cliffs Edge. Don't tell her that – it's useful at times – for food and such.'

'You're very loyal, Miss Leck. She's lucky to have such a friend.'

'Friend! She don't think of me as a friend, Mr Grimshaw. But she's all I've got. So don't be hard on her. She was always as pretty as a picture, as you know.'

Yes,' said Henry.

Lecky gave her odd, grunting little laugh again.

'I've always been as ugly as a dumpling, but I've come

to think it's hard to be like her. A lass would need twice the senses, not half, like she's got.'

'You're very fond of her.'

'Aye. Like I said, she's all I've got. She and the girls.'

'They are all very lucky to have you,' he said.

The big white house, with its columned portico, looked just the same. But no footman opened the door. It was opened by Mrs Jagger herself, wearing a large white baking apron, her arms powdery with flour-dust. She came running down to lift the twins out and to embrace Florence and lead her into the marble-paved hall. The tears were running down her cheeks and her once black-dyed hair was quite white.

The twins stared. *This* was their grandmother? This old lady who looked like a servant and talked with the same rough accent as Lecky? And what was she crying for? And why did Mama stand there looking so frightened?

'Eh, my lass,' said Mrs Jagger, hugging Florence's unresponsive figure. 'I knew tha'd come and help me. I'm that *fraught* with lawyers, and young Henry explaining to me, and your father's illness, I didn't know which way to turn!' She became aware of the staring children and tearfully embraced them. 'Eh, my lovies. And growing so big. This one so bonny wi' her Dad's eyes – and little Maggy, my Lady Margaret all over again. Well, I've baked a nice ham for supper – we're not wi'out food yet . . .'

Her pathetic joke fell on stony ground.

'Mama,' said Florence, stiffly. 'You're wearing an *apron!* What will people think?'

For the first time the reality of the situation penetrated. Poor Mrs Jagger pulled off the offending garment in a bewildered manner.

'You mean it's true? All those horrible things Henry

Grimshaw said? There are no servants here? And you've no money?'

'Aye. So it seems.'

'But where has it gone to?'

'Well, it seems – mind you, I'm not blaming you, love – it seems your father's been sending it all to you and Richard.'

'But Papa is rich. We've always been rich!' she said, accusingly.

Mrs Jagger began to cry again.

'They tell me we're not now. They tell me we'll have to borrow to keep going, or sell up. Eh, I don't know. We'll talk on these things later . . .' There was the sound of dragging footsteps coming from the study, and she whispered frantically, 'It's your Papa! He's been longing for you. You've always been his whole world. Go carefully wi' him, Flo, for he can understand, but only slow like . . . don't upset him. He doesn't realize all t'money's gone, or what he's done. Since his seizure he knows no more than a baby in arms.'

An old, old man came shuffling towards them, peering with wandering eyes and loosely-hanging jaw. He was wearing a dressing-gown, untidy and unshaven, and when he saw Florence his poor eyes lit with joy, and he stretched out his arms, making incomprehensible sounds that he imagined were words.

Both the children, totally unprepared, were terrified. Florence shrank back. This could not be her upright, clever, successful, domineering father who had given her everything she had ever wished for, and assured her that she should want for nothing.

Thomas Jagger clutched at her arm with his shaking hand and pushed his pitiful, dribbling mouth forward for her kiss. She snatched her arm away in senseless denial.

Her horrified disgust penetrated his clouded mind and

52

broke his heart. He fell to the floor at her feet like a pole-axed animal and his wife dropped on her knees beside him, crying, 'Nay, Tom, love, our Flo doesn't mean it. She's a bit scared, that's all . . . come on, love, get up, don't take on . . .' She lifted his head and laid it on her lap and looked up at Flo for help, but Flo was still deep in hysteria. Charmian was clinging to her mother's skirt, bawling. Only Margaret stood silent and still, horrified, but sane.

She ran down the steps to where Henry and the driver were struggling with the heavy luggage.

'Will you please come, Sir, I think my Grandpapa is ill,' she said in one breath. 'Lecky – Mama's having another turn.'

Henry and Lecky ran into pandemonium.

He went to Thomas Jagger's side, saw the contorted face, and shouted to the driver to help lift the old man. Lecky went to Florence, who stood against the wall, screaming and sobbing, 'It isn't true! I won't look! It's horrible!'

'See to Lady Normanby, get her upstairs, and for God's sake keep her quiet!' Henry ordered.

They carried Thomas on to the settee in the drawing-room. Henry felt his staggering pulse and sent the driver back into Thornsby for the doctor. Mrs Jagger stayed with her husband, silent and weeping, and he went into the hall, empty save for the two children sitting on the bottom step, Charmian still sobbing and clinging now to Margaret, who was saying firmly, 'It's all right, Charmy, it's just one of Mama's turns. Lecky will give her some drops and she will be quite all right. Now, don't cry, love.'

'That howwid old man,' wailed Charmian. 'That's not my Grandpa. Where's Lecky? I thought it was going to be fun! I want to go back ho-o-me.'

'Well, we can't yet.' She dried Charmian's tears. 'So it's no use *going on*. Anyway, I'm here.'

She became aware of Henry's watchful presence and stared back at him. Her mouth quivered, but no tears fell. He knelt by them and took their hands, feeling how tense Margaret was, with her slanted eyes and red hair like a little red cat, a little tiger cub.

'Don't be frightened, Maggy,' he said.

'I'm not,' she said, stoutly, 'but what will we *do*? Me and Charmy?'

'When the carriage comes back with the doctor I will take you both to Danesfell Abbey to your other grandmother, Lady Margaret. I don't think you should stay here.'

'You don't suppose,' she asked politely, 'that anyone will die?'

'Oh, no,' he lied. 'Your grandfather has been taken ill, that's all.'

Jany came downstairs, loosening her shawl and undoing her bonnet strings. Her little moon-face had a weary, waxy look.

'She's quiet now. Well, I had to give her a fair dose. How's t'maister?'

'Bad – I've sent for the doctor. Will you take the children into the kitchen and get them some milk and something to eat? I've told the hackney to come back, and I'll take the twins up to Lady Margaret.'

'Aye, that's the best road.' She took their hands and led them down into the big, warm, clean kitchen.

Henry lifted the children into the hackney and took Charmian on his knee. Margaret sat beside him, straight-backed, silent and apprehensive, as the carriage jogged up the winding moorland road. His eyelids began to droop until a long, shuddering sob roused him. He realized that Margaret was crying silently in the darkness, the tears running down her cheeks, biting her lips with the effort to keep back her sobs.

He put an arm around her. 'Come now, you'll be all right, Maggy. But cry if you want to – you've been brave long enough.'

'I can't stop it,' Margaret said, sniffing disgustedly. 'I would if I could. Mama always cries and Charmy always cries, and Grandma Jagger was crying, and it does no good at all. Lecky doesn't cry. She just shuts up and gets on with it – that's what she says to me. She says it's best. I think so, too. I don't *want* to cry.'

So at five years old she had learned to be exasperated by tears.

'I shouldn't try too hard,' he said. 'I should have a good howl. I won't tell anyone.'

'Papa hates whining women. He gets very cross when Mama cries and just walks out. So I thought I wouldn't.'

'Just as you like,' he said, smiling.

'Well, I don't think I want to now.'

Her quaint, grown-up manner was irresistible. He bent and kissed the salty little face, and she said firmly, 'People never kiss me.'

'Why not? Because you don't cry?'

She considered this. 'Well, perhaps. Lecky hugs me. Papa and Mama kiss Charmy because she's so pretty.'

'But you're pretty.'

'No, I'm not. I'm ginger,' she said positively. They jogged along in silence for a minute or so, and then she gave way to a long, weary yawn. 'May I sit on your knee, too?'

He lifted her on to his knee. She was as light as a bird. Within seconds she was asleep.

The great front of Danesfell Abbey rose against the blue night sky in black silhouette. The columned portico rose two storeys to a carved pediment. Henry had not been there since the night of the ball. He lifted a child on each arm and asked the driver to ring the bell.

He was shown into a small panelled parlour, warm with firelight, where Lady Margaret Normanby, Richard's widowed mother, sat with her son George, a newly-commissioned officer, and a dark boy of about eighteen. They all rose as he came in carrying the sleeping children.

'Poor wee things,' said their grandmother. 'George, Bellamy, help Mr Grimshaw . . . put the children on the settee. Markham,' she turned to the manservant, 'get one of the maids to prepare the nursery bedroom, and light a fire there. What has happened, Mr Grimshaw?'

She was in her sixties, but as erect and dignified as he remembered her years ago. She wore a simple black dress and a Paisley shawl, with a triangle of fine lace on her grey hair. Henry explained what had happened at Cliffs Edge.

'Of course they can stay, and welcome. I am delighted to have them. I am tired of writing to their parents asking to see them here. I can guess how things are at Suffolk Street. Richard leaves a trail of disaster, like a comet, glittering but unlucky.' Her mouth tightened. She had wept bitter tears over the son she had loved and spoiled, and knew he would bring nothing but unhappiness.

George Normanby was like her – sandy and steady. The young boy was introduced as Bellamy Chester, the son of George's Colonel, waiting to leave school and join the regiment.

'I am sorry to hear of Mr Jagger's illness and difficulties,' she said. 'We are not much better off here. The estate is being sold. We shall no longer be in Danesfell in the New Year.'

'After two hundred years,' said George. 'It took Dick about eight to smash it all.'

56

'Where will you go, Ma'am?'

'I have a house in Edinburgh. Large enough for me – and for George when he is on leave.' She gave Henry a bright, ironic glance. 'I am a Grant, Mr Grimshaw, Scottish. Even the Normanby charm could not persuade my father to secure my wedding portion to anyone but me. Fortunately, I see now, although at poor Florence's age I thought otherwise. May I offer you some refreshment?'

'No, thank you. I must get back to Cliffs Edge.'

He bade her goodnight – the twins had not stirred.

Thomas Jagger died in the early hours of the morning. Henry had insisted Mrs Jagger get some rest. The dying man's eyes flickered with intelligence, like a candle flaring before extinction and, bending, Henry could just make out the words:

'Take care of my little lass, Henry.'

'I promise to do my best, Sir,' he said, and for the first time it was a burden he did not want to bear.

At Thomas Jagger's funeral he saw his father, his big shoulders hunched forward in the old, bull-like attitude, his long, angular jaw thrust aggressively forward. He looked very self-satisfied. Jagger had failed, he had succeeded. But he was sixty-four now, and he coughed, and looked uncomfortably cold in the biting wind.

'Dad,' said Henry, 'you should get yourself a warmer coat. It's a bitter wind.'

'I'm not soft like some folk,' said Dyson, looking triumphantly towards the flower-laden coffin, as though he hoped Thomas Jagger could hear. 'Are you ready to come back to me at Calder Beck, Henry?'

'I might at that,' said Henry, 'if Britannia has to be sold up.'

'It will be,' said Dyson, 'and I'll buy. Both Britannia

and the Water Meadows Mill.' He saw Henry's eyes light, and grinned. 'You'd like to own 'em?'

'Yes.' He could not deny it.

'So would I. Jagger was a soft fool. Always boasting of that daft wench of his. "My daughter Lady Normanby," dining wi' Prince of Wales, off to Biarritz and Baden-Baden, racing and swank. Nowt but swank. And now what? Dead and buried and broke, leaving a silly old woman and a stuck-up wench.'

His bleak old eyes looked imploringly at Henry. He had a good business and a great deal of money, and what was to become of it all? He wasn't leaving any of it to that fly-by-night Milly.

'Come back to me, Henry,' he said. 'I was a hard father, and I'm sorry. If Mrs Jagger sells, and she'll have to, I'll buy. It will be the greatest business hereabouts. Come and help me.'

Henry felt himself tremble – his dreams for the two mills, Britannia and Water Meadows, and now his father's Calder Beck – the three all united. That would be a cloth empire indeed. It could cover every variety of manufacture from smooth, high fashion, through Army and Navy supplies, to workman's fustian. Organized and modernized, it could be the finest business, as his father had said, hereabouts.

'Give me time, Dad,' he said. 'I can still borrow and keep Jaggers going if those two women agree. It would secure their future. I promised old Tom I'd look after Florence and to keep going would be the best way.' He did not add that to sell, and to let Richard Normanby get his hands on the capital would be fatal. But his father knew, and laughed in his face.

'Tha's wasting thy time, lad. Stop hankering after her. Ten years ago she was worth having, worth a fortune and pretty as a maybud. She's not worth a stick now. I'm your father. I need you.'

'If I can't stop them selling, and you buy, Dad, then, by God, I'll come back and run it for you as no mill has been run before.'

His attempts to keep things going were in vain. Florence would not listen or even speak with him or the lawyers, and Mrs Jagger, like her dead husband, only wanted to see Florence happy so she sold the business. His one victory was to get her to invest enough money to provide a small personal income and to buy an unpretentious villa in Thornsby Town. He could not prevent her parting with the remainder of the money to Florence, who immediately recovered, left her bed, and taking Lecky, returned to London, leaving the twins with their other grandmother at Danesfell Abbey.

Dyson Grimshaw had bought the Britannia Mills and Water Meadows and Henry went back to work for him.

Six months later Henry received an ill-spelled letter, scribbled in pencil.

'Dear Mr Henry, please get her ma to cum heer and help me. Sir R has gone and taken everything, even her jewels, to America, they says, but I dont no, but I am feered for my lady, this time she will go mad I think. She lays in bed and asks only for the drops that make her sleep, and between times is allus at the bottel and talks nonsense about fine friends and balls and such. Folks is allus at the door for money and now there is not a penny in the howse. I go out at night and pawn things – mostly her clothes for he took the silver. Plees send Mrs J or I don't no what. Respectfully, J. Leck.'

Henry's desk was loaded with work to do with the new company. He put it aside, told his father he would be

59

away for a short time, collected Mrs Jagger, and went to London.

Florence was in her boudoir, decked out in chiffon and lace, her face heavily made up between the golden curls. Her slimness was almost skeletal. The sight of Henry sparked off hysteria. She accused him of stealing her fortune while her father was ill, and cheating her of her property. Richard had gone to America to raise some money, but he would return and horsewhip Henry and expose him for the criminal he was.

He left her to her mother and Lecky, knowing how useless any argument was, and arranged for them to take her back to Thornsby. She could barely walk to the cab, she was so stupefied with laudanum.

He closed the house, paid up the outstanding rent and all the tradesmen's debts, redeemed the pawn tickets, and had the gowns and fripperies sent up to Thornsby. Florence might as well have them. She had destroyed herself and her father for such things, and nearly destroyed him, too.

In Thornsby there was a letter from Milly in New York.

'My admirer, Sir Richard Normanby, turned up here like a bad penny. He thought I would be pining for his bloodshot violet eyes. Well, as the Yankees say, he can think some more. He will get nothing from me. I have learned to take only what is worthwhile in life, and Dick Normansby is not worth a fig. Nor is his wife, as you now know.'

Yes, he knew all right. She had been so pretty, and his boy's heart had put her on a pedestal – a little rose-coloured saint to be worshipped, fragile and untouchable. Had it only been lad's love? Romantic and evanescent? Or had Richard Normanby's casual insolence cut deeper than he thought?

Well, it was over and he was free. When the train drew into Thornsby he could see the long green and gilt boards erected on the three mills, stretching half-a-mile along the Bradford Road: GRIMSHAW & SON (THORNSBY), LTD. FINE WOOLLENS.

That year Dyson Grimshaw died in his bleak, comfortless house, the richest and most disliked man in the town, and Henry, his sole heir, became the owner of Calder Beck, Britannia and Water Meadow Mills. He had no doubt at all about his ability, took command of his kingdom and for the first time realized the extent of his freedom. He was rich.

His father's cruelty and avarice had stolen his youth, and suddenly he was hungry for the fleshpots of life. His devotion to Florence had kept him from other women. But Florence was a pretty, silly ghost who only occasionally haunted his dreams. He swore he would never again devote himself to one woman. He found Milly had told him the truth, that he was good-looking, that women liked him. He learned about them fast and from the most experienced teachers he could find. He was rich and handsome and not yet thirty and he would enjoy the pleasures of wealth as no man in Thornsby ever had.

Lady Margaret Normansby left Danesfell Abbey and went to live quietly in Edinburgh. Her younger son, George, was posted overseas. Florence and the twins, with Lecky, went to live with old Mrs Jagger in her modest terrace house on the outskirts of Thornsby.

Florence lived upstairs in her 'boudoir', pretending that nothing had changed. Tomorrow she would hear from Richard to say he was returning with a fortune. She would open up Suffolk Street and buy a new carriage and order clothes from Worth in Paris. The little sips of brandy and drops of laudanum kept reality at bay. The girls grew up accepting the local view that their mother was drunken and mad, that they were poor and to be pitied.

Lady Margaret paid for their education at a good local school and when they were fifteen offered to send them to 'finish' at boarding school in Harrogate. Charmian, nubile and beautiful, accepted.

Margaret, to everyone's consternation, refused. Her six-year-old conclusion that money of your own was the most important thing in the world was not shaken, and she told Lady Margaret that she would like the money to apprentice herself to learn a trade.

Grandmother Jagger was struck dumb, but Lady Margaret, though astounded, agreed. At fifteen, Margaret entered the firm of Madame Rosa's: Fashionable Dressmakers.

Her mother had hysterics and was drunk for three days. Thereafter she invented a story that Margaret went daily to be an unpaid companion to a rich old lady, an illusion which Margaret saw no point in denying if it kept her mother happy.

Within three years, Madame Rosa, who knew a good thing when she saw it, released her from her apprenticeship and made her third assistant with a wage of fifteen shillings a week and twopence in the pound on her sales. Triumphantly she put her red hair up and made herself a smart black showroom dress. Life had begun.

Chapter Three

Madame Rosa Gadsby's establishment in the Arcade in Leeds closed at one o'clock on Saturdays. It was an exclusive shop, and her customers did not come to town at weekends. The carved mahogany door was locked, the blinds of cream silk linen, heavily fringed, with the words MADAME ROSA GADSBY, COSTUMIER AND MILLINER printed across them in gold and brown italic script, were pulled down, and the apprentice and three saleswomen began to clear the showroom for the weekend.

Up two steep flights of stairs in a long attic workroom the sewing girls still toiled under a skylight and would do so until six that evening, or, if there was a rush order or a fashionable wedding, much later. If times were slack, apart from two or three highly-skilled workers and fore-women, they would be laid off. The showroom staff, and Madame herself, left as soon as the shop was cleared and dust-sheeted.

Young Margaret Normanby worked with the concen-trated efficiency of one who never has quite enough time in her day. It was not so long ago that she too had been an apprentice, that despised girl-of-all-trades. Two months in the showroom had taught her that there was nothing there that she could not do as well as, and often a great deal better than, her two genteel seniors Mrs Merrett, first sales, and the languishing Miss Maisy Warren, second sales, so she found the rigid protocol of the showroom irksome.

Madame Rosa was a widow with one son, Mr Willy, a

smart, brash young man, who would have rather done anything than be a shopwalker in his mother's prosperous gown salon. But it would be his one day, and she insisted that he learned the trade. He was good-looking, and inclined to make himself a nuisance with the staff, and at the moment was carrying on a desperate clandestine flirtation with the fair and willowy Miss Maisy Warren. Margaret Normanby he considered too skinny and too young, and she had a quality that intimidated him – his mother had put her finger on it when she had taken her on as an apprentice: 'She's an odd little thing, but she's a real lady. You can always tell. She'll get the county customers, if she takes to the job.'

She had. She was honest, hard-working, and clever, and Madame Rosa was very pleased indeed.

Margaret changed out of her black showroom dress, hung it up carefully and put on a summer dress of white muslin with black polkadots, and a hard black straw sailor hat with a surprising bow of black and white satin, like a magpie's wing, which she had made from workroom scraps.

She was eighteen, so slender that she looked taller than her five feet four. She had all Florence's delicacy of line and bones, but with a springy resilience, like a taut bow. Her eyes were blue as speedwells, clear and shrewd, like her grandfather Jagger's had been when he was a young man, and, like him, there was an inner softness about her, treacherous to herself, which she was quite aware of. Softness, she had learned, got you nowhere. The years had somewhat darkened her aggressively red hair. At home and at school she had been considered the plain twin, such was the contrast between her and her sister Charmian's luscious beauty, and so she still considered herself.

She put on her black cotton gloves and was ready to leave.

Mr Willy came hurrying down the curved stairway from the offices on the first floor.

'Miss Margaret, my mother wants to see you.'

'I shall be late for my train.'

'It won't take a minute.'

'Is it a wigging?'

He shot his cuffs, and fingered his fair moustache.

'I've really no idea.'

'Well, I'd better go and see.'

She whisked past him and up the stairs, displaying neat, high-arched little feet and slender ankles flashing among the spotless white froth of petticoats. She really was a cheeky little thing. Got a bit above herself, he thought, since she had been promoted to third sales.

He picked up his cane and shining top hat and went across to the snug of his favourite public house to meet some of his cronies, to talk about the day's racing and forget the indignity of the gown shop and his mother's firm grip on the purse-strings.

Madame Rosa was a formidable lady in her mid-fifties, rigidly corsetted beneath her expensive black satin showroom dress. Her face was yellow beneath her rouge, and her feet and ankles ached towards the end of the day.

'You wanted to see me?' Margaret said.

'Oh yes.' She was tired.

What Rosa Gadsby needed was someone young to lean on: to shelve the responsibility of a business that was too successful to neglect or give up. With her late husband's and William's weakness where pretty women were concerned, she had tried to employ girls who were efficient and ladylike but not pretty, and when Margaret Normanby had come as an apprentice she seemed to fill the bill exactly. Well-spoken, well-born, thin, freckled and red-haired. Certainly not pretty. But she had style.

She looked down at the figures on her desk noting the list of sales for the month. Margaret Normanby had been third sales for three months now, and her sales were already above those of Miss Warren. Last week she had shifted the whole of a roll of sprigged violet taffeta for a gaggle of bridesmaids for an important wedding. She was young and strong, and had a way of speaking to customers which was neither servile nor bold, which pleased the better-class trade.

'Miss Warren has complained to me that you are stealing her sales? Is this true? You know the rules.'

The rules were rigid. If a personally-known customer entered the shop, Madame herself was summoned. If the customer was unknown, Mrs Merrett the first sales approached her. If she was engaged, Miss Warren, the second sales went forward: if *she* was engaged, the third sales, Margaret herself, had her chance.

Margaret considered.

'Yes, I suppose it is. The question is, which is more important – the rules or the profits?'

'You are saying Miss Warren lets sales go?'

Margaret's face flamed, 'I'm not poaching! I've never spoken to one of her customers while she was engaged with her. Only when she has given up. The wedding order – the sprigged taffeta – they were going out of the shop. The bride, her mother, and three bridesmaids. I picked up the taffeta, and as I walked past they looked at it, and I just said, "Isn't it pretty, Madame? Just the thing for a Spring wedding." They didn't go out.'

'The rule says you should have handed the sale back to Miss Warren.'

'And let them off the hook again?' Margaret gave a small disparaging hoot of laughter. 'No fear!'

66

All three of the bridesmaids were going to have dresses of the sprigged taffeta, and the whole order with accessories and trimmings would cost over a hundred pounds.

Madame Rosa's face was expressionless.

'Miss Warren says that unless you go, she will give in her notice.'

Margaret felt her heart contract nervously. Her earnings, and especially the commission she was beginning to earn, were making a welcome difference to the comfort at home. She knew she had outsmarted lethargic and lovesick Miss Warren, who was relying on Mr Willy to protect her. She knew she had been very pushing for a mere third sales, and also that if she lost her job, there was not another one of this quality in Leeds. She lifted her chin and spoke with all her Normanby authority, cool, well-bred, articulate.

'In that case you will have to dismiss me, Madame, because I am certainly not going to resign. I think, if you examine the figures, you owe me a good reference.'

'Where will you go?'

'I'll have to consider that. Maybe Rosedale's' – they were Madame Rosa's nearest competitors – 'although of course they are not in your class. Maybe to London. There are good cribs there.'

'You'd find it difficult without a family behind you.'

'I could live in. Or take them with me.' She was pale with bravado. 'So? Am I to leave now? Or work until the end of the month?'

'I shall expect you as usual on Monday.' Relief brought colour like a wild rose beneath Margaret's fine, freckled skin. 'I shall accept Miss Warren's resignation. At the end of the month, you will take over as second sales, and I'll let young Lily take your place.'

Their eyes met. Margaret guessed Madame Rosa knew about Maisy Warren's clandestine attachment to Willy.

'Thank you,' she hesitated. 'But I don't want to harm Miss Warren. I just couldn't bear to let the sale go.'

Margaret flew downstairs, out of the shop and down the Arcade, her head in a whirl. It was going to be difficult until Maisy Warren left. She had been lazy, she had bullied the apprentice and attempted to bully Margaret, and she boasted of Mr Willy's devotion to her, and hinted at a secret engagement, wearing a cheap ring which Margaret suspected she had bought herself.

Charmian was now home from boarding school for good. And that was another problem. What *was* she going to do with Charmian, who had elected to accept Grandmama Normanby's offer and be educated as a young lady? Margaret thought of the family as entirely her responsibility, as indeed it was. None of the three grown women in the household could make decisions. Grandma Jagger was too old and crippled with arthritis. Jany Leck, still working from morning to night, was a servant and looked for orders, did not give them. And her mother, the once beautiful Florence, was lost in a mad world of her own drink-induced dreams.

The house in Hollingroyd Crescent belonged to Grandma Jagger and her yearly income came to about one hundred and fifty pounds, which, for some time, Margaret had managed. They just made do on it, keeping afloat on the surface of gentility, until her earnings had begun to ease the situation.

Sometimes sheer panic rose and threatened to drown her, when she wondered what on earth would become of them if anything happened to her.

She would lie awake in her deep feather bed worrying about it. If she worked really hard she might become the first sales lady, or even a manageress. If she saved every penny she could she might open her own shop one day and be rich, like Madame Rosa, and have a hackney carriage to take her home when the shop closed. Then she would look after Mama properly, and give Charmian a dowry so she could marry a gentleman. But those were just dreams.

The best thing that could happen was that Grandmama Normanby, Lady Margaret, should have Charmian with her in Edinburgh where she might find a husband. But Grandmama Normanby was getting old, in spite of her straight back and firm voice, and she did not care to go into society very much. Any money she had saved from the wreck would go to George Wellington Normanby, her younger son, who was now a Major in the Army.

Margaret had long since ceased to believe in the old myth that Mama still told them, that one day their Papa, Sir Richard Normanby, would come home from America, very rich, having made his fortune, and they would go back to Mayfair and London, and the twins would be presented at Court, and marry into great families. Both the girls knew the truth, that their father had been a waster who had ruined his family, stolen all her mother's money, and run off to America. Jany Leck had told them. It was part of their mother's tragic eccentricity to invent the dream of his eventual and triumphant return.

She reached the barrier just as the whistle was blown and raced along the platform, wrenching the nearest door open, realizing at once what a stupidly dangerous thing she was doing. Porters shouted, she felt the terrible drag of the train, knowing if she let go she would be thrown on to the platform, that if she did not she would be slammed against the side of the carriage. Someone thrust the door open, and yanked her up and into the carriage. The door slammed. She sat with her eyes closed, her heart racing, her breath laboured, telling herself she had been ridiculous enough without fainting as well.

'Are you all right, young lady?'

She opened her eyes. It was not her usual third class 'Ladies Only' carriage, filled with shopping matrons. It was empty except for the man sitting opposite her. She was alone, with a strange man in a railway carriage, something she had been warned, all through her life, that she *must never do*. A woman alone in a railway carriage with a man was at his mercy. She looked at her saviour warily through her short, thick, dark bronze lashes. He *looked* all right. Respectable and quite old. Well, over thirty. Miss Warren had said the most respectable were always the worst.

'Thank you very much,' she said shakily. 'I'm sorry.'

'That was an incredibly stupid thing to do,' he said.

'Yes.'

'Then why did you do it?'

'I didn't want to miss the train, and I was thinking of something else. I just – didn't think.'

'Well, if you don't learn to think, you won't live very long. Let's hope you don't do it again.'

'I won't. Thank you, Sir,' she said meekly.

He took the local newspaper out of his square-crowned grey top hat, shook it out and began to read. The conversation would appear to be over.

With her saleswoman's observation she summed him up. Her eye for line and quality approved of the superlative tailoring of his light frock coat. Beside his grey hard hat, which hinted a gentleman farmer rather than a businessman, was a thin leather case with the initials HDG upon it. The sort of case some cloth salesmen carried. But he did not look like a salesman.

His face reminded her irresistibly of a photograph she had seen of a Red Indian carved in the stone of a mountainside in America. The dominant high-bridged nose. The strong cleft chin. The fine-lipped, unsmiling

70

mouth. His eyes were light grey and had regarded her with unflattering exasperation. His thick fair hair, flattened by the hard hat, was already beginning to spring back into waves and curls. One thing for certain. He was a man, not a boy like Willy Gadsby, or the Thornsby lads who tailed round after her sister Charmian like lovesick puppies.

She became aware of the dark blue moquette upholstery and the brass and mahogany fittings, the bevelled mirrors below the tasselled luggage rack.

'Good Lord!' she said, startled. 'It's first class! I've only got a third class ticket.'

He regarded her over the top of his paper.

'Well, there is no corridor, so you're quite safe from inspectors.'

'Yes,' she relaxed. 'I get out at Hornsby anyway.'

She folded her black-gloved hands and shut her eyes. He knew perfectly well that she was regarding him through her half-closed lashes. He could not place her. Her voice, and assurance, suggested a lady, and what was known as a real lady, not just a rich businessman's daughter, of whom there were plenty in Thornsby as he well knew, for Henry Grimshaw, still ummarried, was regarded as a great catch. But if she were either, she would not be travelling alone. Only working girls travelled alone. He knew he had seen her before. About the town? No – he would have remembered. She had something, in spite of her extreme youth, not often seen in Thornsby. Something that devilish sister of his had. Style. Achieved very cheaply, but real style.

He did not care for young girls. In the big cities he visited, selling his cloth, both in England and abroad, there were women with real style; discreet, expensive ladies, of whom he had become a connoisseur. This little creature was as green and sharp as an unripe apple. In spite of her apparent calm he could see the soft young breasts beneath the gathered muslin were rising and falling, and not just because of loss of breath.

'You needn't be in the least afraid,' he said reassuringly. 'You will be as safe in this carriage with me as you would with your own father.'

She gave an odd little hoot of laughter.

He frowned. 'Have I said something funny?' he said stiffly.

'Oh, you didn't mean to. It's just that my father isn't – or wasn't – all that trustworthy from all I've been told. He ran off and left us without any money.'

'You – and who else?'

'My mother and sister.'

'Haven't I seen you before somewhere?'

The vivid blue eyes were instantly wary, and it was Henry's turn to laugh. Young, green, innocent he had guessed, but not naïve.

'I suppose you've heard that before?'

'Lately, yes,' she agreed. 'It's a man's trick to scrape up acquaintance. The girls in the shop say it's something a girl must expect when she goes out to work.'

'Where do you work?'

'Madame Rosa's in the Arcade. A lot's happened today. I was thinking about it when I ran to catch the train. Have you noticed how when things happen, they seem to happen all at once?'

'Yes.'

She was talking as though she had known him all her life, and he was listening with an expression both grave and amused.

'I'm sorry,' she said, 'talking like this. You probably want to read your paper.'

'That's quite all right.' He folded the paper precisely,

and put it back in his hat. 'Would you permit me to smoke?'

'Oh, please do,' she said graciously.

He took out a leather case, extracted a cigar, trimmed it, lit it and drew in a mouthful of smoke, filling the carriage with fragrance. She noticed how white and strong and clean his hands were, and a new awareness moved within her. A sort of stirring which she had never felt before. Unnerving and a little scaring.

'You are perfectly right not to become familiar with strangers,' he said gravely. 'Now, tell me, what was on your mind to make you behave in that suicidal way?'

'Well, I was just leaving when Madame called me and she gave me promotion. To second sales. Well, I'm not long out of my apprenticeship. It means more money, and a better commission. I get twopence in the pound. Now I'll get fourpence.'

'Was there any reason for this?'

'Oh yes. I sold more than the second sales, Miss Warren, last month. And besides, Madame has this son, Mr William, whom all the girls are sweet on, particularly this Miss Warren. She's always saying they will be engaged, but I think Madame would put a stop to that. So I've got her job.'

'Are you sorry for Miss Warren?' he asked unexpectedly.

Again the sharp, inward, self-critical closing up of the childish face.

'I'm not sorry about her losing the job, because she wasn't working at it properly. But I'm sorry for her because she's such a fool.'

'You are an extraordinary little girl.'

'I'm eighteen,' she said indignantly.

'Well, to me you're very young. But you're very quick.

73

If you were a boy I'd take you into my office without any reference. Tell me, do you like being a shop assistant?'

'No.'

'I suppose it's just until some boy comes along and wants to marry you?'

'Certainly not!' He was surprised at the snap of temper in her eyes. 'I want to be like Madame Rosa. Not *like* her, I mean she's old and quite ugly . . . but she's independent. She doesn't even have a husband. I'd like to have my own shop and make the money she does.' He saw the dream rise in her eyes, and remembered his own dreams which were now such concrete realities.

'I'd make more than she does. I've got better taste. In London they say ladies pay a hundred pounds for a ball-dress. Ladies like the Princess of Wales. The society ladies . . . millionaires' wives. The famous actresses. My mother did once – when she was well and rich. I'd like to make really good clothes and have a fashion house in London.'

'And what will stop you?' he asked gravely.

'Money, chiefly. You can't do anything without it – and anyone can boss you about. I want to tell people what to do, not have them tell *me*. Madame Rosa and the other girls will sell anyone anything, so long as they pay. That's *mad*! If you let a customer go out with something that doesn't suit her, she'll hate it when she gets it home, and then won't come again. It's better to let them go with a few ideas in their heads, tell them the colours or styles that would suit them, let them think about it, *then* they'll come back. But I haven't got any money and I've a lot of people to look after.'

'At your age?'

'Oh yes. I've Mama, Charmian my sister, and Grandma Jagger, though she has a bit of money, thank goodness. I'm the only one with any sense. Except Lecky, and I don't think she has much or she'd have left us for a better place years ago!'

His face changed. 'Your grandmother is Mrs Jagger?'

'Yes.'

'Your mother, then, is Lady Normanby?'

'Yes.'

All the kindly amusement had gone. He really did look as though he was carved in rock now.

'Have I said something wrong?'

He had been amused, as though she was a precocious child, but he *had* taken her seriously. He had laughed at her. She guessed he knew about her mother – the titled lady who lived in a tinpot little house and was never quite sober.

'I suppose you know about my mother?'

'Know what?' he had said shortly.

'That she's not well.' The colour that came to the small face this time was dark with shame. 'That she drinks?'

He did not reply.

'She can't help it,' Margaret said passionately. 'She was very beautiful and rich, and then Papa ran away and left her and took all the money. Lecky told me. Lecky's been with Mama since she was a girl. Mama says Papa will come back one day with heaps of money, and we will all go back to London and be rich again. She says a man called Grimshaw who lives in Thornsby cheated her and her father, and stole all her money, but that isn't true either, or so Lecky says. It's one of Mama's delusions. Mama's not made for worry . . . it kills her. So you see I've got to take care of them.'

'I see.'

He picked up his paper, and began to read. But not a word of the print registered in his mind. This child was Florence's daughter. Those kitten eyes, bright blue and fierce, and the aggressive little chin and firm mouth were

75

not like Florence at all. Not like Richard Normanby. His mind ran back to the night when he had driven up to Danesfell Abbey with the two children to deliver them to their other grandmother, Lady Margaret Normanby, the Scottish aristocrat.

He said suddenly, 'Where did you go to school?'

'Miss Sales Academy.'

It was a well-known local school for girls.

'But isn't that expensive?'

'They made a special price. Because we are Normanbys – and Grandmama Normanby paid. It was all she could do for us.'

'I thought all young ladies stayed at school until they were your age?'

'Many did but I *didn't*,' she said positively. 'I told Grandmama Normanby I'd rather have the money to pay for an apprenticeship and she agreed. She said it was a change that one member of the family wanted to make money instead of spending it.'

Amusement rose, unexpectedly, in his hard grey eyes. The straight, hard mouth twitched up at the corners.

'But you are very young to be out working for your living.'

He knew now of whom she reminded him. Her grandfather, old Thomas Jagger, when he had been young and shrewd. The bright blue eyes – the sudden slightly belligerent stare. He wondered if she was as soft-centred as the old man had been.

'You only say that because I talk like a lady. There are girls in the mills in Thornsby younger than me.'

'Yes, I know, and a wicked thing it is.'

He had not employed children since his father had died and the policy of the firm came entirely into his hands.

She was surprised. It was not a view aired among the wealthier manufacturers of Thornsby.

'I was fifteen when I was apprenticed,' she said perkily.

'Yes. Too young.' His eyes were suddenly gentle. 'But you *chose* it, didn't you? And you *paid* for it. And your family don't depend absolutely on your wages. Or you wouldn't wear such a pretty dress. And working in a ladies' shop is not the same as working in a woollen mill. And *why* are you working?'

'To get on in life, of course,' she said defensively.

'And I am sure you will. But the children in the factories have no chance of promotion, or making money, or even learning to read.'

'I thought there was a law against it.'

'Yes. They are not allowed to work in the mills until they are ten years old – but that only applies to the textile trades. There are trades like pottery and match-making where they still employ babies of seven. Such employers are murderers. All decent people should speak against it.'

They fell into an uncomfortable silence, and he felt ashamed when he saw her puzzled, woebegone expression.

'Don't you worry,' he said, 'You've got ambition. You follow your star.'

She gave a little smile. 'I was thinking of our apprentice at Rosa's. Lily. She doesn't have such a good time. She didn't pay, like I did.' She drew in a little breath, as though making up her mind. 'When I get cross with her, I'll remember what you said.'

He was grateful that the little thing had not accepted her mother's lies about him. She was an endearing child. He remembered that hellish evening at Cliffs Edge when Thomas Jagger had died, and it had seemed to him then that the tiny girl was the only female keeping her head. He wondered if she remembered that ride up the moor to Danesfell, crying silently in his arms.

77

He would not speak of it. He wanted no more old memories. Over the years he had changed. Milly said he used women. That he was generous to them but they were for amusement only. Maybe this was so, but it was safer that way.

The train was running into Thornsby station. The Bradford Road ran along by the railway and he could see the tall green billboards with the gilt letters proclaiming his kingdom: GRIMSHAW & SON (THORNSBY) LTD. But now there was no son. He was unmarried. He did not want to marry, but he wanted a son more than anything in life.

The train stopped. He got out and handed her down like a grown-up lady and she flushed with pleasure. He raised his hat, nodded abruptly, and strode off in the direction of the barrier. Margaret followed, somewhat subdued, feeling that she had grown up several years during the short journey.

Charmian Normanby sailed across the Market Square at Thornsby, a vision in pink-and-white check gingham and a small white hat trimmed with a large pink rose. It really was wonderful the way Margaret could make quite stunning little dresses out of cheap materials, raiding the attic storehouse of their mother's forgotten vanities for trimmings. The pink rose, made in Paris, and costing half-a-guinea then, had come off a bonnet Florence had worn once at a garden party, twenty years ago.

Charmian thought that this was the plebeian streak in her sister, who resembled the manufacturing Jaggers, not the aristocratic Normanbys. Sometimes when she saw the yellowing photograph of her grandfather, old Thomas Jagger, in Granny Jagger's bedroom, she had to laugh. The shrewd stare made her think of Maggie – with whiskers! She was no good at such tasks. She played the piano rather nicely, sang in a sweet little voice, and danced beautifully. Mama said often that Charmian was pure Normanby.

Just behind Charmian Jany Leck followed, carrying a shopping basket. She was wrapped in a large grey shawl and an old-fashioned black bonnet was tied on her sparse hair. She was still under five feet tall. She puffed along like a little tug behind an ocean-going yacht, while Charmian did her best to pretend she was not there.

Florence would not allow her to go out into the town alone. The well-to-do young men in Thornsby were all in trade, which in Florence's opinion put them out of the running with girls. Charmian sometimes felt she would explode with frustration.

She was very beautiful, beautiful as only a Normanby could be, with the family bronze-gold hair, the languishing violet eyes, tall, graceful and voluptuous. Men were crazy about her, and she was not even allowed to go to the Town Hall balls. Florence could stage a scene which would shatter her daughters for days if she was really opposed, and now all her confused dreams were centred on a great marriage for Charmian. With this in mind she had been bombarding her mother-in-law, Lady Margaret, with imploring letters. There was no money, of course, but Lady Margaret still had influence. A season in Edinburgh would give Charmian a chance.

Charmian suddenly changed course round the back of a china stall. Bill Heaton, whose father owned a prosperous wine and provisions store, was coming towards her, and she particularly did *not* want to see him. But, with the sure anticipation of a football forward, he dodged round the stall and could not be avoided.

He was a big boy, with big hands, inclined to wearing large checked tweeds. Charmian looked at him indignantly. If he was going to take advantage of a few kisses behind the lilac shrubbery in the park while Jany was dozing, or stolen rides in his high-wheeled gig when her mother was sleeping the afternoon away, he would soon learn better.

Billy, who would have married her tomorrow and laid his life down for her, said imploringly, 'Charmy, what is it? Have you forgotten tomorrow? I'm counting on it, love.' She frowned, fidgetted with a bow, glancing at Jany puffing up in the rear, and said severely, 'Not before the servant, *if* you please, Mr Heaton.'

Not that Jany would ever split on her or say anything that might cause trouble at home.

'*Mr* Heaton.' Billy was aghast. Nay, Charmy, love, what's the matter? Have I said or done anything wrong?'

'Well, yes, but it's not your fault, I suppose,' she smiled, and his entrails melted, and his big boy's body burned. 'But you mean well, Well, I can't come. I can't risk it. Mama heard about my going for a ride with you, and there was an *awful* scene. I just *can't*!'

'But I've told Mother you'd come. You and Maggie and Mrs Jagger.' He took off his hat, and wiped his forehead. He had had great trouble in getting his mother to extend the invitation.

'If tha imagines I want those stuck-up Normanby girls here on a Sunday afternoon to high tea, you can think again,' she had said, and then relenting, 'All right then. But a plain tea, nothing fancy.'

'But, Charmy, it's all fixed, love. I'm bringing the gig to fetch you all.'

'I'm sorry. As a matter of fact, my plans for this Sunday have suddenly changed. I am going away.'

She was quite satisfied with the effect. Billy went white, then red, and cried, '*Away? Where?*'

'I am going up to Scotland, to stay with my grand-mother, the Dowager Lady Normanby, and am expecting to have a most enjoyable time. My Uncle George is back from India and is now stationed there. I shall be gone for some considerable time. So, please, Mr Heaton, leave go my arm. I am going to meet my sister from the train.'

'Heck!' cried the unhappy young man. 'What shall I tell Mother?'

'That is nothing to do with me. I gave you no promise. I merely said I would try to come. It is impossible – you know what Mother is.'

Maddened by memories of the encounter behind the lilac shrubbery, feeling Charmian's tempting young body, and kissing her soft and willing lips, trying to think how he would explain this to his mother, who in spite of her protests had probably done extra baking, Billy said furiously, 'I don't know *what* she is, but I damned well know what people call her!'

Charmian glared at him, drawing herself up imperiously.

'How dare you! I shall never speak to you again!'

With which she swept past, ignoring his apologies and protests, followed by Jany who gave him a sympathetic look and muttered, 'Aye, well, she's like Sir Richard,' and trotted after the queenly figure.

That, thought Charmian, has got rid of him, and forgot all about him. After Lady Margaret's letter had arrived that morning by the second post she had seen immediately that if she were to go to Edinburgh she must not get into any more scrapes with Billy Heaton or any other of her local admirers.

As they went up the steps into the station booking hall, the train was coming in.

Jany, with her basket of shopping, subsided gratefully on to a seat by the barrier. Already her little legs were swollen with veins, cleaning, fetching and carrying up and down the steep narrow stairs of the house in Hollingroyd Crescent.

'Eh, Miss Charmy, you go like a steam train!'

'Don't call me, "Miss Charmy". It is as bad as calling Mama "Miss Flo", instead of "My Lady".'

'Happen I forget,' Jany said imperturbably.

Jany was not the sort of servant Charmian cared to have following her about. Puffing on the station seat with her big market basket and grey shawl like an old cottage woman. She moved away to the far side of the barrier, disassociating herself from the odd, undersized little body.

She saw Margaret coming down the platform, the sun catching her red hair, slim, trim and swift of foot in her black-and-white dress and chic straw hat with its brave magpie wing.

She was always conscious that her sister possessed some quality which she did not understand. Boys did not languish hungrily after Margaret. She would no doubt end up an old maid. But people listened to her, even Mama at her worst. Charmian was a little scared of Margaret. She waved languidly – she had only walked to the station to escape for an hour or so from the unutterable boredom of their home.

One of the first passengers to leave the platform was a wide-shouldered man, exceedingly well-dressed with a grey hard hat set squarely on his broad head. Rich-looking, clean-shaven like an actor, but not an actor at all. The ticket collector touched his hat and a coachman appeared at his elbow.

'Good evening, Sir.'

'Evening, Hutton.'

'The broughman's outside, Sir. I'd best get back – I've left a lad wi' the horse. Will you be going to t'club?'

'Not tonight, Hutton. I'll come right away.' Henry caught sight of Jany dozing like a little Buddha on the seat near the barrier, and a look of startled recognition came over his face. He hesitated, and went over to her.

'Miss Leck?'

Jany's eyes flew open.

'Oh! Mr Grimshaw.'

He held out his hand as though she were a lady. Margaret had come through the barrier and was standing by Charmian, both girls listening and staring.

'It's been a long time,' he said. 'Especially as we live in the same town.'

Jany struggled to her feet.

'Aye, it is that, Sir. I reckon we're both kept busy.'

'Yes. Let me take that.'

Mechanically Jany let him take the heavy basket and he took her arm. He had to bend to do so, because she did not reach to his shoulder. As though in a trance she let him lead her to the entrance of the station. The two girls followed just behind, glancing at each other in astonishment. Maddeningly they were now just out of hearing.

'How are things with you, Miss Leck?'

Her small, pursed mouth gave a grim little smile.

'Much the same so far as Miss Flo goes, and t'owld lady is very shaky.'

Town gossip had told him about Florence over the years: Jany's brief comment confirmed it. He was not going to speak about Florence to her or anyone.

He took a guinea case out of his waistcoat pocket, and pressed some coins into her hand, calling the boy holding his own carriage horse.

'You look tired, Miss Leck. Take a cab home.' He gave the boy some coppers, and told him to fetch a hackney, then for the first time became aware that the two girls were in fact with Jany. He glanced from one to the other. A brief nodded acknowledgement of Margaret.

83

She saw his eyes kindle when he saw Charmian, the automatic reaction of any man to her burgeoning beauty.

'This is my sister, Charmian, Mr Grimshaw,' she said with dignity.

Charmian drooped her long eyelashes, then suddenly raised them with a little smile; lips half-open, pink from a quick tongue-lick. She practised it in the looking-glass and on her admirers, with devastating effect.

His smile was kindly, but indifferent. He judged the pretty sister to be a highly-sexed, potential trollop, but the freckled one was right to stand up for her.

'Miss Charmian,' he bowed to the flustered girls. He was a man quite out of their experience. The colour shot up beneath Margaret's freckles, the lovely rose-colour troubled his memory, remembering her mother. 'And you are the elder, Miss Normanby?'

'Yes, by ten minutes. We're twins. I'm Margaret.'

'It has been a privilege to meet you,' he said, raised the immaculate grey hat, and without another word stepped into his smart carriage and was driven off across the Market Square.

'Well,' said Charmian outraged. '*Miss* Leck indeed. Just as though she was a lady!'

'Well, he was always a nicely-spoken lad,' Jany said smugly.

The boy came back with the hackney. 'Well, since he's paid for me to ride home, we might just as well.' She opened her little work-worn hand. In it were three golden guineas. The girls gasped.

'What fun!' Charmian jumped into the cab as though it had been ordered for her. Margaret took the heavy basket from Jany and helped her in, because her short little legs found the high step awkward, and got in beside her. They jogged off across the Market Square, feeling rather grand. Carriage rides even of the meanest kind were very rare in their lives.

'So *that's* Mama's monster,' said Margaret thoughtfully. 'The man who never forgave her for marrying Papa, and in revenge robbed us of everything.'

'So she says,' Jany said indulgently. The unexpected ride over the steep half-mile home was sheer luxury to her, 'but you know better than to believe everything your Mama says.'

'Yes, oh yes,' said Margaret with a laugh that was half a sigh. 'I know better than ever today.'

'He did his best wi' her, like we all did.' Jany leaned back rocking gently as the horse began the long pull up the hill. 'But you mustn't blame her. She would never believe a word against your father, I'll say that, and if it comforts her to say what she does, well it does no harm. Certainly not to Mr Grimshaw.' Her eyes closed again, then snapped open. 'But don't say a word about this to her, if you don't want tantrums. We've had a reight nice day too, since your Granny wrote from Scotland.'

'Oh, yes! All this made me forget,' cried Charmian. 'What *do* you think, Maggie? Mama had a letter today from Edinburgh and Grandmama Normanby wants us to go and spend the rest of the Summer there. Uncle George is back home and he's stationed there. He's a Major now, and there'll be parties and dances and heaps of officers for partners. And Grandmama Normanby will come here, and take us back with her so we'll be properly chaperoned, and we might *even* be presented at Holyrood.'

'I can't go,' said Margaret flatly. Charmian gave a small, protesting wail. 'You know I can't. You know what happens to Mama when I'm away for long.'

It was only her control of the purse-strings that held her mother back from complete self-destruction.

'Besides, I've not told you my news. I've been given promotion. I'm second sales lady now. More chance to sell. More money. I'm not going now. I could have waited years for this.'

'But, Maggie, Grandmama Normanby knows *all* the very *best* people, and we'll have wonderful chances there.'

'For you, perhaps. Not for me. It's not the sort of chance I want. You know that.'

Charmian was near tears. She did know, and thought Margaret mad. Mad to work like any common girl in a shop and to talk about owning her own one day. As though anyone would *want* to be in trade.

'Don't cry,' Margaret said gently. 'You'll go. You'll have a lovely time and perhaps marry that Duke Mama is always on about for you. I'll manage Mama. Besides, you'll need a lot of new clothes, and it will be easier to afford clothes for one rather than two.'

Jany opened her calloused little hand and exposed the three guineas there.

'Happen you could use these?'

'Oh, Jany! What a love you are!' Charmian's greedy little hand was stretched out for the money, when Margaret slapped it. Not very hard, for she was fond of her sister, but determinedly.

'*No!* It was given to Jany.' She put the money into Jany's worn old purse. 'Buy yourself some new shoes, Jany, and put what's left into the Penny Bank.' An overwhelming tenderness for Jany made her hug the little woman. 'Thank you for offering. Oh, here we are. Better get down out of sight of the house.'

They paid off the cab, and entered the garden by a wicket gate in the stone wall. The gate was concealed from the house, and Charmian's admirers were wont to wait outside on Summer evenings, like prowling tom-cats. She would hold court there sometimes, surrounded

86

by the eager young men who were never allowed to enter.

Hollingroyd Crescent consisted of ten tall granite houses standing in a half-circle, overlooking a lawn and shrubbery, with a fine view across the smoky town to the moors beyond.

They were awkward houses, with two large rooms on each floor, and a clutter of attics, the floors linked with narrow, dark, crippling stairs. The big, light, warm semi-basement kitchen was the most pleasant room in the house. Florence never came down there – indeed she had never seen it. She lived upstairs. The girls and Jany went in by the tradesmen's entrance, which was beneath the tall flight of steps leading to the pretentious front door, with its blue-and-red stained glass and a stucco pillared portico, already peeling and showing signs of disrepair.

Old Mrs Jagger, stout, arthritic and grey-haired sat close to the hearth, a shawl about her shoulders. Although it was a warm day, there was a fire in the large black cast-iron cooker, as it was the only means of cooking or heating water. It shone like a polished top hat, and every bit of brass on it glittered, burnished by Jany's magic hands.

Mrs Jagger's cheeks were bright red with the heat, but she could never be persuaded to move. The girls kissed her, sat down and chattered their news. Tea was already laid on the big kitchen table – a substantial North Country tea. On the dresser Jany had laid the 'upstairs tray' for Florence. Bone china in rose and gilt, a Waterford claret glass – the only one left from the Suffolk Street days – a white damask table napkin in a silver-gilt ring.

This was the children's hour, when, from their early days, they had been taken, brushed and be-frilled, to spend half-an-hour with their mother before she dressed

87

for the evening. It was one of the rituals which Florence maintained.

'Come on, Charmy,' said Margaret. 'Get your hat off. Let's see what we can do.'

They went up the steep dark stairs into the narrow hall, where the shabby walls were speckled with blue and golden lights from the glass in the front door. It was in the two connecting reception rooms on this floor that Florence Normanby spent her life. She never went out. Here the Suffolk Street boudoir had been recreated.

The delicate colours glowed, the worn-out patches on curtains and upholstery did not show in the shaded lamplight. The curtains were never drawn, even on the finest day. The room was full of bits of silver and porcelain, of photographs of aristocratic house-parties. In a place of honour stood the Royal photograph, autographed to 'Dear Dicky and Flo'. There were fresh flowers in the vases. A fine portrait of their handsome father hung over the hearth. A faint, sickly smell of brandy permeated the air.

Florence was sitting on her chaise-longue and she looked up at her daughters with her meaningless little smile. She wore an afternoon robe made for her by Worth twenty years past, and a small lace cap as became a young matron in the early sixties. Her haggard eyes peered out between bunches of false golden curls fixed to her own lank, dyed hair. Her porcelain fragility had become a painful thinness. She had not changed. She was as silly and shallow and pretentious as she had always been. Only her beautiful youth had gone.

'Come in, my darlings, just for a minute with Mama. I shall not come down to dinner tonight, I'm not so very well. Just a little something on a tray.'

She never did eat with them. She was *never* very well. They kissed her dutifully.

'I suppose, Margaret, Charmian has told you the news? That you are to go to Edinburgh for a season? Of course, the Scottish season is *not* like the London season, but it will give you a chance to try your wings. I don't wish you to be presented just yet. I must get better, so I can present you myself. I think eighteen too young. I was twenty when I first went to Court. Dear Lady Maberley presented me. But then I was a young married woman and had my beloved Richard by my side. He told me afterwards that HRH said young Lady Normanby was the prettiest woman that season.'

The twins had visited their grandmother at the tall old house in St Andrew's Square before. Charmian found it very dull. Tea-parties, museums and boring Scottish castles. But this time, with Uncle George, their father's younger brother, stationed there it should be different. Balls, parties, dances and well-connected young officers. She was sick with anxiety that all should go well.

'You will need two new walking-out dresses each, and several ball-dresses. Your grandmother knows all the best families and you will be asked everywhere. I've already spoken to Granny Jagger and she is quite willing to pay for your new clothes . . .'

The girls exchanged patient glances. If their grand-mother could do any such thing, it would be no more than three pounds each for material, for the household existed on her small annuity.

'Mama,' said Margaret firmly. 'I can't go. Mrs Gadsby can't spare me. It's better that Charmy should go alone, then there will be twice the money for her dresses.'

Florence's glance wandered. She knew perfectly well that Margaret worked, shamefully, at some common-place job in a shop, and not as a refined companion to a wealthy local lady, which was what she told the few

89

snobbish women who called, because she was, after all, still Lady Normanby.

'Oh dear, what a tyrant that woman is. Surely she could spare you for a little while? We don't want to offend Grandmama Normanby.'

Margaret did not reply.

'For goodness sake, don't sulk like that, Margaret. A sulky girl is such a *bore*!' Florence's spite was like a cat's pounce. 'Your Papa couldn't endure a sulk.'

'I can't leave you, Mama, when you are not well, with only Jany. Grandma Jagger is not well either. Let Charmy go alone, and I will have my chance later.'

'Chance? What of?' Florence said haughtily. 'Unless you learn to have more charm, Margaret, you won't have *any* chances. Unless you behave like a lady. But have it your own way. You are stubborn and silly, and will never get a husband. Now come and kiss me.' She pulled Charmian down and kissed her affectionately. Charmian drew back hurriedly, and when Margaret bent down Florence turned her head and presented a dry, raddled cheek. Margaret kissed it dutifully. 'Now run along, and tell Lecky to bring my dinner, and later, if I am awake, Margaret, will you come up and read to me?'

'Yes, Mama.'

'Run along then, children.'

As the door closed behind them they heard the clink of decanter on glass.

'Granny Jagger to pay for dresses! It's ridiculous,' said Charmian pettishly. 'Oh, God! Wouldn't it be wonderful to have some *real* money? And a real mother, who would chaperone one into society? And she *could*. That's what makes me mad. Even if we haven't any money she *is* Lady Normanby, and if she didn't swill brandy all day she *could* introduce us, and people *would* receive her!'

'Never mind. I can manage the walking-out dresses.'

'But I shall be going to parties and balls,' wailed Charmian, 'and I don't want to look a dowd.'

'You won't,' Margaret said and pointed upwards. 'Let's have a treasure hunt!'

They went up into the attics. There lay the long, flat boxes, like ten-inch deep coffins, pastel-coloured and gilt-lettered, layered, and begrimed with dust.

She took off a lid, and pulled back the yellowing tissues, lifted out the dress with its enormous full crinoline skirt and began to undo the wrapper. It was of pale lilac moiré, covered with white gauze, the gauze caught up with clusters of violets, each cluster sewn with tiny paste dew-drops that glistened in the light of their lamp.

'It's pretty,' Charmian faltered, 'but it's old-fashioned. No one ever wears that style now.'

'You're not going to wear *this*. I'll unpick it. There's stuff enough for three dresses here.'

'Oh, Maggie! Can you really? And make me a smart dress? With the new line . . .'

They carried three of the dresses downstairs, like smugglers escaping with their loot, and spread the silks and chiffons out on the cleanly-scrubbed kitchen floor. The colours and richness filled the homely room, turning it into an Aladdin's cave.

Chapter Four

Henry Grimshaw was not the only manufacturer in Thornsby who could afford to ride in his own carriage, but he was certainly the only one who still lived in the town. Thomas Jagger had started the exodus twenty-five years before, and prosperity invariably took people out of the smoke and fog to the new, pleasant suburbs up on the moors.

Henry lived in the old Master's House at Britannia. His excellent housekeeper, Mrs Sykes, came in daily to run it for him. He had no domestic problems. He mixed very little in the social life of the town. In the evenings he read in his well-stocked library, worked at his personal investments or urgent matters of business. His pleasures he kept well out of Thornsby, and mostly out of England. He made frequent business trips travelling for the firm in Europe. Very few men had such a peaceful and comfortable life.

Meeting young Margaret Normanby in the train had brought back painful memories of Florence. But for Florence he would have been married by now, perhaps with a son of Margaret's age to follow him into the firm.

His own father had lived meanly, and died as he had lived, but at least he had achieved what he had wanted – money, power, and a son to follow him.

Tonight the sight of the mills, the long rows of windows lit for the late shift, did not bring Henry his accustomed glow of satisfaction. He walked through the weaving sheds. He always did this on his return, no worker or foreman knew when or where he would appear. They

92

respected and feared him: nothing ever escaped his notice.

Quality was the policy of the company. He had built up a trade of superb cloths which were in demand by wholesalers throughout the world. Gentlemen in Moscow, Chicago and Adelaide wore Grimshaw's fine suitings. Millionaires and royalties had them cut and fitted in the exclusive tailors in Savile Row. It was a trade demanding meticulous attention.

At last he left the works and went into the house, shutting the door on the noise and smell of the yards and sheds.

A childhood made bleak by his father's parsimony had made Henry appreciate quality. His bachelor apartment on the first floor of the old Master's House was extremely comfortable, his taste was simple and discriminating. Fine Eastern carpets. Solid, plain mahogany furniture. Warm curtains. The small dining table covered with white damask, laid with good silver and heavy cut Waterford glass. The smell from the kitchen was delicious. But this evening he felt restless and lonely. He needed a woman's company, therefore he was delighted to hear the jingle of harness as a carriage stopped outside, knowing it would be his sister, Millicent known as Emilia de la Cartier, the celebrated young comedy actress, recently returned from her triumph in America. He knew she was playing in Leeds that week.

Cosmopolitan sophistication emanated from her like scent as she swept across the pavement to the door, people stopped, vehicles slowed down, children hung together, staring open-mouthed. She accepted their attention as her due, her red lips in a half-smile, her black eyes indifferent and calm.

'Mrs Sykes,' shouted Henry like a boy, 'Miss Milly's

here. Lay for two will you – perhaps she'll stay for dinner.'

He threw open the door, and she was in his arms, all silk and smoothness and scent and laughter.

'I heard what you said – of course I'll stay.' She kissed him heartily on both cheeks. 'Why do you suppose I've come? To see you? No, for Sykesy's cooking. It is roast beef and Yorkshire. I can smell it. Sykesy . . .' she ran into the kitchen. 'I've come to dinner.'

'Eh, Miss Milly, love,' Mrs Sykes straightened up, her oven red face beaming welcome. Millicent's visits were always something to talk about. 'Eh, what a picture you are. If your poor Ma could see you now.'

'And if my Pa could he'd turn in his grave.' She looked round at the clean, convenient kitchen. 'My goodness, you do keep comfy here, Henry. I'm weekending up at Danesfell Abbey. Mr Hengrave has a house-party. I told him I must run away for one evening to see my dear old brother. But really I wanted a good plain meal, not fourteen courses and a lot of chit-chat with the ladies afterwards.'

'You are just the same as ever.'

The power to charm was her most valuable asset. 'It's quite true. Honestly, society women bore me stiff. Men, yes, they can all be human. But these trilly, shrilly, nothing ladies. *No!* They're best in the stalls when I'm on stage. Not to talk to.'

Henry listened with indulgence. The close affection between them had grown over the years. Dyson had left her nothing, but when the estate was settled Henry had given her the option of having a third of his father's money, or taking shares to the amount when he made the firm a limited company. She had taken the shares, and had never had occasion to regret it. She had done well in America – good parts, and successful tours, and generous,

94

rich admirers. She lived grandly in London in one of the new apartment buildings near Victoria Station, mixing in a smart, but Bohemian society, with successful theatre people, writers and artists as her friends. When Henry was in London, he always stayed with her. On occasions they had travelled abroad together. Each one lovingly thought the other a trifle absurd.

'How long can you stay?'

'Until about ten-thirty. That is when the card tables come out and I find it amusing.' She took off her hat and gloves, looking round her. 'Henry, you're getting to be the perfect old bachelor.'

She saw a shadow cross his face, and linked her arm over his. 'What about a drink? A hock and seltzer?'

'Of course.' He went to the sideboard, and opened a bottle of hock, half-filling a long glass, topping it up with the seltzer water. 'There. It's good to see you, Milly. Today I was feeling a bit down.'

'And I was too.'

'Why?'

Mrs Sykes came in with a china boat of gravy, and an oven pan in which was a batter pudding, golden, crisp and perfect, spattered with gravy droppings of the joint.

Milly's eyes lit up with delight.

'Heaven!' she said. 'I only ever get it here. When I get married, I shall have a Yorkshire cook as well as a French chef.'

'Well, get on and eat it then, love,' said Mrs Sykes, 'while it's hot.'

She cut it in four, put a portion on each of their plates, poured the gravy, and stood waiting. Milly forked a bit into her mouth.

'Perfect!' she said, closing her eyes.

Henry refilled her glass with claret. As soon as the

door closed behind Mrs Sykes, he asked, '*When* you get married?'

'Yes. I'm thinking of it.'

'You've had an offer?'

She exploded with laughter. 'Oh yes, dear Henry, I've had many offers of every kind, and some of them I've taken up. Marriage is a serious business and I can afford to be choosy. And this man is right for me.'

'Well? Who is it?'

'Hengrave.'

'But he's a millionaire.'

'There's no law against marrying money, love,' said Milly, and took some more Yorkshire pudding. 'Even if you don't need it. Look, I'm sick of the stage. I thought I would never be, but I am. I want to settle. To have a country house and to entertain. To move in society, but not Court society. No aristocrats for me. Their relations are such bores. I like interesting, creative people and so does Johnston. He is very rich. Very cultivated. He can teach me a great deal. He is sixty – twenty-four years older than me. He has a grown family, so does not want children, and neither do I. I'm too selfish now.'

'You don't think the age difference is dangerous?'

'Why?' she said with sharp perception. 'Are you feeling age? Attracted by some nubile Thornsby girl?'

'Don't be disgusting!' snapped Henry, and she laughed, knowing his preference for mature and sophisticated women.

'It's time you got married, Henry. You're a born family man at heart.'

'Yes. But who? A local young girl would be no use to me.' Amusement lit his rock-carved face, making it extraordinarily attractive. 'And the ladies I like would scarcely be suitable for a respectable cloth-maker. Can you imagine Nina de Malvette living in Thornsby?'

Nina de Malvette was an exotic dancer, an expensive queen of the Parisian *demi-monde*.

'Imagine the Worth gowns and the famous diamonds sweeping into the Mayor's ball!' She laughed so much that Henry began to laugh helplessly too.

He shook his head. Millicent was always a tonic to him.

'You don't need a rich husband, Milly.'

'Oh, I always need money – it is the only thing that makes me feel safe. I'll end up as an old miser woman wondering whether to leave her millions to a cats' home. You'd better marry, Henry, and have some kids for me to leave it to.'

This time he ignored the hint. He knew it was true. He knew the lack of marriage, the lack of children was at the root of his growing dissatisfaction with his life.

'Does Hengrave know all about you, Milly?'

'You mean about my past? He's never asked. He's not straight-laced, but I guess he values his personal dignity. So do I. He knows that a woman of my age who has been on the stage all her life is no shrinking violet. The truth is, Henry, I have come to know my limitations as an actress. I'm clever, good-looking, sexually attractive, can wear clothes, have a good sense of comedy and timing, and I've been lucky. But I'm not *great*. And I've seen and met the greats now, and I *know* the difference. Terry, Duse, Bernhardt, Rachel. I don't think it's worth the struggle and heartache if you've not got that real gift. So I'd like to be married. I'd like to queen it at Danesfell Abbey, now Johnston's bought it, and spend part of the year at the high spots – Deauville and Nice, Baden-Baden, Cairo – share the good life with a fellow sybarite who loves me. Johnston and I will be very happy.'

'But you don't love him?'

Her black eyes levelled with his. 'I've said before – what *is* love?'

'You were in love with Richard Normanby,' he said, tight-lipped.

'Oh, Christ, every girl was in love with Dick Normanby. I was sixteen and wild about him. He was a very skilful lover. He followed the company for about a month, and then disappeared, and the next thing I knew he had married Florence Jagger.'

Henry went scarlet, 'By God, if I'd known . . .'

'But Henry, you didn't know. I had a bad time. It was as much my fault as his, I suppose . . . young girls are dangerous cattle. Looks and sex, that was all there was – to him – nothing else.'

She did not tell him of the ugly, back-street abortion, and the time when, jobless, she would have starved without the money he had sent her. She smiled into his stiff, disapproving face.

'You don't hear from him?'

'No. When he arrived in New York he turned up on my doorstep – I didn't let him cross it. He threatened to blackmail me, and I told him to go ahead – but he didn't. I was not going to have him fleecing my friends – or me. I had some very rich friends. Dick is nothing but an aristocratic con-man. He went through the money he had stolen from Florence, and he lived on his title and looks, and rich women, and then when he got too well-known he left for the West. I've never even heard of him since!'

Mrs Sykes came in and removed their plates. Henry carved the succulent beef. There were roast potatoes and a perfectly cooked cauliflower, English mustard and horseradish sauce. Millicent clapped her hands.

'Delicious! What's for pud?'

'An apple pie, Miss Milly.'

'And Cheddar cheese? Perfect.' She raised her glass.

'Here's to you, Mrs Sykes.' When the door closed behind the smiling woman, she said, 'and to us, brother Henry. To a more satisfactory future. To my marriage with a very nice man, and to your marriage too. That's what you want, isn't it?'

'Yes,' he smiled, forgetting his disapproval. 'Yes. But how to go about it? It's funny, it's the one thing I just don't know how to plan for.'

'I'll think about it.'

She stayed until nine, and then summoned the carriage, put on her pretty hat and went out, all smiles and scent, and sweeping taffeta skirts, making an exit as only she could.

She paused at the carriage door, and turned back to him.

'I'm staying at Danesfell for some days. Will you come up there and meet Johnny Hengrave?'

'Up with nobs? If you wish. You've made up your mind on this marriage, then?'

'I'm going to tell him "yes" tonight.'

'You always were one for quick decisions. Well, the best of luck.' He meant it sincerely, and she gave him a quick, grateful kiss.

'And you, Henry. If you want to catch a wife, you ought to move, buy a good house where you can entertain some of the local girls. Suitably *chaperoned*, of course.' Her face was wickedly solemn. 'Give a few parties.'

'Get along with you,' said Henry, slapping the curve of her fashionable bustle as she got into the carriage. 'You'd flirt with the devil himself.' Then unexpectedly, 'Do you ever get clothes in Leeds?'

'In *Leeds*?' she stared, astounded. 'No.'

'Well, why not? Most of the cloth you wear comes from here anyway. All right – *don't* tell me! Monsieur Worth has no branch here. But in the Arcade there is a

nice little shop called Madame Rosa's. There's a young
girl working there who is very hard-working and
ambitious and whom I would like to help, and I understand that they get commission on sales.'

'Whom shall I ask for?'

'Oh, well . . .' he hesitated. 'Ask for Miss Margaret.'

'I suppose that this is the nubile girl who is turning
your thoughts to matrimony?'

'You are quite wrong. My thoughts are turning to
marriage because I want a son. I have a great business,
and a large amount of money. I need someone to work
for. This little Miss Margaret is just someone I wish to
help, and whom I'm sure is too proud to accept a
handout.'

'H'm,' said Milly. 'A likely story.' He closed the car-
riage door and waved to her as she went jingling away in
Johnston Hengrave's beautiful carriage to be back at
Danesfell by the time the card tables were set.

Henry turned back into the bleak old house in which
he had created his snug, bachelor home. He rubbed his
strong cleft chin with his thumb, and poured himself a
second tot of brandy. She was a card, all right, his sister,
Milly.

A month later, hearing that Cliffs Edge, the house at
Upper Thornsby which Thomas Jagger had built for his
beautiful daughter over twenty-five years ago, was up for
sale, he bought it. He had acquired his kingdom, he had
made a success, and now he would become a householder,
and perhaps a married man.

Two or three days later Miss Emilia de la Cartier,
accompanied by her new fiancé, Mr Johnston Hengrave,
walked up the Arcade, looking ostensibly at diamond
rings, although they had no intention of buying the
engagement ring in Leeds. It was simply, Johnny said, to

get an idea of the sort of thing Milly wanted, although, heaven knows, she had enough diamonds already to last a lifetime.

Johnston Hengrave was a cool, pleasant, well-preserved American. He had been born with a large-sized silver spoon in his mouth, in the shape of a steel company in Pittsburgh, created by his father and grandfather. He was a millionaire. Johnny, however, had never worked in the business. He had devoted himself to enjoying life. He had married early, done his duty to the family by producing two boys and a girl, before he and his wife had divorced by mutual consent and with some relief. Divorce in the USA was not looked upon with royal disapproval as it was in England. His ex-wife lived in New York and Massachusetts near the children. Johnny preferred European society. He was, in fact, a popular, discreet, cosmopolitan gentleman. The sort of man Henry affected to despise – but in fact he became very fond of Johnstone Hengrave.

Milly saw Madame Rosa's shop with its plate glass and handsomely-carved mahogany front. In the window were just two garments, and a scatter of beautiful artificial flowers across the pale felt of French grey which lined the floor, all of which picked up the shades of a small toque made entirely of pale amber and salmon-coloured ospreys. A fold of fine amber cloth was draped over a gilt chair, and against it was a French fashion plate, illustrating a walking-dress in the very latest fashion and a pair of exquisitely stitched cream kid gloves. Milly stopped. Someone who knew about display had fixed that window.

'Oh, Johnny, isn't that charming? I really do love that hat. Perfect for Autumn racing.'

'Well, go in and buy it then,' he said indulgently.

'But what will you do?'

'Oh, I'll have a walk around – I don't know this city at

all. I'll take the carriage and go on a bit of a tour. It seems very dirty but full of life. Not the kind of place one could live in.'

'Give me – half-an-hour, then?'

She went into the shop. A tall, middle-aged woman in rustling black taffeta, with the questioning smile of the saleswoman, came forward.

'Can I be of assistance, Madame?'

Milly glanced around. 'I was told to ask for a Miss Margaret. Is she here?'

The tall lady bridled. '*I* am the first sales, Madame.'

A stout, tired, overdressed and over-dyed woman appeared as though by magic. She had evidently been listening and was the owner of the shop. 'Mrs Merrett,' she said sharply, 'if the customer asks specifically for an assistant, it is her privilege. Mr Willy . . .'

A good-looking, discontented young man appeared. He was flashily well-dressed, and showed an overwhelming amount of white cuff and collar.

'Yes, Mama?'

'Will you tell Miss Margaret that she is wanted in the showroom?'

'Of course.'

Willy eyed the tall, graceful lady and recognized her at once. He flew up into the workroom where Margaret was helping with a difficult draping.

'Maggy,' he burst out, 'you're to go down – there's a customer asking for you. Personally. Old Merrett's in no end of a stew. It's the actress, Emilia de la Cartier. She's ever so famous.'

Margaret rose, glanced at herself in a tall mirror, smoothed down her dress, and her hair. She washed her hands at the sink. Perfectly clean, well-groomed hands were important.

'Hurry, hurry.'

'It's no use getting all puffed out,' she said sharply. A final twitch to her cuffs, and hands folded neatly she went skimming down the stairs with her quicksilver motion, stopped and permitted herself a faint false smile of recognition and delight, for she had never seen Emilia de la Cartier before, although she had, of course, heard of her.

'Madame de la Cartier,' she said, 'What a pleasure to see you.'

Millicent saw a slender young red-head with blue eyes full of intelligence, incredibly neat and formal, but with none of the fawning gentility of the average 'shop lady'. She understood flair when she saw it. It was what she had herself.

Margaret's glance rested admiringly on the apricot tussore walking-dress. 'You want to see the little hat in the window? It would be perfect with your gown.' And before Madame Rosa, Mr Willy or Mrs Merrett could draw breath, she had the pretty hat out of the window.

'Your dress is beautiful,' she said shyly. 'Was it – could it be by Mr Worth?'

'You know about him, then?'

'Oh yes, of course,' said Margaret, who read everything she could lay her hands on about the great couturiers.

'No. It was made for me by a friend of mine – a very talented designer. Ferdinand Leon. He works for Marischelle & Staynes in Regent Street. He would like to open his own house, but alas, he is a creator and not an organizer. But he's very good.'

'Indeed, he is. I like simplicity.'

'You admire Monsieur Worth?'

'Ye-es,' said Margaret doubtfully. 'But sometimes – there is too much of everything. Too many trimmings . . . I think a dress should stand on its own. Like yours. And the little hat will set it off perfectly.'

It was well over an hour before Millicent left, wearing the osprey hat, and leaving Madame Rosa's in a chaos of tulle and silk and tweeds. Three times Mr Willy had been sent down the Arcade, his coat-tails flying, to tell Mr Hengrave that Miss de la Cartier would only be another ten minutes, and Mr Hengrave had leaned back good-naturedly in the carriage, and lit another cigar. Three dresses had been ordered, the first measurements taken, and Millicent said she would come in for the first fitting when she returned from Europe. Mrs Merrett murmured something about a deposit, and was silenced by a sharp dig in the ribs from Margaret.

'I will drop you a line as soon as I get back,' said Millicent, 'and will either come here, or perhaps you will be able to come out to me at Danesfell? My London dressmaker always comes to me. I shall want these dresses for the Autumn season in town. Who shall I write to here? Miss Margaret? Is that really your only name?'

Madame Rosa put in eagerly, 'Her name is Miss Normanby.'

The penny dropped. Henry had sworn never to have anything to do with the Normanbys again and here he was, on the sly, helping this young girl, a girl who, in other circumstances might have been his own daughter. Milly could have laughed with amused exasperation.

'You are related to the Normanbys of Danesfell Abbey?'

'Yes,' said Margaret shortly. She obviously resented Madame Rosa's vicarious pride in the aristocratic connection.

'I am about to marry Mr Hengrave, who owns it now. I suppose you lived there once?'

'No.' Margaret was tight-lipped. 'I stayed there when I was very small, with my grandmother. For a very short while.'

'Well, Miss Normanby, you must certainly bring my dresses to be fitted. It will interest you to see Danesfell again. You will be able to spare her for the day, of course?'

'Of course,' Madame Rosa was ingratiating. The order was over a hundred pounds.

'Good day, and thank you. I've had a lovely morning.' Milly sailed off down the Arcade to join her betrothed in the carriage, leaving Margaret standing in the chaos of the shop.

'Well,' said Mrs Merrett spitefully, 'I hope she pays.'

Madame Rosa's tired shrewd eyes went to Margaret.

'With that kind of customer,' Margaret said evenly, 'you don't ask for deposits. She will pay. But even if she did not, the prestige it will give us, when people know she has bought here, will be worth it in the long run.'

Defeated, Mrs Merrett said angrily, 'Actresses! What a performance! And who is going to clear up all this mess and fold all the bales? Five bales out for every dress she chose. Who does she think she is?'

'A very clever, very successful, very important lady,' said Margaret. She bent over the order book, checked the entries carefully, totted up the amounts. 'One hundred and sixty pounds. Will you initial them, please Mrs Merrett?'

The head sales had to initial her junior's orders.

'I'll initial it when you've cleared up this mess.'

'I'll initial it myself,' said Madame Rosa sharply. 'It's a grand order. Lily . . .' she called down the basement stairs into the stockroom.

Lily Oglethorpe was a pale girl of sixteen who had been promoted to third sales. She was devoted to four-penny novels about poor but virtuous girls who married into the nobility, and regarded Margaret with a kind of holy awe, not because she was good at her job, or that she did not bully her like Mrs Merrett did, but because she was born a 'real lady'.

She appeared at the top of the stairs like a jack-in-the-box.

'Get this showroom cleared up, lass, and be sharp about it. Mrs Merrett – will you give Lily a hand.'

'Wait,' said Margaret. 'I must put the materials aside for Madame de la Cartier's order, and they must be taken up to the workroom to have the lengths cut. I'll do that myself. You do these.' She sorted out the unrolled bales of silks which Millicent had rejected. Mrs Merrett stood, her hands stiffly clenched, not moving a muscle.

'It is no part of my duties to clear up after other assistants, nor to take orders from my juniors. I may even have lost a customer. Mrs Shaft came in for a summer blouse and with all the fuss Miss de la Cartier made, she could not decide, and went without buying. In my opinion she will not come in again.'

Margaret kept her temper.

'Don't be cross, Mrs Merrett. Mrs Shaft will be back, and she'll bring plenty of her friends . . . right now she'll be telling them that she was in Madame Rosa's at the same time as Madame de la Cartier, the famous actress. It will fly round Leeds like – like a boomerang.'

Mrs Merrett began, huffily, to help clear the showroom. What was the point of being a 'first sales' Margaret thought, if you were not three times as clever as the other two? The day's commission would pay the Hollingroyd Crescent coal bill for next winter, and help with Charmian's new dresses for Edinburgh, and even give her a little bit for herself. For a new dress? Why not?

William Gadsby was suddenly taking an interest in her, and although she thought him ineffectual and tied to his mother's apron-strings, it had given her a new sense of being grown-up. He was not a real man – not like Mr Grimshaw. She often thought about her brief adventure in the train, and was disturbed that she could remember every feature of Mr Grimshaw's craggy Red Indian face, while Willy, whom she saw every day, vanished from her mind the minute she left the shop. But he was good-looking, well – if a bit flashily – dressed, and was generally thought of as a good catch.

By casual questioning of Jany Leck and her grand-mother, Margaret had learned a good deal about Mr Grimshaw. That he had once been deeply in love with her mother. That he had done all he could to save her mother's money and the firm her Grandfather Jagger had built, and that it was due to him that old Mrs Jagger had at least the house in Hollingroyd Crescent and a small income. She knew that he owned the three great mills along the Bradford Road, and that he was very rich and quite old and he was not married. The last fact gave her an odd sort of comfort which she could not understand. Having lived for thirteen of her eighteen years in Thornsby, and never having crossed his path during that time, she thought it very unlikely that they would meet again.

So William Gadsby was a much more likely proposition, and he really did want to take her out, which was flattering. Because, accustomed to young men being reduced to emotional jelly by Charmian's violet-blue eyes, Margaret had always thought of herself as 'the plain one'.

That evening Madame Rosa Gadsby, accompanied by her son, got wearily into the hired cab to drive back home. Mrs Gadsby pulled off her tight shoes and put her feet up on the seat opposite with a sigh of relief. She also took off her large be-flowered hat, and leaned back, taking out a thin dark cheroot. Willy bent forward and lit it for her, and she offered him one for himself.

'Thank you, Mother!'

Rosa Gadsby sloughed off the ultra-gentility of manner once she took the smart shoes off her aching feet, and relapsed into the earthy speech of her youth.

'I wrote to Rowes of Birmingham today. They were asking for a reference for Maisy Warren. I gave her a damn good one. She'll get that berth.'

William was relieved. The clinging Miss Warren had been on his conscience. He should never have mentioned an engagement to her. But a chap had to say something to get started with that kind of girl.

'It was a near thing, our Willy. I've told you before to keep away from t'shop girls. Only a fool fouls his own doorstep.'

'Yes, Mother.' He was sick of hearing her say it, although it was true. But it was hard, when one was thrown in contact with the workroom and shop girls all day. And some of them were smashers.

'So, keep off them . . . well, all but Margaret Normanby.'

Her calculating dark eyes watched him, and the tell-tale colour rose in his fair-skinned face.

'Ah,' she cried triumphantly. 'I've seen you taking a good look up her skirts every time she goes up to the workroom. No hanky-panky there, Will. She's a real lady. She's more than that. Her old man was Sir Richard Normanby, who used to own Danesfell Abbey. No good, of course, and no money. But she's a lady.'

'You mean you don't *mind* if I ask Maggy to come out with me?'

'Haven't you already done so?' His ears went bright red. 'You're wondering how I know. Well, if you must know, Miss Maggy told me herself.'

His mouth fell open. He could not believe it. It had never happened with any of the girls before.

'She *never* did!'

'Oh, yes. Cool as a cucumber. Said you had invited her to walk out with you on Sunday, and had I any objection, because she values her job, and would rather not accept if I had.'

He was astounded and humiliated. It was what he ought to have done if he had had the nerve. But he was afraid of his mother. She had plans for him, and she held the purse-strings.

'What did you say?'

'I said I had no objection so long as it was kept on a friendly footing only.' The tired eyes under the hennaed bouffant fringe were amused. 'She said that was exactly what she thought. She'll be a hard nut to crack. So don't you try.'

He settled into his corner and shook out the evening newspaper, thinking of Maggy Normanby as a saucy bitch, but also thinking of the small, pretty, elegant ankles, and the soft young curve of her breasts beneath her well-fitting dresses. There was a sharp sweetness about her, refreshing after Maisy Warren's languishing.

'You can bring her up home to tea if you like,' said his mother. 'Give me a chance to talk to her outside the shop. Rub my insteps, that's a good boy.' William obediently put down his paper, and rubbed his mother's small swollen feet. 'She's a card, that Maggy Normanby. She took that de la Cartier woman along today – well, it was a treat to listen. She only came in because a friend had recommended us. But she put in an order of a hundred and sixty pounds. It's a pleasure to watch Maggy handling a customer. Like a chap landing a trout. She's got real style and a head for figures like a boy. I'll make her first saleswoman this year if she goes on like this.'

'What will old Merrett say to that?'

'She'll put up wi' it,' said his mother shrewdly. 'She's over fifty, and on her own. She'll never find a better crib. And the little Normanby will handle her. Come to think of it, in a few years' time she could handle the whole shoot, as manageress. Give her an interest in the shop. Then I could put my feet up for a change and leave her to it.'

'What kind of interest?'

'What kind do *you* think, lad?'

'You mean – I might *marry* her?'

He was aghast. He was only twenty-three and no such thought had entered his head.

'You think on it, Willy, lad. A real lady and a first-rate manager. There's nowt like having your own working for you, Willy. When it comes to brass tacks, they're the only folk you can trust. It would be your shop, of course, eventually, when I go.'

'Don't talk about that, Mother,' he said. But he thought about it. He also thought of opening a small turf commission agents. Or a pub. Anything but a ladies' dressmakers. One day, when the business was his to sell. But in the meanwhile, with a girl like Maggy in charge, there would be precious little for him to do – he might relax a bit – and enjoy himself.

To Charmian the evening had been like a dream. She had been in Edinburgh a month, and up to the present it had all been rather stuffy and prim, because Grandmama Normanby was a great one for culture and history, which Charmian decidedly was not. She was sick of being walked up the steep and tiring Royal Mile, peering into smelly wynds, with a guide book, and being told boring things about John Knox, and Mary Queen of Scots, who must have been an idiot to stay in such a country when

110

she could have gone back to France and had a good time. Of course there were parties and visits, and an occasional dance, rigorously chaperoned by Lady Margaret Normanby. George lived at home unless he was on duty at the Castle, and his friends came and went, and as the rumour of the beauty and charm of his young niece grew, the house seemed to be full of red-coated young men, bringing Charmian posies, and hanging over her chair with adoring eyes.

The most assiduous was Lieutenant Bellamy Chester, a handsome, ambitious young officer, twenty-nine years old, on furlough from India. Everyone said Bellamy was set for a great Army career. He was not fantastically rich, but very well-to-do, and his family were Scottish aristocracy, with a castle somewhere up on the Pentland Firth and a house in Edinburgh. People, including Lady Margaret, had begun to notice his attachment to Charmian, and tongues were beginning to wag.

Charmian herself was sure he *would* eventually ask her to marry him and was quite sure she would accept. But Bellamy was a little too correct, a little too worshipping. He did not excite her at all.

'I shall never forget being at Danesfell when you and your sister were brought there as children. Your grandfather, Mr Jagger, had died, and this Yorkshire chap, his manager, brought you to Lady Margaret – he carried you in and set you down, half-asleep, all golden curls, and those pretty eyes full of tears, a little rosy, china doll,' he had said adoringly. 'You haven't changed a bit.'

'Oh, haven't I?' Charmian thought a trifle rebelliously. It was one thing being adored, but there was also such a thing as fun. F-U-N. And she was only eighteen. She remembered Billy Heaton and the lilac shrubbery, and the delicious thrills that powerful if common young man

111

had aroused within her, and she began to wish Lieutenant Chester were not quite such a chivalrous young gentleman, or that his chivalry was of a more urgent kind, like young Lochinvar, and he would snatch her up, and ride away with her to his castle.

But that would be quite shocking unless it was after the wedding, and he had not proposed yet, and she wished he would because he was due to go back to India in a very short while. And – terrible thought – supposing he proposed and left her, an engaged girl, for months in England, until the hot season was over in Calcutta. Months with a fiancé on the other side of the world! And in *Thornsby*! With all those local boys after her? She would go mad! She would run away, make a bad marriage, or do something shocking like making love properly in the way people never mentioned. With Billy Heaton. Or anyone. They all wanted to – and so did she.

She would feel her breasts prickle, and hug herself, arms closed round her urgent young body, and wish passionately that the honourable attentions of honourable gentlemen were not so boring.

But this ball, given at the Castle by the Commanding Officer, was particularly exciting. The regiment was there and there was no doubt at all who was the queen of the ballroom. She had saved her most beautiful dress for it. Margaret had made it from the pale lilac crinoline which Florence had once worn to a ball at Devonshire House. It was low cut, and draped closely, displaying Charmian's magnificent figure, her white shoulders veiled in gauze, her dark golden hair crowned with pale violets, her lovely eyes glowing with excitement. Lieutenant Chester, when he led her into the ballroom, was overwhelmed with desire, pride and terror at the thought that before the night was out, this exquisite creature would be promised to him.

Before every dance there was a cluster of red coats about her. Lady Margaret sat among the ranks of chaperones and watched, and thought of her son, Richard, and saw again all the signs, the arrogance and invitation in the violet eyes, the reckless disregard of propriety when pleasure was offered, dangerous in a man, fatal in a girl of eighteen. The sooner Charmian was safely married, the better.

It was at this point that Lieutenant Angus Black of the Ghurkas, also on furlough, made his entrance into the ballroom, late and spectacular, and a flutter went over the assembled ladies, their heads bending towards him like a cornfield beneath a southern breeze.

Angus was six-foot-two, of a slender strength, ruddily handsome, with thick coppery hair and a full, red mouth. He looked superb in his dress uniform. His yellow hawks' eyes moved over the women and stopped when he saw Charmian. He had little money, a bad reputation as a womaniser with a reckless disregard of reputations. Colonel's lady or private's missus, it was all the same to him.

Charmian, surrounded by importuning young men, met his eyes across the ballroom, and felt the authentic thrill of sexual excitement. She was her father's daughter, she knew already the power of her attraction, and the delight such contacts brought her. What she did not know was how to control or disguise them. She had no real society experience, and no finesse. So she smiled, and Angus, being what he was, crossed the room, scattering the surrounding opposition – a hawk hovering for the kill.

He turned to Bellamy Chester, who stood beside her with the proprietorial air of one who has already an established claim, and said shortly, 'My dear Chester. Will you please introduce me to this charming lady?'

113

'Miss Charmian Normanby,' Bellamy said stiffly. 'Miss Normanby is engaged with me for the supper dance.'

'Oh, come on, Bellamy, old chap. You've been here all evening. Have pity on a latecomer . . .'

His hand was already on Charmian's waist, and without waiting for her consent or Bellamy's answer he swung her on to the floor among the swirling dancers.

They did not speak. She did not dare look up although she knew his eyes were raking her flushed face and the whiteness of her neck and shoulders. Under the gauze and lace of her draperies she felt his gloved forefinger insert itself beneath her arm, into the warm depth of her armpit, under the silk of her bodice; touch, hidden, the upper curve of her full young breast and slide towards the red nipple, suddenly proud with terrifying desire. She stopped and his arms dropped from about her. For a moment she thought she might faint, but she knew that he was as aroused as herself. She had no knowledge of passion, other than the unskilled fumblings of boys like Billy Heaton, but her instincts were true so far as men were concerned, and she knew that this was the real thing.

'It is so hot,' she said.

'Shall we take a turn along the battlements?' This burgeoning beauty was worth the kill. What he had not anticipated was the overwhelming urgency of his own desire. He took her arm and they turned towards the door, and in that moment Lady Margaret rose from her seat and sailed across the floor, and confronted them.

'You are not feeling well, Charmian?' she stated, rather than asked. 'Come along. I will get you some cool water. Here . . .' she took out a small crystal flask of smelling-salts, and thrust it firmly beneath Charmian's nose. The fierce perfumed fumes hit Charmian's olfactory nerves, and jerked her head back like a curbed horse. She felt as

114

though she were being forcibly and painfully revived from drowning. Her grandmother took her arm. 'You will excuse us, Mr Black.'

She sailed off, taking Charmian with her to the room which had been set aside for the ladies' cloaks, where she made Charmian take off her tight white gloves, and rinse her wrists in cold water. Then she took her firmly along a corridor into what were obviously private apartments, and sat her down at the table, taking a seat opposite her.

'Where are we?' said Charmian faintly.

'These are Lord Eckersley's quarters. I know them well. He will not mind. Now, listen, Miss. What do you want of life? Your sister Margaret seems to know very well what she wants. To be independent. But what of you?'

Charmian flushed, and drew herself up indignantly. She was recovering and on the defensive.

'I don't see why you are so stern, Grandmama.'

'Oh yes, you *do*! I know your kind of Normanby, Charmy, because your father was the same, and you are very like him. Idle, dishonest, vain, beautiful and very dangerous.' Charmian stared, shocked; Lady Margaret had never been so angry with her before, and the sharp old eyes made her feel like some little maidservant. 'You're mad if you think you can handle Angus Black. He's no Thornsby lad. He's like your father but more dangerous.'

'I wasn't doing anything.'

'You were about to make a public spectacle of yourself and lose your reputation and any chance of marrying Bellamy Chester, who I may say has already spoken to me and asked my permission to propose to you.' Charmian's defensive protests went unspoken. The swooning sexuality vanished, her beautiful eyes became bright and eager. Lady Margaret sniffed, and her Scottish r's rolled more threateningly than ever. 'Well, now, what *is* it you want? To go back to Thornsby to that mad mother of yours or to marry Bellamy? He is returning to India within six weeks. It is a very short time – not really long enough to arrange a really great wedding. But as your mother and Grandmother Jagger have no money, and I have very little, that can be dispensed with anyway. He has told me he is so in love with you he wishes to take you back with him.' Her knowledgeable eyes were suddenly gentle. After all, the child was beautiful, born for trouble, and so like Richard it made her heart ache. Fate had given Margaret all the character, and Charmian all the looks. 'It's up to you. You either stay here, accept Bellamy Chester, and I'll arrange everything. Or you go home to Thornsby tomorrow. You may be sure that I will not keep you here to ruin your reputation and your life with a rake like Angus Black and make my name a thing of talk and gossip about Edinburgh. Well, Char-r-mian?'

'Oh, Grandmama,' said Charmian, her eyes filled with genuine tears of regreat. 'I *am* sorry. I don't know what came over me.'

'I do,' said Lady Margaret, with grim amusement.

'I would like to marry Bellamy. I think he is very nice.'

'H'mph,' ejaculated Lady Margaret. Personally she thought Bellamy Chester too much of an inhibited Scottish gentleman to manage a girl like Charmian. There was bound to be trouble one day, but better that it should be within the iron circle of a marriage. 'Strike while the ir-r-on is hot. Bellamy has secured places for us with his parents for supper . . . let us go . . .'

So they went to the supper-room, and Charmian apologized so charmingly for her slight indisposition that Bellamy's parents were quite won over, especially the old Colonel, his father, and pronounced her a delightful, beautiful child, and during the entire evening she danced with Bellamy and only once in the early hours, when they were going down to their carriages, did she look over her shoulder, with a fleeting glance of farewell to where Angus stood watching her departure.

He called, he wrote, he waited about St Andrew's Square like, Lady Margaret said, a dog who has got the scent of a bitch on heat. Once the indomitable old lady went out and told him, if he did not clear off, she would have a word with his commanding officer and Lord Eckersley. Bellamy proposed. Charmian accepted, a wedding was hurriedly arranged at St Andrew's. Florence, to her daughter's infinite relief, did not come up to the wedding, pleading indisposition; nor did Mrs Jagger, whose arthritis ruled out a long railway journey.

Margaret travelled up to Edinburgh. She took on all the organising, and made the wedding dress; she was so quick to grasp and act it sometimes took Lady Margaret's breath away. She should, the old lady said, have been a boy. And yet, when she followed Charmian up the aisle, her only bridesmaid, wearing a dress of pale lemon taffeta, and a single pale yellow rose, catching the short lace veil to the thick, shining bronze of her hair, she looked every inch a woman, a lady, and a Normanby; and in the church, crowded with the military, aristocratic and literary cream of the city, she was by far the most elegant figure present.

Her grandmother sighed, and shook her head. That was *her* girl. What a wife *she* would make for a great landowner. Why in the name of all that was wonderful did she want to be a shop assistant?

At the back of the church, Black, beset with a burning frustration watched Charmian married to that stiff prig, Bellamy Chester. He would get her one day, he told himself. In the Army and in India anything was possible. The longer the stalking, the more triumphant the kill.

* * *

117

Margaret went back and found Madame Rosa and William full of eager welcome after her three weeks of absence, and the whole staff, even the threatened Mrs Merrett, relieved to have her back. Madame Rosa offered her the position of first sales. Mrs Merrett could take second assistant's place or leave.

Mr William Gadsby proposed marriage.

Margaret sorted the whole thing out with extreme tact. Why not create the position of manageress for her? Then Mrs Merrett could stay on in her present position as first assistant? Then no one would be upset and it would give Madame more time to rest. Madame Rosa accepted gratefully, and Mrs Merrett became her grateful slave.

With regard to the proposal of marriage, she told William she would think about it. She was too young to take such a definite step. She had not really considered marriage. She could not leave her invalid mother or her ageing grandmother. Besides, her mother would be opposed to the marriage, which might be prejudiced, but was understandable. She was, after all, Lady Normanby. Willy heartily agreed. He was more than a little afraid of her.

With Margaret in the business, he could pursue his pleasures, take the odd day out per week to go to the races with his pals. Madame Rosa's was now Margaret's kingdom, she drew a good salary, and commission – but no profits. She could wait for that. Meanwhile, she would make it the smartest establishment in Leeds.

Charmian sailed to India with her new husband, delighted that they would be stationed in Calcutta. She was warned by old India hands of the appalling Summer heat, and the long yearly separation from one's husband in the cool of the hills – so trying to young wives. Charmian did not think this would be trying at all. The Vice-Regal Lodge was in Calcutta, the Government was in Calcutta, Society was in Calcutta. She did not want to be stuck away in some remote place with Bellamy and she had been told that the life in Simla and the hill stations was enormous fun.

The Normanby girls were separated for the first time in their lives, and they missed each other with a yearning that perhaps only the twin-born can understand. Charmian missed Margaret's protective loyalty, and Margaret missed her pretty baby sister, the only outlet for the frustrated depths of affection she kept hidden in her heart.

The voyage out, surrounded by jealous wives and importuning officers and ICS men was not easy, and Bellamy, an impassioned though not skilful lover, became more like a gaoler than a young husband, shocked by her abandon and sexual urgency, which was not quite lady-like: it increased both his need for her and his profound distrust. She became like a drug which he could not do without, an addiction which he despised in himself.

Margaret waited anxiously for word from Miss de la Cartier, who was now Mrs Johnston Hengrave. The three expensive dresses, cut out and tacked, hung in their muslin wrappers, unpaid for, awaiting her return. It was the slack season, but the sewing hands could not work on them before another fitting. Madame Rosa muttered about laying some of the girls off, which Margaret could not bear. She knew how much they needed their money.

Mrs Merrett was obviously thinking, 'I told you so'. Willy hinted that actresses were always unreliable and that the wealthy Mrs Hengrave might not come back for her gowns and they would be left with a bad debt. Margaret resisted the temptation to write to Danesfell Abbey for reassurance.

Then, at last, it was late September and trade picked up, and one day Mrs Johnston Hengrave came sweeping in to the shop, and had her fitting, expressing delight with everything; she brought new fashion plates from Paris, and wore a sable cape from Vienna, and patting Margaret's cheek said, 'What a young lady you are growing, my dear. You must bring the dresses up to Danesfell for the final fitting next week. I shall be going back to London for the little season at the end of October. You'll have them ready?'

'Of course.'

'I may need some other things.'

'Now we have your pattern that will be easy.'

'Pattern? Oh, you mean *toiles*! In Paris, that is what they call them. That's dandy. Next week?' A small leather-and-gilt *aide-memoire* was slipped out. 'Wednesday afternoon? I'll take some lace patterns now – I need some blouses. Will that be convenient? Would you like to come to Danesfell?'

Margaret assured her that she would. She escorted her to the door, sending Willy Gadsby to carry the box of lace patterns to the carriage.

'Don't forget,' she whispered as he passed, 'to open the carriage door, hand Mrs Hengrave in, close the door, and bow. Then wait until the carriage starts.'

He gave her an exasperated look and rushed out after Millicent.

As at Millicent's previous visit, the showroom was strewn with bales and trimmings. Margaret turned to the electrified staff, smiling round at them. 'Well,' she said quietly triumphant, 'Let's get this cleared up, then.'

This time no one protested.

Chapter Five

Henry Grimshaw moved into Cliffs Edge at Upper Thornsby. With his usual efficiency he had replumbed and modernized, installed two bathrooms and easy-working kitchens, with service elevators or dumb-waiters, which he had first seen on a trip to New York, to save the servants' legs; had given a famous London furniture store a free hand to fit him up with the best-quality carpets, furniture and hangings, installed Mrs Sykes, together with her husband, as housekeeper and general handyman, with a couple of daily girls to help them.

Henry lived in a very plain bedroom and living-room, identical with the ones he had inhabited at the Master's House. The same Turkey rugs, the same fine but now outmoded mahogany furniture, the same huge glass-fronted bookcases filled with his books. This was his place. The impressive luxury of the rest of the house, the overstuffed velvet sofas, the grand piano, the glittering chandeliers and the oval dining table which could seat twenty, were all for entertaining, and characteristically, having decided to get married, he set about it in a businesslike manner, making schedules, planning dates, sending out invitations to local families with likely daughters, who were all delighted to accept his lavish hospitality. He knew nearly all the fathers – he had met them in the Wool Exchange, the club, and in business generally. The women of the family he did not know – they were not his kind of women, and they did not attract him in the least.

He was always delighted when, after an enjoyable

evening, his guests departed, leaving him to himself, and so far all the girls, though nice, well-brought up, and many of them good-looking, left him cold. He was filled with an ironic pity as he watched their attempts to catch him, and a cynical regret that he was not a boy in his twenties just coming into his father's business, but instead a man too worldly and too experienced to be attracted by these delightful but, to him, boring young girls.

After a bout of entertaining he would slip across the channel to Paris, and meet up with Liane, or Nina, or Chou-Chou, delighting in their charms, and their skill, and the way they walked into the Cascade or Maxims, and the way they wore their clothes, and talked, or danced, or just listened, and the way they were in bed. And after a weekend he was just as bored with them and came hurrying home to Thornsby, convinced that work was the only real thing in a man's life.

He knew what the matter with him. Somewhere, hidden away, was that terrible tender memory of love – when Florence Jagger had been the centre of his existence. Not Florence as she had ever really been, spoiled, selfish and neurotic, but Florence in the glory of her fragile young beauty. He could not endure to suffer that again.

He found it amusing that now he was rich, powerful and eligible, women fell in love with him. Many of the virgin daughters of Thornsby society, who came eagerly to his house with their Mamas and Papas, gazing at him with doe's eyes full of hope, trembling at his touch or word. And many also of the Ninas, Lianes and Chou-Chous, who professed a longing to be one man's mistress. But when he saw their eyes melt and their lips open and felt their silky arms cling when morning came, his instinct was to put an end to it, leaving them hurt and bewildered, wondering where they had gone wrong.

Mr and Mrs Johnston Hengrave returned to Danesfell

Abbey from a protracted honeymoon. Henry liked Millicent's husband and his sister was his only close friend. When she returned and they opened Danesfell Abbey for the Autumn with a series of brilliant house-parties for the hunting and shooting, he was their first and constant guest.

They dined, the three of them together. The great old house was now splendidly restored and furnished, staffed as only a great fortune can staff a great house. They told him of their Summer in Europe in the smart resorts and elegant towns, and he told them of his search among the young ladies of Thornsby for a bride, so drolly that they roared with laughter at his self-mockery.

Milly was looking magnificent and very happy. Watching her glowing dark beauty over the dinner table, he wished he could find a girl like her, and said so.

'Oh, don't be absurd,' she said. There were just the three of them, so she sat with the two men over their port. 'Here you are, the richest, and quite the handsomest man in the district, and you can't find a wife. It's ridiculous!'

Tonight Henry was particularly attractive. The strong face, which had made Margaret Normanby think of a Red Indian carved in a rock-face, came alive when he laughed and was animated, and his light grey eyes shone with self-mockery. The shaded table lights accentuated the shadows under his high, lean cheek-bones, and picked out the fading gilt in his thick, fair hair.

'You don't laugh enough, our Henry,' Millicent lectured, 'and you're *too* choosy. You want a young girl, of blameless reputation, who makes love like Nina de Malvette, is a perfect lady, and . . .'

'And dresses as well as Mrs Johnston Hengrave,' finished Henry. '*You* advise me, Johnston, you've picked a good one. Where shall I look for a wife?'

'Well, you could advertise for one, like they do in Bombay,' said Johnston, smiling. 'My dear boy, how can I help you? I didn't even *want* a wife. I'd been married for many years and was enjoying being a middle-aged bachelor. I just met your sister and became completely besotted with her.'

Henry's strong face darkened warningly.

'I'm beyond that kind of thing, Johnston.'

'*You* are?' Hengrave laughed. 'And how about me? I can certainly give you twenty years. I thought I must be in my dotage.' He took Millicent's hand. 'But it was just love.'

'It's not a wife our Henry wants,' Millicent said drily. 'It's a woman to mother his children.'

'Ah well, I've done my duty in that respect,' smiled Johnston, 'and to tell you the truth, although I have found inherited money pleasant, I have never felt the dynastic urge. But Henry tries to organize the whole darn thing like a sales campaign or the re-organization of a factory.'

'It's the only way I know.'

'H'mph,' said Milly, 'a likely tale. I'll have to see what I can do.'

'That is exactly what I hoped.'

'Well, now I'm here I'll do some entertaining for you. I think, Henry, love, that you should stop looking in Thornsby. Why not try among the local gentry? Many of them have very pleasant girls.' She puffed at her small, yellow, Russian cigarette, her head on one side, her eyes mischievous, pretending to consider. 'You ought to choose a lady. You appreciate refinement. Not too rich, then she'll appreciate you. Not too clever. Pick from a big family so you will be certain she can breed.'

She caught him on edge, and he coloured angrily. 'I'm not buying a brood mare.'

'Well, isn't that so?' she said innocently.

Johnston rose, intervening, 'Don't tease, Milly. Would you like to play pool, dear boy? I can see you two are heading for a squabble so I'll go ahead and see the table is ready and tell the man to put up some Bourbon and sandwiches.'

He went out and Millicent's dark eyes were bright with affection.

'He's a dandy. He knew we wanted to talk alone. He's the most tactful guy alive.' She rose and sat on the arm of Henry's chair, her arm round his neck. 'Henry, love, you can't have everything in one person. It's impossible. You have to be satisfied with the best you can get and be thankful, and sometimes it can be very sweet. If someone really loves you, as I know Johnston loves me, it creates its own response.'

'Is it enough?' he asked harshly.

'That's what I'm trying to knock into your stupid head. It *has* to be enough. You and I have both had our great passions, Henry, and what were they? Mine was a thief and yours was a fool, and marriage to either of them would have been a disaster. No. After thirty you have to compromise. Look for the best, value it, and stick to it.'

'Oh, philosopher . . !' mocked Henry rising, laughing at her. 'Come and play pool with your admirable Johnston. You'll end up being madly in love with him.'

She rose, taking his arm, smiling.

'Not *in* love – and never madly. Never again. But yes, . . . I do love him. He is a dear companion.'

So Millicent went to work and gave dinner-parties, and small dances, and weekends, and shooting-parties and invited the 'local gentry' as she called debutantes of the district. And Henry found himself seeking out more and more a certain Miss Angela Torrance.

He liked her. Her father was a gentleman farmer, a

125

tenant of Johnston's. His wife, a formidable lady, came from what she termed, a *better* family, in that her father had been a bishop and an aristocrat. It took Mr Torrance all his time to support his family and send his five boys to good schools. He made do on his large-holding, but he preferred hunting to farming. Angela, at twenty-seven, was the eldest, and already considered well on the shelf. She spent her time running the house and helping her mother care for her five brothers and two younger sisters. She was capable and pleasant and rather shy. She rode well to hounds, worked for the church, and did some district visiting.

A tall young woman with a fine figure. Fair-skinned and rosy cheeked; her hair was poor and colourless, smoothly braided, her eyes an undistinguished blue-grey. She was thrown into a panic of fear and gratitude that the rich, good-looking Mr Grimshaw should show an interest in her. If, as her mother insisted, he was not quite a gentleman, she did not care. She thought him a fine man and she adored him which was extremely gratifying to Henry.

Millicent watched with some amusement. She quite liked Angela. A *good* girl, undoubtedly, but was goodness enough? She did not seem to have much intelligence, and she certainly had no sparkle. Henry would be kind, generous, and discreet, but she did not think he would be faithful – but then how was a wife in Cliffs Edge to know what her husband did on long trips to Paris or Vienna? Milly shrugged. *Chacun à son gout*. Angela loved Henry, that was obvious, and after battling with the inconveniences of the Jacobean farmhouse that was her home, she found Cliffs Edge a palace. That a man should give thought to making a house easy to run was a miracle in itself. She thought Henry perfect, which was as it should be.

The Hengraves gave a dinner-party before they left for London for the little season and to travel on to Egypt for the bleak months of January and February. They were not hardy hunting folk, but sybarites. Millicent invited Angela, her eldest brother, and her parents – 'to give Henry a chance,' she told Johnston, 'to get the matter settled. It's not fair of him to keep the poor girl in suspense.'

It was a beautiful late Autumn day, the bracken red on the fellside, and Henry decided to send his man ahead with the evening clothes and ride across the moor to Danesfell Abbey. Angela's chief accomplishment was riding. He would never be a brilliant horseman but he enjoyed the exercise and she taught him a great deal about handling a horse on their rides together, always with a groom or one of her sisters in attendance. Henry, still unsure of his intentions, strictly observed the proprieties.

He rode contentedly, thinking Angela might do very well at Cliffs Edge, and that it would be pleasant to buy her some decent clothes, and spoil her – and to take her away from 'that harpy of a mother'. She did not arouse any urgent desire in him – but she was a lady and would never let him down.

Below, the curlews were calling across the Autumn ploughing, and the farmhouse chimneys sent smoke straight up in the clear and breathless air. Beyond Upper Thornsby the ground dropped in a high grey stone cliff, so from this part of the moor the town of Thornsby itself was hidden, and only the cloud of murk, pouring up from the mill chimneys and narrow streets of workers' houses, marked its presence.

He turned into the long main drive of Danesfell Abbey, between the wide wooded paddocks where cattle and deer grazed. It was still as unreal to him as it had been that night when he and his father had come up here to the ball where Florence had first met Richard Normanby. Reality was down there in the hidden town, in his weaving sheds, in the rows of little terrace houses, and the busy market place.

He saw a hackney carriage trotting up the driveway ahead of him towards the house. It drew up before the long pillared portico of the main entrance just as he rode into the gravelled forecourt. Two young girls alighted and proceeded to unload several long, dress-makers' boxes. Hengrave's butler, flapping like a disapproving crow, came running down the steps.

'You must take these round to the tradesmen's entrance, young Miss,' he said severely. 'And wait there until Mrs Hengrave can see you.'

The elder girl spoke in a cool authoritative voice: I'm sorry, but we have already unloaded the boxes. Mrs Hengrave particularly wanted her gowns today to be packed for London. I am certainly not going to load them all back again.'

Henry found he was smiling. It was his odd, funny little girl from the train. Florence's girl, with the red hair and freckles, and direct blue eyes: the gutsy, positive, ambitious little creature who should have been a lad – who might, in different circumstances, have been his. He unmounted, and went forward, told the man to call a groom for his horse, and to have the boxes carried up to Mrs Hengrave's boudoir, and to tell her that Miss Normanby had brought them from Leeds and was waiting on her.

The man's manner altered immediately. 'Mrs Hengrave will not be in for another hour,' he said. 'She and Mr Hengrave drove over to Abbey Farm for lunch.'

128

'Well, take the dresses up, then, and bring Miss Normanby and me some tea in the small parlour. Pay off this driver.' He turned to Margaret who stood demurely, glittering with inward amusement. 'Have you driven all the way from Leeds?'

'Goodness, no! We took a hackney to the station, then a train, sitting in the luggage van with the boxes to guard them, and then another cab from Thornsby station up here. I should love some tea.'

'Come then,' he took her arm, and became aware of the gawping Lily. 'Hawkins, take this young lady to the housekeeper for tea and look after her well. And take care of those fripperies, or Mrs Hengrave will have your ears off. Come along, my child.'

He took her arm and they wen- into the great house together, both conscious of a strange elation at meeting each other again.

'Have you had anything to eat all day?'

'No.' She realized she was starving. 'But it's all right. Lily is staying the night with us at Hollingroyd Crescent and we shall eat then.'

'But you will eat something now,' he said, and rang the bell. When Hawkins came he told him to bring Miss Normanby something substantial.

It was very pleasant to be taken care of – she sometimes got sick of looking after everyone else. Mama, Charmy, Grandma Jagger, Jany. The shop, Mrs Gadsby, Mr Willy, Lily. They all turned to her for decisions.

She followed him into the small panelled parlour she remembered from Lady Margaret's day – but it was much prettier now, with flowery chintz, a bright fire burning, vases full of brilliant autumn flowers.

'Sit down, sit down. Take off your hat.' She sat down near the fire, and the winter sun lit up the flame of her hair. She looked older, not so childish, more decisive.

129

But prettier. He realized she was not, as he had thought 'a little creature'. She was quite tall, but slender and delicately boned, the look that had given Florence her enchanting fragility. But there was nothing fragile about Margaret – she was more like sprung steel. 'You would like a sherry?'

'No, thank you.'

'You don't like it?'

'I've never tried – with a mother like mine, would you?'

'Ah!' A shadow crossed his face. 'I had forgotten. But it's not hereditary – it's a question of character, and you are quite different from your mother.'

'You mean I'm not pretty?'

'I didn't mean that at all. I meant you have a strong character, and your mother never had. My mother died of drinking. She was gentle, generous, soft-hearted. My father was cruel, mean and harsh. But strong. I think both I and my sister have inherited a lot from him.'

'Did you hate him?'

'Yes. My sister hated him still more. In the end I was sorry for him, being so rich and lonely, with no appreciation of the good things in life.'

'You have a sister?'

He was startled. 'Did you not realize that Mrs Hengrave is my sister?'

'But she was Madame Emilia de la Cartier before her marriage.'

'That was her stage name – she was Millicent Grimshaw of Bradford Road, long before that. She used to keep house for my father when we were children. He would not even pay for her to go to school. She was nothing but an unpaid servant at home.'

Margaret's eyes opened wide. 'And now she has all this. How?'

'Hard work, hard thinking, knowing the right people . . .' He stopped and was surprised by the wry irony in the tired young face.

'And she is beautiful and has that – that something that attracts men.' She gave a forlorn little sigh, 'which I *don't* have. Charmy does, my sister. In fact she has too much of it – it's a nuisance to her. And to everyone.'

'Sexual provocation?' he said, and she flushed, suspecting he was trying to shock her.

'Yes. It's almost as bad as being hump-backed or squinty. Every man she meets is just mad about her. But she hasn't the brains to control it. Your sister has.'

'Oh, yes, indeed,' said Henry, not able to disguise his amusement. 'Very much so. But being an actress has taught her a great deal.'

'Charmy isn't clever enough to be an actress,' she shrugged, and smiled. 'Not that Mama would have allowed it. But anyway, Charmy's married now, to a Lieutenant Bellamy Chester, and now she's gone off to India with him.'

'I hope she will be very happy.'

'Well, she's not my responsibility any more. Thank heaven. I hope she won't get into some awful mess.' She looked up suddenly, puzzled, and said, 'It's a very funny thing but I can talk to you as I can to no one else. Not even Lecky, because she would not understand, and you seem to understand everything.'

'Almost as though I was your father?' he asked wrily.

'It's not a bit like that!' The pure colour flared up her face at the admission.

When he filled the sherry glasses, his hand shook very slightly. 'Now, you've had a long and tiring day, and this tiny drink is not going to turn you into an habitual drunkard.'

Hawkins came in with cold food on a trolley, and

131

Henry dismissed him and served her himself, then sat opposite her, watching her with pleasure, loving her quick precise movements, the quick flash of her interest, and finding himself extraordinarily stirred by the naïve admission that she found him attractive.

He talked about his work, the mills, and the cities he knew in Europe and America. The people he had met, but not about the lovely ladies. He was a great reader and theatre-goer, interests which she had neither the time nor the money to pursue. Her own busy life shrank down to nothing – Thornsby and Leeds – home and shop. Only when people like Henry Grimshaw and his sister came fleetingly into her life did her horizons expand and she had a glimpse of a great world far outside her experience. She gave a long, long sigh.

'I don't suppose I'll see any of those places.'

'Why not? I didn't think I would at your age.'

She brightened. 'It's easier now Charmy's gone, and I'm earning more money. I'm the manageress. I pay Lecky now – five pounds a year. I'll pay her more when I can.'

'But it's not quite what you wanted?'

'Oh, yes. More than I expected.' Again the long childish sigh. 'It's funny, isn't it, that you work and work to get something, and then when you get it, it's never *quite* what you want. There's always something wrong or something else. Do you think anyone ever says – "Yes. This is *it*! This is what I *really* want? I'm happy *now*! I can't ask for any more." Do you think it's possible?'

'Not any more,' he said. 'At your age I did. You are wiser than I was to doubt it.'

He put out his hand and his long, well-shaped fingers cupped her chin, and raised it, looking into her eyes, watching the colour shift under the fine skin, smiling.

'Do you remember the night your grandfather died?

132

When I brought you and your sister up here? Into this very room? To your Grandmother Normanby. Do you remember in the carriage? Your sister fell asleep and you cried in the darkness until I took you on my knee. I've never forgotten that little girl trying so hard to be brave.'

She rose, eyes alight. 'Yes. I remember very well. I was so frightened until you took charge of us. I hated feeling helpless, even then. That's why I work so hard – because being poor makes me feel helpless and I'm never going to feel helpless again. If I can help it.'

'You are *wonderful*!' he said, and took her hand, drew her up to him and kissed her as he had kissed her when she was a small girl of five. She was so young and sweet, yet so strong. He did not mean to rouse her, or himself. It was an innocent and thoughtless action – as though she was the weary, silent, plucky child of thirteen years ago.

And then like a flash, desire came. He was angry with himself for his lack of control, but Margaret was swept away by the power of feeling. She sprang to her feet, raised her face again, firm flesh lips parted with a fervent response.

'Again!' she said imperiously and his arms closed about her.

'What the devil made you think you are not attractive to men?' he said, uncertainly, still half in mind to put her away from him, but suddenly unable to. He took her lips again and their kiss had all the blind, mindless delight of complete consummation.

He heard her gasp, felt her tremble, felt the cool lips warm and melt, and the thin girl's body sag yieldingly against him, and his own body harden in responsive desire.

He knew he had made an unforgiveable error. He set her down. He still held her upright, or she would have fallen. Her neat little hat had slid backwards, her face was a triangular patch of rose against her cloud of coppery hair, her blue eyes melting and heavy.

'Miss Margaret,' he said stiffly, 'please forgive me. I forgot you are now a grown young woman and I must not take such liberties. You were not shocked? Or frightened?'

She was coming slowly back to earth. She smiled enchantingly. Quite unashamed. 'No. I never did it before. I know what Charmy means now, when she says she is carried away. You carried me away.' She was suddenly very serious. 'Do you suppose that anyone else . . . I mean any other man will ever carry me away?'

He began to laugh helplessly. She was as naïve as a baby, for all her cleverness.

'I am sure that many handsome young men will want to.'

'I don't see what handsomeness has to do with it. You're quite old. And you're like a granite Red Indian. But you carried me right away, Mr Grimshaw.'

He could not speak. She was artless. So bold and innocent. So utterly without guile. His experience had only been with exceedingly practised ladies. She made him feel young, and foolish and tender. Between his hands he could feel her delicate rib-cage, and her heart beating wildly within.

'Little Maggy Normanby,' he said. 'You are adorable.'

There was the sound of high, well-bred women's voices . . . his hands dropped as though she burned him and she nearly stumbled. Past the long windows that looked over the rose-garden came Millicent and Johnston, with Mrs Torrance, a lady with an air of forbidding aristocracy, and her daughter Angela.

They stared through the window at this compromising scene. With great presence of mind Henry crossed the room and opened it, greeting the Torrances. Millicent's dark eyes were full of wicked mischief. Margaret sat down again, paralysed.

'Have we disturbed you, dear Henry? Mrs Torrance and Angela have come to see the new puppies . . . I have told Angela she can have her pick. Won't you join us?'

'Of course. But Miss Margaret from Madame Rosa's is here with your clothes. She has been waiting for you.'

Millicent glanced at Margaret's pink cheeks – really the child was admirably calm.

'I'll go up to my boudoir at once,' she said. 'You come and show Angela the puppies . . .'

Margaret could have laughed if she had not wanted to cry as well. The back of his fair head and his broad shoulders looked absolutely furious. He was angry with himself. She could sympathize. Did he think she would give him away? Or behave like Charmian, all tears and poutings, and soft touchings of inviting little hands. But she was not Charmian.

'Well, now my sister is back, you had better call your assistant and get off upstairs,' he said abruptly. 'When you have finished we'll have a carriage to take you to Thornsby.'

'Who were those people?' she asked.

'Mrs Torrance, and Miss Angela Torrance, from Abbey Farm. They are friends of my sister's.'

'Miss Torrance would be handsome, if she wore the right clothes.'

'But she is not rich,' he said, feeling unreasonably angry, as though she were criticizing one of his possessions.

Margaret looked at herself in the mirror, adjusted her neat hat to an impeccable angle, glanced at her beauti-fully-fitted simple little dress, and said, 'Neither am I.'

Henry made his escape. Margaret met Millicent's twink-ling dark eyes, and blushed again, but said nothing. Lily,

135

gorged with unaccustomed good food, was summoned from the kitchen and they followed Mrs Hengrave up into her boudoir.

The clothes were a great success, and Milly was delighted with them. She put each garment on, critically observing and approving each detail. The designs had been taken from *La Mode*. The ball-dress in amber and flame was a triumph.

'Are you pleased?' Millicent asked.

Margaret hesitated. 'Yes,' she said. 'Except that I wish we had designed them ourselves.'

'Have you ever thought of designing?'

'Yes.' Margaret bit her lip. 'It's not in me. Not that I want it. I know everything else. When I send a dress out, it's got to be perfect. I can sell and manage staff. I can cost every job in the whole place. But we take our designs from the fashion plates. We're not original.'

Millicent regarded her silently, then patted her cheek.

'My goodness, what a perfectionist. I'll keep the amber for Sandringham. We have a weekend down here. What shall I wear with it? Jewels?'

'Not many. One, perhaps – in your hair . . . the dress is flamboyant enough . . .' She added, 'If all the customers could wear clothes like you, how easy life would be!'

'Thank you. But I'm trained to wear clothes – part of being an actress once. It gives me an edge on all the well-bred ladies, who are mostly trained to ride horses.' They laughed together, 'I'll talk about you, child, in London. How are things going for you? At the shop? Is it all right?'

'Oh yes, for the time being. I want my own shop one day. But I'm not ready yet. I've got to learn to buy – Madame Rosa hasn't trusted me with that yet.'

'She will.'

'Yes . . . when her poor legs get too tired to come to the shop.'

'Aren't you afraid of becoming like that?'

'No.' She lifted her skirts, showing strong, slender legs. 'Mine are made to last.'

'I'll order some tea before you go.'

'Thank you.'

Henry came out into the hall as they were leaving. He turned sharply to his sister.

'Have you paid Miss Normanby?' he demanded.

'Oh, no . . . I'll send a cheque . . .'

'*Now*, dear sister. Miss Normanby does not get her commission until the cheque is paid . . .'

In spite of Margaret's protests, he insisted, and Millicent sat down and wrote out a cheque.

'Thank you.' Margaret glanced at it, put it away in her bag. 'You are very kind . . .' The cheque shut a door against her – she was just the dressmaker again. Mrs Hengrave was too wordly-wise to bother about her brother's behaviour, and Henry obviously wished to forget. Margaret felt humiliated, but not surprised. The afternoon had opened her eyes. She had been astounded by the unknown depths within herself. Without flinching, she made her goodbyes, and took her departure.

Lily, overcome by their condescension, was quite flushed.

'I didn't know great folk could be like that.'

'Yes, they were very kind.'

'But they're not great folk, are they? Mrs Merrett says they're jumped-up working people. Your mother, she says, is the real thing.'

'My mother?' Margaret repeated bleakly.

'Well, she *is* Lady Normanby.'

'Oh! Oh, yes.' She leaned back in the carriage, closed her eyes and began wearily to laugh. 'Oh yes. We're certainly the real thing. And much good has it ever done us.'

'You like that little Normanby girl?' said Millicent in her boudoir before dinner.

'I told you so. She's got character,' Henry said indifferently.

'Well, why don't you ask her up to Cliffs Edge?'

'With her drunken mother as chaperone?' Henry said grimly.

'No, that is a problem. But I'm sure I could find a chaperone.'

'You'll do nothing of the sort. I won't have you trying to run my life, Milly.'

'But you find the girl attractive. What's on your mind?'

Johnston sat silently, his fine white hands folded, his cool pale eyes going from one to the other appreciatively, like an umpire at a tennis match.

'What is on my mind is that I've been what I swore I never would be again. Soft over a woman.'

'But you're in the market for a wife. You could marry her.'

'I'm not looking for a child-bride. I'm over twenty years her senior.'

'Well, Johnny is a whole lot older than me, and we manage very well.' She stretched out her hand to her husband, who took and kissed it with smiling, good humour, and a little warning shake of his head. But, undeterred, Millicent continued to bait her brother. 'One would think you were one of those lecherous dotards out of a Dickens novel. You are just over forty, you are extremely attractive, amusing, interesting and very rich. I tell you there's not a mother in the country who would not hand over her sheltered sixteen-year-old and be grateful. The little Normanby girl told me today that the son of the proprietor, of Madame Rosa's, has asked her to marry him.'

'A very good thing for her.'

'He's not good enough for Margaret Normanby. But he'll own the business one day, of course, and what she wants is her own business.' Her eyes were bland. 'It might, as you say, be a very good thing for her.'

'You are not manipulating me, Milly. I'm quite aware that the child has quality. But she is Florence Normanby's daughter and I want nothing more to do with that family. I would be grateful if you would not speak of this matter again.'

Johnston's quizzical brows switched to Henry, as though to point out the ball was still in his court. Henry was furious.

Millicent's maid knocked to say the guests were arriving. Johnston rose punctiliously, offering his arm, his thin, distinguished face alight with amusement. 'We must go and greet them – however fascinating this discussion. Come, honey.'

Millicent went to his side in a sweep of velvet, a rustle of taffeta, a gleam of diamonds, taking his arm, ignoring Henry's tramline scowl. Every gesture she made to her husband held a caress. She shot a dark-eyed Parthian glance at her brother. 'Are you sure that poor crazy Flo has anything to do with it? Or the girl's age? Isn't it that you can't forgive her being Dick Normanby's daughter? Or do you perhaps think that little Maggy Normanby might be a bit too hard for the great Henry Grimshaw to handle?'

Henry followed them, glowering. The smooth, beautifully tailored broadcloth of his evening clothes slimmed down the muscular aggression of his broad shoulders, and the lights shone on his well-groomed hair – so fair that the streaks of grey were almost indistinguishable.

But the old fighting-bull Grimshaw stance was much in evidence.

But inwardly he was back to the raw boy in cheap, ill-fitting clothes and Richard Normanby and Florence were laughing at him. Did it still rankle as deeply as Milly said? He did not know. He only knew that this afternoon Richard's daughter had smashed his sober plans to pieces. He wanted a good reputable wife and boys to follow him into the business. He did not want to think about a kitten-faced red-head called Margaret Normanby.

Angela wore a missish flowered taffeta, quite unsuitable for her stateusque figure. Her fair broad face was flushed with health and emotion. Her parents, poor and well-born, were consumed with anxiety to achieve the admirable match. The virtuous Mrs Torrance would make nothing of the scene in the parlour. She would not have done so, Henry thought, if he had been the devil himself.

Marriage was a decision to be made, like buying a new machine or investing capital. You looked at everything available and picked the best. Yesterday it had seemed an admirable idea. Tonight it had more the temptation of a safe bet – the respectable married state. *Marry Maggy Normanby!* Milly was mad! Maggy Normanby could not begin to be the reliable wife and devoted mother he was looking for. That night he asked Angela Torrance to marry him.

Margaret read the announcement in the local paper and was shattered as though by a bereavement. Outside business she was starved of companionship, and the two brief meetings had been illuminating. The powerful man, so much older than herself, had caught her imagination. The touch of his lips had aroused her unawakened young body with a rapturous urgency. She did not think of him in the way that Angela did – the chance of a lifetime, a prospective husband – but she passionately wanted to see

140

him again. The announcement was like a door slammed in her face.

When she took the train home every evening her glance searched the platform. Once she had caught a glimpse of the broad shoulders and square grey hat and fled to a compartment at the far end of the train.

Her mother spoke maliciously about the wedding. 'That horrible Grimshaw man is getting married,' she said. 'I read it in the newspaper. What kind of woman would consider such a man?'

'Miss Angela Torrance is of very good family.'

Her mother's raddled face made a dismissing grimace.

'Farmers, aren't they? Your dear Papa would never have allowed us to mix with such people.'

Margaret rose, unable to stand her mother's company, but Florence's thin hand came out like a claw catching her skirt.

'Don't go,' she commanded. 'I get very lonely now Charmy has gone. She used to cheer me up with her gossip. You never talk to me.'

'I'm sorry, Mama.' She sat down again. 'I'm quite tired when I get back from work.' Florence ignored this – she never admitted that Margaret worked.

'I've been very good lately.' She bridled a little. 'You *know* I have.'

'Yes, Mama. You have been good.'

She had been good because Margaret had kept the bottles locked up, like medicine. She had also forbidden any laudanum unless she permitted it. Florence's condition had improved; she had been sober but irritable. Drunk or drugged she forgot her boredom, envy and loneliness and could still pretend she had kept her beauty.

'You know I have always been delicate. Ask Lecky. I was seventeen when she came to me, and even then was constantly under medical care. You must know how I

141

miss my baby, Charmy. Now, just a tiny brandy, and sit with me, and read her darling letter again. Is it not wonderful she has made such a success of life? That she's having such fun? And she's only a child. She could have done much better than Bellamy. Her Grandmother Normanby was too precipitate in pressing the match. Such nonsense! A session in London was what she should have had. She would have married a duke.'

Margaret sighed, sat down again, patiently measured out a small glassful of brandy, and began to read Charmian's last letter for what seemed to be the hundredth time. It had been written two months ago. Charmian, it appeared, was having a wonderful success. Bellamy was attached to the Residency. They had a pleasant bungalow in a cantonment outside the city, and life seemed to be a long sequence of balls, race meetings, receptions, and entertainments.

'*You cannot imagine what it has been like, and how lucky I am to be here, and not away in some awful station, miles from anywhere. At one reception the Viceroy actually introduced me to a real HRH, an Austrian archduke, whom I danced with. Your little Charmy was the belle of the ball, and poor Bellamy was so jealous, and I thought he would be so pleased and proud. Husbands can be so difficult at times.*'

'She is a *naughty* flirt,' Florence said in delight. 'I was *just* the same. Darling Papa would get mad with jealousy.'

'*There are men dressmakers here called darzees or something, who sew most wonderfully, and can copy any smart gown at absolutely ridiculous prices – Maggy would die at the cost. A few shillings for a beautifully-sewn dress. Anyway, please Maggy, send me all the very latest fashion journals and plates, and any new ideas about fashions. Materials here are cheap and some are very beautiful. Wonderful silks and Kasmiri shawls. The receptions at the*

Vice-Regal Lodge are very grand and one must look one's best. You should see the rajahs in their satins and turbans, with pearls like pigeons' eggs and diamonds and rubies, and some of them fat and old but some of them very attractive men, but I would not like to be a ranee, shut away in purdah, though I think my dear old Bell would sometimes like to shut up his naughty wife when she flirts too much. But Bellamy is very well thought of and very kind and generous to me, and should soon get his captaincy. I try to put his mind at reast, but I cannot help it if the officers and officials make a great fuss of me. I think he should be proud. After all I am not yet twenty and I want to have a good time now while I am young and unencumbered by a family.

'It is beginning to be hot so soon I shall be going up to Simla where it is cool. I am going with Mrs Armstrong, the Colonel's wife, as Bell has to stay on duty at the Residency, although he will get some leave to join me. She is a stuffy old dear, but has taken a fancy to me, so I shall have to be very good.

'Now it is getting really hot. There is nothing to do but take a siesta until people drop in for tea or a chota-peg, which is a little glass of whisky. There is a beastly bird which makes a tink-tink noise all day, and drives you crazy. I'm longing to go to the hills. My love to you both, hope all is well, don't forget the patterns, Maggy. Your own Charmy.'

At Millicent's insistence, Angela went to Madame Rosa's for her trousseau. It was to be a very grand wedding, entirely at Henry's expense. Angela was reluctant, remembering the brief glimpse of that slim body and red head so close to Henry, but when Margaret greeted her in the showroom, the tumultuous hair neatly braided, gravely polite and efficient, she began to wonder whether

143

her shortsightedness had deluded her. And no one, either her mother, Henry or Millicent had ever referred to the scene.

Margaret thought Henry's prospective bride totally undistinguished and was ashamed of herself for being glad. Beside Millicent Hengrave she was like a milch cow next to a thoroughbred horse. Later she would run to heaviness, and her legs, when she was pared down to her heavy flannel and cambric petticoats for a fitting, were heavy.

Besides the wedding dress, there were three small bridesmaids, two grown ones, a light suit to go away in – the honeymoon was to be spent in Paris – day-dresses, evening-dresses, ball-dresses, charming hats and accessories – everything but underwear. Millicent was ordering that from London.

Extra hands were taken on to cope with the order and Madame Rosa's buzzed with activity for eight weeks. The clothes were delivered and on the wedding day the Hengraves' landau was sent to take Margaret and Lily to Abbey Farm to dress the bride. Lily loved these excursions into the homes of the rich. She loved staying overnight at Hollingroyd Crescent, and listening to Florence's stories of her social triumphs. She always called her 'My Lady', and was beginning to emulate her high, rather affected upper-class southern accent.

Margaret had taken a great deal of trouble with Henry's bride. She had chosen a dress of stiff white satin, sculptured over Angela's fine breasts and firm waist. Her hair was dressed very simply with a coronet of white gardenias and orange blossom to hold the long lace veil in place. She looked – for once – quite beautiful. Like a Grecian marble, which Millicent brought to life with subtle touches of rouge and a pale rose-coloured lip salve. Angela, horrified at having her face 'painted' was amazed when she saw her completed self in the long pier glass. She turned to the women about her. 'I do look – *nice*, don't I?'

'You look lovely, my dear,' Millicent reassured her. She glanced at Margaret's slim, erect figure. She was not wearing the humble black of the shop assistant – she had left that to Lily. Her close-fitted dress was in a fine dark blue wool, piped, collared and buttonholed in dramatic emerald-green velvet. Every time Millicent saw her, Margaret had changed, was more poised, better dressed, more assured. Privately Millicent thought Henry a fool.

'Now,' she said to Angela, 'I will go in the first carriage with Miss Normanby, who will be waiting for you at the church for a final inspection. The bridesmaids will go in the next carriage, with your Mama, and your Papa will go in the bridal carriage with you. Wear your furs, Angela – it's turned cold. We don't want a blue-nosed bride.'

Margaret put on her hat which was made of emerald-green leaves with small, frosted blue berries. Her outfit was new. She had wanted to look well today – she wanted Henry to see what he was saying goodbye to.

'I'll be waiting at the church, Miss Torrance,' she said. 'Lily will help with your train into the carriage.' She hesitated, then said steadily, 'I wish you every happiness.'

Angela smiled her gratitude. 'Thank you, Miss Normanby.'

The big carriage bowled down the moorland road. Millicent's lovely sables filled the air with musky perfume. They had a warm rug over their knees, warming-pans in the muffs for their feet. Margaret, kitten-like, enjoyed the luxury.

'You've done very well with the gowns,' said Millicent.

'Thank you.'

'And you look very stylish yourself.'

'Thank you again. I wear the best we have at this sort

145

of affair – like a mannequin. I'm told in the French salons they have girls parading in their latest fashions. I've found if I dress well it puts ideas into the customer's head.'

'Have you everything you want at Rosa's?'

'Not everything. I'm starting to buy now – when I've learned that I don't know what I'll do. I'll have to think about it.'

'You ought to go to London.'

'I haven't the money.'

'That might be arranged.'

Margaret's sharp blue eyes lit with interest.

'You mean you might lend me some?'

'I would, of course. And so would my brother.'

'No,' Margaret said violently. 'Not him!'

'Ah,' said Millicent comprehendingly. She buried her face in the small bouquet of Marshal Neil roses which she carried. 'When I was your age, I found it better to work out the alternatives before making any move. What are yours? Your alternatives?'

'Oh, I haven't any,' Margaret sighed. 'But I know what I want. My own firm – or a good partnership.' She wailed suddenly, 'Why the devil aren't I thirty-five with twenty years' savings in the bank? My trouble is I'm too damned young.'

Millicent Hengrave burst out laughing. 'Be glad of your years of youth – they don't come back. Though I will say, I've preferred being over thirty myself.'

'I want so much. Money, experience – and opportunity. I could move to another job, but it would be hard to get better terms or a better establishment in the West Riding.'

'Or you could marry Mr William Gadsby – as you told me some while back.'

'Yes.'

'Why don't you?'

146

Margaret stared straight before her, her pure young face as hard as nails.

'It would be *his* business. Not mine. I don't want to spend my life working for someone else. Your brother said to me when we met in the train – and I chattered like a fool because he'd practically saved my life, and I didn't know how to thank him – he said Madame Rosa knew when she was on to a good thing. So does Willy.'

'You don't love him?'

'No. I don't hate him either. He can be quite nice.'

'You are tempted, then?'

'Why not? I'd be Mrs William Gadsby. The way the other girls go on that's *supposed* to be something.' Millicent waited, knowing there was something else, and then Margaret said, 'A woman isn't expected to be calculating.'

'But women are. They often have to be.'

'I calculate everything. Willy hates the dress trade. If his mother died, he would sell the business over my head. I might find myself a publican's wife. Or an amateur turf commission agent's.'

To her surprise Mrs Hengrave burst out laughing again.

'You are in such a *hurry*, Margaret, anyone would think you were a Grimshaw not a Normanby. My advice, for what's it worth, is turn him down.'

'Have you ever done that? Turned down a good chance?'

'I once turned a man down whom I desired and – yes, if you like it – loved. Let's say it was my first great passion. But he was worthless. A gambler, a thief and a cheat. Like you I wanted to go up, and I knew he would pull me down, as he had pulled down his wife and his family and anyone who loved him.' Her great, dark theatrical eyes burned into Margaret. 'It was your father.'

The silence in the carriage was so intense you could

hear the curlews crying across the moors. The clop-clop of the hooves were like irregular heart-beats.

'Well,' Margaret said calmly, 'it's nice to know the truth about him. Mama makes him out to be a sort of knight errant – *sans peur et sans reproche*. She writes to him – long sentimental letters, as though she were still seventeen. He doesn't answer. She hates your brother – says he stole everything from her.'

'He was very much in love with her,' Millicent said drily. 'If it had not been for him you would have had nothing. He saved Hollingroyd Crescent for your grand-mother, and saw she had a small income when everything had been paid up.'

'I knew Mama was telling lies . . . she does. Especially to herself. I've been told of her fabulous beauty – it's hard to believe. She cannot mention your brother civilly. Even now.'

'Perhaps because she wishes she had married him. Then she would have been sheltered and cared for all her life instead of being robbed and deserted. Perhaps she feels ashamed because he gave so much and was repaid with insults.'

'She lives in dreams,' Margaret said, and gave a deep shuddering sigh. 'I suppose that's why he dislikes me.'

Mrs Hengrave gave her characteristic little hoot of laughter.

'*Dislikes* you? A *likely* tale!'

The carriage stopped before the lych gate of the Parish Church and Angela's good-looking brother opened the door and helped them alight. The wide flagged pathway was lined with people. Henry, typically, had made it a Thornsby wedding, giving his working people the day off and contributing generously to their tea-parties. He and Angela would tour the parties in their carriage on the way to the station that evening; a private carriage had been reserved for them on the London train.

The church seemed full of the Torrance family. One of the young Torrance brothers, seeing Margaret standing to one side, came to ask whether he could show her to a pew.

'Thank you, I'll slip into the back,' she said smiling. 'I'm here to see to Miss Torrance's dress. I'm her dressmaker.'

When Henry arrived, he saw Johnston Hengrave waiting for him. An elderly best man, but the only friend he had. Within an hour he would be married to a nice, worthy young woman whom he supposed, a little wrily, he was lucky to have found.

He heard a clear, bright, girl's laugh, turned his head sharply and saw Margaret laughing with one of the young Torrances. She had grown up so much since he had first seen her. His plain little girl in the train; the funny, positive, odd, ambitious child; in less than a year she had learned more about being a woman than Angela would ever learn.

He was filled with an overwhelming, aching emptiness, and at that moment she turned her head, and saw him, and they stood frozen, looking at each other. The sudden unguarded longing in her face told him all that was in her heart. He told himself she belonged with the youngsters like this big, fair brother of Angela's, but he knew she belonged to him.

Johnston touched his arm.

'Come along, old boy, we ought to get down to the altar.'

'Yes, yes, of course.'

'The bridesmaids are arriving.'

'Yes. Let us go.'

He went down the aisle with his elderly best man.

Margaret stood motionless. Then the two young Torrance girls came chattering in in their bridesmaids' gauze, and she was straightening garlands on curly fair heads, and at last Angela arrived, tall, nervous, very handsome in the wonderful dress that she had created. She spread the train, smiled, said, 'You look wonderful, Miss Torrance,' and stood back and watched her go down to the altar on her father's arm to marry Henry Grimshaw.

So the great wedding was over, and she had helped Angela change into the pale blue dress of very fine cloth, with the cascades of lace at her throat and wrists, and the small blue hat with white and blue quills, and the long stole of sables, the present from the groom to the bride, and she and Lily saw that all the trunks and cases were packed and sent down to the station, addressed to the Hotel Spendide in Paris, and the personal luggage put into the landau for the overnight stay in London, and then from an upper window she watched Angela's brothers hurrahing and throwing confetti and tying white satin shoes to the rear springs, and her mother dabbing her eyes, and Mrs Hengrave dabbing hers, because she loved her brother very much, until the carriage vanished down the moorland road, to make a tour of the factory streets where the parties were in full swing, and thence to Leeds to catch the express to London. She watched Henry's fair head and broad shoulders, saw him grasping well-wishing hands, willing him to look up once, just once before he drove away. But when he did, his glance raking along the Abbey Farm, she stood back behind the curtain where he could not see her. Then she looked round at the turmoil of Angela's simple, poorly-furnished bedroom, and said, 'Well, Lily, let's get this tidied up, then we'll get back. We'll get someone to drive us down, then you can catch an early train back to Leeds. Tell Madame I will be in as usual tomorrow, and that it was a great success.'

* * *

Margaret heard the screams as she came up the path to the front door, and ran up the steps to her mother's room. Lecky was pressed against the wall, her moon-face terrified, and Florence was pacing round the room, her skeletal figure sweeping her old-fashioned velvet gown about her, knocking the silver frames and china knick-knacks down to the floor, her hair wild, her face convulsed, tearing a newspaper to pieces.

Margaret went straight to her, and grasped her wrist.

'Mama! Be quiet!' She turned accusingly to Lecky. 'She's been drinking.'

'Miss Maggy, I don't know where she gets it from. How can she? She doesn't go from the house.'

'I do. It's that new scrub woman. There's no one else. Look here!' Behind the pretty gilded chaise-longue were empty gin bottles. 'Get rid of her tomorrow. We'll get someone else. Pay more money, and get someone better.'

'I can manage without, Miss Maggy.'

'Do as I say. Sit down and be quiet, Mama. Do you want all the neighbours to hear you?'

It always quietened her; although she despised them, she hated them to look down on her.

Margaret took the paper from her hand, an evening paper, and on the front page there was a long account and full description of the town's great wedding.

'I didn't think,' said Lecky. 'I just brought her up the paper. I didn't think of Mr Henry's wedding . . .'

'Go down. Make us some coffee.' She sat by her mother. 'It's all right, darling, you mustn't be silly . . .'

'He was just a common boy . . .' The old tale she had heard so often came rambling out once again. 'He was mad about me . . . you should have seen him at the ball at Danesfell, in that awful suit . . . breeches, like a farmhand, we laughed at him, your dear Papa and I. A *nothing*! Son of that awful old miser Dyson Grimshaw.

He wanted to make a match between us. As though my Papa would consider it.' She suddenly rubbed her eyes, and stared in bewilderment. 'When I was a little girl I used to play with Henry in the Water Meadows . . . we'd get through a hole in the fence. No one knew. Mama wouldn't have allowed it. Princess he called me . . . so did Mama and Papa . . . our little Princess . . . but your Papa was my Prince. You *wait*! Wait until he comes home again. He'll deal with this Grimshaw.'

'All right, Mama, drink this up . . .' she took the coffee and made her mother drink, listening to the old anguish, the resentment, the jealousy.

'There,' she said gently. 'Now, Lecky, the drops . . .' She measured them carefully, held the glass to her mother's trembling lips, put it aside, took out a comb and straightened Florence's hair, adjusted the fragile lacy cap. 'There . . . now you look pretty . . .' She kissed the thin, rouged cheek, but Florence, as always, turned away from her.

'Don't fuss me, Maggy! You make such a fuss . . . just because I'm not very well . . .'

Her eyes began to droop. Margaret took the laudanum bottle and locked it away, and picked up the empty bottles.

She threw a light rug over Florence who was now deep in her drugged and comforting sleep. She looked down at the thin, rouged, haggard face, and understood more than she had ever done about this wrecked woman. 'Poor Mama,' she thought, 'to have had the chance of such a man and to have been such a fool as to let him go.'

They went downstairs into the warm, clean kitchen. Old Mrs Jagger was sitting in her usual place by the fire. She did not turn her head as they entered.

'Aye, well,' sighed Lecky, 'I'll get the old lady her tea

now. She's been none so well. I've had a proper mucky day with the two on 'em.'

She took the big black kettle to fill at the sink.

Margaret suddenly put down the bottles. She bent over Mrs Jagger and touched her surprisingly white cheek, felt her pulse, turned and flung out her arms to Jany who ran to her side. Mrs Jagger would not waken again.

Margaret grieved for her grandmother who, foolish though she had been, had always been loving and kind. The doctor came, and the lawyers, and Lady Margaret Normanby travelled from Edinburgh to be with her. Florence, of course, did not attend the funeral. The very idea of death sent her terrified mind scurrying in search of oblivion, and in sheer compassion Margaret allowed her drops to be increased that week.

But many Thornsby folk came. Mrs Jagger had lived in the town all her life and people had liked her, remembering her as a simple, generous soul, worshipping her pretty, snobbish daughter to the point of idolatry. There was a large wreath from Mr and Mrs Henry Grimshaw who were, of course, still away on their honeymoon.

Margaret learned that Mrs Jagger had left her the house in Hollingroyd Crescent and the small income of one hundred and fifty pounds a year. She had managed both for many years and now this small independence was her own.

'Well,' said Grandmother Normanby before she left, 'you've money of your own now, Margaret. I'd be happy to have you with me, and your poor Mama, if you will give up this idea of being a shop assistant. I'm not rich, but there's a well-bred, cultivated society in Edinburgh, and with George being stationed at the Castle, you'd get some good invitations. No doubt you'd find yourself a worthwhile husband, like Charmian.

'No, thank you, Grandmother. I've decided not to marry. This money is just the beginning. Now I can do what I want – not just what Fate offers me.'

Now she need not marry Willy, or anyone. She had money of her own. She was young and, as Mrs Hengrave said, she could afford to wait.

She pushed the thought of Henry Grimshaw away. That was just spilt milk, and spilt milk was no use crying over. She must work and learn and watch the chances life would bring. There were some women who did not need men. Perhaps she was one of them.

Chapter Six

Captain Bellamy Chester was sweltering in the unbearable heat, agonizing about his beautiful young wife.

Tomorrow she was going to Simla accompanied and chaperoned by Mrs Armstrong, the Colonel's wife, a redoubtable memsahib of impeccable reputation and many years Indian service. This yearly separation was unbearable to Bellamy, but he could not condemn Charmian to stay in the heat of Calcutta. And Charmian adored Simla with its beautiful mountain scenery, and the riding, picnicking, dancing, theatricals and flirting. What was an agony of separation to Bellamy was for her a delightful escape.

The creak of the punkahs could be heard along the verandah, the brain-fever bird was practising its maddeningly uneven scale, and the men were beginning to go down with heat-stroke and fever. Each day was a gruelling effort.

The parades and drills were held early, before the merciless sun took full possession of the land; the sweat poured down Bellamy's back staining great dark patches on his uniform jacket. The winter visitors had all departed for England, for green fields, sweet-smelling ploughlands with the curlews crying above them, and there would be snow up on the mountains in Scotland.

Bellamy's love for Charmian had grown into an obsession. He could not bear that she should be away from him, but when she was with him he had no peace. Her enormous social success during her first two brilliant seasons only brought him a gnawing jealousy. He began to understand the Indian custom of purdah. He dreamed sometimes of having her safely imprisoned in a silken harem where no man but himself could look upon her face.

Marriage had increased Charmian's beauty to a luscious ripeness, and success had given her sophistication and a greater power over men. She dressed beautifully – every post brought her fashion plates and periodicals from Margaret, so that the darzi with his sewing-machine, a new and magical wonder, was almost busy making and altering her dresses. The new fashions were daringly revealing, draped to the figure to swirl over the bustle at the back; cut low, revealing the shape of her lovely breasts, exposing her gleaming shoulders and delicate tapering arms.

He could not forbid her to dance with other men, he could not imprison her in the bungalow when he was on duty and could not watch over her all the time. She looked at all the men as she looked at him, with melting eyes and soft promising mouth, and she drove them all wild. So far there had been no scandal. People talked – especially jealous women – but Charmian had betrayed no preference for any of the men who flocked about her.

'Don't be so stodgy, Bell,' she said. 'They're only boys. The more I flirt the safer it is.'

His perpetual questioning irritated her like the pestering Indian flies.

'*I* don't ask where *you* have been all day,' she pouted. 'I always believe what *you* tell me.'

'I know what some of those chaps are.'

'*I* don't know if you have some fast little milky tucked away somewhere. I've *heard* about these half-caste girls.'

'You ought not to know about such things!'

'Oh, *fiddle!* I declare I shall run off with one of my beaux if you don't stop being silly. It's horrid being

156

suspected of wickedness when I'm as good as gold. Have I ever done anything wrong?'

The inviting eyes belied her prim indignation.

'Well, then! Don't nag, or I shall go home to Maggy and Mama! Maggie will send me the money for the passage if I ask her to. Then you'd be all alone, and it would serve you right for being such a jealous old thing.'

He could never resist her. It always ended in kisses and usually in bed.

The thoughts of the months without her tormented him. Sometimes he would awake in the night, rise on his elbow, turning up the lamp, having dreamed she had run away, sick with relief to see her beside him, her red lips softly parted and the dark gold curls tumbled childishly across the pillows, her bare breasts like pink-tipped flowers, naked beneath the sheets. He would take her in his arms, his mouth moving hungrily over her, and she would awake, cross and sleepy, pushing him away, protesting, 'Bell, don't, please . . . it's so *hot*. I want to sleep . . . I shall look a sight tomorrow . . .' Or, just as often, the sleepy eyes would glisten, and the silky arms creep around his neck, and she would offer herself with an abandon and skill that frightened him. He remembered before he had ever met her, the mess talk among the officers, talk which he himself had taken part in, amused comment on the season's girls and young married women. Which one was the prettiest, which was the least guarded? Or talk about the Anglo-Indians, daughters of mixed marriages, received in neither Indian nor white society, but smart and seductive, eagerly imitating English ways. The milkies, with their creamy, shadowed skins, and fabulous dark eyes.

The men would talk over their drinks, laughing as men do. Such a girl was a likely 'kill'. 'A hot little number.' He wondered if men talked about Charmian like this.

Charmian had spent the day packing. She was taking all her loveliest clothes. Before she had left England Margaret had unpicked and pressed out yards of her mother's forgotten crinolines, and bought her bales of materials at cost price. Some of the other young wives, neither so rich as the young Chesters nor so chic, grumbled at Charmian monopolizing the best darzi on the cantonment.

That night she was particularly loving, pouring Bellamy's drink herself, and sitting on his knee, but Bellamy could not contain his fears. He implored her to remember his honour and her reputation while she was away. Hill station flirtations could get out of hand. Scandal could ruin his career. She lost her temper.

'One would think you had married a whore. Oh, *Lord! Now*, you're shocked again! Really, I'm at my wits' end how to please you. You seem to want me to be a whore for you and a prig and a prude for everyone else. I tell you, I can't *stand* it! You're upsetting me with your suspicions. *You're breaking my heart!*'

She burst into furious tears, and shut herself in her bedroom.

She had a new novel and she lay sipping lemonade and reading, until she heard Bellamy cross the living-room and call her name, when she hurriedly pushed the book under the bed, and took out her handkerchief, and turned her face into the pillow.

Bellamy fell on his knees by the bed.

'Charmy . . . please . . . Charmy, forgive me.'

She raised the long, gold-tipped lashes, her red lips trembling, her violet eyes filled with tears. He took one small hand in his, and pressed it to his lips.

'Charmy, forgive me. I know I'm unjust. But I am just so crazy about you . . . I know it isn't fair. I wish we were having a baby.'

158

Her eyes flew wide open. '*A baby!*' she exclaimed in horror at the mere thought. Nine months getting enormous and missing all the fun! 'Bell, I'm not old enough. I would be so frightened. I might die. Lots of women die out here, having babies. You said you'd wait until we were due back in England.'

'It will be two years. I know. You are too young, and too sweet and gay . . . such a child. But – I thought it might steady you. Make you different. Give you an occupation, something to hold on to, instead of this endless round of pleasure and flirtation . . .'

Charmian regarded her distressed young husband with some distaste. But she must be careful. He could insist on her staying with him – it would be too cruel. She could not stay and get all yellow and ugly with the heat, old before her time, with children round her heels worrying everyone with their fevers and boring illnesses.

She put her arms out, and the tears ran down her face, crying quite genuinely from tension and self-pity. 'Oh, Bell, darling, please, let us not quarrel tonight. It will be weeks before we are together again – I had planned a lovely dinner, with some champagne, and I had this nightdress made, and a beautiful negligée, just to look lovely for you, because I want you to think of me up there in Simla, waiting for you, and I want you to think of me as pretty and just yours alone . . .'

Bellamy gave a groan, put his arms about her, pressed his lips to hers, and she melted and sighed, and did not do the naughty things that shocked him and which roused her to transports of pleasure, but was tender and passive. Afterwards, she rose, and put on the new pale rose-coloured kimono embroidered with fights of silver birds, and he opened the champagne and they dined amicably and lovingly, before going back to bed. She must be in bed early because the Armstrongs were coming with a gary to fetch her, and the train left quite early, so he must just lie and kiss her, so she could go to sleep.

Mrs Armstrong was on time and Bellamy drove with them to the station. They found their carriage – Bellamy had booked a whole private first class compartment for them, because he was so anxious that Charmian should be properly chaperoned on the journey.

There was a company of Ghurkas entraining, small dark men, very clean and smart, in a rather exotic uniform, with kilts like Scotsmen, turbans with dashing ties, like smart Paris hats, and white spats. They were in the charge of British officers. A tall lieutenant strode down the platform, speaking to the men. Charmian nearly choked, her heart seemed to stop with excitement, her body experienced an orgasm of shock and delight. It was Angus Black.

She prayed to God, feverishly, like a child for a treat. 'Let him see me. Please God let him see me. Please God don't let Bell see him, but please let *him* see *me*.'

And as though he had received a message Black turned, and his reckless eyes were looking straight into hers.

'Christ!' he thought, 'it's that hot little beauty from Edinburgh.'

He moved forward, but she shook her head warningly just as Bellamy returned with fruit for the journey. She gazed down at him, the picture of a loving young wife. The whistle sounded, the train began to move, Bellamy let go her hand, and over his head her beautiful eyes met Black's, and she smiled, a smile of recognition, as inviting as that of any practised harlot.

'Well, I'll be damned!' thought Angus. He was as aroused as though she had stripped herself naked. 'The bitch,' he thought, 'the bonny little bitch!'

The train moved out of the station.

'Don't cry, my dear,' said Mrs Armstrong kindly. 'On

the Indian service one has to get used to partings. The time will soon pass. And in Simla you'll be the belle of the town.'

'You are so sweet to me,' Charmian mopped her eyes and managed a smile. 'Mrs Armstrong . . .'

'You must call me Edith,' said the Colonel's wife. She was forty, plain, yellowed by Indian suns, and a little in love with this pretty creature, who was about the age her own little girl would have been had she lived.

'Edith. Those funny little soldiers on the platform. What are they?'

'The Ghurkas? Oh, excellent soldiers. Hill men. Very splendid.'

'Will they be going to Simla?'

'No, my dear,' she laughed. 'Though not so far away. Up to some frontier station, I expect. We get a lot of their officers in Simla for short leave, you know. It's very dull at those hill stations, and it makes a change for the poor chaps.'

'Not the little men?' said Charmian ingenuously.

'No, my dear, the men don't come . . . just the officers when they get a little leave. Nice chaps, too, although they get a bit wild. They're really very harmless.'

Charmian closed her eyes – it was unbearably hot and stuffy in the carriage. She thought of Black's predatory eyes and temptingly sensual mouth. She prayed as she had always prayed, quite thoughtlessly, to God or Father Christmas, to give her her heart's desire. She tried to make plans – but Indian was so large, and the Army was spread so thinly over its great cities and plains. They might never meet again. He would surely know where she was going. The whole train was filled with army and ICS wives and children going to the hills. He would remember, get leave, come to Simla for her. He *must*. She loved him, she wanted him, she could not do without him – or so she told herself. But she had nearly forgotten him, and it was five years and several lovers later before he came into her life again.

Henry and his bride travelled to London in the utmost luxury. By the time they boarded the Paris train Henry already knew that from one point of view his marriage was a disaster, but that it was not the commonly accepted one of sexuality. It was true that Angela was totally ignorant, inexperienced, inhibited and shy, but he was sensitive – he knew that side of marriage must be a shock to any really innocent young woman. He realized his wife was nice, good and so anxious to please him that she was nearly tongue-tied, absolutely in awe of him because he was her husband, and therefore her master.

In the train to Paris Henry pretended to doze, watching her covertly. Now, thinking him asleep, her anxiety was not hidden. Her big well-shaped hands fiddled nervously with the fringe of her mantle and the beads on her reticule, twisted her wedding ring and the splendid engagement ring – a half-hoop of diamonds – furtively wiped away the tears that started from her eyes.

If the marriage was to work, it was up to him not to push her beyond her understanding.

He kissed her, stroking her worried face, and felt her respond gratefully to this gentling.

'It is a pity Milly is not in Paris,' he said. 'She would take you around, introduce you to the best shops.'

'Oh, I'm so glad she isn't,' said Angela unthinkingly. Mrs Hengrave made her feel like a lump of clay. 'It's much nicer just being with you.'

It would be better when she became accustomed to marriage. There would be a family soon and he was sure she would be an excellent mother, kind but firm, as she

162

had been with her young brothers and sisters. It would all be as he had planned. He had done the right thing.

He took her to see the famous places, the parks and palaces, the Opera and the Comédie Française. But Angela, though a gentleman's daughter, had been meanly educated. She did not speak French and had no ear for music. The few acquaintances Henry had in Paris were rich businessmen. They had good bourgeois homes and smart, competent wives. The dinner engagements were of such length and variety and the conversation, even when in English, so incomprehensible that her self-doubt deepened and her panic grew. She began to hate France, and Henry, watching his tall, handsome English rose wilting in the hothouse of Parisian life, terminated the honeymoon.

'Don't you worry, my dear,' he said, smiling at her, 'I enjoy a simple life and plain cooking at home, and if you don't like this sort of thing, you shan't put up with it. Tomorrow I'll take you home.'

'Oh, thank you Henry . . . I am so sorry . . . and really, I have had a lovely time.'

He burst out laughing. 'You've hated every minute of it. We'll get back to Cliffs Edge, then your own family will be near you.'

'You are so good to me,' she faltered, then with a sudden burst of courage, 'I've wondered what you saw in me, Henry. I mean, I'm not pretty, nor rich, and I'm not – well, not really young any more.'

He could not pretend to a grand passion, and knew she would not believe it if he did.

'I just liked you very much,' he said, quite honestly. 'And I thought you would be a perfect wife for me, and I could give you the kind of life you wanted, and we would raise a family, and our boys would follow me into the business.'

163

Her eyes shone happily, and she said, 'That's what I want.'

'That's what you shall have.' He rose, and said, 'Now, as we are going to leave I will go down and give our courier all the instructions, and I think you should have an early night. I am going out to see Monsieur Jacquier as we have some business to finish . . . will you have dinner sent up? Shall I order it for you?'

'Oh please, dear Henry.'

He ordered her a simple dinner. He changed into his evening clothes and went out. She did not notice that the shining black topper had a slightly more jaunty angle than usual as he placed it on his broad, blond head.

Henry drove up to the theatre where Mademoiselle Nina was appearing and went up at once to her dressing-room.

There were several men in the room, some of them of great family and members of the Jockey Club. But Nina, dressing behind a tall Japanese screen, had eyes only for Henry.

'*Mon bon anglais*,' she cried. ''Enri – for so long you have been away. *J'etais desolée!*'

A lovely, brilliant, common creature, bright as an exotic bird, filling him with an uprush of desire. One paid for Nina, but by God, she was worth it.

He took her hand and kissed it, biting the tips of her fingers, his eyes devouring her. He felt her shiver, saw the pink-tipped breasts lift, and heard her breath quicken.

She authoritatively told the other men to leave.

'Tonight I am with 'Enri,' she declared. 'It is *longtemps* since 'e was in Paris. Tonight you all go away and amuse yourselves in some other way . . . I want only 'im.'

It was about five o'clock when he returned to the hotel. Angela, reassured because she was going home, was fast

164

asleep. He slid quietly into the big bed beside her, and was instantly asleep.

On the way home he remembered Nina de Malvert with some satisfaction, but also, to his chagrin, he remembered young Margaret Normanby. The bright blue eyes behind which a quick mind darted. The thin, quicksilver body. The lemon-sharp tang of youth. Unlike either Angela or Nina she was essentially a female who did not know her place. She had flashed through his life like a shooting star, or a bright kingfisher, and now he would have to forget her, and he was distressed to discover this was not an easy thing to do.

Angela ran his house admirably, entertained local people when he requested it, without brilliance, but with dignity. Henry had frequently to be away either in England or on the Continent on business. She did not mind him going. He always seemed so glad to come home, so refreshed, bringing presents, good-tempered and charming, and for a while his love-making would have a new ardour. But Angela did not become pregnant, and it was a source of grief to both of them, because they knew that children were the only reason for their marriage.

He still made dutiful love to her. He still was a gallant and attentive husband in public, thoughtful and kind in private. But she had an aching sense of loneliness and became obsessed with the thought that if only she could conceive then he would really love her. His polite tolerance was perhaps the heaviest burden she had to bear.

It was a Sunday, and it was Margaret's twenty-first birthday, and it was a queer feeling to think that Charmian, in far-away Calcutta, was also twenty-one. Charmian had written her the usual gossipy letter. She wished Margaret a happy birthday, and was glad everything was

165

going well; she had received a nice-ish pearl necklace from Grandmama Normanby, a card from Lecky, and Maggy's lovely parcel of fashion plates, French gloves and silk stockings. 'Much love' from their 'devoted Charmy'.

Margaret had also had a 'nice' pearl necklace from Lady Margaret. Half of a long string, an heirloom, white matched pearls, which she had saved from the wreck, and had split for the twins. It was the first valuable possession Margaret had ever owned, and she loved its fine quality.

'I remember your grandmother wearing them at dinner-parties at Danesfell Abbey,' said Florence, handling the smooth, faintly irridescent globes. 'They say they go yellow if one does not wear them.' An impatient expression crossed her face. 'Your grandmother should not have split them. The original necklace must have been worth five hundred pounds. She should have let Charmian have them – after all she leads a full social life, while you have no need for such things.'

Margaret linked the pearls around her long white throat, and smiled. They were beautiful. They suited her.

'Charmian has a rich husband to buy her jewels if she wants them. This is all I have. It was very generous of Grandmama Normanby to keep them for us, when she had to sell up so much when Papa left.'

'I don't know *when* you'll wear them.'

'I shall wear them today,' said Margaret, 'I am going out for luncheon for my birthday.'

'By yourself?'

Margaret shook her head. 'No. A young man whom I know is coming to fetch me. A Mr William Gadsby.'

'Do I know him? What is he? Who are his people?'

'You don't know him. His mother owns the place where I work.'

'A tradesman!' said Florence horrified. 'I forbid . . .'

166

'Mama . . .' Margaret shook her head teasingly. 'I'm twenty-one today. You can't forbid me to do anything any more. So you'd better face up to what I am – I'm in the dress trade. I am the manageress. I am learning everything about the trade and one day I shall own my own shop. You need never speak about it, if you don't wish to, but that's how it is. Oh, Lecky . . .' Jany Leck came in carrying a tray with champagne glasses, and a bottle of the wine. She looked more rested, younger, quite spry in her black dress and white apron, her thin spare hair under a neat starched cap. She had old Mrs Jagger's bedroom on the kitchen floor now, to save her short little legs. Margaret paid her ten pounds a year, as well as her keep. She was appreciated and it showed. Her funny little moon-face glowed. She kept the house immaculately. If she had been in love with the young Florence and the pretty baby Charmian, she worshipped 'young Maggy'.

'If yon had been a lad,' she told neighbours, 'I reckon she could have done owt she set her mind on.' Two years ago this same thought had crossed Henry Grimshaw's mind.

'I brought some champagne, Mama, and Lecky's made a cake – you brought a glass for yourself, didn't you Lecky?' She ignored her mother's protesting frown at the inclusion of a servant, and opened the bottle, filled three glasses. 'Well, here's to the future for Charmy and me. Success to both of us, whatever we do in life.'

'And happiness, Miss Maggy, love,' said Jany earnestly.

'And happiness,' agreed Margaret, adding drily, 'whatever that may be.'

'To me it means your dear father's return,' said Florence. 'And I am sure that this year it will come.'

Margaret smiled and kissed her – she said it every day, every year, like a litany; whether she really believed it, it

167

was impossible to tell. There was a sharp knocking at the door and Margaret put on her hat and picked up her gloves.

'That will be Mr Gadsby. Would you like to see him, Mama?'

Florence froze. 'Certainly not! I do not approve and you know it. You are Sir Richard Normanby's daughter. For you to go out with this person is bad enough, but that you should go unchaperoned is terrible.'

'It's quite all right for a working girl,' Margaret said cheerfully, and went out.

In the New Year Willy Gadsby had bought himself a gig and a strong carriage pony. The gig was a sporting affair with high yellow wheels, and he felt a great swell in it. He wore a check suit, a high curved grey billycock hat and chamois leather gloves, and the ends of his fair moustache were highly waxed and twisted up at the ends.

They drove out of town towards Ilkley, where they stopped at a pleasant inn for lunch.

He admired her neat hands, her warm pale grey suit with the small grey squirrel collar and muff. She ate with no affectations, no fancy finger cockings, no flirtatious glances over the wine glass rim. She drank very little, but appreciated the good food.

Afterwards they went for a walk in the unseasonable March sunshine, finding a bench overlooking the moorland stream which gushed over the stone outcrops on its way to join the wharfs and the sea.

'It's a grand day,' he said.

'Hot enough to give me freckles.' She turned her face up to the sun, her hair glowed, her eyes were azure, and her firm full mouth a delectable pink. He put an arm along the back of the seat.

'Well, Willy,' she said, 'what is it you want to say?'

He laughed and let his arm drop round her small waist.

At lunch he had drunk most of the bottle of wine. It had been a pity to waste it.

'Come on now Maggy,' he said. 'You know well enough. It's a while since I first suggested we might marry. You said you weren't old enough; you said you had to look after your mother and grandmother, to wait until you were twenty-one. Well, your granny's dead. And today you're twenty-one. What's it to be?' He bent forward and kissed the pink curve of her cheek. 'I haven't bought you a birthday present, because I want to make it an engagement ring. What do you say?'

She turned suddenly, so that the charming, petal-shaped face was close to his, the eyes unutterably blue. Disconcertingly calm. Not a blush, or a flutter of coy withdrawal.

'Willy, I'm not the sort of girl that you – what do they say? – *fancy*. I mean, if you wanted to go to bed with a girl, I'm not the kind you'd want, am I?'

His jaw dropped a little and he drew back, shocked.

'*Maggy!* That's *not* a ladylike thing to say!'

'I'm not concerned with being ladylike. You're quite nice, but I don't love you. I know you don't love me. Love's a different kettle of fish. What are you offering me?'

'I don't understand you!' His face was very red. He withdrew his arm and stares sulkily at the river. It was all wrong – a girl ought at least to pretend to some sort of feeling. 'Is it because your mother's got a title?' he sneered. 'You think you're a cut above me?'

'No, it is *not*. That's nothing but a nuisance to me. It's just common sense. You want to marry me: so you *say*. I don't want to marry you really. You want a manageress, not a wife. I want my own business. Well, what are you offering?'

'Well, I don't know . . . I mean you'd be as you are

169

now. Already you're in full control . . . but you'd be my wife as well. You'd live with Mother and me, and you'll agree it's a very nice house? If we go on doing well, we could have a carriage – as well as the gig.'

'It would be just the same as now. Except we would be married? We'd live together?'

'Yes.'

'And I'd have to keep my mother and Jany at Hollingroyd Crescent?'

'Well, that would be best.' He attempted a playful smile. He had brought her out here to propose, not to strike bargains. 'Two mothers under one roof wouldn't be such a grand idea.'

'It would be impossible,' she agreed. 'Well, let's see. I would want a full partnership, legally drawn up, so that if you ever decided to sell I would be entitled to half the business.'

'*Maggy!*' He was horror-stricken. 'You'd be my wife!'

'And what would that secure to me? I have a house and a small income – as my husband you could claim that. I would want them secured to me too – legally.'

'You bargain like a Briggate backer.'

She flushed crimson. 'Maybe. But they have to bargain for their living, and so do I. If we loved each other, that would be different. If we trusted each other too. I'll have my own business anyway, but maybe not until I'm nearly forty. A real partnership now would be worth it. You have to decide.'

'You know it's not my business yet. Mother would never agree.'

'Well, ask her. She would like to retire. It's the only way *I* would agree.' She jumped to her feet, buttoning the fluffy grey collar beneath her chin. She smiled down at him, bright-eyed, pink-cheeked from the moorland breeze. 'Don't worry, Willy, I'm not holding you to anything. Let's forget about it, and walk back along the other side of the river. It's so lovely. I'll race you across the stepping stones.'

And before he could protest she had run forward across the swirling stream, going from flat stone to flat stone, sure-footed, light as a swooping bird, turning to laugh at his clumsy progress, as he followed her.

She was in the office the following week when a card was brought to her. She had been buying since the New Year, but this card did not suggest a traveller.

> *Ferdinand Leon,*
> *designer to*
> *Marischelle & Staynes, Ltd.*
> *Court Dressmakers,*
> *Regent Street, London.*

She searched her memory for the name and found it. The first time Mrs Hengrave had come into Madame Rosa's when she was still Emilia de la Cartier, and playing at the theatre. She could see Millicent's dark grace in the superb apricot-coloured walking-dress, and remembered how she had asked if it had been made by Monsieur Worth of the Rue de la Paix. Ferdinand Leon? Marischelle & Staynes was a fashionable and very expensive store. But it was not a wholesalers. Why should they send a representative to see her?

'Please send the gentleman in.'

Lily went out and a few minutes later ushered in one of the best-looking, best-dressed men Margaret had ever seen. She could not guess his age – over forty, certainly. Perhaps over fifty. His centre-parted hair and small imperial were just a little too dark for nature. His skin was olive, his eyes brown, his teeth perfect beneath the small, neatly-clipped moustache. His frock coat was the acme of West End tailoring. His topper shone, his linen was spotless, and there was a good pearl in his silver-grey cravat. She caught a whiff of good cologne. What did this exquisite gentleman want with her? She rose and extended her hand.

'Please sit down, Mr Leon. What can I do for you?'

He sat down opposite her. They faced each other across the desk.

'It is a question, Miss Normanby, of what we can do for each other. Mrs Johnston Hengrave has spoken to me about you.' There was the faintest French accent, although his English was perfect.

'And to me about you. I have admired the clothes you have made for her.'

'And I have admired the workmanship of the clothes you have made for her.' He smiled his charming smile, a studied charm, using the full flattery of his fine eyes. 'I have come to Leeds, Miss Normanby, to ask you to lunch with me.'

'All the way from London?' she twinkled disbelievingly.

'All the way from London,' he said solemnly, 'and it is a matter of some secrecy. Better if we discuss it over lunch than here.'

'Ah?' Was this exquisite gentleman going to buy Madame Rosa's? Or offer her a job? She glanced at the little gold-and-enamelled watch hung on a chain around her neck. 'I must go at once if I accept: I have a personal customer coming at two-thirty.'

'That would suit me splendidly.'

He took her to the best restaurant in the city. He put his proposition to her directly. There was something ingenuously impulsive about him that appealed to her. He had none of the cautious deliberation of a business-man. He had an idea and he told her what he wanted,

172

spreading his cards on the table without reserve. She liked him very much.

'Miss Normanby, to understand my proposition, you must know I am an artist. I design clothes for beautiful women: I create them. For many years I have worked for this firm of Marischelle & Staynes, running their bespoke department, and I have made it the best of such departments in London. I want to start my own business.'

'So Mrs Hengrave told me.'

'And she told you, also, that I hate business – I hate the whole thing. The organization. The book-keeping. The choosing and engaging of staff. The bother of keeping them happy. I lose my temper, when they are stupid and slow, and roar. I do not wish to bother. I particularly hate *costing*! I wish only to see beautiful ladies, to choose the right materials for them, and make them clothes that turn them into stars of fashion, leaders of the *dernier mode*.'

'But can you make it pay? For one woman of taste whom you enjoy dressing, there are many who have no taste at all. But they pay their money like the rest.'

'But they *see* the stars, and *try* to look like them, which is where money is made. The stars know their own beauty. They are in love with it. The others follow, and pay for the illusion of beauty.'

There was a small silence.

'Quite,' she said in total agreement. 'Mrs Hengrave said that these difficulties prevented you from starting on your own.'

'Yes. So – I am now at a crisis,' he made a small, desperate, expressive gesture. 'I have been offered a very good lease on a house in Hanover Street. I can raise the money. Mrs Hengrave alone would give me guarantees. It is a big house, a big light basement for the workroom, four grand reception rooms for salons, and upstairs pleasant rooms where I could live and have an office; it would be admirable. It is now – or never. I am not so old – but not so young. If I do not start now, I shall work for others all my life, and never receive just payment. I need a manager.'

'Me?'

'Yes. Mrs Hengrave says that you run this place. That you know everything about such things, although you are so very young.'

'I've been here since I was fifteen. Six years. Plenty of time to learn.'

'Mrs Hengrave says you have made Madame Rosa's one of the best businesses in this city.'

'*The* best,' said Margaret succinctly. 'What are you really offering me? Just a crib?' She deliberately used the slang term for a shop assistant's job, flipping it at him in her well-bred Normanby voice.

'And you are totally in charge here? Workroom, fitting, accounts, buying and design?'

'Ah, I *cannot* design. I pick out designs from the plates, and copy them. But the rest – yes. I made myself learn everything. It was the only way. It's not such a big staff. Four in the salon. The workroom varies with the seasons – I always keep the best girls on. The best workers are always worth hanging on to. Their loyalty means a great deal. It pays to pay them well. You can't run this kind of women's business with a lot of jealousy and backbiting. Jockeying for position. People ought to know their position, and their rights, and so should the boss. How many will you be engaging?'

He spread his hands. 'That I don't know. That is what you will have to tell me. I can count, *j'éspère*, on twenty good clients.' She noticed his strange, yellowish hands, very beautifully kept – an intaglio set in gold on the little

174

finger. 'You must come to London and see the premises. We must be better, and at first a little cheaper than the others. I will choose the decor. Offices, workroom, staff-rooms, store-rooms – that will be for you. It must be perfect. I aim to open for the Autumn season.'

'But what are you offering me? To be manageress? With that responsibility I shall need more money. Madame Rosa will offer me a partnership rather than let me go.'

'In Leeds?' he said scornfully. 'With me you will learn the West End trade. You will serve the highest in the land. I *mean* that. I aim to have the Royal appointment one day. You will have to travel to Paris, and Vienna to buy, as I do now, and although you will work under my supervision at first, I expect you eventually to take complete responsibility. Your starting salary will be three hundred a year, with commission on the takings. What do you say?'

Her delicate, fine-boned, cat-like face was blank with concentration. He was to know that look very well in the years to follow. He found her charming. He had worked too closely with women all his life. He disliked their use of their sexuality to manipulate their needs. She made him think of a boy, the blue eyes with the thick, brown lashes were so frank and direct.

'I'm scared.'

He felt a warm, unbusinesslike rush of kindness.

'You don't have to be.'

'I am too young. But if you'll help me I'll take a chance if you will.'

'It's a deal then?'

'Thank you.' She held out a small, firm hand. It was as steady as a rock.

'I'll have to give them a month's notice. It's only fair.'

'Of course. I should expect the same. You will need

175

another month to move and get settled in London.' He hesitated tactfully. 'Can you afford that? I could arrange an advance for you.'

'No, that's all right.' She had saved hard over the past years for just such an opportunity as this. 'Is there anything else you want to know?'

He regarded her with great gravity, and said, 'What is your opinion of the creations of Monsieur Worth?'

Equally solemnly she said, 'Nothing much. Now. He is behind the times. He has a great name. His day was in the Empire, when the Empress Eugenie went to him – the crinolines of my mother's day, all the women swimming in yards of tulle, like water-nymphs. Today women are different – they parade their . . .' she hesitated, then boldly used the word, 'their sexuality.' Leon blinked, and began to smile. 'The skirts flow behind like a mermaid's tail, but from the front the gowns are sculptured round the body to display it. They don't need these frills and ribbons and swags of flowers and fruit . . . the extended buttocks . . . the bustle . . . I don't like it. The style needs simplifying, not decorating. A woman should know she looks perfect, and then forget it.'

He rose, seized her hands, and kissed each one.

'*Parfait*. We shall get on like a house on fire.'

Her tension vanished and she laughed.

'What a lark,' she said delightedly. 'Wait until I tell Willy and Madame Rosa.'

Who Willy was Ferdinand Leon did not know and did not care. He was by character euphoric, given to bursts of soaring optimism, and Margaret had gone to his head. He had not expected to find a young provincial either so talented or so ambitious. He liked her clothes and her graceful figure. He did not find the opulent femininity of breast and hip that typified the Prince of Wales' favourites at all attractive. And she was every inch a lady. Brought up behind counters, painfully acquiring gentility, he appreciated that. It was arranged that she would give in her notice and as soon as possible travel up to London.

Willy came into her office the next morning. He had had a bad day with his mother, extracting the conditions that Margaret demanded. Both of them thought the offer of marriage would have been sufficient.

'I spoke to Mother, Maggy. She has agreed to you having a share of the profits. I think that's right handsome of her. Many chaps' wives work in the business for nowt.'

'Then their wives are fools.'

'Well, how about it, then?'

'No.'

'No?' he said, astounded.

'I've had an offer to go to London and run a new business there.'

'To *London*!'

She was irritated at his repetition. As though there was nowhere else but Leeds and no opportunity other than Madame Rosa's.

'Yes. I've decided. I'm going to let the house at Hollingroyd Crescent and take Mama and Lecky to London.'

'But in London there's a lot of great shops. Competition, love, not like here where we've made ourselves the best.'

'*I* made this shop the best. I'll find out what I'm made of in London – I want to give in my notice. A month. You should be able to find someone else by then.'

He stared in dismay. She really meant it.

In the bar of a second-class hotel in San Francisco Sir Richard Normanby sat with a glass of champagne in front of him. He had the authentic confidence of the aristocrat, and was still very handsome, although the violet-blue eyes had faded, and the whites were yellowing and bloodshot. His features had thickened, the arrogant, classic nose reddened. His hair had lost the red-gold splendour of his youth, and, like his moustache, was touched up a bit too brassily. His hands were still beautiful, slender, long-fingered and well cared-for, his voice had the assured, slightly patronizing drawl of his class. To the average American he was a dude, to an Englishman he seemed a well-born old roué, perhaps down on his luck although everything he wore, from the wideawake hat to his hand-made shoes, was expensive and in excellent taste.

He had come by stages across America, striking it lucky in some places, down on his luck in others, haunting the gambling parlours and race tracks.

So here he was in San Francisco.

He set the felt hat back on his head and sipped his champagne. The truth was he would like to go back to England. At least he wanted to go when he felt low. Then he heartily disliked this great, busy country where everyone worked so hard in pursuit of the dollar, and leisure, as he understood it, was unknown.

A familiar accent caught his attention – a sea captain at the bar with an unmistakable West Riding accent, making him yearn suddenly for the high moors, and farmlands, and Danesfell Abbey in all its glory. The man, also far from home, was glad to play pool with him and gossip. He lent Richard some old local papers which he had just picked up with his post from home. Richard's face reddened with growing anger. Mr Johnston Hengrave, the American gentleman who had bought Danesfell Abbey, and married Miss Emilia de la Cartier, the popular actress, was to re-open the North Fell Pit by drilling a new shaft through the moor to the unreachable coal.

Emilia de la Cartier, that black-eyed bitch Milly Grimshaw, whom he had followed, eager with desire and full of plans, to New York, only to find she was not having him in her life again, and no amount of threats, from suicide to blackmail, would change her mind. He read on irritably. Miss Charmian Normanby, the daughter of Sir Richard and Lady Normanby, had been married in Edinburgh to Lieutenant Bellamy Chester, and Lady Margaret Normanby had given the bride away in her father's absence in the United States. Lady Normanby had unfortunately not been present, owing to ill-health.

'Owing to nips of brandy,' Richard thought sourly.

And then in a more recent edition he came upon the report of Henry Grimshaw's wedding to Miss Angela Torrance of Abbey Farm, and suddenly it all came so much nearer home. He read that Grimshaw was now the prospective candidate for the Borough, standing for the Liberal Party. That vulgar lout with his farmers' breeches was standing for Thornsby, the seat which had by tradition belonged to the Normanby family for generations. There was a picture of Henry, and the firm-jawed, wide-browed face looked out at him from the surrounding newsprint with grim mockery. Richard noted that his hair, although he must be over forty, was as thick as ever. He looked every inch a prosperous provincial gentleman. He owned Cliffs Edge, which Thomas Jagger had built in the height of his prosperity. And Milly, the sister, the player girl, lived at Danesfell Abbey. These people whom he had despised now had everything that should have belonged to him. Like Florence he considered they had cheated him; like Florence he could never admit that any calamity was his own fault.

The same edition contained an obituary of old Mrs

179

Jagger, and her Will, leaving a small amount of well-invested capital and a house in Thornsby to her grand-daughter Margaret Grant Normanby. Sir Richard considered this.

It might be an idea to write to Florence – just in case his present luck did not hold. Her letters, imploring, incoherent and highly romantic, occasionally caught up with him. He hardly bothered to read them.

So he took some hotel notepaper and wrote as he had written when he was pursuing her, when she was a young, lovely, mindless creature, her golden head swimming in dreams, the heiress to Thomas Jagger's considerable fortune.

'*My dearest little wife, my own beautiful girl, I wonder if you have forgotten all about me?*'

It was the first of many such letters, always pleading ill-luck, always assuring her of his love, always asking for money. But it was the first, and Florence had waited for it for sixteen years.

Chapter Seven

The small house in Juniper Place on the East side of Regent Street was almost a replica of the house at Hollingroyd Crescent. It had a big, light kitchen basement, with three floors above, on the second of which Florence was housed in her boudoir and bedroom in the utmost comfort.

It was nearly midnight and Jany Leck dozed before the glowing embers in the shining black kitchen range. As she had once sat up for Florence, now she sat up for Margaret and would not think of going to bed until she was safely home and everything locked up for the night.

During the past five years life to Jany and to Lily Oglethorpe, who had come to London with them, was sheer heaven. Margaret was making money. She had a position. The salon – 'Maison Leon' – it was not called a *shop* – was a great success. Now they were in this cosy little house, with every convenience. Jany had a washerwoman and a young housemaid to help her. Every one of them was paid. Margaret was seldom there during the weekday; she worked long hours, arriving at Hanover Street at eight o'clock and rarely leaving before seven in the evening. And she often went out with Mr Ferdinand and his smart friends. Mr Ferdinand Leon thought a great deal about Margaret Normanby.

Lily opened the kitchen door and came in to bid Jany goodnight. She was already in her wrapper, her hair beneath a frilled nightcap was in tight curling rags which drew her eyebrows up into an expression of perpetual surprise. And indeed she was still surprised to find herself in a warm clean house, and at long last getting enough food to eat, and enough money to send some home occasionally to her mother in Leeds.

She was devoted to Florence whom she found a continual source of wonder and amazement. Every evening after supper, she read to her ladyship, sharing her passion for highly coloured romances of life in high society. Florence's accounts of her own life 'when my dear Sir Richard was with me' were as real to Lily as the sufferings of the fictional Lord Nigel over the proud and heartless Lady Gwendoline.

When Richard's first letter had arrived from California shortly after Margaret had brought them all to London, Florence had demanded that Margaret should immediately send five hundred pounds to 'Poor brave Papa, trying so hard to make money for us in that awful country.'

Margaret flatly refused, and Florence predictably made terrible scenes. Margaret agreed to send small regular sums, ten pounds four times a year, and thereafter the intervals between the letters became longer, although when they came they always asked for money and described, quite eloquently, her father's sufferings and privations, bravely endured for the sake of his beloved wife and little girls.

It was well over a year since Florence had heard. She did not really mind. Richard had become the leading character in her world of romantic make-believe, in which the 'young Normanbys' were still the most beautiful couple in London. Lily never tired of hearing about them. Margaret was grateful to Lily. Her belief in Florence's fantasies kept her from drinking and neither Jany Leck nor Margaret had time or patience for this nonsense.

Florence's 'friends' had begun to call soon after her arrival in London. They were all noblewomen. Beautiful young Lady Derring, the Duchess of Denton, Lady Maberley and even HRH the Princess of Wales occasionally called, although Florence with many warning glances, insisted that this must *not* be spoken of for fear of causing *jealousy* at Court.

At first Lily had believed these high-born ladies actually called at Juniper Place when she was at work, but Margaret explained drily, that although her mother had known them briefly in the butterfly Summer of her youth, Lady Derring was nearly fifty, the Duchess of Denton was dead, and the Princess of Wales was by now quite unaware of Lady Normanby's existence. To Lily this made Florence even more fascinating. It was 'sort of' true. She *was* Lady Normanby. She *had* once rubbed shoulders with the great. Lily would stand outside the boudoir and listen to the high, affected voice within chatting away to thin air of long-dead scandals and fashionable gaieties, and never let drop a hint that she knew it was make-believe.

'You off to bed, Lily, love?' asked Jany.

'Just come for my milk. We finished the book tonight. It was real sad. Her ladyship's asleep.'

The milk was seething gently in a pan on the stove. Jany poured it for her, and gave her a piece of jam pasty. Lily sat and nibbled as contentedly as a sleek little town mouse.

'She was good as gold this evening,' said Jany, 'when I put her down. She looked lovely in her little lace cap. She does, without all that stuff she puts on her face . . . Her hair's gone grey, but it's a sight prettier than those wigs she wears. She's not that old.'

'How old?'

'She doesn't like to say,' Jany sighed. 'Maybe forty-five – forty-two – maybe less, I don't rightly know.' Her loving indulgence towards Florence had worn thin over the years, 'Aye, but she was right bonny once. Like a little angel when I first served her.'

'And he – Sir Richard? Was he really like she says?'

'He were very handsome,' Jany conceded. '*Very* handsome. They were the handsomest pair in London. And the gayest.'

'And the happiest?'

'Well, if they weren't she'd never let on. Miss Flo'd never let on to anything she didn't like. She just pretended it worn't there.'

'In a way that's wonderful, Lecky. It's as though she's writing a book – like the ones I read to her, only it's her own life.'

'Aye, well, let's hope there's a happy ending.' Jany stirred the fire, put some coals on, and set the kettle on the hob. 'It's getting late. Miss Maggy ought to be back soon. She'll want some tea.'

'It's but half-past eleven. Do you think Sir Richard *will* come back and bring all that money like her ladyship says?'

'Who knows?' Her little mouth set with wry amusement. 'It depends on how his luck runs.'

'In the last letter he said he was mining gold, working real hard, with rough men, in the bitter cold.'

Jany's face was a study. 'I said *luck* not *work*. You don't want to believe all he says, any more than you do her. Now get you off to bed.'

There was a sound of a carriage driving up to the door and Mr Leon's voice and Margaret's answering, light and clear. Lily's romantic heart fluttered. Mr Leon was so handsome. A lot of the girls at work were in love with him, but he took no notice of them.

'This Ferdi . . ?' began Jany.

'You mean Mr Leon?'

'Aye. Is he really sweet on our Miss Maggy?'

'So everyone says at work. Some of them says he's not a marrying man. But he thinks the world of her – she is in charge of everything.' She rose, taking her milk. 'I'll get upstairs before she comes.'

She took her candle and had reached the top of the hall stairs when Margaret came in. She was wearing a dress of pale lemon silk faille, with a cream Chinese shawl, embroidered with brilliantly-coloured flowers and birds about her shoulders. She held a small posy of white flowers, and was looking down at them, smiling thoughtfully, the yellow light from the hall gas-bracket shining on her cloud of copper-coloured hair.

She looked up and saw Lily and her smile deepened. She seemed happy.

'Just off to bed, Lily?'

'Yes, Miss Margaret.'

'How was Mama tonight?'

'Wonderful – Lecky was just saying so. After dinner, I read for over an hour, and then Lecky put her to bed.'

'You're a great help, Lily. Mama likes you.'

Lily did not answer. She was filled with troubled guilt.

'Goodnight, my dear,' said Margaret. 'Sleep well.'

'Goodnight, Miss Margaret.'

When Lily had returned from work that evening the late post had just been delivered. She had taken a letter out of the basket, and knew with a thrill of excitement that it was from Sir Richard. She had taken it straight to Florence, and they had read it together. Florence had put a dramatic finger to her lips.

'Shut the door, Oglethorpe,' she had whispered. 'Has anyone but you seen this letter?'

'No, your ladyship.'

'Say nothing about it. To Lecky or Miss Margaret. Promise?'

'Why yes, of course, if that's your wish.'

185

'It is an order. Now come near me. I must speak quietly.'

She clutched Lily's hand and drew her down beside her on the chaise-longue. She was shaking, her sunken eyes wild with excitement. 'You can keep a secret?' Lily nodded. 'I always knew Dicky would come back to me. They thought I was mad. But I knew. I knew he would come back and take care of me again. Do you think I'm a fool and a madwoman?'

'Your ladyship,' protested Lily. 'I don't. I never have. Nobody thinks so!'

'Oh yes they do,' said Florence petulantly. 'That fool of a doctor thinks so too. Lecky thinks so, though of course she is devoted to me, the poor simpleton. And my daughter Margaret certainly does.'

'No, Madame, no, your ladyship. Miss Margaret works that hard, all day to make money to keep us . . .'

'Don't mention what Miss Margaret does! It's a disgrace that she should work in a shop like any common girl.' She glared indignantly at Lily, who thought of the show-rooms in Hanover Street, all cream and gilt, the ten lady assistants, the five juniors, the forty workroom girls, the doorman, the page, and the office staff. 'I cannot think what he will do when he comes back home. Go and drag her out of that *place* and lock her up in a boarding school until she learns better.'

'But, my lady, Miss Margaret is twenty-five.'

Florence ignored this. 'Just think of it. He is in San Francisco, and he has had such adventures, looking for gold.'

'Has he found any?'

A shadow fell across Florence's face, and the faded eyes darkened warily as a breath of reality threatened. She glanced vaguely about the room, a look that Lily had come to dread, searching for drink or the laudanum,

186

which she sometimes hoarded and hid. Then a sly, childish smile lit her eyes.

'If Margaret is making so much money why doesn't she send a proper amount to Sir Richard? Last time she sent ten pounds. A pittance to a man like that! As he says – it is an insult.'

Sir Richard had apparently journeyed up to the goldfields in terrible conditions and managed to stake a claim, but the vein of gold had run out a few yards further up the valley, so he had to sell all his equipment to get back to civilization:

'Sweetheart – I do not like to ask you for money, and the little gift you sent last time is really an insult. Not enough to pay my boot-maker. But you say Margaret holds the purse-strings. Cannot you persuade her to let me have a substantial amount – something in the region of, say, five hundred pounds? Or even three? I would pay my passage home. I know you'll try. Meanwhile, dearest, lovely little wife of my dreams, I send you my eternal love, and a thousand kisses until I can take you in my arms again.'

Florence took out her handkerchief and wept.

Lily sighed and sniffed. 'It's a beautiful letter.'

'And we are separated just because he had a little bad luck. If the North Fell coal seam had not run out we should still own Danesfell Abbey. If someone had lent us a few thousand pounds when my Papa died, my dear Richard would never had had to leave England. And now, because Margaret is mean and cruel, I cannot even send him his fare home.'

The North Fell coal seam had been successfully opened up by one of Johnston Hengrave's companies, but this was never mentioned to Lady Normanby.

'Surely she'd like her Dad back again?' said Lily.

Florence drew her narrow shoulders together and

assumed the dramatically disapproving look she used when speaking of Margaret.

'I don't like saying this, Oglethorpe, not to you, because you are devoted to Miss Margaret, but there is a hard streak in her. She never really loved her father as he deserved.'

'But she was only a little girl when he went away.'

'Perhaps. But children can be cruel. The twins were always as different as chalk and cheese. Charmy all life and fun, and so beautiful, and Margaret so stiff, and disapproving, looking at me with those eyes of hers, like a nasty little spiteful cat, a spinster from babyhood. I always told her so. "Charmy," I said, "will marry a duke, but you will *never* marry. You have no charm".'

'Oh, *no*, your ladyship . . .'

'That's enough!' Florence said haughtily. 'Allow me to know my own daughter. I'm beginning to think I can't trust you.'

Her voice rose sharply to that note which could precede hysteria.

'Oh, you can, really, you can trust me,' Lily said terrified. 'I won't say a word.'

'Well, then, we won't say anything about this letter. It is a secret just between us two. I will write an answer, but first I'll search through my things, and see if I can't find anything – I have a few small valuables still. Then perhaps you'll go on a little errand to a jeweller in Holborn, where Sir Richard did a lot of business in the old days. We'll see if we can raise the money for his passage.' She clasped her thin hands together childishly. 'What fun, what a day it's been! And my darling Richard is alive, and is coming home to me.'

Up in her small, neat bedroom Lily blew out the candle and got into bed. It *was* a nice letter. She could not see any harm in keeping her ladyship's secret, and she could, of course, tell Miss Margaret at any time. But even Lily, devoted as she was to her mistress, did not really believe that Sir Richard Normanby would ever come home.

Margaret went straight downstairs into the kitchen. Jany was scalding the tea. Their two cups were set out on a tray with the milk-jug and sugar-basin, rose-patterned bone china which she had bought Jany one Christmas, and which was reserved for this cosy nightly ritual. Margaret drew a footstool to Jany's feet and sank down on it. The red embers in the fire glowed, lit up her hair and her glowing eyes.

'Something's happened,' said Jany: she stirred the teapot, poured out, handed Margaret her cup. 'Well, happen you'll tell me if tha's a mind to. Is it that Mr Leon?'

'He's asked me to marry him.'

'He's *niver*!'

Margaret burst out laughing.

'Like Mama and Charmy *you* thought no one ever would!'

'Nay,' protested Jany. 'I never said that. I just thought with this grand shop you're at and such, you'd be too fussy. You allus look down your nose so. Chaps are scared to speak.'

'Well, this one isn't. And I'm not losing the shop. I'm marrying it. It's all signed and sealed, a junior partnership. Like a man.'

'Oh, aye,' Jany said sceptically, 'that's a queer kind of marriage.'

'Lecky, it will suit me. Can you see me running a house? I can't boil an egg.'

'You're right about that. But what does *he* get out of it?' She spoke roughly. If Margaret married she would leave Juniper Place. Who then would be responsible for Miss Florence?'

189

'Well, he's getting me. Don't you think I'm worth anything?'

Jany rubbed her eyes and her little red nose. The days when she had been alone with the young Lady Normanby, with Sir Richard off to America, taking all the money and all the jewellery, leaving them with two young children and hardly a penny to buy a loaf, were never far from her memory. Florence's rapid descent from the starry heights of fashionable beauty to a shattered wreck always haunted her.

Margaret hugged her. 'Don't look like that, Lecky. I'll always look after you. I won't be living here – but very near, just on the other side of Regent Street. I'll come in every day. Everything will be taken care of. I'll be able to afford more now. It will be all right.'

She put her head down on Jany's knee, and the little workworn hands pulled the combs and pins and loosened her tumultuous hair so that it fell in waves and ripples across her white apron. She took a comb and two brushes out of a drawer, a hard brush and a very soft one, and began to comb and brush the waving coppery hair. Every night she did this for Florence, and every night, since her nursery days, for Margaret. It was her nearest approach to demonstrative affection – she had never kissed either of them in her whole life. She felt the girl leaning on her lap relax under the brush-strokes like a purring cat.

'Well, do you care for Mr Leon?'

'We've become good friends. We understand each other, I think. I enjoy his company. We have just taken the house next door in Hanover Street which we are opening for tailor-mades. English women are taking to them for day wear. I have engaged a master tailor, and extended the workroom. I want them severe, but chic and feminine, smart for the street as well as for sportswear

190

and the moors. To be worn with a really attractive hat . . .'

'But you're still on about the business, love. You're going to marry a man.'

Margaret's flushed face came up, gravely considering the matter.

'What do you think of him, Lecky?'

'He seems a very nice gentleman . . . a bit fancy like, but then he's a shopkeeper.'

'You awful old snob. I'm in my twenty-fifth year, Lecky. Nearly on the shelf. Charmy was married when she was eighteen.'

'Miss Charmian would ha' married the sweep if there'd been no other chap about.'

'Yes, but the sweep would have died for wanting her. No man has ever felt that for me. Once . . .' she stopped; no use remembering Henry Grimshaw. No use speaking about it. A girl's foolishness. She gave a long sigh, like a child does after drinking or crying. 'So! Mr Ferdinand Leon wants to marry me. We like each other, we work in harness like a well-matched pair. We both love the business. He has many talented and amusing friends. He is clever and cultivated and has taught me a great deal. True, he's a good deal older than me, but I've always preferred older men. We shall have a fine appartment over the business – and I shan't just be Miss Margaret, nearly on the shelf. I shall be Madame Leon – the boss's wife and partner, and I shall like that.'

'You deserve someone to tek care of you, you've spent your young life looking after others.'

Margaret smiled her sparky, confident, three-cornered smile.

'Looking after a business is different to looking after people, Lecky. Especially when you're getting a third of the profits. Now every time I go in, every order I take, I

191

shall think that a bit of it is mine. I shall think I am only twenty-five and one day it may all be mine.'

'Well, once you've made up your mind, Miss Maggy, that's it. There's no changing you. There never was. Finish your tea, and get off to bed.'

'And you'll be able to manage Mama?'

'Now, don't you fret about me, Miss Maggy, love. I'll look after your Mama, as I always have. I just hope you're doing the right thing.'

She was not sure at all. She could not imagine her Miss Maggy trotting demurely in harness. What she needed was a firm driver, and a touch of the whip sometimes.

Ferdinand bought Margaret a beautiful ring, and the engagement was announced to a great deal of comment and speculation among the staff and Ferdinand's friends. They would get married in mid-July when the season was ending, and go to Paris and Vienna during August, where he would introduce her to the foreign wholesalers and his circle of Parisian friends.

During the last week in June, just as trade was slacking, Mrs Hengrave came in to order some new clothes for travelling. Millicent looked older, her bold good looks tinged with anxiety. Johnston Hengrave was ailing with a mysterious complaint of the nerves, slow and insidious, undermining his capabilities, like a premature senility. They were going to consult a foreign specialist in a desperate attempt to find a cure. She was astounded at Margaret's news.

'You mean you're *marrying* Ferdi Leon? He's too old!'

'Oh, not that old! And you married an older man.'

'But he had been married before.'

'So you don't think it a good idea?'

Millicent's dark eyes were quizzical.

'A very good idea for dear Ferdi, no doubt,' she said

drily. 'You've helped him create a fine business. But is it such a good idea for you? You're not in love with him.'

A little irritably Margaret found herself defending her position again.

'We're very close friends. People are talking.'

'And?' Millicent challenged.

'It's a proper partnership. I'm to get a third of the profits. The running of the place, apart from the designing and buying, will be entirely in my hands. It will give me stature in the business. And I shall have a very presentable and delightful husband who is a good friend and a wonderful teacher.'

'You have it all worked out.'

'Of course,' Margaret said. 'He is the best designer of women's clothes in England – perhaps in Europe.' She laughed. 'What is it, Millicent? You introduced us. You have always liked him.'

'Everyone likes him. But to marry him?' She shrugged expressively. 'You could have done it all on your own, you know.'

'No. Ferdi is the creator. Our sort of business is built round the designer. Without we'd just be an ordinary house.'

'Well, have it your own way – and good luck to you.'

Ferdi designed Margaret an enchanting trousseau. Almost nightly, after business hours, they were out together. He was attentive and charming, and his circle of clever and often very distinguished friends entertained them royally. When they were married, Ferdi said delightedly, they too would entertain.

He was busy planning their apartment above the new house in Hanover Street. The tailoring department would be on the ground floor, the offices and counting house and his studio on the first floor. The two upper storeys would be their apartment. He searched through Libertys,

Maples and Heals, choosing fabrics for curtains and hangings, and bought antiques, china and pictures at the quality auction sales. Margaret was quite happy to leave it all to him . . . she had complete faith in his good taste, and she was very busy. They had an excellent season, the last orders before the mid-Summer slack were in the process of being made and delivered. She began to look forward to married life. It was going to be smart, successful and a great deal of fun, and she had not had much fun. They kept Ferdinand's manservant, Judson, as butler, and his wife as cook, and engaged two maids. There was an excellent stable behind the house where, as well as their chic grey-and-gold delivery waggon, they could keep their own carriage. Ferdinand squired her gallantly through the smart, high-artistic, Bohemian set in which he moved, and if Henry Grimshaw's craggy Red Indian face haunted her nights, she forgot him in the delight of her full and amusing days.

It seemed to Charmian that she had been in India for a lifetime, and the years had whittled down to unrelieved boredom until Bellamy was posted to Bombay. That there were a great many young, frivolous wives among the Army mems was true, but there were also many serious women who went in for good works and charitable efforts to make the soldiers' wives, in this uncomfortable life of the lines, bearable, who interested themselves in health services and education. Pretty Mrs Chester was *not* one of these. She found them exceedingly dull.

She was now twenty-five, no longer the girlish bride whose charming indiscretions could be laughed about in the clubs and cantonment. She was a magnificent, voluptuous woman, drawing men about her like a magnet. The wives of the Army community tended to isolate her as her reputation spread.

In Bombay, with its fresher air and more cosmopolitan society, Bellamy had hoped their growing estrangement would ease, but her indifference to him grew, and his possessive desire for her fed upon her indifference.

There was nothing positive – no open scandal. The bazaar gossip went from servant to servant, running round the verandahs of the cantonment, leaking quietly upwards into the drawing-rooms. The Chesters had no children. It was rumoured that the *dais* – the midwife from the bazaar who dealt in such magic prescriptions as burnt snakes' skins, and plasters of cowdung, who told fortunes, and could help ladies in all kinds of predicaments, was often to be seen sitting on the Chesters' verandah in the long, hot, idle afternoons. Someone's bearer told someone's ayah that the young Chesters had no longer shared a bedroom, that they had bitter quarrels and that the memsahib had threatened to return to England alone.

Charmian had no intention of returning to England. It was a threat she used to reduce Bellamy to an abject state of fear, when he would agree to almost anything she wanted rather than lose her. Since her last visit to Simla she was living on a knife's edge of sexual excitement, for she had met Angus Black again. In her first season in Bombay she had drifted from the Army set into the wealthy, cosmopolitan merchant society surrounding the millionaire, Baron Philippe Abderhazy.

She boasted about him in her letters home. His great house in Malabar Hill, his riding- and racing-horses, the steam yacht, the shooting lodge at Simla, the myriads of white-turbanned servants who appeared like genii to serve everyone's wish, and the indulgence with which he regarded every pretty woman in his multi-racial society, where creed and colour did not seem to matter, only elegance, good looks and the urbane surface manners of high society. After the teas and bun-fights of the cantonment life, it seemed to her sheer bliss. On her last visit to Simla he had invited her to stay for a weekend at his shooting lodge. Angus Black was also a guest. For five years she and Black had remembered each other – but India was huge, and the Army widespread, and their paths had never crossed. And then, in that last hill season, they met again.

Abderhazy's heavy-lidded black eyes had summed up the situation between them at a glance, and found it amusing. He was a rogue male in the conventional life of the hill station. Of mixed Persian and Hungarian blood, it was rumoured that he was a Moslem, and that he had more than one wife in strict purdah who never appeared in fashionable society.

He found it entertaining that these self-righteous rulers of the British Raj should succumb to the blandishments of his wealth. He was accustomed to the under-cover setting to partners in the great country houses of England and France, and thought that hot little beauty, Mrs Chester, deserved some fun when she was away from her burned-out stick of a husband, and if ever two human beings were ravenous for each other, it was Charmian and Angus.

So he invited Angus for a weekend and he invited Charmian and – of course – Mrs Armstrong too, for Bellamy only permitted Charmian to go to the hills for the hot season in Mrs Armstrong's company. It was a pleasure to Mrs Armstrong because Bellamy paid her expenses. It was a shackle to Charmian who was beginning to detest the Colonel's wife.

The shooting lodge was a fine white house with a balcony running above the wide verandahs on which the guest bedrooms opened; far more convenient, Baron Philippe explained in his too-perfect English, than the creaking oak-floored corridors of great English country houses along which even royalty had to creep in stockinged feet to attain his beloved's bed. And Mrs Armstrong was housed on the opposite side of the house.

'So much nicer for you,' Abderhazy insinuated, 'away from the smoking-room where we men make such a racket at night, and it is the new part of the house with every possible amenity and overlooking the garden. No jungle noises to disturb you. No balcony. Panthers have been known to go up the balconies at night.'

The first day the men went out after small game, the ladies drove into Simla, a picturesque town with its hills and precipices, its breathtaking views of distant mountains, and its neat villas and bungalows with unlikely names like Westgate, and The Ould Manse, or Clematis Cottage. The new Vice-Regal Lodge stood on Observatory Hill and the Vice-Regal establishment moved into residence when the weather became unbearable on the plains. The ladies wandered about the steep narrow streets, bought trinkets and presents, visited the library and drove back through the lush mountain scenery with occasional glimpses of the eternal snows. At the Lodge there was a long and magnificent luncheon, and afterwards some of the women settled down to bridge. Charmian went up to her room.

Lying naked under her thin wrapper she tossed and sighed the hours away until the men's return. There *had* been talk of a panther in the district, and she dreamed of the beast's hot green eyes and its fangs sinking into the flesh of the decoy goat. It seemed that Angus was the panther and she the panting decoy waiting with fearful joy to be taken and destroyed. Her heavy eyes looked as though she had taken one of the dais' love-potions. Her hands moved over her smooth, warm body, her nipples were swollen like ripe fruit, her long, lovely thighs sprawled loosely. She half-wished that Bellamy had been with her to prevent the inevitable. She felt bold, yet terrified, knowing quite well where she was going, knowing she could destroy her reputation and the careers of both men, yet quite unable to draw back. At last she heard the sound of the men returning, the first dressing bell, and summoned the ayah to help her dress.

It had been a white night with a full moon. The brilliant light, the fierce black shadows, the glitter of leaf and petal, the diamond flash of the fountain basin were incredible, theatrical and unreal, the air heavy with the perfume of flowers.

There was an undercurrent of sensuality about the women in their light dresses; in their hair and eyes, the whites gleaming in the shadows of the verandah, their teeth sparkling when they laughed, the shirts of the men, patches of reflected light.

Abderhazy's dinners on these occasions were not stiff and conventional; the food was exquisite, the service silent and swift, a turbanned servant behind each chair, the wine cold and delicious, the guests drawn from the rich, self-indulgent, easy-going, cosmopolitan crowd. Charmian was in her element.

Afterwards there were cards and baccarat, and a small orchestra played for the younger people to dance. She and Angus had been seated opposite at dinner, and over the bank of maidenhair, jasmine and roses, she dare not meet his eyes. But as soon as the music started he claimed her.

The imperative sexual urgency they aroused in each other reduced them to helpless silence. There was no attempt at flirtation. No laughter. No formal banter. He did not say, 'Do you remember me from Edinburgh, Mrs Chester? Before you were married? At the Castle? We danced there.'

Nothing like that. Just his powerfully aroused body touching hers in the dance, his predatory fingers stroking the bare skin of her arm, his strange, hawk-like eyes, mindless with desire, staring at her lips and shoulders, and the transparent chiffons above her beautiful swelling breasts.

They stopped dancing. Their proximity was painful, and he led her out on to the verandah which was lit with the coloured globes of Chinese lanterns. Couples whispered in the shadows. The white-turbanned, dark-faced servants served champagne. Abderhazy, the magician, moved among his attendant genii, ensuring that every pleasure was served.

Charmian skimmed down the verandah steps into the garden. Beneath the casuerinas, the jacarandas, the tumbling climbing roses, the paths were broad and paved, brilliantly lit, so that a snake could easily be seen. Small striped squirrels darted, thinking it was daylight. She walked with her bare shoulder touching Angus's arm.

'I can't dance with you,' he said incoherently. 'You drive me insane. How long since I saw you? On the station at Calcutta?'

'Nearly five years.'

'*Christ!* So much time wasted. Why the hell are you married?'

'I'm not all that much married . . .' Her attempt at flirtation faltered and was silenced by his savage look.

'Don't play with me, Charmian. I have the room next to you. The Baron has arranged it.' His strange primitive face was agonized. His control was at breaking point. She had the excitingly delirious feeling that he might take her there in full view of the house, or murder her. 'You will not refuse me if I come to you? I think I will kill you if you do.'

Her hands fluttered to her throat in excitement. Her body was pulsing with anticipation.

'If you don't come,' she said softly, 'I think *I* shall die.'

Abderhazy was ironically kind to them. He made things easy. He wanted her himself, but not with this young animal's urgency. He did not want any scandal. She was a woman who would create her own scandal, given time, and later would be grateful for his protection. One day she would come to him, but not yet. When she did she would be more experienced. More useful to him. He could wait.

So he gently replenished Mrs Armstrong's glass so that, sleepily, she was glad to retire, and the ayah who waited in her room, chinking with the soft metallic sounds of anklets and bracelets, made a last cup of tea, helped the unsteady elderly lady into her bed, and fastened the mosquito curtains. The tea contained a mild sleeping draught – Mrs Armstrong would not awaken early. And Charmian too made her excuses and went up shortly afterwards to her bed.

She undressed, washed, rubbed her white body with cologne. She did not put on a wrap but waited, naked and exquisite on the bed, her curling red-golden hair about her shoulders. In the five years she had been in India there had been other infidelities, other affairs, but this was the one she had been waiting for. A man who could match her sexually.

When Black opened the door from the balcony, she saw his tall figure silhouetted against the moonlight, and the pleasure began to well up within her.

He padded in like a cat, like a panther, closed and barred the shutters, stripped, never taking his eyes from her, drew aside the nets and came into the bed. No preliminaries of affection. Instant and overwhelming possession.

She had to hold her hands over her mouth to stifle the agonized and ecstatic cries that rose to her lips. It was what she had always known it could be and had never been before. Mounting waves of pleasure engulfed them, rising to an explosive climax, followed by sleepless bouts of rest, like the trough between breaks in a storm. When he left her and crept out into the lemon-coloured dawn she rolled over on to her face and slept as though she had been pole-axed.

If they had been normal people Charmian and Angus might have got away with it. But they were not – they were crippled in character as a hunchback is physically. They were too physically virile, too beautiful, too vain, too spoiled, too shallow. And both of them had been frustrated to a point of insanity by their lives in India.

Charmian had been subject to a possessive obsession that was bringing Bellamy towards impotence, and Angus to the womanless rigours of a frontier post, with only the relief of brief leaves to assuage him, for his fastidious love of his splendid body would not allow him the relief of native brothels, and the hill women were fierce, religious and dirty and not willing to risk their lives by concubinage with a white officer.

Perhaps, if Abderhazy had not been there, cynical and sensual, amused by their childish efforts to conceal their passion, they might have escaped, but he created opportunities for them, and promised his help when she returned to Bombay.

In the few days he had left in Simla they could no more hide their desire than handsome animals in season. Hands touching, eyes meeting, cheeks colouring, speechless with longing, and by the time he had to leave for the frontier every native servant, and every household in Simla knew of the rides into the hills, the secret, reckless meetings, and when poor Mrs Armstrong, shocked out of her senses at finding that Angus was creeping into her bungalow at night, reprimanded Charmian as she would have an erring daughter, she merely produced fury and hysteria.

Charmian said unforgivable things. 'What in God's name do you know about it? You've never come to a man in your life. You and your old stick of a Colonel! What does a dried-up old woman like you know about love?'

Mrs Armstrong could not turn her out. They stayed together until their return to Bombay, but she never spoke to Charmian again. Bellamy did not know the reason but he was not surprised. He had been surprised that the friendship had lasted so long.

In Bombay, Abderhazy drew Charmian into his set, and she loved it. He invited the young Chesters to his dinners, balls and garden-parties, his race-meeting picnics, the tennis afternoons, particularly when they clashed with Bellamy's duties. Bellamy would not permit Charmian to go alone but there were always charming women friends of Abderhazy's who were delighted to act as chaperone to the beautiful Mrs Chester.

Then Angus Black came to Bombay. He had been posted to Egypt, and was awaiting his embarkation orders. He implored Charmian to leave Bellamy and go with him to Cairo.

Charmian revelled in the drama. To her overheated romanticism they were like the doomed lovers in her favourite novels. These might be their last days together. They must seize every precious moment. Danger of discovery lent excitement to every meeting. Abderhazy was most kind. In the wall of his extensive garden there was a wicket gate to which she was given a key. Just within the wall there was a charming pavilion created for

202

clandestine affairs, where the Baron and his lovers, or his favoured friends and their lovers, could meet discreetly.

But Charmian was not discreet.

Every evening she attended some function and Lieutenant Black was always present. They left early, within minutes of each other. They were seen driving away together. The British community was ringing with the scandal, and Bellamy was the last to learn the truth. Colonel Armstrong sent for him.

He was a civilized man, leather-brown from many Indian summers, and fond of both Bellamy and Charmian. But he must crush this scandal and he did not want any dramatic fireworks within the regiment. And he did not like the look of Bellamy Chester. That driven look, as though the brink of endurance had been reached, which was not an uncommon thing in India.

'I don't want to lose you, Bell,' he said kindly, 'but things are getting a bit out of hand.' Bellamy's blank bewilderment told him he did not know what was happening. He changed course. 'Your little mem, now, she's too pretty by half. Not really made for the life out here. She's lost her head about young Black. Well, she's not the first one – he's an attractive young animal. Now, why don't you let me fix you up with some home leave? You've done a long stint. A few months at home would break the whole thing up.'

Bellamy felt his bones melt with fury.

'Can you give me specific details of the conduct you object to, Sir? I cannot allow accusations to be levelled against my wife without evidence.'

'Don't be a fool, Chester, the whole of Bombay is talking. You don't think I would have approached you if it was not true?'

The Colonel shifted some objects angrily about his desk, as though they were people he would like to move out of the way. 'Lieutenant Black has been in Bombay for two weeks. Mrs Chester has been seen driving alone with him. He will be here at least another month before he sails for Cairo. It simply doesn't do, Bell. My mem has told me about what went on up at Simla. It upsets the women. The natives talk and it's bad for morale. Makes us a damned laughing stock. Now, do as I say. Apply for leave, and I'll see you get it. Fix up a passage as soon as you can. And apply for a home posting, that'll do the trick.'

Bellamy's hands were shaking. His mouth worked as though he was about to have a seizure. The Colonel felt very sorry for him. There were some women who should never come out East – they arrived like flowers and ripened into poisonous fruit. Charmian Chester was one of them. Already the lines of sensuality were deepening about her soft, rosy, childish mouth, and the beautiful violet eyes had lost their innocence. The admiration she had aroused was changing – men now spoke of her in furtive undertones, stirred by her very presence. Armstrong pitied Bellamy Chester, although, like most men, he envied him. To possess a girl like Charmian would be something few men experienced.

He added, paternally, 'When you get her home, start a family. Give the little woman something to do. Keep her out of mischief.'

Bellamy's long, well-bred face looked yellow. He gave Armstrong a long, derisory, furious stare, and said, 'If you will excuse me, Sir. I will do my best. A scandal must be avoided at all costs.'

He went out. He had the corporal on duty call him a rickshaw with some excuse about not being well. It was true he was shaking as though he had malaria. He wondered if the fellow knew. Of course, God damn it, they all knew and most of them were laughing. Particularly the men. She was probably the new subject for bawdy barrack-room jokes.

He moved off through the crowded streets, his eyes fixed on the rippling black shoulders of the rickshaw man. *He* probably knew too. Everyone knew. Every gossiping woman, every officer in the mess, every salaaming servant, all of them smirking and whispering about her.

And worst of all, there was Abderhazy, the man with money, who had no responsibility to the Army or to the Empire. The pirate magician, thinking them all fools and puppets. It was said in the mess that the garden pavilion at Malabar had two-sided mirrors so that Abderhazy, unseen, could watch his guests coupling.

'I'll kill them,' Bellamy said out loud.

'Sahib?' the rickshaw man slowed, glanced round.

'Nothing, nothing. *Imshi*, you fool.'

'Sahib.' The man ducked and increased the speed of his tireless jog-trot. He knew nothing of the Chesters, nor cared. A little money, a little food, a little hashish before he stretched out on the floor at night and slept, was all he expected.

The bungalow was empty when Bellamy got home. The startled bearer, aroused from his afternoon sleep, said that the memsahib had gone driving with Madame de Marcos. Bellamy knew the handsome Portuguese woman, one of the Abderhazy set. He told the man to bring him whisky and sat in the drawing-room drinking. He could not let her go. *He could not live without her*. What did Armstrong know of the love that destroyed a man's peace of mind? She had starved him for sex until he could have howled like a tom-cat for it. She might bolt with young Black, and if it was not him it would be some other prowling scoundrel. When he had met her in Edinburgh, he had thought that because she was so young, a virgin, such a lovely child, he could mould her to his ways, the ways of his family, a good and faithfully devoted wife.

He burst out laughing, and went into her room and began to search through the drawers and cupboards. There must be some evidence. He had not to go very far, for Charmian had stuck Black's letters in the most obvious place – at the bottom of her jewel case under the velvet tray. Not very good love letters, and not particularly well-spelled – but terrible in the directness of their message, and damning in their explicit sexuality:

'*When shall we meet again? When will we be in bed together again. I think of nothing else. I remember the last time, the way your breasts filled my hands. You are like no one else. The only woman for me. I care about the Army, but I would rather give it up than give you up. Come with me to Egypt. If I have to resign I have to. It does not matter. Tomorrow we shall be together. Abderhazy has a tennis party. At about four I shall slip away and go down to the pavilion, and will meet you there. Two hours in each other's arms.*'

She would be there now with him. Even while he was sitting here agonizing, Charmian was giving herself to Angus Black. Bellamy put the letters away. He took a shower, changed into tennis clothes, and had Lal, the bearer, call a gary. Then he took his raquet, and from the desk drawer his service revolver, and told the man to take him up the hill to Mr Abderhazy's residence.

Chapter Eight

Margaret Grant Normanby married Ferdinand Pierre Leon at St George's, Hanover Square, in July. She was twenty-five and still a virgin, and he was fifty-four, a Frenchman by birth, although he had lived in London all his adult life. Margaret had no idea of his age until she saw it on the wedding certificate. She was astonished. With his slim, graceful figure and smiling charm, she had thought him younger.

Ruthlessly practical Margaret did not allow herself to think about Henry. One of her tenets, ingrained through the years, was that it was pointless to fret over anything irrevocable, and her life was busy enough without the wearing waste of useless yearnings. A lesson learned at her mother's knee indeed.

They were deep into the building alterations to the adjoining house in Hanover Street where they were to open their new tailoring department in the Autumn and Ferdinand, as always, left all the practical details to her, quite apart from the day-to-day management of what was becoming a smart and profitable business.

He limited his work strictly to personal conferences with distinguished or beautiful customers, designing their clothes, and searching through the warehouses for the exact materials in which to create the gowns. He was like an artist choosing his palette. If he wanted pale sea-green, then the silk had to be the exact colour his imagination demanded. The practical buying of linings, stiffenings, sewing silks, whalebone, trimmings, lace, braids, was all in Margaret's hands. He had far more free time – and no family ties at all.

But he organized their very smart little wedding. He invited a scintillating party of actors and actresses, writers, journalists, painters, models, wits and pretty women, the *haute bohème* among whom he spent his evenings. The only support Margaret had in the church was little Jany Leck in her best blacks and a new bonnet.

Florence would not even discuss the matter. But Lady Margaret Normanby, her grandmother, too old to travel to Edinburgh, sent a small pendant with the Normanby crest in diamonds. The reception, held in a private room at Romanos, was very gay, with lobster and caviare and a great deal of champagne, with brief and witty speeches and a large, elaborate cake with a sugar mannequin atop in pink spun sugar.

Ferdinand had designed the wedding dress, a chalk-white moiré silk in a simple Princess style, with tight wrist-length sleeves, and a swept back, flowing skirt. Instead of the conventional veil and wreath Margaret wore a small toque of orange blossom and white roses, and carried a posy of the same flowers. The whiteness set off her clear skin, and her crown of brilliant hair. Leon had aimed to do her proud, and he had succeeded. His eyes lit up with pleasure when he saw her dressed.

'You are more distinguished than any lady we have ever served,' he told her. 'I am proud of you, and I am proud of the firm.'

He looked the very acme of elegance, perfectly dressed from the pearl pin in his grey satin stock to his pale grey spats and highly-polished patent boots.

One of Ferdinand's closest friends, a popular actor, was his best man, and he proposed their health, referring to 'These two shining stars of the fashion world, of whom it may be truthfully said they are "the glass of fashion and the mould of form".' There was amused applause. 'Which one of us here, *Ferdi's friends*, ever expected to see the day when he would marry . . .' A murmur of laughter – 'But he has, and he has chosen, I believe, the perfect partner for both his business and for life.' Prolonged applause, more kisses and congratulations.

Margaret drove back to Juniper Place with Jany to change into her travelling clothes.

That morning, before leaving to go to the church she had gone to her mother's room in her wedding dress. Surely for once Florence would say she looked pretty? Surely she would kiss her and wish her well? But Florence, her false curls awry, and her sunken eyes glittering, was holding forth to an invisible Lady Derring who had called, apparently, to commiserate with her on this new humiliation. She gave one stony look at Maggie's slender, white-clad figure, and continued her one-sided conversation with the empty air.

'My dear May, it is so good of you to be with me on this terrible morning. My daughter Margaret – yes, the red-headed twin, always a stubborn and difficult girl – has decided to marry a draper, and there is nothing one can do about it. She is of age. What her dear father will say when he learns about it, I dread to think. You may be certain we shall never receive such a person, either here or at Danesfell.'

Danesfell, in her foggy meanderings, was once again Normanby property. The only reason they did not go there for the shooting was because Florence was too delicate to cope with the entertaining. 'This – Mr Ferdinand Leon – whoever heard of such a name? He must be a Jew from Cheapside. I think one must draw the line somewhere, although HRH has made a fashion of receiving these Jewish financiers, but royalty is a law unto itself. *I* shall never receive him. My daughters have been a sad disappointment to me – they have no ambitions and no pride.'

Margaret knelt down, her rustling skirts billowing around her, and took her mother's thin hands in hers, her other hand pulled Florence's withered face round to face her.

'*Mama*. Mama, please wish me happiness and give me your blessing. Just once in your life wish me joy. I *am* getting married.'

Florence drew away, her fan making a small barrier of disturbances as though she was afraid Margaret would kiss her.

'I don't know what you mean! Will you kindly *not* interrupt. Cannot you see I am speaking with Lady Derring. Go to the nursery at once and tell Lecky to keep you out of my sight.'

'Mama – I am twenty-five.'

Florence's voice began to rise towards the threatening heights of hysteria. Margaret rose and left her. Jany and Lily Oglethorpe were waiting to drive her to church.

'Let me stay with her, Miss Margaret,' said Lily eagerly. 'I do understand her, she's upset today.'

'If you don't mind, Lily.'

But after the ceremony, when Margaret returned to change to go on her honeymoon, it was to disaster. Florence was drunk as she had not been since they had arrived in London.

'Now then, love,' Jany said quickly, 'don't you fret. You get changed and get away. I'll deal with her. I've dealt with her many times. She's only being contrary.'

'But where did she get it from Lecky? The money?'

'Who should know – summat we've overlooked. She's right cunning when she needs it. I'll give her something to make her sleep, and you get off. You've spent your young life on her. It's time you cut away from it all.'

Margaret went up to change into her going-away clothes, stony-faced, stony-hearted. She was married. Lecky would stay at Juniper Place and so would Lily Oglethorpe, whom she had persuaded to give up her work at Maison Leon to become Florence's personal maid.

She would do her duty. Her mother would never want, but never again would she live with her; never give way to the foolish hope that some day Florence might love and respect her, treat her with affection and be a little grateful.

She heard the carriage draw up outside and, giving Jany a brief hug, ran down to join her new husband, not looking back as she drove away.

Leon and Margaret travelled down to Dover and stayed overnight at a hotel to catch the early morning packet to Boulogne. He had engaged a sitting-room and two bedrooms. She did not know whether to be surprised or not. They had been affectionate friends, but never lovers. That was a Rubicon she would have to cross tonight, and she hoped he would help her. She was no longer a silly girl whom a touch could arouse, when the sap rises, and the heart sings and reaches out recklessly towards its desire. She was relying on Ferdinand's wider experience to show her the way.

After dinner they walked along the seafront in the golden sunset. A large harvest moon was rising, orange against the intense azure of the night sky. A honeymoon night.

Ferdi took off his top hat, and let the breeze cool his forehead, blowing his fine shining hair.

'Tomorrow, Margaret, I shall introduce you to Paris. I've been longing to do so. To the great fashion houses, to the wholesalers where we buy our silks and trimmings. And especially to my many friends. It is a beautiful city

211

of many contrasts. Exquisite, sordid, amusing, bizarre, artistic, bohemian, everything. One is never bored in Paris.'

'Are you bored now?'

He smiled and kissed her on the cheek, affectionately as he had often done over the past year, but not even a fragile shiver of desire rose between them.

'This time tomorrow we will be in my lovely Paris, sitting at the Café de la Paix, watching people pass. You will see many handsome women, but you will outshine them all. They can boast of Monsieur Worth but we will show them what Maison Leon can do. You will wear your blue velvet. We will go to Maxims for supper, and you will see the queens of pleasure stalking their prey.'

'Prey?'

'Men. Rich men. Come, let us go back to the hotel and get a good night's sleep – we don't want to waste a minute of Paris tomorrow.'

They went back to the hotel. In the comfortable room overlooking the sea, she undressed and put on the new nightdress and negligé. Not the conventional white cambric, high-necked and long sleeved, but the most beautiful garments which Ferdinand had ordered for her from Vienna. Apricot satin, appliquéd with cream lace and embroidered.

She had let her hair down about her shoulders, and its coppery thickness shone about her pale triangular face. She rubbed her cheeks to bring colour to them. Should she put on rouge? She had never worn it in her life. She waited, her knees drawn up, slim hands linked about them, praying that he would come, and that it would be all right.

Ferdinand knocked. He was still dressed, immaculate and very good-looking. He carried a tray with a bottle of champagne and glasses, which he put down on the table by the bed, sat down on the edge, and took her hand.

'Margaret, you look really lovely. The negligé is perfect with your hair.' He touched her hair gently, and she shivered with fear because no desire rose within her. Her loins felt like clamped steel. Her breasts cold as porcelain. He picked up a small comb, and wound an amber strand round his finger, smiling to see it spring into a perfect ringlet. 'What lovely hair. Shall I brush it for you?'

'If you wish.'

He took off his coat, folded it neatly, and sat on the edge of her bed, brushing her hair with more gentleness and care than Lecky ever had. When it was spread in a shining fan about her shoulders, he rose. 'There. I'm well-trained at looking after lovely ladies. Mama was very beautiful – and very exacting.'

'I shall not be that.'

'I know,' he said gratefully. 'My little partner. My dearest girl, we are both tired. Rest now, and tomorrow we travel to Paris.' He kissed her head, and then her cheeks. It was charming, kindly, affectionate. 'Goodnight, my dear.'

He went out, carefully closing the door.

Margaret was drowned in mindless panic. She sprang out of bed and ran to the door, irrationally feeling she was locked in. The door opened, pride suddenly clamped down just in time to stop her running barefoot down the corridor, imploring him to stay with her.

She saw his well-tailored, jaunty back swinging down the corridor, stopping to unlock the bedroom door at the farther end. As far as possible from her? She closed the door, and leaned against it, shivering.

'Oh God, oh Christ,' she said. 'What is the *matter* with me?'

The old doubts, the old cruel mockeries. She could

hear her mother and Charmian from over the years. She was a born spinster, that dreadful hair, the lack of charm, of attraction, of sexual response – that had been Charmy. 'You're cold, Maggy. A fellow likes to feel a girl wants him. Or at least knows what he wants from her.'

The seductive figure in apricot satin with the red hair shimmering about its white shoulders reflected in the mirror was a mockery.

She could not understand. Ferdinand had *wanted* to marry her. He had pursued her. They were very close. He valued and admired her. Did something about her repel him? Her breath? Her body? She stumbled back into the bed and drank the glass of champagne, filling her glass three times before she turned down the light and lay in the darkness, her vibrant young body burning for the reassurance of passion, and Ferdinand, jaunty, elegant, menacingly faceless, stalked through her fevered dreams.

They sailed early next day and the excitement of the crossing and the arrival in Paris, Ferdinand's devoted attention and the fine Summer weather made everything different.

Paris was a revelation. They spent the afternoon in the Rue de la Paix, visiting the most exclusive establishments. They spent much time in the high temple of fashion, Worth's, both wondering at the organization and beauty of the workmanship, both agreeing that they would not want to run such an enormous establishment. They called in on some of the wholesale houses where Ferdinand was a valued customer. He introduced her proudly as his wife, and partner. Bales of the latest materials were unrolled before them, trimming of a variety she had never dreamed of, artificial flowers as beautiful and more exotic than anything nature could devise, plumes and ostrich fronds, fans and furs. Ferdinand was right – Paris was magnificent.

The Hotel Ventura Royale was on the Champs Elysées, a huge, new and magnificent edifice. Again Ferdinand had booked a drawing-room, two bedrooms, and two bathrooms such as Margaret had never even imagined. She could have played with the complicated showers and taps and sprays like a child; the bath was large enough to swim in, the cream-coloured tiles had a pattern of roses and butterflies, the thick towels hung over heated rails. It took her breath away.

'It's like ancient Rome,' she exclaimed. 'It's like a pagan city . . . people here worship their bodies. Cleaning them, dressing them, displaying themselves to look beautiful, eating perfect things. All the money spent on themselves. This hotel, it's like a great new, luxurious temple to Mamon.'

'Tonight, I will show you the night-life of Paris. It can be rich like this, and it can be sordid, but even then it is fascinating – and picturesque . . . go and rest, and enjoy our temple . . .'

Obediently she went to rest. The head and foot of the bed was decorated with gilded wickerwork and carved with swags of gilded flowers. The quilt was of rose-coloured satin. But she could not rest – she went to the window and watched the sunset flare behind the Arc de Triomphe, and the lights come up among the trees. The extraordinary, glorious city had an aphrodisiac quality about it, redolent of wealth, luxury and sex which set her nerves throbbing. Some hidden stream of profligate Normanby blood stirred within her. If this self-indulgence was not her way of life at least while she was here she wanted to taste the city's pleasures. Perhaps Ferdinand had known that, and made her wait. Perhaps tonight it would be different.

The evening-dress he had created for her was of a velvet so fine it could be pulled through a wedding ring. It was dark blue, so dark it was almost black. It had demure elbow-length sleeves, with falls of white lace that nearly touched her wrists. The neckline was scooped daringly low and fitted so closely that her small, full breasts were half-exposed. The front of the dress was cut in one piece outlining her fine long hips, and draped back into full folds, making a small train, for she disliked the bustle, which extended the buttocks with an ugly frame, overloaded with bows and frills and flowers. On the boulevards she had seen ridiculous exaggerations of it. Her only trimming was one huge shell-pink rose fastened below her left breast, and, instead of a mantle, or the ubiquitous shawl, she wore a long cloak of the same velvet, lined with shell-pink and collared with the pale pink roses. The dress was a triumph – Ferdinand at his most inspired. Her hair, usually plaited and bound as befitted a capable young businesswoman, was worn loose and flowing in a cascade of curls and waves on the nape of her neck.

What jewels? The diamond pendant from Grandma Normanby? Her pearls, of course. When she lifted the string from her case she stared in disbelief. They were not the Normanby pearls, but a cheap link, the skin already peeling off the glass beads beneath. She recognized them as belonging to her mother.

So that was how Florence had found the money to get drunk yesterday, to drown the disgrace of her daughter marrying a dressmaker? But who had sold them for her? Who had made the exchange? Lily, of course. She remembered the girl's anxious face and evasive eyes. What tale had Mama invented to persuade her to do this? She dropped the beads back and put on the gold chain and the Normanby pendant. With its quivering tremblant drops it hung provocatively in the cleft between her white breasts. She went out into the drawing-room where Ferdinand waited for her, the black and white of his evening clothes enhancing his slim, youthful figure.

His eyes lit with triumph and admiration. He kissed her hand. 'You look like a Princess,' he said, and meant it.

They drove East at first, away from the fashionable centre.

'I want to show you where I was born, Margaret, and where I lived as a small child.'

They stopped outside a tall, dark house in a narrow crowded street near the Place de la Bastille.

'Here?' she asked, startled.

'Yes.'

'You are going in?'

'God forbid,' he said vehemently. 'My mother was a sempstress, and very beautiful. I adored her. She was seduced by some young aristocrat. She was very ambitious for me and I for her. We were to make money, have a fine house and I was to marry a lady. Well, I've made money, and I've married you.' In the light from a street-lamp she caught his faint, quizzical smile. 'She would have been very proud of you.'

She thought of her own mother rambling on about her hallucinations and lost youth. Was she always to be enmeshed in other people's dreams? She who was so practical and worked so hard?

'She worked at Chabrier's and got me in there as a messenger, and Chabrier took a fancy to me. I matched for him, ran about buying silks and trimmings, held his pins while he cut and fitted, and finally he sent me to an atelier to learn to draw. After the fall of the Empire, Mother and I came to London – I had a small shop in Soho. I wish she could have lived to see Hanover Street –

217

and to see you. Like you she took everything off my shoulders, leaving me free to design.'

She remembered pink-faced, ham-handed Willy Gadsby at Madame Rosa's in Leeds. Another mother-ridden son? She did not want a man who wanted to please his mother, be she alive or dead. She wanted a man to want *her*, and not just as they had wanted Charmy, to get their hands on her body, but *her*, no one else, because she meant something special to them.

Ferdinand touched her arm; she blinked; her throat was dry, she had forgotten him and Paris. The fiacre was drawing up outside a large corner café. Ahead, across the wide square, the ornate bulk of the Opera House was silhouetted against the blue night sky.

'We are here,' he said, and she realized that his urbanity had disappeared, and he was eager and excited as he searched the groups of people sitting at the tables before the café. 'I have written, telling my friends I shall be here tonight . . . ah, look, yes!' He leaned from the window, removed his hat and waved it towards a large group sitting round two tables drawn together. 'There they are . . .'

He sprang out, leading Margaret forward with the other hand, like the star of a theatrical show. They were all silently staring at her.

There was something a little bizarre about them. Clever faces, clothes somewhat *outré*. One woman in long embroidered robes like a Rosetti painting; a small lady in a mannish high collar and Homburg hat. A large handsome middle-aged Englishman, very correctly and elegantly dressed, with a heavy, sensual face, and a green carnation in his buttonhole. Several vivacious girls, very smart and shrill, several very young good-looking men. Margaret was conscious of critical scrutiny and silence.

She was also conscious that her elegance outshone them, and that Ferdinand was inordinately proud of her.

'*Mes amis,*' he said, 'may I introduce my wife.' The silence cracked into greetings and exclamations as she took a seat among them.

'*Elle est belle, n'est-ce pas, celle-là?*'

'Margaret – fair Margaret – *une perle, vraiment.*'

'Come and sit by me, darlange,' said the little lady in the Homburg hat. She was smoking a thin black cheroot, and sported a monocle. 'This is an astonishment to us. One never imagined it of Ferdi! But you are a lovely child – are you a mannequin?'

'No, I am his general manager and partner.'

'*Mon dieu.* And so charming.' Laughter and compliments showered. Champagne was called for, and opened. Ferdinand, sitting by her side, was obviously triumphant at her success. Their health and happiness were toasted.

They bombarded her with questions. Her French was inadequate, but she explained, laughingly, that she had worked for Ferdinand for five years. That she was the general manageress, that, yes, he had designed the velvet dress she was wearing; that they had had a busy and successful season and had taken a second house and when they got back were going to open a tailoring department; yes, she was most impressed with what she had seen of Paris, but for her, the clothes were too ornate, and concealed rather than emphasized a really good figure.

She suddenly became aware that she was the only one speaking – that the company about her was quite silent, and standing beside Ferdinand was a boy of about twenty with a beautiful, dark, delicate face, with thick brown hair worn rather long, and light grey eyes with soft thick Italianate lashes and a red-lipped, childish, sensual mouth.

He was dressed in a white tropical suit and carried a soft

panama hat; his beautiful face was alight with surprised delight. He bent and kissed Ferdinand on both cheeks – but as the red mouth crossed from one cheek to the other, it brushed gently across Ferdinand's lips with no attempt to conceal the provocative sensuality of the caress. She heard the intake of breaths, like a faint hiss, go round the table.

'My Ferdi! Why did you not write to me you would be here in Paris? I have waited to hear that you were coming for so long. I have been desolate. Sometimes it has seemed that for me life is over. And now, here you are! You thought to surprise me, no?' He pulled out a chair and sat down at their table, glancing indifferently at Margaret, and went on, 'You remember how you said I could go with you to Vienna? This I have dreamed of. It has been hard for me . . .' The beautiful eyes were sad. 'My Papa insists I return to Orleans and soon I must, because I shall have no money . . . and he will not keep me here in Paris. I cannot stay at the university, because I have failed my degree . . . but last Spring when we had such fun and pleasure together how could I work?'

'Raoul!' The words seemed to force themselves out of Ferdinand's mouth. 'This lady is my wife.'

The boy turned his beautiful eyes on Margaret. He went white. He was shattered.

'It is true?' he demanded. 'I cannot believe it.' He looked wildly round the company. 'Tell me this is not true!'

Ferdinand jerked his head in an odd, convulsive movement. Under the thin moustache his lips were working as though he was on the brink of tears.

'It is true, Raoul.'

Raoul put his hands over his mouth, the big eyes staring above them, like a veiled Arab woman.

'Then you no longer *care* for me?'

He rose to his feet. So did Ferdinand. 'Raoul, there is no need for a scene. I did not say that. Sit down, and we will talk. You will adore Margaret, when you know her. Please, please, my dear child, don't be foolish . . .'

But the boy was weeping openly. He snatched up his hat from the table and rushed off into the crowd towards the Opera House, his white suit conspicuous among the promenading people. No one spoke. They were all watching Margaret.

The Opera was brilliant with lights. Carriages were drawing up before its ornate façade and people were ascending the steps to the grand foyer. As the carriages passed, one could catch the glitter of jewels, the gleam of bare shoulders and of silks.

She said to the little mannish lady next to her, 'There will be English women there, I expect. If we were near enough I could point out some of the gowns Ferdi has designed and I have made.' The little lady did not reply and Margaret realized she had not spoken aloud. She had a feeling of losing control.

Ferdinand turned to her, his face taut with anguish.

'Margaret, forgive me . . . I *must* go to him. He – he is *so* excitable . . . he might do *anything* . . .'

She found she could not speak. She smiled. It seemed to crack her face as though it was enamelled, and she made a gesture of permission, vague, stiff, like a mechanical doll. She found her voice at last.

'Please, go and console your friend, Ferdi. It is quite all right. I do understand.'

He vanished into the crowd in pursuit of the boy. About the table Ferdinand's friends began to talk in a high-pitched chatter. She looked down at her immaculately gloved hands, and her glass filled with vermouth, and lifted it to her lips. The tiny knot of anger grew

221

within her, wiping away the whiteness of her face with a high, bright flare.

Not at Ferdi – he was what he was – but at herself. How *could* she have been such a fool? Why had she not seen? His friends in London, the many charming young men, the smart, sexless women with their witty tongues. Ever since she had known him; the over-graceful manner, the love of silken, feminine things. She knew about such people, she knew them among his friends; she held no particular opinions or prejudices. If people were charming to her and amused her, what did she care? It was one of the things he had loved her for – she was so tolerant about people. Yet in Ferdinand she had not seen it. Or she had chosen not to see it, because he had been her friend and companion, her employer and mentor, and, simply, like any stupid little girl in her own workroom, she had wanted so much to be married. To have that mysterious status with which a woman commands respect in a masculine world.

She drew in a long breath and her chin came up, met the eyes of the elegant, dissipated Englishman who had moved into the seat by her side.

'You didn't know?' he asked.

Her violet-blue eyes sparkled, her small head moved with Normanby dignity: she smiled. 'Of course I did,' she lied. 'Ferdi and I have a very civilized relationship. *Chacun à son gout*, my dear Monsieur.'

There was a burst of laughter round the table, and she rose, drawing her cloak about her shoulders. 'I think it would be superfluous for me to wait, my friends. It will obviously take a long time for Ferdi to console his emotional young friend. Would you ask the waiter to get me a cab?'

He sprang to his feet, a fiacre was called, and he

offered his arm and escorted her across the pavement, his big coarse-lipped face alight with admiration.

'Will you please tell my husband that I have gone back to the hotel?'

'Of course.'

'Good night, and thank you, Sir.'

'Good night, and thank you, Madame Leon, for gracing our company. *Au revoir*.'

He handed her in, lifting and neatly folding her train. She drove back up the Champs Elysées to the hotel. Not until she was safely back in their suite did she collapse into a small attack of hysterics, all by herself, and then, when it was over and she lay on the bed, shaken after the storm of laughter and tears, she was surprised to find she was not unhappy at all. She was relieved that Ferdinand had not wanted her, because she had never for a single moment wanted him.

He had not cheated, because he was giving her all she had really wanted from him, a brilliant partner, a shield against the wagging tongues of disparagement in her status as a married woman, a share in the business which she loved, had helped to build, and had such great hopes for – all the rest had been pipe-dreams, expecting something from him which he could not give, and which she had always known in some secret way that he could not.

Well, she would make Maison Leon the finest fashion house in Europe. She would show these French frill-makers that an Englishwoman could beat them at their own game. She could not do without Ferdinand Leon, the designer, but she could do without a man as a lover – unless it was the one man she really wanted – and he was married to a dull, worthy lady and was beyond her reach.

Chapter Nine

Henry and Angela had dined alone at the 'little table' which was set in a deep half-circular window which overlooked the front gardens and the sloping moorlands to the town. In the distance they could see the three belching stacks of Britannia, Water Meadow and Calder Beck Mills, and after dark their plumes of fire would glow above the trees, marking Henry's kingdom. The kingdom was still without an heir after five years of marriage.

Angela was now thirty-one, and if she was not deliriously happy at least marriage had given her dignity and a very proper appreciation of her position. She was Mrs Henry Grimshaw of Cliffs Edge. Henry had been Mayor of Thornsby twice, and would be the next Parliamentary candidate for the Liberal party. She was also the daughter of Mr Torrance of Abbey Farm. With Henry's shrewd advice and ready loans, Abbey Farm had become a very considerable property. Her brothers had done well, her sisters were sought-after young ladies – life was very different from when Angela had cooked and worked and mended on a shoe-string to keep things going. She was happy that her parents were prosperous and her family held in high repute in the county. She had put on a little weight. She carried herself with matronly assurance in her public duties, and never forgot that it was all due to her wonderful husband, and that she ought to be the happiest woman in the world. But she was not.

There were no children, and she had always known

that Henry had not married her for love, but because he wanted children.

Tonight, sitting near him, she was filled with pride and love. She always was. He was so clever, so powerful, and so handsome, looking so very young, trim and lean-waisted for, in spite of wealth and good-living, he was a moderate man.

His grey eyes were as clear as ever. If his hair was greying about the temples, he was so fair that it was hardly noticeable. It was still thick and curly. When they were home together, which was not so often these days, she loved to watch him. The two lines between his brows, deepening with the years. The finely-carved strong face, the high thoughtful brow, the square capable hands, always so immaculately clean, although she knew he could set a machine and get down to a job in the works as well as any hand on the place. 'The place' being his life's work – the three big mills in the valley.

People in the valley speculated about who would inherit the kingdom. Both Henry and Millicent were childless. Henry had offered to take one of the Torrance boys in with him, but they were gentlemen born and bred. Industry was not for them.

Angela prayed nightly that she might conceive. The times when he came to her room became more infrequent. She could accept that she did not attract him, but she could not accept her childlessness. Even a girl would prove she was not barren. If there was one child others might follow. She tried to conceal her agonizing disappointment and to be everything he wanted in a wife.

Henry put down his dessert spoon, and smiled, congratulating her upon the meal which was, as always, perfectly cooked and served, but unimaginative, like herself. And having harboured this disloyal thought, he immediately felt guilty, and exerted himself to be charming. Tomorrow he was going to London and on to Paris carrying his samples for the spring. Tonight he would be very nice to her.

'Let us take our tea in the conservatory,' he said. 'You shall show me your latest treasures.'

She rang the bell and told Mrs Sykes, who still waited upon them personally, to serve tea there, and they went together into the warm, moist, leafy place.

Henry was proud of Cliffs Edge. Old Thomas Jagger had built it for his lovely daughter, and he, Henry, had enlarged and improved it as a home for his children. Two disappointed men.

At least poor crazy Florence had children. The twins. The pretty one with the eyes of a whore, and Maggy, clean and sharp as a lemon, vibrant with eager youth.

Even today he felt ashamed and disturbed when he remembered how much he had wanted her. It had been indecent in a man of his age. But now it seemed a hundred years ago. Both his boy's passion for Florence, and his brief but intense interest in her daughter. It seemed that he and Angela had been locked together in their comfortable, mutually respectful, married life since the beginning of time.

So they sat in the charming, flowery bower with its exotic plants, its goldfish and cage-birds, and catching Angela's shy, entreating glance, he took her hand and patted it. He was always very kind to her, and tonight he felt guilty because it was such a relief to be going away.

The tray, set with silver-and-gilded Crown Derby, was brought in and put on a low table. Henry took tea in the Russian manner with lemon and no milk, and when he took his cup he remembered that Nina de Malvette had first made it for him that way. His smile vanished and the tram-line frown between his straight dark brows deepened

226

irritably. Once going to Paris had meant going to Nina – but now she was beginning to bore him too.

As his interest in her waned, hers intensified. She was still the most exciting woman in bed that he had ever known, but she was becoming possessive. She demanded more expensive toys; jewels which she could display to her friends were her only proof that her power over him was still strong. It was not. And she knew it. And this time he had not let her know he would be in Paris.

'Henry,' Angela said timidly, then again louder, '*Henry!*'

He stared, and smiled, and put down his empty cup. Usually about now he would go to his small study, and read or work, or write letters.

Angela, so far as he knew, knew nothing of his life in Paris. But she was jealous of the fact that he so obviously enjoyed being away from home. If she knew of no other women, she was always apprehensive about them, as though he was venturing into a jungle of predatory female cats, and Paris was enjoying a worldwide reputation. *La Belle Epoque*. Sodom and Gomorrah, Mrs Torrance called it. Angela was a strict churchgoer and it hurt her that he never went to church with her. 'What,' she asked, 'will people think?'

'They'll think the Bishop's granddaughter has married an awful sinner,' Henry had told her, smiling.

But tonight he must be kind. He must stay and talk about flowers, and horses, and the house, and the neighbours and her family – one of her brothers was ordained, and her two sisters had married clergymen. When she said again, '*Henry!*' he started, and turned to her with his charmingly apologetic smile.

'My dear, forgive me, I was miles away.'

'Henry,' she said gravely, 'if there was anything wrong with you, you'd tell me, wouldn't you?'

'Wrong with me?'

'I mean, seriously wrong. Your health. You would tell me.'

'I would, of course.' He was bewildered. 'But why should you imagine such a thing?'

She gazed at him helplessly. She knew he thought her apprehensions foolish.

'Angela, the Dover packet will not be sunk in a storm. The cab horses in London will not plunge me into the Thames. The express to Paris will not be derailed.' He was laughing at her. 'You go out riding on the most spirited animals – am I an indifferent husband because I get on with my business and don't shiver in dread until your return?'

'Yes, but . . .' she stopped. She had been about to say that the difference was she loved him and he had never loved her. Her dull cheeks flushed, and she said stiffly, 'I'm sorry. I'm silly. One reads so many dreadful things. I worry when you're away.'

'Well, worrying about them won't prevent them. But this is a new one – that I should be ill. And *not* tell you?' He threw back his head, and gave his great boy's laugh. 'In God's name, Angela, I make such a damned nuisance of myself if I have a cold, d'you suppose I'd suffer in silence?'

She managed to laugh this time, for he was a notoriously bad invalid.

'Now come on, out with it. I can't go off abroad and leave you fretting. What awful fate have you thought up for me this time?'

'Well . . .' she said uncomfortably, 'I couldn't help knowing, for Mrs Thornhill saw you, and told me, that you were at Doctor Merryett's in Leeds . . .'

'The devil she did!' he said irritably. He rubbed his long chin with his thumbnail, and his smile deepened

228

ironically. 'Dr Merryett is a gynaecologist, Angela. Did you think I might be having a baby? Oh, my dear, I'm sorry.'

She was as stricken as though he had hit her. 'I know babies are no joking matter between us. No. I will tell you. I have heard it might – *could* be – possible to tell which of a childless couple is sterile.'

She stared in disbelief. '*Which?*'

'Oh, yes. It could be the man or the woman. I thought, my dear, that it might be me.'

She turned bright red and murmured, 'But Henry, it can't be you.'

'Virility has nothing to do with it. I had a very interesting talk with Dr Merryett. In fact we have arranged to dine together on my return. He is a man who has a great deal of knowledge, and the subject of fertility is fascinating. He thinks in the future we shall be able to impregnate the infertile, and decide the sexes . . . have a boy or girl, according to order. But, alas, as yet we cannot say which party causes the infertility, and we have no choice about the sex of the child. All he could say was that it is possible to find out if the woman has any real defect, and so far as he is concerned you are perfectly healthy and normal, and science has not yet found out enough to tell whether I am to blame. So, my love, don't blame yourself if we don't have children. Just look at me, and say to yourself, "It might be Henry".'

'I should think no such thing!' She was deeply shocked, drawing her shoulders up like a ruffled bird. 'It would be disgusting!'

'No, my loyal love. But you won't think I have a flaw, and alas, I have so many.' He moved his chair next to hers, and put his arm round her. His affection welled with tenderness and the tenderness aroused a mild and pleasant desire for her tall, strong body. She was still timid and unrelaxed in his arms in spite of all his skill. 'Tonight, let's go to bed early. *Now!*'

'Henry! What will the servants think? It's but eight-thirty. It is still daylight.'

'What the hell do we care what they think?' he laughed, and touched her heavy breast through its stiff silk casing. 'They will think I want to go to bed early. I have to rise very early for my train.' He put his arm through hers, and lifted her gently to her feet. 'Off you go. I'll be up in a jiffy . . .' He could see her breasts rising, her breath quickening, and touched her mouth with an experienced finger, then brushed it gently with his lips, so that she gave a soft, bewildered cry, as she had always when roused. 'Off you go.'

She fled from the room, and he watched her go, smiling, shaking his head ruefully. Compensation for his indifference? Maybe tonight he would break through her tension and her appalling modesty, her rooted belief that sexual pleasure was unnatural for a good woman. Unladylike. The kind of thing only common women could enjoy.

He went down to the cellar and found a vintage champagne, and took it up to her neat, flowery room, with the romantic engravings of young lovers and pretty children, in idyllic gardens, sentimentally petting charming ponies, kittens and dogs.

He opened the door before she had finished undressing. Her upper body, with the fine shoulders and large sculptured breasts was bare, her petticoats about her feet. She snatched up the long-sleeved, high-necked nightdress. She was never naked before him.

He had already drained a tumblerful of wine downstairs. He was suddenly exasperated with her ridiculous modesty. He snatched away the nightdress and lifted her into bed. She was a heavy armful. He could feel her shaking as though she was being raped. He filled a glass with champagne.

'Here, drink this, a woman must be relaxed to enjoy love.' Her reproachful eyes filled with tears. Had he given himself away? He pulled off his jacket and shirt, while she sat, gulping down the good wine like medicine, the sheets pulled up to her neck. Was he going to rape his own wife? No, not good, gentle Angela, for whom he had a positive, if lukewarm affection. 'I'll just go in here,' he said reassuringly, and went into her dressing-room to take off his other garments. He found a towel and went in to her, girded like an Indian, his muscular torso bare.

'Henry!' she exclaimed, deeply shocked.

In the blue twilight the harvest moon shone like a yellow coin.

'Look,' he said, 'how beautiful it is. There will be a good harvest.' His eyes teased her as she refilled her glass, 'for us, too, perhaps my dear.' She gulped down the wine and he got into the billowing feather bed beside her. Her heart was racing, terrified, excited. Tonight was so different. 'Don't be so scared, Angela,' he whispered laughing, 'we have been married for five years . . .'

It seemed a long while afterwards when he awoke, but it was only just after midnight. The endless night stretched ahead. She lay beside him, wakeful, still breathing fast, and when he lit the lamp he met her astounded eyes, and knew she had experienced true pleasure for the first time. The imperative urge to rise and leave her possessed him, as it always possessed him, with any woman. To be private and alone again, but he put his hand on her, and asked, 'You were happy?'

'It must be wicked to feel so happy,' she said.

'Don't be stupid, my dear . . . if the good God had not intended us to enjoy sex, he could have invented some

231

other way of reproduction.' He got out of bed, reaching for his dressing-gown.

'Henry,' she said suddenly. 'If I never have a child . . . What will you do? You won't leave me, will you?'

'Oh, Angela, my dear, forget about it . . . the more you worry the less likely it will be.'

'If you have a child – by someone else – and I could not have one. I would bring it up as ours. If you wanted it . . . and you would want it, wouldn't you? Just as long as you stayed with me.'

He gave a little groan of impatience and sat down by the side of the bed, and drew her against him. Since they had married he had discovered a worrying, over-anxious nature beneath her rather stolid outward calm. And unlike him she could never forget their childlessness. He had his work, the mills, his travels, his mistresses, and she had nothing but this comfortable home and the restricted life of a provincial lady. He got back into the bed with her. It was the first time he had spent the whole night with her since they had been married.

'You're so good, Angela,' he said ruefully, 'too good for me.'

And he took her again, and for the first time since their marriage she was relaxed, and responsive, giving herself eagerly, awaiting her reward, and when it came, crying with pleasure. She conceived that night. But by the time she knew it had happened, he had met Margaret Normanby again.

Henry crossed the channel on the night packet and got into Paris the following morning. He sauntered out of the Gare du Nord, following the blue-clad porter carrying his case, and surveyed the Rue Lafayette, crowded with morning traffic.

The pleasant feeling of anticipation, being back in this

city whose language he spoke, which had given him so much pleasure, entertainment and relief, failed him.

During the past few years he would have arranged no business appointments for this first day and driven straight to Nina's charming apartment near the Parc Monceau always giving her a tactful warning, to be greeted by cries of delight. The maid, the two snow-white poodles, and Nina herself, all in an ecstasy of welcome. They would take coffee, sending the girl out for fresh croissants, lingering over breakfast, going back into her large, gilded bed for the morning, or for the whole day, until she was due at her performance at the theatre in the evening.

Usually he took two weeks when he travelled. A week of work, a week of pleasure. This time he did not know what to do. He had no desire to travel alone. Send for Angela? She would come, but she would hate it . . . she was an entrenched Yorkshirewoman, believing that no life was as good as in her own county. He could go and see the Hengraves in Geneva, but the sight of his ailing brother-in-law and Milly, shadowed by anxiety, was not what he needed. He decided to get all his appointments into three days, and go home. At least, in Thornsby, there was work, and if one did not know how to amuse oneself, what else was there in life?

His last day, the second Thursday in August, he kept for Paul Jacquier, the proprietor of a wholesale house which sold to the high fashion trade of the world. He and Jacquier had become friends over the years. He was welcomed with pleasure. Henry's swags of samples were spread out over the table before Jacquier and his chief assistant. In Paris Henry sold quite a different class of cloth to that he sold in London. Finer, brighter colours, contrasting and brilliant checks and stripes.

Paul was amused by them.

'It is extraordinary to me, *mon ami*, that you, so

masculine a man, and so conservative an Englishman, should produce these so charming feminine fancies.'

'I don't design them,' explained Henry. 'I have a staff of skilled designers. I have three factories. In the Calder Beck Mills, which belonged to my father, we do the heavy-duty stuff: uniform for the Army and Navy, working men's liveries, hard-wearing Sunday-best stuff. At the Britannia and Water Meadow Mills which I acquired and have extended and modernized, we do the high fashion tweeds which you so much admire. And mourning. Mourning is one of our largest products since Prince Albert died. We aim to meet every demand, but of good quality. Grimshaw's don't make shoddy.'

Paul Jacquier placed a good order. He picked up a black-and-white herringbone. 'This I like so much,' he said, 'it reminds me of a bird.'

'A magpie,' said Henry instantly remembering Margaret Normanby in a white dress sprigged with black, and a hard black hat with a flash of white satin, set straight a-top her red hair. The memory was as vivid as though it had only happened yesterday.

The small, triangular, intelligent face, the slanting blue eyes, the lashes thick and short, and tinged with copper. The way she had talked, nineteen to the dozen, straight like a boy, with no coquetry. How often had he met her? Was it really only three times? In the train. The time when he had been fool enough to yield to his imperative desire to kiss her. And the last time, at his wedding to Angela, waiting to fix the bride's train, add the final touches.

The look in her eyes, the turn of her head, the colour fading from the fresh young cheeks, the instant of naked longing between them.

It was ridiculous that after all this time he could feel the intensity of his desire. A girl of eighteen, the daughter

234

of the woman he had once thought he loved. He shook his head shaking the absurd memory away, feeling bored and old.

'Yes,' he said heavily, 'like a magpie. Come, Paul, you have made your decisions, and I promise the order in good time for the Spring buying. Let us go to lunch.'

Jacquier rose, taking his shining top hat from a stand, glancing in the mirror at his portly reflection.

'How do you keep so young and slender, my friend? You eat as well as I. You spend your nights in Paris with our most famous ladies of the town.'

'Not this time,' said Henry, 'I'm sick of dissipation.'

'Ah yes, we all come to it. When the pursuit of pleasure becomes an obsession, it is time for a wise man to desist.'

Henry shuddered, thinking of the rich, world-weary men who hung about Nina de Malvette. Was he becoming like them? He looked anxiously into a pier glass but his alert, youthful reflection reassured him.

'You should settle down,' said Jacquier.

Henry burst out laughing. 'I *am* settled down. I am an old married man of five years standing.'

'When the children come, it will be different.'

'Ah, yes. *When!*'

There was an uncomfortable silence, then Jacquier gestured towards his office door. 'Come, let us go to lunch.'

He opened the door which led into the main showroom. An elegant bearded gentleman, wearing a perfect frock coat, a flower in his buttonhole, and pale grey spats stood in animated conversation with a slim red-headed girl. She was also very soignée, too much so for her age. She was talking with a brilliant smile like an animated puppet. She turned and the light caught her face, and Henry felt his heart constrict and, for a moment, was paralysed.

235

Then he said slowly, 'Maggy. Maggy Normanby, Christ almight . . . *young Maggy Normanby!*'

Jacquier, puzzled, followed his glance.

'This is Madame Ferdinand Leon. Her husband is a fine designer. They own an exclusive business in London. He is one of my best customers. You know him?'

'I know the young lady. She is from my home town. I knew she was working in London. You say she is married? To that *pouf*?'

Jacquier made a little reproving gesture. 'Monsieur Leon is highly respected in the fashion world. They are married only a few days. She is truly a clever and capable young woman with excellent taste. But . . .' his shoulders went up to his ears, 'In Paris Ferdi Leon is known as a paederast. Very discreet. But she seems a sophisticated young woman. Could it be possible that she did not know?'

'Possible?' Henry repeated. He was thinking of her at eighteen. The blazing innocence of her self-confidence. The burning ambition. 'It is possible. Excuse me, Paul,' he said, and ran down the circular iron stairway into the showroom, strode across to the Leons. Ferdi looked at him with polite enquiry. Margaret stood quite still, waiting.

'Miss Normanby,' said Henry. 'Paul Jacquier has just told me that you are now Mrs Leon. Allow me to congratulate you.'

'Mr Grimshaw,' Margaret inclined her head. 'Ferdi, dear, this is Mr Henry Grimshaw from Thornsby, who manufactures the beautiful suiting we have just been ordering.' The two men bowed correctly. She lifted the edge of a very fine tweed in pale grey with a jade and pink check line in it. In the selvedge were printed the words Grimshaw & Son (Thornsby) Ltd. 'When I saw it, it brought back many memories. How is Mrs Grimshaw?'

236

'She is well.'

'She is not with you?'

'She does not care for foreign travel.'

There was an edgy little silence.

'I have ordered a bolt of the tweed,' said Margaret. 'We are opening a ladies' tailoring department – my husband has taken the premises next door.'

'Indeed,' said Ferdi graciously, 'it was Margaret's idea. She feels the *costume tailleur* has come to stay in England. Not just for Scotland and the country, you understand. For town wear too.'

'Quite,' said Henry.

Paul Jacquier had joined them.

'It is very suitable for the tall, fair, slender, English lady,' he said.

'With horse's teeth?' Margaret said wickedly, her own pretty teeth flashing a smile. 'All Frenchmen think English ladies have horse's teeth, *n'est-ce-pas, Monsieur*?'

Jacquier blustered into animated protest, then stopped, smiling, and said accusingly, 'You make a joke?'

'Yes, Monsieur Jacquier,' Margaret's pretty smile teased, her extended hand reminded Henry of Lady Margaret, her grandmother, receiving at Danesfell years ago. 'I'm sorry, it was naughty of me. Forgive me. I think we have concluded our order, Ferdi?'

'Yes, indeed. And it is time for lunch.'

She was going. Panic seized Henry.

'Paul and I are lunching at the Cascade,' he said. Jacquier raised his brows, they had agreed upon a reasonable nearby bistro. 'Won't you join us? Mr Leon? Maggy?'

The name slipped thoughtlessly off his tongue. For the first time he saw her colour change, and felt an unbearable excitement. Ferdinand glanced at her for a decision. She gave a small smiling nod.

'That would be charming,' he said, 'you are most kind. We have a carriage waiting . . .'

Margaret sailed ahead through the showroom with Paul Jacquier; Henry followed with Ferdinand.

'You are staying in Paris long?' he asked.

'Alas, no,' sighed Ferdinand. 'A circumstance has arisen that I have to go to Vienna. Furs . . .' His shoulders drooped as though weighted with sable. 'Margaret has not yet touched upon this side of our business so she has decided not to go with me. We do not make furs, you understand. We use fur for trimming but for the coat, cloak and jacket there is no place like Vienna. Vienna, Mr Grimshaw, stands between Europe where furs are worn for luxury, and the great forests of Eastern Europe where the skins are trapped. The Viennese furriers are a class on their own. They handle furs like I handle silks, cutting it and shaping it . . . like Worth cuts velvet. We are speculating, my wife and I, whether to import one of these craftsmen from Austria and start our own department. We should have room now we have taken over extra premises. The trouble is these workers are nearly all very orthodox Jews and are reluctant to leave their community . . .' He stopped. Henry was not listening.

'Mrs Leon, then, has a say in the policy of your business?' Henry was shocked. The idea of a woman having power in any real business was something he could not comprehend. At their last meeting Margaret had been an underpaid employee at Madame Rosa's in Leeds.

'Oh, indeed,' said Ferdinand. 'Margaret is my junior partner. She is an extraordinarily capable girl. She has ambition, foresight, and taste. She can handle customers and staff. Since she joined me we have become a house to reckon with. I am left entirely free to create our models. She is a businesswoman to her fingertips. We have a very rewarding partnership.'

Henry regarded the slender, straight back ahead, the pretty hat like a flower, turning graciously to Paul Jacquier as he handed her into the carriage, and once again knew the tender amusement of their first meeting.

'It must be a wrench to part from her. Can she not go with you to Vienna?'

Ferdinand's eyes blinked evasively.

'Alas, no. We cannot both be spared for so long from Hanover Street. I take the train from the Gare de l'Est this evening and Margaret returns to London tomorrow morning.'

'How rotten for you!' exclaimed Henry, and his silver-grey eyes smiled. He made a gesture towards the carriage door, politely removing his square grey topper, 'After you, Sir.'

His thoughts were in a turmoil. The woman of twenty-five disturbed him even more than the piquant child of eighteen. Was she aware of it? Did it please her? Was she laughing at him behind that pink-and-white porcelain façade? What had she been doing during these years? Sleeping with this *type*? He could not believe it. Had she had lovers? The very thought made him hot with jealousy. Had she thought about him at all? She still had that drift of freckles across her nose, and the fresh untouched look of girlhood, for all her elegant sophistication.

They had a charming lunch in the beautiful restaurant in the Bois. Henry entertained them royally, ordering like a potentate. Margaret's vivid face beneath the flowery hat revealed nothing. He felt she must know what he was thinking. When she met his eyes hers were as blue as periwinkles and calm as summer skies. Leon was leaving early for Vienna, and tonight she would be alone in Paris. Tomorrow she would return to London.

He found himself bending towards Leon and saying

239

with the utmost civility, 'If you are leaving this evening, Mr Leon . . .'

'Please,' Ferdi gushed a little, 'call me Ferdi – as would any friend of Margaret's.'

'Ferdi,' Henry swallowed, very conscious of Margaret's amused blue eyes. He felt his neck go red over his high collar. 'May I have your permission to wait upon Mrs Leon tonight? Perhaps she would dine with me? And, as I also have to return to England in the morning, we might travel together. It is not too pleasant for a charming young woman, however independent, to travel alone. I should be happy to accompany her. With your consent, of course?'

As Ferdi turned questioningly to his wife her fine brows went up like two small ironic half-moons. How pretty she was, Henry thought. How very pretty, still with that lemon-sweet sharpness, that edgy appetising stimulating vicacity.

'That is very obliging of Mr Grimshaw. I shall be delighted to accept.'

'At eight?'

'At eight,' she agreed calmly, although her heart was racing to the point of suffocation. 'We are at the Hotel Ventura Royale.'

'I am there too.'

'What a coincidence,' she said, taking Ferdinand's arm, 'and so convenient.' She stepped into the fiacre and they drove away.

'*Un peu indifférent, celui-là!*' said Paul Jacquier.

'Cool,' Henry said smiling, and he stood and watched until the carriage bearing the flowery hat a-top the red hair had quite disappeared.

At eight o'clock precisely he sent up his card, and in a few minutes a page came down to inform him that Madame Leon would receive him. He had purchased a bouquet of red roses: a stiff posy in a holder and a frill of gilt lacy paper and tulle. He had never bought flowers for a woman in his life – Angela had a conservatory full, and Nina had preferred jewels. The florist had assured him that red roses had a romantic meaning all ladies understood. He felt like an idiot as he went up in the gilded cage to the second floor.

He knocked and she called out for him to come in.

It was an ornate sitting-room, cream and gold, with heavy satin drapes, and elaborate over-upholstered furniture. He stood with his hat in one hand, and the red bouquet clutched against his stiff white shirt-front. Margaret was wearing her blue velvet dress. He presented the flowers.

'Thank you.'

'You have many flowers.' Indeed the room was full of them.

'We are good customers in Paris. Won't you sit down?'

'Thank you.' He sat stiffly on the edge of one of the over-stuffed boiserie chairs. She buried her face momentarily in the bouquet. He suspected she was laughing at him and anger touched the edge of his desire.

'May I offer you a glass of wine, Mr Grimshaw?'

'Please.'

She put the bouquet on the edge of a small table, and turned towards a cooler in which stood a bottle of champagne. He rose quickly, 'Allow me.'

'Of course.' He opened the bottle, filled two flat, hollow-stemmed glasses. Margaret drank, a very little mouthful, licked round her red lips, and put the glass down. Then she took up the bouquet, tugged one of the red roses out, unwound the thin wire, then delicately pulled at the low-cut decolletage of her gown, and slid the flower between her breasts. She looked up at him and smiled. It was a blatant invitation. He dropped his glass which rolled across the carpet, took her into his arms and ravished her face and throat with kisses. He felt again the vibrant, youthful eagerness, and desire stung him. She was fire and ice, youth and laughter and recklessness. He felt as though he was being awakened from a long, boring dream.

'Margaret,' he cried, 'why the hell did you marry him?'

Her eyes sparkled.

'Why the hell did you marry her?'

'That's different. He's – well, anyone can see what he is.'

'What's so different? Your virtuous marriage doesn't stop you chasing the grand whores here in Paris.'

'How the devil . . .'

'Oh, Ferdi's set here know all the scandal. I've learned a lot. Everyone to his taste as they so glibly say. Ferdi likes pretty boys. You like loose women. I like – you. I'm older now. I've learned a lot. I'm not the little innocent whose urgency so embarrassed you at Danesfell.'

'You little bitch,' he said. 'You little devil, you drive me out of my mind, I want you so much.'

They were standing near the door – she slid the brass bolt across.

'Maggy . . .' he was at a loss. Never in all his experience had a woman taken the initiative like this. Even Nina pretended to be besieged. And she still looked so bewilderingly young, so pure, fresh, girlish. But he was no longer in control of himself; he picked her up and carried her into the bedroom beyond.

It was only when she cried out in pain, and then her thin white body wound more freely about him, demanded that he should ignore her pain and penetrate her completely, that he knew that he was the first man she had ever had – or ever wanted – and that at forty-seven he was hopelessly in love.

* * *

242

Charmian heard a tenative knock and woke in the large circular divan in the central room of Abderhazy's pavilion. A dim, rose-coloured lamp faintly illuminated the room. Her tumbled clothes were on a chair, and Angus's white tennis shirt and flannels strewn on the brilliantly-patterned Persian carpet. His muscular back was turned towards her, the skin gleaming with a moon-like sheen, his closely-cut ginger head was deep in a satin pillow, his mouth beneath the silky sandy moustache slightly open, showing his white and regular teeth.

They did not lie in each other's arms in tender closeness. They drove each other's bodies with fury, seeking ever greater explosions of pleasure, then slept in stunned, impersonal unconsciousness.

Charmian looked at him in triumph. She had exhausted even his much-vaunted virility.

The small noise came again. It was the Indian woman who acted as lady's maid to her on these secret afternoons. She rose quickly, snatched up her things and went into the dressing-room, and the Indian woman silently followed her, anklets clinking, to lace and hook up corset and underwear and gown over the luscious, full-fleshed nakedness.

Charmian hurried, snapped at the woman, snatching the comb from the thin brown hand.

'For Christ's sake, you stupid cow, hurry. Get my hat and parasol. Go and see if the carriage is waiting. I have to get home, and change and get back to the ball.'

The woman handed jewellery, handbag, hatpins, gloves, and stooped to tie the small white shoes. When Charmian hurried out she went to the ewer and washed her thin brown hands with a gesture of disgust.

At the door in the wall one of the white-coated, scarlet-turbanned manservants waited. He salaamed and unlocked the wicket gate. The carriage was waiting outside. The man shut and locked the wicket after her and spat eloquently on the spot where the high-heeled shoes had left small indentations in the soft, damp sand of the pathway.

He went up the steep, winding pathway, overhung with trees, to the pavilion, to awaken Angus who was to leave through the house and main entrance. There was tennis that afternoon. Angus would slip in among the guests who were still watching the game from the terrace. Later the bearer would call him a rickshaw to take him back to the barracks to change for the ball Abderhazy was giving that night. It was a farewell ball. The Baron would shortly be leaving for Shanghai where he had shipping interests.

As the man neared the pavilion he heard a shot, and stopped alarmed. One shot. But no one appeared. He could hear the laughter and applause from the tennis courts on the far side of the house up higher on the slope. But he was in no doubt about the sound. He began to run towards the pavilion.

Charmian lolled back contentedly in the carriage. Like everything Abderhazy owned it was perfect. She knew he wanted to own her, and found him both frightening and exciting with his heavy-lidded black eyes in which there was no gleam of infatuation. He selected a woman as he would select a racehorse.

But to live in such blissful luxury. To travel, to escape the boring monotomy of Army life – was a temptation. She played with the idea of sailing with him to Shanghai – or running off with Angus to Cairo – either of which would destroy her socially, and her marriage, and cause a great scandal. But at least, she thought childlishly, it would not be boring, although, of course, she had no real intention of doing either of these things.

The carriage descended the hill between the mansions of the rich and powerful. Small striped squirrels played in the trees, kite-hawks hung in the hot air. Glimpses of the harbour, the busy shipping and the small green islands showed between the buildings. It was hot. She knew she would have to end the affair with Angus Black.

Physically they were satiated, and the romance was wearing thin. He had no money but his pay, which would not cover her dress accounts for a month.

If she ran away with him to Cairo, he would have to leave the regiment. And what could he do but soldier – and make love? And would Bellamy divorce her? And if he did, a divorced woman was unacceptable in society. Oh, it was just another of her scrapes, and she had always managed to extract herself from them. No use worrying.

She must make it up with Bellamy. She had been very cruel to him. He was such an old woman. So weak. Yammering for love like a baby for the breast. But she had no doubt whatever that she could make him forgive her; she would simply stop refusing him, let him paw and mouth her, for that was almost all he was capable of now.

When she arrived home the bearer said that he had been in and gone out again. She supposed he had gone to the barracks. They were both due at Abderhazy's ball that night. She went to her room to rest before changing.

It was nine when Bellamy arrived home, and she had already dressed. Her ball-gown was a spectacular affair made from two saris of rose-pink gauze spangled with gold. She had had it copied from a design Margaret had sent her, and the delicate material was swathed and bunched over an under-dress of ivory satin. She pinned the fine half-moon diamond brooch Bellamy had given her on to the lace that barely covered the sumptuous lift of her bosom, and fastened her pearls round the strong

245

white column of her throat, pleased with the opulent reflection.

She heard Bellamy moving about in the drawing-room and the clink of bottle on glass, and went to join him, all smiles and radiant welcome.

He had collapsed into a chair, his head buried in his hands. He stared up at her, his thin face yellow, his big, sentimental eyes sunk into dark hollows. His uniform jacket was dark with great patches of sweat. When she bent to kiss him he smelled like a frightened horse when it lathers up with panic.

She sank in her froth of gold and pink on to his lap, her soft arms about his shoulders, her perfumed breasts level with his distraught face.

'Bell, my dearest, what is it? You're shaking. You must have fever. We must get a doctor. I'll send Lal across for Major Graham.'

'No,' he cried. 'I'm not ill.'

'Then what is it?' Her beautiful eyes were full of reproach and alarm. 'Bell, you haven't been listening to any silly stories about me and that boy again?'

'Silly stories?'

'Of course they are.' She kissed him on the mouth, opening his trembling lips with her soft, probing tongue. 'It's just nasty gossip. These jealous women make such a song about the smallest flirtation. What is there to do out here but flirt?' She tilted her head charmingly and kissed him again, instantly arousing him so that his arms tightened about her helplessly. It was so long since she had been like this. 'Oh, you foolish old Bell to get into such a state over gossip. You know I'm never serious about anyone but you.'

He jerked open the desk drawer and took out Angus's letters, spreading them before her like a pack of cards. She was startled, but not afraid.

'Is this what you call a flirtation?' He began to read from one of the letters. '"*I remember your body moving beneath mine and the feel of your breasts in my hands, and the fire rising between my legs . . .*"' He dropped the letter, sobbing with disgust. 'He wrote this – *filth* – to you! No man would dare to write like this to an innocent woman.'

Charmian rustled to her feet, covering her face, genuinely weeping from anger. How could she have been such a fool? She should have destroyed the letters. She shook with the fury of her sobbing.

Bellamy clutched at the gauze skirt, and said pathetically, '*Don't – don't cry!* I can't bear it. Don't leave me. It all happened because I could not stand the thought of you leaving me.'

She turned, the train of her gown lashing round like a cat's tail, the tears quivering on her lashes.

'Leave you? Why on earth should you think that?'

'Here . . .' he lifted one of the letters. 'Here, he says he has your letter, saying that you will join him in Cairo.'

She laughed. 'Oh, Bell! I only said that to make him want me. Run off with Angus! I'm not mad. He's just a stupid boy with too much . . . well, you know . . . he has no self-control. There's a crazy strain in his family, everyone says so. Oh, Bell, dear, listen . . .' She went down on her knees, and put her head on his lap. The silky waving hair fell apart at the back of her long neck, the white nape of which, encircled by her pearls, seemed so slender and delicate, reminding him of the young girl he had first danced with in Edinburgh. He put his hand on her head, gently ruffling her curls. It would be so easy to slip his hand around that slender throat and strangle her. Best, perhaps, for them both if he did. But he could never hurt her.

'*I* thought you meant it,' he said.

'Bell.' She did not raise her head, her voice was muffled; he could feel her lips moving against the bones of his knees. 'Forgive me. I am a bad girl. I know. I must be like my father. But really it means nothing. Bell, please forgive me. Can't we go away, you and I? Can't we go home? I'm beginning to hate India.'

'It was what the Colonel advised. He said he would grant me leave, and that I should ask for a home posting. But it's too late.' He sat back in the chair. 'I killed Black this afternoon.'

Her head jerked up, her mouth dropped open, her eyes stretched with horrified disbelief.

'I went up to Abderhazy's. There was a tennis party. I went in with the other guests, but I went down into the garden, into the trees behind the pavilion. I saw him come down to the pavilion in his tennis whites. I saw the servant let you in through the door in the wall, and watched you go up the path to join him. I waited there – an hour . . . more . . . I just stood there, waiting. The birds and squirrels came quite near me, I was so still . . . I saw you leave, and then I went down into the pavilion and shot him. He was sitting on the bed, naked, pulling his white tennis flannels on. I shot him straight through the heart.'

'Oh, God,' she said. 'Oh, *God*! You *are* crazy. Did anyone see? Does anyone know?'

'Adberhazy knows. And his servant. So, it's no use any more, Charmy. The game's up. I'll just wait here until they come for me.'

She rose, poured some brandy, sat down in a chair opposite him, and drank it down slowly. She could not think what to do – she never had. She had just followed her instincts and her vanity. Would they hang Bell? Or put him in prison for the rest of his life? Or shoot him? Did they execute soldiers in the Army by shooting? No one would hurt her. But no one would speak to her. Her name would be in all the papers. Maggy and Mama would read about it in London. No one would receive her. She would be branded all her life.

'Are you sure?' she said, like a puzzled child. 'You didn't dream it?'

He gave a crooked smile.

'Quite sure.'

The bearer came in, and said, 'Sahib, Sahib Abderhazy has sent flowers for the memsahib to wear tonight. The servant wishes to see you.'

Bellamy stared apathetically. It did not occur to him that there could be any solution. He had seen the small red wound on Angus's white flesh, and the ginger head pitch forward on to the Persian carpet among the scattered clothes.

The tall, hawk-faced native who guarded the gate appeared in the doorway behind Lal. He carried a gilded basket full of orchids, roses and stephanotis arranged among maidenhair fern, damp and sprinkled, grown in the famous cool-houses at Malabar Hill. He looked expressionlessly from Bellamy's haggard face to Charmian's and made a small dismissive movement of his head in the direction of the waiting Lal.

Charmian said instantly, 'That will be all, Lal. You can go.'

He went out. She went to the door and opened it, looked out, made sure there was no one listening and came back. 'Well?'

Abderhazy's man put the basket on the table beside them, and took Bellamy's revolver from beneath the flowers. It was wrapped in a white silk square.

'Where is this kept, Sahib?'

Bellamy was speechless, frozen. Charmian spoke quickly.

249

'In the drawer of that desk.'

The man opened the drawer carefully. He was wearing white butler's gloves. 'Bullet?' he asked.

'In the box.'

The white-gloved hand opened the box, slid a bullet into the revolver, and put everything back into the drawer.

'It is all as it was,' he said. 'My master sends his greetings – he expects the Captain Sahib and the Memsahib to the ball tonight, and to dinner before. He says it is most important that you should both come. He will send a carriage for you in one hour.'

'We shall be ready,' said Charmian.

The hawk-like face was totally expressionless. He made a low salaam. 'In an hour,' he said, and went out.

Bell buried his face in his hands.

'What the devil is Abderhazy playing at?' he groaned. 'It's useless. I'd better go to the police myself now.'

'You will *not*!' she said. The softness of youth had gone. The pretty mouth set, the blue eyes were black with anger, the pupils distended. But she was not trembling. She took him by the shoulders, and shook him. '*Do as he says!* Get dressed. You're fighting for your life, Bell. You've always been such a weak whining fool. If you'd been a real man, I wouldn't have looked at a boy like Angus. You say you love me. Now, *show* me! You say you were afraid I'd leave you. Well, I won't. I swear . . . I'll never leave you if you do this now . . .'

'You mean it – you really mean it, Charmian?'

'I swear to God.'

He pulled himself to his feet, swaying a little. She filled a glass with brandy and gave it to him.

'Go on. Get dressed. It will be all right. Philippe will help us. He knows how to keep secrets. Do as he says. Do you want to destroy us both?'

250

He looked at her with a strange, wild glance, drank down the brandy, and went into his room, calling to Lal to put out his dress uniform. Charmian collected the letters, searched the drawer, checking that they were all there, then she put them on a brass Benares tray and set light to them, and when there were only ashes left, dusted them out on to the calla lilies growing below the verandah.

Captain and Mrs Bellamy Chester attended the ball at Baron Philippe Abderhazy's house – it was the most brilliant ball of the season. The young couple were together nearly all the evening. Mrs Chester seemed anxious about the Captain. He looked pale and said he thought he might be in for a bout of malaria. He insisted on his wife having one duty dance with their host. When it was over she returned immediately to his side, whispering to him solicitously. She seemed most concerned about him.

Colonel Armstrong began to wonder if he had not made a mistake. If the talk had not been the malicious gossip of jealous women and envious men. But he had his own wife's word for Charmian's outrageous behaviour at Simla last year. He was glad they had decided to leave.

What Charmian had whispered to her husband was brief.

'Philippe says don't worry. Everything has been attended to.'

It was nearly a week later that it was reported that Lieutenant Angus Black was missing. He was in transit, not attached to any particular unit, waiting for a passage to Cairo. The mystery was slow in growing. By the time it was being buzzed about the clubs, drawing-rooms and cantonments, the Chesters had sailed for home. Bellamy, it was said, had gone down severely with malaria and had been told to leave as soon as possible.

Young Black did not reappear. There was a police enquiry which led nowhere. He had been seen leaving Baron Philippe's tennis party, and had bidden his host goodbye. Two servants of the house said they had seen him leave.

'He left alone,' said the Baron, shrugging, smiling smoothly. 'I believe to meet a lady. With Angus there was always a lady of some kind.'

He sailed for Shanghai at the end of the week, having large shipping interests there. He went in his own ocean-going yacht.

Bombay buzzed with talk for a while. It was rumoured that Black had been messing around with a native woman. He was always crazy – he must have known to pursue a virtuous Indian wife or daughter was asking for trouble.

Months later an unrecognizable body was dragged up in some fishing nets far down the coast. A young white man, killed by multiple stab wounds, no recognizable bullet wound, weighted with rope and boulders. The sharks, the crabs and the small carnivorous fish had done their work. It was presumed to be Lieutenant Black. No one could be sure. Death by a person or persons unknown. The body was buried in the military church-yard. He had not been stationed in Bombay and few people knew him. In Scotland his parents and clan wept for their lost lad.

Margaret and Henry Grimshaw walked down the steep hill to the harbour, sauntering hand-in-hand along the quays. They had left Paris as originally planned, but had stayed on in the old town at Boulogne in a comfortable hotel within the walls, instead of crossing to England.

The sky was the pale yellow of a Summer sunset, and the Cathedral and the walls were black against the saffron glow. Along the quays fishing-boats with coloured sails and painted effigies of saints on their masts were casting off and sliding out on the evening tide, the large sails billowing as they cleared the harbour-mouth to the ink-blue twilit sea. In the deep green water by the dockside some nearly-naked boys were swimming from the slimy stone steps, holding their noses, leaping in, dog-paddling and shouting. Henry and Margaret stopped, her arm about his waist, his about her shoulders, to watch.

He was hatless, the light breeze lifting his fair curling hair, his jacket slung over his shoulder, his shirt-collar open. He looked as though the years had slipped away during the days they had been together, leaving him a young man again.

Margaret's hair was loose about her shoulders, she wore a blue cotton gown sprigged with pink daisies which she had bought in the market place, and a straw sunhat, like the peasant women wore working in the fields. Sunlight and sea air had brought a scatter of pale freckles across her nose. All her Paris finery had been shipped back to London. They had been in Boulogne for seven days.

Henry threw some small silver to the swimming boys who dived like frogs to recover it, surfacing with the coins between their grinning teeth, shoving each other out of the way, calling for more. He tossed down the last of his small change and they turned back towards the town. The harbour smelled of tar and fish. Some old men in clogs and blue overalls were sitting along a wall smoking. It was very peaceful. Time had stopped.

'I never learned to swim,' he said. 'Some of the lads at the mill offered to teach me in Calder Beck, but Dad found out and beat me. He said it was all right for them to waste their time, but Calder Beck would be mine one day and I must never forget it. He did not let us play. Neither Milly nor me. I never did, except sometimes, with your mother, when she was a child and lived at Britannia Mill Master's House.'

'Mama lived at the Mill?' she said incredulously.

'Did she never say so? She was ashamed of it, even then. Her father, old Tom Jagger, spent a fortune building Cliffs Edge for her, and she was ashamed of that too, when she became Lady Normanby. But I used to sneak through a broken fence to meet her in the Water Meadows. It was never for long. Her mother or a servant would come looking for her.'

'Was she very pretty?'

He smiled, shook his head. 'I suppose so. To me she was – like a vision. Her life was so different from ours.'

'What did you play at?'

'It wasn't a game – it was a kind of play, like in a theatre. She was the queen and I was the devoted servant. She always thought of me as that. She did not like it when I stepped out of my role and grew up, and fell in love with her, and tried to make her see sense.'

Her face pressed against his arm.

'Does it hurt you – knowing what she has become?'

'Not now. I think I knew, quite early on, that nothing would ever get her to face up to reality.' He raised her hand to his lips. 'That's how you caught me. That first time in the train between Leeds and Thornsby . . . when I realized who you were I couldn't believe it. Such a funny, freckled girl . . . so down to earth, so determined to beat the world.'

She smiled. 'As a child I only thought of getting money, to pay Papa's debts and bring him back to her. To make her stop drinking and be happy because she was rich again. She was ashamed of me too – because I worked. I was vulgar, she said, like the Jaggers . . . I would never be a lady, a true Normanby.'

'Thank God.'

They laughed, walked on linked together. A ship's siren hooted and they saw the packet entering the harbour. They would leave for England in a few hours – they had not spoken of their future.

Her cheek was against his shoulder, her eyes alight with love. She irradiated happiness.

'This week,' she said, 'we have had more happiness than most people find in a lifetime.'

'Oh, Maggy Normanby,' he sighed, and bent to kiss her with the hard hunger of uncertainty. 'We've got to have more than a week. We have to make it a lifetime. I love you.'

'Shall we climb that great hill again, back to the hotel, or shall we get a fiacre and drive up there quickly? We do have just a few hours left?'

'We shall drive, of course,' he said, smiling.

They drove back, and went to their room, and made love until it was time to go down to the port and board the cross-Channel packet to Dover. On the train from the coast to London they had their first quarrel.

In the isolation of their first class carriage Henry said, 'I won't be able to come to London for another ten days at least. As soon as I know when I'm coming I will write and tell you . . . it will be quite different when we get a place of our own.'

She did not reply but suddenly sat up. She had been leaning softly in the circle of his arm. Her small, cat-shaped face with its dominating blue eyes was sharp with question.

'A place of our own? What *do* you mean?'

He kissed the questioning face indulgently.

'Well, you cannot possibly go on living with Leon. I would like you to move out before he returns from Vienna. I will instruct my agents right away to find a house or apartment. Somewhere furnished. Later, when we've time to think, you can choose whatever kind of place you want. Anything you like . . .' he smiled into the unsmiling face, wondering at the purity of her skin, so white, so softly flushed over the cheekbones, the small gold-brown freckles over her nose, adoring her youth. 'I can afford to spoil you, Maggy.'

'And where is this love-nest to be? Near Hanover Street?'

'It would be more convenient for me if you came up North,' he said. 'We should see each other oftener. And you won't need to be near Hanover Street now.'

'Why not?'

'If you are going to leave this man, you can't continue to work for him.'

'Why on earth not? I've no quarrel with Ferdi. I work for myself. It is partly my business.'

'But, Maggy, my love, I can give you anything you want.'

'And what about Juniper Place? What about Mama and Lecky and Lily Oglethorpe? Are you taking them on too?'

'Maggy, I am trying to tell you I am *a very rich man*.'

'How much do you propose to pay me as your mistress?'

He frowned irritably. 'I don't care for you to speak like that.'

'Well, that's what you're proposing, isn't it? I like to know where I am.'

'Rest assured that you will never want,' he said stiffly. 'What on earth has got into you, Maggy?'

'*You!*' she said furiously. 'You are *telling* me – not even *asking* me – to give up my independence. Well, I'll tell you what it's worth. At present I am getting eight hundred pounds a year out of the business, of which I am a legal partner, taking a third of all profits. My last cheque for twelve months' trading came to that much again. Next year, when the tailoring is open, Ferdi and I expect to clear ten thousand. Are you offering as much?'

His face fell incredulously. 'You earn *so* much, Maggy?'

'I do. And for a businessman you are an idiot. You know we buy from you, your finest and most expensive materials. How do you think we can afford to do that if we are not doing well? Oh, Ferdi and I are not like Worth with a thousand sempstresses. We have forty. We have ten showroom girls and five models. When we open the new tailoring section we shall take on a small number of first class tailoring hands – the bulk of the work will be done outside. We have a hall-porter, two pages, and six cleaners, a coachman and groom for the delivery van and horses. I run all that with two clerks leaving Ferdi free to design and buy. We don't want to be any bigger. We are doing very well.'

'You cannot go on living with that effeminate sodomite . . .'

'I am *not* living with him. And don't call him names! I am married to him but I shall not live with him. We will live under the same roof, because I am never, never going to live with my mother again. We have worked together now for nearly five years and been good friends. I can't see why it should end.'

'But don't you want to live with me, Maggy?'

'*No*. I want to love you when I can . . . what in God's name should I do all day, hanging about for you to come when you were free? No, thank you!'

The two deep tramlines appeared in Henry's forehead. He would always respect Angela's position and dignity as his wife. But she must understand that his interests lay elsewhere – it was a situation he had frequently met with among business and political friends. So long as the decencies were observed it could be managed very well.

Boulogne had been a playtime, a romantic re-discovery

257

of his youth. Margaret was his passionate and enchanting little love. That she was not prepared to give up everything and come to him simply had not crossed his mind. He was furious.

He withdrew his arm from her waist and staring at the seat opposite, his mouth set like a trap. If she thought she could get round him with her pretty cajolery, she was wrong. She made no attempt to.

The train was running into Victoria. Margaret reached for her hat and put it on, drawing her veil tightly, pinning it firmly, pulled on her gloves, and collected her handbag.

'It seems to me that we might just as well forget the whole business,' she said briskly, but her lips were trembling.

'Maggy!' He was outraged. 'After what has happened!'

'Well, as Lecky would say, it's plain daft! I'm certainly not going to abandon Ferdi and my business. If you won't accept that, there's no point in bothering. I'm in love with you and I thought you were with me. It has been a wonderful week, and now it is at an end. I had hoped we might be able to do this often – get away together. No one need know. I never thought it would involve altering our lives in any way. If that's what you want, it's better to end it now.'

He did not answer. He could not. He had thought of her as unlike her mother as it was possible to be, and so she was. But now he could see the Jagger stubbornness in her. The ridiculous thought which had occurred to him at their first meeting returned poignantly. She should have been a boy. His boy, not his girl-lover. A son. Clever, practical and ambitious, stubborn and clear-sighted as a businessman should be. Not afraid to make decisions and act on them.

The train stopped. He descended and handed her out punctiliously. They walked through the barrier without speaking. She glanced at her watch, a pretty jewelled thing on a long golden chain.

'I shall be in by the time they open up. Good,' she said.

The porter, wheeling their luggage, asked if he should call a cab.

'Two please,' said Margaret. 'The gentleman and I are going in different directions.'

The porter whistled and two growlers came trotting up in procession. She indicated which was her luggage for the men to load in it for her. Watching the small, precise figure, authoritatively directing them, Henry felt the melting, tender twist of laughter. He had never had a quarrel with Angela in the whole of their marriage. At his slightest hint of displeasure she was fussing about him with placating spaniel eyes. He took Margaret by her stiffly averted shoulders, swung her round, and kissed her lips.

'Do what you damned well like, you little devil, but stay with me.'

'Oh!' she gasped, straightening her hat. 'You're always knocking my hats off. Write me – at Hanover Street. When you're coming up to London.'

'I'll fix something. Soon.'

'I should have died if you'd gone away,' she said. 'I'm mad about you, Henry.'

She got into her cab and drove away. Henry suddenly burst out laughing, overtipping the porters, and drove across London to catch a train to the North. Never had he felt so reluctant to go.

At Hanover Street the doorman had just unlocked the main entrance, and the cleaner came out with her buckets and brushes to clean the steps.

Margaret's sharp eyes took in everything. The window-boxes needed watering, and the brass was not as bright as it should be. The decorators had not finished the outside painting, which they had promised to do by her return. It was already fifteen minutes past eight and the doors should have been opened at eight sharp. By now the cleaning staff should have finished the outside work.

Huggins, the doorman, got the sharp side of her tongue before he could greet her.

She went up to her office just as the two clerks were taking off their frock coats and putting on their alpaca jackets in the counting-house outside. She asked if the goods she and Mr Leon had ordered in Paris had been delivered yet, and sat down to go through the invoices and the week's mail. There was a card from Ferdi saying he would be back the following day, and had bought some very beautiful furs in Vienna.

A rustle went through the whole house from the basement workroom to the gilt-and-cream salons at the sound of her voice, and everyone moved quicker, took more care, glanced warningly when her voice was heard.

Monsieur and Madame Leon's honeymoon was over. Madame was back. The whole tempo of the place quickened, and the staff moved about their appointed duties like a team of circus horses in unison to the crack of the ringmaster's whip. Between themselves – well out of her hearing – they called her "The Bitch". She knew and did not care.

Chapter Ten

Sir Richard Normanby, still in San Francisco and down to his last few dollars, was relieved to get a letter and money from his wife. Four hundred and fifty pounds. The wild, unsteady hand looked as though it would run off the page. He thought she had probably been drunk when she wrote it. She had always tippled. But at least she had come up with some cash. Good old Flo.

He read indifferently through her romantic vapourings. She had been wild with joy to hear he was coming home to her. She had sold some jewellery to send him the money for his passage home.

So far as Richard knew there had been no jewellery left when he had departed. If Florence had kept any she must be less of a fool than he remembered.

The letter rambled on about the Duchess of Denton, Lady Allyson, Lady Derring – he could remember May Derring: a fast little devil. He had had her once in Derring's closed carriage on a wet day in the Park. But she must be sixty now, if she was a day. It seemed that his wife was as snobbish and as crazy as ever.

He threw the letter aside. The money would come in handy. He would pay his landlady and get his watch and better suit out of pawn, then take a trolley down town and try his luck at one of the gambling houses. As yet he had no intention of returning to England.

In late October Maison Leon opened its new tailoring department with a very exclusive afternoon reception and tea. At three-thirty Margaret and Ferdinand made a final inspection of the preparations. She looked enchantingly young and slender in a suit of fine gentian-blue tweed faintly flecked with green. A high-necked lace blouse, pearls, her hair dressed loosely in the new, full style.

The showroom was ready – Gunters had set out the trays of foie gras, salmon and cucumber sandwiches, the little sugar cakes, the tea-urns, the gilt chairs and small tables, and the major domo, impressively frock-coated, stood with his team of waitresses ready to serve.

The florists had arranged yellow roses, copper chrysanthemums and pyracantha in tall golden baskets. The new tweeds and worsteds were displayed on stands. The five pretty model girls were already dressed, hatted and furred, waiting to walk among the ladies as soon as they arrived. The cream-and-gilt decoration of the first house was continued through the large opening which had been knocked through the main wall, connecting the two premises, but while the gown department was Spring-like with curtains and carpet of pale green, the tailoring department was amber coloured for the Autumn.

Margaret and Ferdinand stood side by side, sharing the excitement like two actors about to go on in a new play. He had created a superlative collection, practical yet exceedingly chic: the famous English tailored suit made essentially feminine.

Margaret had supervised and organized the building and decorations, replanning the house, costing it to a fraction. They had sunk last year's profits into this new venture.

The workrooms were in the large, light semi-basement. The showrooms and fitting-rooms took up the whole of the ground floor. The offices were on the first floor. Their new, spacious apartment occupied the attic floors of both houses.

It was as they had dreamed and planned. What more could she want?

Ferdinand saw her secret, almost mischievous little smile as she stood waiting with him for their first customer-guest to appear. He was happy too. He admired her new, restrained voluptuousness. She was growing into the type of woman he most admired – a woman of the world. He knew she had a lover and had a shrewd idea who it was. They made no confidences and asked no questions. They worked smoothly in harness. What could be better?

'Well, my dear? It's a great moment.'

He kissed her hand. He wore a very pale yellow carnation in his lapel, and she noticed a new and beautiful carved amethyst signet ring. He was beginning to go a little grey and his smooth hair and small beard had been skilfully touched up by his barber. The pleasantly matt surface of his heavy features suggested the use of *poudre de riz*. She made a mental note to tell him, very tactfully, to be careful, London was not Paris. But her criticism was edged with affection. She respected and admired him immensely.

'It's a great collection, Ferdi.'

And you have presented it perfectly.' He linked his long thin hands together, pressing the knuckles against his lips, swaying his svelte figure as he was inclined to do when filled with enthusiasm. 'It's exactly the effect I wanted – not bleak and wintry . . . but warm, and golden . . . like today's Autumn sunshine.'

Margaret laughed, patting his arm. She was very fond of him. They lived and worked together in a kind of fraternal intimacy. She could not imagine why Henry still resented her marriage. The two men never met. Her love affair with Henry was conducted in brief interludes, snatched whenever he was free to come to London . . . she lived for those escapes into passionate friendship.

They had taken rooms in a charming, old-fashioned fishing inn up the Thames. There they spent their stolen days, rowing in the golden sunshine, driving through the sleepy riverside villages, talking interminably, quarrelling, sometimes quite fiercely, making up with kisses and laughter, making plans. Next year they would go abroad together. He would show her the cities he loved and knew so well. In the Winter they would find an apartment in London when the dank November mists came down on the river. They created a series of small delicious holidays to break up their hard-working lives. She felt neither guilt nor shame – she was very happy.

The first arrivals were announced: Lady Lucaster and Miss Violet Lucaster. Margaret and Ferdinand went forward to greet them.

It was a great success. Nothing quite like it had happened in the West End before. The ladies were shrill with enthusiasm, as they sipped their tea and spooned their ices, their accompanying menfolk smoothing their moustaches and covertly eyeing the pretty models displaying Ferdi's beautifully-cut *tailleurs*. The Leons were really a charming couple, not like tradespeople at all, but then he was French, and she had been a Normanby. The family had come down in the world, and the mother drank, yet of course blood will tell. Margaret, quite aware of these comments, kept herself slightly aloof. She did not believe in making friends with customers. Except, of course, for Millicent Hengrave, whom she hoped would be able to come.

No doctor had been able to cure her Johnston or offer any hope. He was now a bed-case and she devoted herself to him and was rarely seen in society. Therefore, when she arrived Margaret was delighted to see her.

In her forties, Millicent's turbulent dark beauty had been tamed by anxiety to a thin distinction. Her big, dark eyes had lost their boldness, her bright, hard personality was shadowed by sorrow. She embraced Margaret warmly, observing the change in her, the assurance and lack of tension, the confidence of a woman who has found herself in every possible way.

'Why, Maggy Normanby, how splendid you look. Like that cat who stole the cream.' Millicent offered her cheek to be kissed. 'Success suits you.'

'Thank you, Mrs Hengrave. I'm so glad you could come. When did you get back to London?'

'Oh, a week ago. I'm taking my dear old chap up to Danesfell tomorrow.'

'How is Mr Hengrave?'

'I'm afraid he will not leave Danesfell again.' Her voice was quite calm. 'He is dying, Maggy.'

'Oh no!' Margaret was shocked. 'I had no idea.'

'No. Well, we kept it to ourselves. I couldn't believe it myself at first.' The handsome, pale face crumpled a little, and her elegantly gloved hand pressed momentarily against her mouth. 'There is nothing any of the great doctors can do, nor any of the quacks and cranks and therapists and faith-healers. No one knows what causes a healthy man to lose his faculties in an insidious, premature senility. I asked him if he would like to go home to the States, but he said Danesfell was his happiest home and he would like to be there.'

'Oh, Millicent – how terrible!'

Millicent smiled into Margaret's stricken face. 'Don't look so sad, love. We've been very happy. I thought I knew all about love, but until this past year I knew nothing about it. I've been carting an elderly and ailing man about Europe in search of a cure and learning every day just a little more about what we've come to mean to

265

each other. But I had to come along when I received your card, so I slipped away while Johnston took his afternoon rest.'

A pretty showroom girl passed, wearing a fine tweed suit in yellows and muted browns with a small stand-up Elizabethan collar of golden brown mink, and a toque and muff to match. '*Charming!* I see you use *demoiselles de magasin*, like the great house of Worth.'

'Models,' Margaret said firmly. 'Ferdi likes to use the French terms. *Vendeuse, toiles, Monsieur le Directeur, tailleurs* . . . all that. *Not* me. Many of my best and richest customers come from round Leeds, and they come because I was Margaret Normanby who did right well for them when I was at Madame Rosa's in the Arcade.'

'Isn't it a little late for an Autumn opening?'

'Yes, but we didn't secure the lease until June, and then we got married, and went to Paris, and Ferdi went on to Vienna.' Margaret spoke as though her marriage was the most normal and delightful thing. 'He has designed some really beautiful suits. So we thought we would take a chance and open in October. After all, it is the little season, people are back from Scotland and preparing for Christmas country parties. And, as you see,' she regarded the room crowded with eager chattering ladies, 'it's a success.'

'Will you expand any more? Into a big store?'

'No. I want to be my own boss. I don't want a board of directors breathing down my neck. I want a mangeable business, small and exclusive, practical, and with a reputation for good taste. I want Ferdi free to do his best work. Our aim is to make the well-bred lady look her best, and the not-so-well-bred look like a lady.'

'You're a sight too clever, Maggy Normanby,' Millicent smiled affectionately, glancing across to where Ferdi was draping a length of red-gold tweed over his arm for a lady customer, hand on hip like a Spanish dancer. 'And are you happy?'

'Oh yes,' Margaret said. She smiled dreamily at her friend, giving nothing away. 'At the moment I am blissfully happy. Ferdi is an admirable husband for me.'

'H'mph!' Millicent emitted the rather crushing little snort with which she greeted any doubtful statement. She knew that the willowy, fiftyish Ferdinand Leon had not brought about the change in Margaret. 'How's your pretty sister?' she asked casually.

'Charmy is well, but her husband is not. They are coming home.'

'And your mother?'

'Only her illusions change,' Margaret said drily.

'You see her frequently?'

'Nearly every day. She lives just across Regent Street in a small house I took for her. She now imagines that my father will return from America with a fortune made in the gold fields. Although the gold rush is long since over!'

'He must be over fifty,' Millicent said slowly. She remembered the beautiful, worthless young man of twenty-five, and how once she had burned for him; what an alley-cat of a girl she had been then.

'She still thinks of him as twenty-five, just as she imagines that she is eighteen. But he writes occasionally.'

'Asking for money?'

'Oh, always! She sold my pearls and sent him the money for his passage, since when she has not heard a word.'

Millicent laughed ironically. 'He doesn't change.' Richard Normanby had no interest for her now. 'I see you are using a great many of the Grimshaw fine tweeds. That will send my dividends up. Does my brother call on you with his swags of cloth?'

267

'Oh, no,' Margaret said lightly. 'We cannot use enough cloth to buy from him direct. We buy from the wholesalers in Paris and in the City of London. His orders must run into hundreds of yards. We can only take a few bales. I buy the suiting materials – Ferdi buys for the *grandes toilettes* – the silks, satins, lace and furs . . . the glitter . . . the ball- and court-gowns are what he really enjoys.'

'So I would imagine,' said Millicent. Margaret did not flicker an eyelash at the dry comment. She was perfectly aware that Millicent's sophisticated eyes had summed up Ferdi long ago. There was a small silence. Millicent began to draw on her gloves. 'I must get back,' she said.

A very young man, with a pleasant, ingenuous manner, immaculately frock-coated, made his way unobtrusively through the crowd of chattering, fashionable women, and handed Margaret a blue Express letter.

'It just came for you, Madame.'

'Thank you, Roy.'

'You have floor-walkers too?' commented Millicent. 'In such a feminine business.'

Margaret smiled. 'One. Roy Brinkley. He came here several years ago as a page, and has made himself so useful, we've promoted him. Ferdi and I share him – as a general assistant.'

'The ladies seem to like him.'

'He's an attractive boy.'

Margaret had recognized Henry's writing. Just occasionally he would appear unexpectedly, and they would meet and spend the evening together, and these stolen meetings were inexpressibly sweet.

Her heart seemed to race, skid, right itself. She was furious to feel herself change colour beneath Millicent's perceptive eyes. She began to talk, a little too quickly.

'I am a terrible saleswoman,' she said. 'We have done

nothing but gossip. Is there anything you want, Mrs Hengrave? Have you everything you need for the cold weather at Danesfell?'

'We shall not be entertaining. Or only just family. Henry will come, for he and my Johnston are friends, and I expect that means my admirable sister-in-law and her very boring mother. And Johnston's son may come over from the States. No big parties. I *would* like one of your pretty new *tailleurs* . . . the average tailor-made makes one look like the mannish lesbian ladies of the Left Bank. But we go to Yorkshire tomorrow so I cannot come for fittings. I am a lot thinner than the measurements you have in your book.'

'Let me call a fitter and take new measurements, and I will send you patterns to Danesfell – and I will send someone there to fit you. I might even come myself.'

'You could stay with us. I should like that. Illness cuts one off from one's friends. They do not mean to be unkind, it's simply that healthy people are so busy.'

She followed Margaret into one of the resplendent new fitting-rooms, lined with mirrors, but small compared to those in the gown salon where space had to be allowed for sweeping evening-skirts and trains. Margaret rang for the fitter who came in, black-gowned, obsequious, her pin-cushion on her wrist, and the new measurements were taken down.

Millicent lingered, making rather a business about tying her veil and adjusting her hat, talking to Margaret indirectly, through the mirror.

'Henry is with us in London at the moment. With Angela and her mother. Angela is pregnant.'

She saw Margaret's face change, and knew immediately why. She had guessed that Angela's jealous suspicions about another woman, which Mrs Torrance had tactlessly confided to her, were not without foundation. The fact that Henry had told her nothing had made her suspect it was a serious affair.

'Angela is not at all well. Very nervous. She can scarcely bear him out of her sight. It is really extraordinary that such a fine strong girl, from a family of good breeders, should make such heavy weather. They have been consulting specialists. A gynaecologist and a nerve man.' She turned to face Margaret who managed a politely interested smile. 'But, of course, she is not young for a first attempt. She is very apprehensive. It would mean a great deal to Henry to have a child. Particularly a son. It is what he has wanted for years. Why he married. He would do anything on earth for her now. Goodbye, my dear.' She drew Margaret towards her and leaned a perfumed cheek gently against hers. 'I'm glad you're so successful and happy. Don't you think, after all these years, we could drop the Mrs Hengrave?'

Margaret flushed gratefully. 'Thank you, Millicent.'

She watched her cross the pavement to the carriage, smiled and waved, then turned and fled upstairs to the apartment, leaving the mid-Autumn opening to get on without her. She tore open the blue envelope. It read briefly:

'*Meet me at Waterloo at seven o'clock. Imperative. H.*'

It was five o'clock. Downstairs people were beginning to leave. Since their meeting in Paris she and Henry had met at Waterloo and travelled down to their riverside haven together. He always wrote to her, and wrote briefly, for neither of them could express their feelings on paper – but never anything as authoritative and brief as this. And his wife was pregnant! She rang for the butler and ordered a cab.

She read the brief, imperative message again. Her face flushed and her blue eyes sparkled with temper. Henry could both soothe and provoke her as no one else could.

How dare he write to her like this?

The speaking-tube whistled – it was Ferdinand, shrill and agitated. People were beginning to leave. Lady Lucaster had placed a very good order; what on earth was she thinking about not to be there to see her out?

'All right, I'm coming!'

'Are you all right?' he asked anxiously.

'Of course I am,' she said irritably, wishing Lady Lucaster to the devil. She thrust the blue envelope away into her purse and ran downstairs, catching Lady Lucaster as she went through the hall, accepting her congratulations on the new salon, and accompanying her to her carriage. She was a bad payer but a very important customer, influentially near the Court. Ferdinand looked sulky and a little reproachful when she returned.

'I'm sorry,' she said, then burst out untruthfully, 'Heavens! One *has* to get away sometimes.'

'I thought you might be ill,' he said, hurt, 'not to be here when important customers are leaving. It's not like you, Margaret.'

'I'm sorry,' she said again. The crowd had thinned out but a few latecomers were still lingering over the beautiful heathery tweeds. 'Oh, why *don't* they all go!' she said impatiently.

He looked at her as though she had gone mad.

'But it has been most successful,' he stammered. 'We've taken over a thousand pounds in orders this afternoon. If this goes on we shall have to take on extra hands before Christmas. You're tired . . . well, it's been a triumph, and it is all due to you.' She went with him into his office. At a large table Roy Brinkley was checking the lists, attaching patterns and numbers to order forms. At a word from Ferdinand he left them alone.

'Sit down,' he said. 'Relax.' He looked at the bright flag of colour in her cheeks, her blazing blue eyes. He had never seen her like this before. 'Margaret, why don't we go out to dinner tonight – a little celebration. Verrey's, perhaps? Or the Café Royal?'

'I am going out. I have to see someone.'

'Margaret, if there is anything wrong, anything you would like to tell me, or if I can help in any way?'

She took a small, chic hat of iridescent feathers from a stand and pinned it on thoughtfully.

'We must be very careful, Maggy.'

'Oh, yes,' she said gently mocking his earnestness. 'We must indeed. I don't know how long I'll be. Don't wait dinner for me.'

She picked up her handbag and gloves, and went out. He went to the window and watched her swift, light figure run across the pavement to the waiting cab.

Angela had missed her period during the time Henry was in Paris in August. Dr Ramsden advised no cohabitation for two months after the first sign of pregnancy. He advised her to rest in bed for four weeks, or until conception was confirmed.

She did not tell Henry or anyone. She cancelled her morning ride and waited, wanting to be absolutely sure – but as the days passed, and the unmistakable symptoms appeared – nausea; morning sickness; heaviness in her large, fine breasts – the certainty did not bring her the expected happiness.

She had longed for him to return rom Paris, and was eager and shy, remembering that last night together and his courteous indifference shattered her. What had been a revelation of passion to her had obviously meant nothing to him. She had expected a new and tender relationship – she was distraught to find that nothing had altered, or, if it had, it was worse. He made no approach to her. He did not come to her room. There was something about

272

him which she could not place; a strange renewal of his youth.

He was away far more frequently, and he had changed. He laughed more easily, he seemed more relaxed, began to enjoy his political career – he who had been a loner in the community became popular.

That there was a new and secret influence in his life became obvious: a long, curling red-gold hair on a jacket shoulder; the smell of a sweet-sharp lemon flower perfume about his linen. It ate into her peace of mind. The announcement that she had been going to make so triumphantly went sour on her. She had prayed and waited so long for this, and now she wondered if it was going to bring her happiness after all.

The weather in the South of England was glorious, and Henry had returned from a long weekend with Margaret late on a Monday afternoon. The moorland skies were slate-grey, and the rain driving across the moors as he drove home from the station. The golden Autumn sunlight flaming upon the woodlands at Cookham Reach, and Margaret in a yellow dress, with her straw hat sliding back on her red hair; like a child as he taught her to steer their boat – it seemed another world.

He had begun to dread these returns to Cliffs Edge and Angela's patient presence was a reproach to him. She made him feel guilty at being so happy and, like most men, he hated feeling guilty.

He was like the man in the old Norse tale, who fell in love with the Elf-King's daughter who could be possessed in love, but who disappeared with the first cock-crow. Margaret was like an elf with her pointed face, her small pointed ears. Margaret. Such a quiet, cool name for such a mocking, mischievous girl. She had filled his sober, childless life with her gaiety, and his starved heart with her reckless love. She entranced, provoked and exasperated him. She had renewed his youth and set his life at odds – he could never have enough of her.

A chill wind had blown along the river that weekend and he and Margaret had pulled the feather quilt about them as they lay together, naked in their warm, white nest.

'Do you remember asking me, that day at Danesfell when you came with Milly's dresses – you said, "Do you think that anyone ever says – 'Yes, this is it – this is what I really want. I am happy now'." I could say it truthfully now.'

He felt her shiver. 'You said I was wise to doubt it,' she said.

'Then *don't* doubt it now.' He lifted her on to him, for he loved to hold the fine delicate body above him with her breasts touching his and her lips hovering, bee-like, above his own. She was delicate yet fierce in her lovemaking. 'Now we know it's true. Tonight we could both say it – "Yes, we are happy *now*!"'

The inn bedroom with its sloping dormer ceiling was the home of his heart now. Cliffs Edge, large, luxurious, rather pretentious among the gardens and paddocks of which he had once been so proud, was a prison.

There was a high-wheeled gig standing in the drive, and he recognized it as belonging to Dr Ramsden from Thornsby. He ran up the steps and met the doctor in the hall.

'Is someone ill?' he asked anxiously. 'It's not my wife?'

'No, no, indeed,' Dr Ramsden said cheerfully. 'Quite the reverse. What a year it has been for you, Mr Grimshaw. Chosen to represent Thornsby at Westminster, and now *this*. . . Congratulations, my dear fellow, congratulations.' He seized Henry's hand and began to pump it up and down.

'On what?'

'Of course, Mrs Grimshaw has not told you. You are to be a father, Sir.'

Henry had waited years to hear this. He waited now for the sense of joy and triumph, and it did not come.

'Are you sure?' he asked.

'This time it is quite definite. Not quite out of the wood yet, though. Mrs Grimshaw will have to take care. Her legs are not very good. She is inclined to blood pressure. She is very nervous. I have been telling her mother, I would like her to travel to London, and see Sir Malcolm Hesketh. He was my Professor at Guy's, and he has very good ideas about the female nervous system. There is a reason why they become fanciful at times. A disturbance of the gland secretions.'

'Of course, if you say so,' Henry said woodenly. 'We will consult anyone you advise. My wife must have the very best care.'

'Precisely. I can only advise you. Mrs Grimshaw is depressed and worried, and she will not tell me why.' Henry made to pass him, but the doctor caught his arm. 'Her mother, Mrs Torrance, is here. I think you should speak with her first. Daughters tell mothers their worries. If we can find out what is causing this painful depression, we might remove it. Eh? Well, just go in and see Mrs Torrance. She is in the Winter garden. Call me at any time. But, yes, I think a consultation with Sir Malcolm would be a good idea. Don't worry. Babies usually arrive safely in the end. Good evening to you.'

He trotted off down the marble steps and into his smart new gig.

Angela *nervous? Fanciful* and *depressed?* His stolid, unimaginative Angela? Henry could not believe it. He threw his hat on to the hallstand and ran through the drawing-room into the Winter garden.

Mrs Torrance, a formidable gentlewoman, rose to greet him rather coldly. Her manner suggested that if anything was wrong, it was all his fault.

'But . . . she's not in danger of losing the baby, is she?'

'Apparently not,' said Mrs Torrance in irritable bewilderment. The mother of eight healthy children, like Henry she was completely taken aback by Angela's behaviour. 'But she is very hysterical and has behaved very strangely, and said some very embarrassing things. But Dr Ramsden says that this is all *nerves*!' Her long, aristocratic face stared at him with indignant accusation. 'No one in *our* family has *ever* had nerves before.'

'What exactly has she told you?'

Mrs Torrance coloured; she was ashamed of Angela. Her behaviour was not ladylike. One did not make scenes.

'Well?' Henry said impatiently. 'What has Angela said? And what *is* the matter?'

'She hasn't stopped crying all day.'

'For Christ's sake, what's she crying *about*?' cried Henry, losing patience, and then, remembering Mrs Torrance was a Bishop's daughter, apologized. 'I am sorry, Madame, but I really am very anxious about my wife.'

Mrs Torrance swallowed her indignation, and drew a deep breath. Dr Ramsden had said she must confide in Henry, and however embarrassing, she was determined to do her duty.

'She seems to think that you have another woman. I suppose it is her weak condition, but in my opinion a lady would say nothing about the matter, whether it were true or not, which I *hope* it isn't. Things . . .' she shrugged, 'go wrong with the best of marriages,' Henry suppressed a desire to laugh. Everyone knew Farmer Torrance's reputation. His mother-in-law would never

276

employ a good-looking maid-servant. 'Things work out. One prays for guidance, and keeps one's head.'

'I will go and see Angela,' he said, and turned to the door.

'Henry,' said Mrs Torrance in a stifled voice, 'be careful. She is . . . she's not herself. The servants sent for me this morning because she attempted suicide.'

'She *what!*' He was frozen with horrified disbelief.

'Her maid found her out on the balcony of her room, trying to drag herself over the balustrade. She managed to calm her and bring her back. She said she did not seem to know what she was doing.'

'In God's name,' snapped Henry, 'why couldn't that old woman, Ramsden, have told me this at once?'

He ran up the stairs to Angela's room, and opened the door. She was not alone. Her maid, a faithful local woman whom she had brought with her from Abbey Farm, sat by her. Henry jerked his head, and the woman shot to her feet and went out like a scared rabbit.

Angela was sitting up in bed. He was shocked at the change in her. She looked like one of the mill women who would go on working long into their pregnancies, anxious to earn until the last possible moment. The yellow pallor, the triangular discolouration on her cheeks, the hollow shadows round her eyes.

The luxury of her bedroom, the lace-trimmed pillows, the embroidered silk bed-jacket, the satin bow tying back her lank, light brown hair, seemed to accentuate her curious, frightened lethargy.

Coming from Margaret, young and fresh as the buds in May, he could not avoid the comparison. He was filled with compassion and guilt. He had never loved her, but he had never wanted to hurt her and he thought that she had all she desired. Those accusing, tear-filled eyes told him he was wrong.

'I didn't know what I was doing,' she said defensively.

'Angela, my dear.' He sat on the edge of the bed and took her hand. 'Promise me you'll never attempt to do such a thing again.'

'How can I promise?' she babbled feverishly. 'I didn't know I should want to die.' She picked at the lace edgings of the pillow. 'I've worried.' She gave him a furtive, timid glance. 'You do still want a baby, Henry, don't you? I mean you want *my* baby, not just a baby by any woman, so long as it is yours.'

'My dear, you know . . .'

'But I don't,' she said furiously. 'I don't *know*, anything any more. I thought I did. I knew you didn't love me. You just wanted to be married and have a family. Then that night before you went to Paris it was so different . . . you never made me feel like that before. You stayed all night . . . I thought we had found love. And then, when I realized there could be a baby I was so happy. I waited for you to come back, thinking it would be like that again, but you didn't seem to remember.'

He had never known her speak like this. He held her dry, pale hand, trying to find words of comfort.

He remembered his nights with Margaret Normanby. Nights when they had not even made love, but lain in each other's arms in happy silence, or talked quietly, or quarrelled fiercely, and made up with wanton and urgent passion. Something of his thoughts must have been reflected in his face, for Angela suddenly started to cry.

'You're not even *listening* to me now. You never have understood that it was like a miracle. You choosing me. I didn't mind until I thought that at last you loved me. But if *that* time, *that* night was just to get this damned baby, then I don't want it, and I don't *want* to live with you, and I *can't* live without you, so I'll jump out of the window, and then perhaps I can have a little peace . . .'

He put his arm around her and tried to quieten her, but she could not stop now. The fears and doubts and insecurities of the loveless years came pouring out.

'Angela, you are all worked up and foolishly imagining things. I shall be home with you now, and you'll see it will be different.'

'I might die,' she said, going off on another tack, following the stream of unhappy thoughts. 'Women do. The baby might go wrong. Be lame or blind or something. It might be a girl – you don't want a girl do you Henry? You want a son for Henry Grimshaw & Son . . .'

'Son or daughter, it does not matter.'

'I don't believe you.'

'Angela, you don't have to do anything you don't want to. You've just to be happy and well.'

'The only time I've been happy is when I've been riding. When I'm off on Merlin over the moors . . .' She saw the expression in his eyes and said slyly, 'But I'm not allowed to do that now. For the sake of the baby. Everything I do is for the baby. *I* don't matter at all. But I could take Merlin out and ride all day, and then this baby might not come!'

His patience snapped. The anger in his voice made her shrink back on her pillows.

'Angela, don't be ridiculous! Do you want to murder this child?'

She was silent, sullen, tense with resentment.

He said, more gently. 'What is the matter with you? You've never been a silly, vapouring woman. We have always wanted a child and now we're having one, you should be the happiest woman in the world.'

'I can't go through with it alone,' she wailed.

'But you won't be alone. I'll be here with you.'

'You're never here . . .'

'That's not true. I have to go away sometimes, but I am here more often than not.'

'Not with me. You don't see me. I ask you things, Henry. I want an answer, even if they are trivialities. But you just say, "Do what you like my dear", "Wear what you want", "Ask whom you please" . . . and you won't see me, or hear me, or care, because there's someone else you're thinking of.'

He stiffened, his complacency shaken, furious that she should question him and that she had not been deceived.

'I have always treated you with consideration.'

'Consideration!' she cried scathingly. 'One is considerate to servants. I am your wife. I know how bored you are here. You want a different kind of woman, a woman who is full of wit and laughter, a pretty woman, a young woman, a woman who is wanton in bed like a street woman . . .'

'*That will do!*' He rose as though to go, but she caught his arm.

'Henry, whoever she is, give her up. Please! I know there is someone. Your clothes smell of her perfume, you smile when you think of her . . . ever since you went to Paris in August, you've changed.'

She stopped and lay back, exhausted, and his anger evaporated. He lay beside her on the bed, and drew her into his arms, kissed and caressed her until she sighed and trembled and clung to him with newly-awakened desire. Not yet, he said. For a little while they must do nothing to hurt the baby. Or herself. He must take care of her. And presently she was clinging tearfully to him, and, because she was Angela, was apologetic and ashamed. But there had been a deadly undercurrent of purpose in her hysteria; if he had not come home today perhaps she would have jumped.

So he stayed with her over the next week, devoted and

attentive, and when she felt better he took her to London to see the specialist, who was a little dissatisfied with her condition, and advised return home and a month's bed-rest, just to settle things down.

On their return to Millicent's London house Henry insisted that she go straight to bed to rest up before their journey back to Yorkshire. He told her that he had to meet a business acquaintance at his club and would be back about ten. They were not to wait dinner for him.

'And I am not going to meet a lady-love,' he teased.

Angela went red and hung her head, bitterly ashamed of her *crise de nerfs*.

He went to the nearest Express office and sent a message to Margaret at Hanover Street. The thought of being without her sent him crazy, like a drunkard trying to give up spirits.

Both Henry, marching across Hungerford Bridge, and Margaret, driving down the Strand, were incredibly alike. Ambitious, hard-working, dragging themselves out of difficult early years to wealth and independence, nothing infuriated them more than their plans being set awry by fools. They approached Waterloo station and their meeting in an equal state of simmering anger.

Margaret saw him first, and was shaken by the emotion that swept over her, leaving her weak-kneed, her heart in her mouth, defenceless as any girl in love. There he was – her man – leaning on his stick, his carved, alien face set in a furious scowl beneath the brim of his hard grey hat. He was forty-seven, rich, powerful and experienced. He should have managed things better.

She marched through the homeward-going crowds and stood before him aggressively, tense as a fighting cat.

'Millicent told me.'

He was startled. 'About what?'

281

'That your wife is pregnant. What has that got to do with us?'

'Is that all she told you?'

'*Is* there anything else? I hope there is. Or why should you send for me like this . . ?' She flashed the offending Express letter before his eyes, '. . . as though I was the under-housemaid?'

'Maggy, for Christ's sake, don't *you* start to make scenes,' he said roughly. 'We must go somewhere where we can talk.'

'Where do you suggest? There is a train leaving in ten minutes. Shall we go to the inn?'

'Maggy, I have told them I will be back at ten. We leave for Thornsby tomorrow.'

'We?'

'Angela and I, and her mother.'

'Oh!'

The colour flared in her cheeks. Her eyes sparkled blue fury.

'Well, in that case we had better forget it all. Goodbye!'

She turned her back on him and made for the station entrance. He caught her arm savagely, dragging her to a halt. 'Maggy,' he shouted, 'hold your temper.'

'You hold yours!' She turned blindly southward, walking away from the bridge into a district of small, cheap hotels and lodging houses. 'What does it matter to me if she has a hundred babies! So long as she doesn't know about me, what harm can it do?'

The self-contained Madame Leon had vanished. The passionate egotism of her youth was shattered by his threat to her love. Beneath the smooth blue jacket he could see her breasts trembling with sobs.

'Maggy, Angela suspects that I have another woman.'

She turned so abruptly that he bumped into her.

'That you *have* another woman? Or that you are *in love with me*?'

'Oh, my dearest, listen to me. She is in an acute state of nerves. She is not herself. She really suspects I have another woman.'

'Why? Or rather how? Has someone seen us together?'

'No. I've been too happy. I suppose I've been really happy for the first time in my life and I did not trouble to conceal it. I suppose I was careless, just thinking of the things you do and say and smiling to myself.'

She was defeated. Her arms went round him. 'Oh, my Henry – my own darling!' He kissed her. 'Honestly, what difference can it make if she doesn't really know? I am not jealous of her.'

'You have no cause to be,' he said grimly.

'We must just be patient and discreet. You may not come down to London quite so often, but you can still come, surely?'

'She said – if it were true – she would take her life.'

For a moment she was frightened, then a lifetime's knowledge of blackmailing hysterics made her scoff at him.

'Some women are like that. Mama is – *you* should know. They do it to get their own way. Great heavens. I've had staff – *and* customers doing it. Scene-makers. I abhor them.'

He shook his head.

'Angela is not like that. She is patient and long-suffering. She nearly did it – she was caught in time. I cannot risk it now there is a child on the way.'

Now she really was frightened.

'This baby means so much to you?'

'Everything.' He was caught in currents he could not control, and like her, he loathed it. 'I married her for a family. She has always known this was the reason for our

283

marriage. Now I must take care of her. I must respect her wishes. I owe it to her – and to myself – and to the business. It is a great business, and I am a rich man, but unless I have children – what purpose is there in it all?'

'So we won't meet any more?'

'Maggy – not for a while . . . When a year has passed . . . When the baby is safely here, and Angela strong again, perhaps it will be all right. With a child she should be happier. Have more to think about. I don't know, I shall soon be fifty, Maggy . . . a man should be settled at fifty.'

They were walking aimlessly through the shabby streets – there was the smell of a market nearby, oranges and rotting cabbage leaves. Little shops and pubs and the small, shabby hotels.

'What a lot of them – is it because of the station?'

'Many of them are places of accommodation.'

'Accommodation?' she repeated blankly. 'Oh! You mean people who want a bed for a night – or an hour or so?'

He was silent. He had spoken thoughtlessly.

She stopped before one of the tall narrow houses. The curtains looked clean. The steps were whitened, and the brass polished. Through the glass door she could see a red-papered hallway and potted palms; pinkly-shaded lights; a man in a black coat at a reception desk. She started up the steps.

'Maggy!' he protested, horrified, holding her arm. 'Come down. You can't go into a place like that.'

'Why not? It's just the place for people like us. People who only want to be alone for a short while.'

She pushed open the door and went up to the reception desk. The proprietor eyed her doubtfully. The thin young arrogance, the authoritative upper-class voice and Ferdinand's beautifully designed blue tweeds, were not usual in his customers.

'Have you a double room?'

'Yes, Madame.'

Henry was frozen with angry embarrassment. The man looked towards the door for a cabby bringing luggage, thinking that such obviously rich people had made a mistake. But there was no luggage.

'How long will you be staying, Madame?'

'Oh, about an hour or so,' said Margaret loftily. 'That should be quite enough for our purpose.'

He handed her a key. 'Number two, on the first floor.'

'Thank you; can you send up some champagne?'

'Certainly. But, of course, Madame . . .' he spread his hands, 'we have to ask first for the money . . . I am so sorry. It is a custom.'

She would have opened her handbag, but Henry furiously, red-faced, banged a note down on the desk. At that moment he hated all women. But he followed the slender blue back up the narrow stairs into the room, and as she turned and looked at him desire rose so imperatively it destroyed his anger and he wanted her with an aching, painful urgency. The curtains were drawn and the shutters closed. There was a glimmer of gas in a bracket, shaded by a rose-coloured glass globe. She turned it up. The room was clean, a white bed, a washstand, a bidet – austere, a monk's cell devoted to lust. They did not speak, and after an interval during which the man had obviously sent out for the champagne, it was brought up. He looked anxiously at this unusual couple. He wanted no trouble, no scandal. No scenes or suicides.

'Is there anything else, Sir?'

'No. Keep the change.'

The man went out.

The scarlet flags of defiance had gone from Margaret's cheeks. Her small, triangular face seemed all eyes, dark and intense. She looked ravished and terribly young, like a tragic girl-child facing her first seduction.

'Maggy,' he said in agony, 'I never meant it to end like this.'

So it was at an end? Margaret broke down. The tears poured down her face and her mouth was open, half-choked by her sobs. With a groan of tenderness and desire he took her in his arms.

'I do not want it to end at all,' she cried. 'I just wanted it to go on for ever and ever as it was. It was perfect. I want nothing else. I can't bear it – I can't bear it. We've only had such a little while.'

She began to take off her hat, her jacket, undo her blouse, throwing the garments furiously on the floor.

'Damn her, and your beastly baby!' she said childishly.

She stripped off the new expensive suit – the blue cloth woven in his mills, made in her workrooms, with such infinite skill. Piece by piece she shed her underwear, the exquisite garments of cambric and lace, the fine black stockings, the little pale blue satin corsets, and stood naked, white and fragile as an ivory statue as his need of her became unbearable.

He took her, but it brought them no comfort.

Outside the street-lights were lit, the traffic clopped and rumbled, the newsboys' voices shouted raucously. They stayed for two hours, and every wild, ecstatic climax subsided into a panic of despair that made them cling together, kissing with tears salt on their lips, because for the first time their love-making was joyless. No laughter, no tenderness . . . no future.

It was nine o'clock when they rose and dressed. The anger and resentment drained out of her. She lifted her white face like a child for his final kiss, and as he held her, and kissed her gently, it was a child he kissed; the

286

child of his heart that he had hungered for for so long and found too late in this young and ardent lover.

Outside he called a hansom cab and she drove westward back to Hanover Street. He walked all the way along the Embankment to Millicent's in Cadogan Square, suffering as he had sworn he would never suffer over a woman again.

Chapter Eleven

On a cold Friday night in December, after the staff had been paid, Margaret was working alone in the office. Ferdinand had gone out earlier – he did no office work.

She went through the order-books, checking the work completed and delivered and planning the schedule for the week ahead; all the details which Ferdinand found boring she found fascinating – it was like keeping her finger on the pulse of their success. She always worked until about eight o'clock, finding she could concentrate and think clearly when everyone had gone. She liked sitting there at the heart of it, hearing the footsteps of the departing staff clatter along the marble hall to the back entrance, and the hall-porter go round with the keys, locking each door before he left. Somehow the business seemed entirely hers then, and she could see all the individuals and the departments as a comprehensive whole.

But tonight she was totally unable to concentrate. She sat shifting the schedules on the desk unseeingly, making foolish little calculations in her head.

The tailoring department, which had succeeded beyond their wildest dreams, had opened in the last week in October. She had not seen Henry since and had not expected to. He would keep his word to Angela. They did not write. The lack of him was unbearably painful and work was her only solace. This year had been the turning point. Up to now they had been building. But the coming year was going to establish Maison Leon as the most successful fashion business in London.

The shock and humiliation of being discarded was slowly diminishing; but now her work was not enough. The business which had been her whole life was now also a prison.

The porter came in from the office bringing her the keys. He was a sober, working-class man out of his plum-coloured livery and top hat. He bade her goodnight, took his wage packet, and left. Now the only person in the whole large building beside herself was young Roy Brinkley, working in the outer office at a big mahogany counter, unpacking the day's deliveries from the manufacturers, unwinding the bales of satin and chiffon and lace, of tweed and lining silks, examining each piece for any flaw or damage before wrapping them, entering them in the stock book, and stacking them away on the glass-fronted shelves. He was a conscientious worker and never left a task unfinished, but tonight he was hurrying, glancing at his watch. As she sat idly, neglecting her own work, his busy-ness irritated her. She rose and opened the door, and asked, 'Have you an appointment, Roy?'

'Yes, Madame.'

She wondered which of the showroom girls had caught his eye, and hoped it was nothing serious. Emotional entanglements among staff were usually tiresome and he was a good-looking boy, but she thought he had the sense to keep his nose clean.

'Well, just put a dust-cover over the rest of the lengths until tomorrow, because I want to go out too. But run down and get me a cab first of all. I'm going round to my mother's in Juniper Place.'

'Yes, Madame. Right away.' He put aside the bales with relief and started towards the door.

'Has Mr Leon gone out?'

'Yes, Madame, some while ago.'

'Very well – get a cab for me, then you can go too.'

289

It was bitterly cold outside. She put on her new coat of grey squirrel fur, collared and cuffed with pale grey fox, and a small hat of tightly packed dark violets which matched her fine wool dress. She stood, tying her veil, looking at her elegant reflection.

Eight weeks since she had parted from Henry. Ten since she had menstruated. Unlike Angela she was not wild with hope, nor was she afraid. It was something she could not associate with herself at all. Her life in Hanover Street had no place for a child. She was certainly not going whining to Henry about it.

Brinkley returned. 'There is a cab waiting, Madame.'

'Thank you.'

He hesitated, the colour coming and going beneath his fair skin, and she waited, guessing he had some request to make. For a rise? Or a confession of some error?

'Is something wrong, Roy?'

'No, Madame.'

'Well, then, off you go.'

'Thank you, Madame.' But he still lingered.

She said unthinkingly, 'Where are you off to tonight, Roy?'

He replied, 'To the Café Monico, Madame,' and then stopped, rigid, aware that he had betrayed himself. He was well paid, but they both knew he could not afford to go to the Monico, or to take a girl there.

'You are meeting Mr Leon?' she said instantly.

Amazement, fear and relief flooded through him.

'Yes, Madame. You knew, Madame?'

'No.' She did not say that she had not dreamed that Ferdinand could be such a fool. 'But I do now.'

His fresh young face was filled with anxiety. 'Mr Leon said not to say anything to you. I wanted to just now, Madame, but I was scared that he would sack me if I did.'

'Oh, come now, what nonsense. Mr Leon is very kind and generous, and he likes young people. He is a little indiscreet, he forgets favouritism makes for bad feeling among the staff.'

Roy lived in the West End in a cluttered block of slum flats in Seven Dials. His father was a bouncer at a big public house in the Strand and his mother a theatre dresser. He was physically innocent, but not unsophisticated. He had found it difficult to keep Ferdinand at arm's length. Not that he disliked or feared him; he was simply a girl's fellow, and proud of it.

His calm returned. He admired Madame Leon intensely – her looks, her style, her ability. She was, of course, old. Must be thirty-five. But there were no flies on her. If she was going to play it discreetly, he quite understood.

'I think it better, Roy, that Mr Leon does not invite you out again. I will speak to him.'

'I would be glad if you would, ma'am.'

'You don't like my husband's company?'

In his relief at being rescued from an untenable position he became garrulous, losing a little of his acquired refinement.

'Oh, yes, Madame . . . I like going to nice places where you see the toffs. You learn about life. How to order at these swanky places, and what to say, and to talk proper . . .'

'Properly.'

'Oh, yes, Ma'am – properly. But I'm not one of . . .' he stopped just in time.

'No. I can see you prefer going out with people of your own age, particularly girls.'

He blushed again, his big bright eyes apprehensive, wondering how much she knew about the odd kiss that could be harvested in the long corridor to the employees' entrance.

She suddenly buried her face in her hands. The slender, erect body sagged with weariness; when her hands dropped and she looked up at him he realized with astonishment that she was not a woman of thirty-five, but a girl at least ten years younger. He was overwhelmed like a rush of protective concern.

Mr Leon was a wonderful designer, but he was a soft old touch where a good-looking boy was concerned. It was Madame who kept everything going, whose eyes were everywhere, who never overlooked an error, whom everyone respected. But now her tired young girl's face was shadowy with anxiety, and the cool, commanding blue eyes were full of weary tears. Suddenly she seemed younger than himself.

'Don't you worry, Ma'am,' he blurted out. 'I won't say a thing to anyone. I promise. I shouldn't have said I'd accept, but you know how it is . . .'

'Yes,' she said, 'I do indeed,' and smiled and searched through her bag for a handkerchief. He pulled out his own, and thrust it across, bursting with longing to comfort her. 'It's clean, Ma'am.'

'Thank you, Roy.'

She wiped her eyes and handed it back to him.

'I don't know why,' she said, 'but lately I've felt very tired.'

'You do three people's work,' he said. 'Don't think I haven't noticed.' He waited, but she said nothing. She had taken a small vial of salts from her handbag and was inhaling its scented pungency. Manfully he decided his own fate. 'I'd better send in my notice, Ma'am, if I'm an embarrassment to you. I will. I'd only ask for a reference. I'd need that to get another job.'

Impulsively she gave him her hand. He held it awkwardly – it felt so small and cold. She looked down at the thin wrist and boyish knuckles.

He was a really good boy. He could have gossiped all over the firm. He could have blackmailed Ferdinand. She knew he was her man now, and would do what she wanted, and generously, although she valued him, she decided to let him go.

'No, Roy, wait. Look around for a new place. Something with a future. I hear Willis & Harrington are looking for senior staff.'

'I'm not old enough, Ma'am.'

'Roy, you could pass for twenty-one. Who is to know? Grow a moustache if you can.' They both laughed. 'I will see you get a first-class reference. That way it will be tactful and raise no suspicions. And there *is* no scope for promotion here.'

'Yes.' He sounded doubtful. 'I've often thought so. But now I feel you need some help.'

'I shall manage. I always have. I shall rely absolutely on your discretion.'

'Of course, Madame,' he said proudly. 'With Mr Leon, it would be better just to employ young females. I shall miss you, Madame.'

'And I shall be sorry to lose you, Roy. It's a great pleasure to work with friends. His face glowed with pleasure. Gently, she withdrew her hand.

'And we won't refer to this matter again – any of us?'

'Of course not, Madame.'

She rose, picking up her gloves and bag.

'Madame,' he said awkwardly. 'Shouldn't I . . . shouldn't someone let Mr Leon know. He will be waiting for me.'

'Ah, yes . . . at the Monico you said? I'll pop in myself before going to Juniper Place.'

'*You*, Madame?' He was horrified. 'You can't . . .'

'It's not quite the place where ladies go alone, I know,

293

but it will be only for a minute or so and I shall be quite all right.'

A small, grim touch of amusement shone in her eyes. 'After all, my husband will be there waiting for me.'

He rushed to open the door for her, and ahead to open the cab door, and hand her in, overcome with emotion when the small gloved hand rested on his arm. She looked down from the cab and said, 'Thank you, Roy. You've been very understanding, and behaved like a true gentleman.'

He stood rooted to the pavement as she jingled off towards Piccadilly Circus, cursing Ferdinand and the bad luck that was forcing him to leave just as he had realized how wonderful she was, and how, in other circumstances, he could have helped her.

At Piccadilly Circus Margaret dismissed her cab and went into the Lounge Bar of the Monico. It was early and not yet very crowded. She was aware at once of the type of woman sitting at the small tables. High-class prostitutes; young, smart, vulgar women from the music halls. The raffish, sporting men gathered at the bar, all looked at her with curious eyes.

The Monico Bar was not Ferdinand's milieu at all, and Margaret guessed he did not want to be seen with Roy by any of his particular clique of smart friends. He was sitting on one of the velvet upholstered banquettes, an ice-bucket beside him on the marble-topped table, planning a pleasant evening.

The door opened, bringing in a gust of wintry air, and he met her grave glance. He was so shocked he forgot what he was doing there and for whom he was waiting.

'Margaret!' Then he remembered and changed colour. There *was* only one person who could have told her where he was, Roy himself. He rose, took her arm a little roughly and began to hustle her towards the doors. 'Are you out of your mind? You can't come into a place like this.'

'*Ah* – I forgot that. I came to tell you that Roy won't be coming.' He stood silently, furious, shamefaced. 'Well, shall we go?'

'I thought you were going to Juniper Place to see your mother?'

'I was about to when Roy spoke to me.'

'Why did he tell you? Was it blackmail?'

'No. He was afraid you'd dismiss him if he did not meet you. And he did not want to.'

That was the bitterest blow – that the boy had found his company distasteful. 'But you dismissed him all the same?'

'No. I asked him to look for another post and assured him we would give him every assistance and a good reference. He said that he thought it better if we only employed women in future. He will make a very intelligent manager.'

Ferdinand shivered inside his fur-lined overcoat. No wonder the staff called her 'The Bitch'. He said with angry petulance, 'When we came back from Paris you *said* you understood! That we would work as before, keeping our personal lives apart. I never interfered when you were going off for the weekend with Grimshaw. Oh, yes, I knew who it was,' he answered her questioning look. 'It wasn't very difficult. I could see what was going to happen. He could scarcely keep his hands off you in Paris – even in your husband's presence.'

'Ferdi,' she said, gently, 'please don't be silly and coarse. It isn't like you. I do understand, and you must be miserable. It's always miserable to be humiliated in love.' The desolation in her voice made him take her arm; the gesture was quite involuntary, they were now such old and close friends. 'Brinkley is not yet twenty.

He is an employee and a good, clever, hard-working boy. And if you had succeeded it would have been not just a scandal, but a criminal offence. You could ruin us.'

They had left the Circus with its circulating strollers, the women in their harsh finery, the night-hawks in their black evening clothes.

They walked up Regent Street. Here the wind blew directly from the North, sending the stragglers into shop doorways. On Summer nights the street was full of flashy young clerks and shop-walkers, aping their betters, but tonight only beggars and the desperate lingered. In a lighted doorway two young men in thin flashy clothes stood shivering, the yellow gas-light darkening the rouge on their cheeks. One smiled at Ferdinand.

'For God's sake, let's get a cab,' he said. He hailed a passing four-wheeler and its musty interior seemed like a haven. He reached out blindly and took her hands. In the darkness of the cab she could not see his face, but when he spoke she knew he was in tears. 'I'm sorry, Margaret. I really am sorry.'

She sighed. 'A year ago I could not understand why people in love did such stupid things. Like children. Why didn't they *think* first? I know now. I understand them all now.' She patted his gloved hand as though she were the elder.

'I can't change myself, my dear, I've tried. When we were married I hoped it would change me. I was so fond of you. We were so right together, I thought we might be in that way too. I knew it was useless from the first night. I could not make myself come to you. But I swear I'll never take this sort of risk again. You won't desert me, will you, Margaret?'

'I'm not going to leave you. I can't. I need a husband now more than when I married you. I'm going to have a child.'

The cab had turned off along Marlborough Street. A light snow was falling and there seemed no other sound in the world but the clip-clop of the tired horse dragging them through the cold night, the frosty air steaming round its nostrils.

'So – he left you?'

'Yes.'

'How long have you known – about the child?'

'Two weeks. For sure.'

'There is no need for you to have it, Margaret. I know people who will arrange it. Reliable people.'

'No!'

'You *want* a child?' he said incredulously.

'I don't know! I think I want Henry's. Or I want him to know I can have a child, because he wants a child so much.'

'But the business?'

'I shan't be away, or not for long. A few days. But I need to be married.'

'Will he support you?'

'I won't ask him,' she said flatly. 'It will be mine. I can afford to give it everything. And if we are parents, Ferdi, who will talk scandal about you? Who will whisper and hint? We will be a respectable married couple with a family to prove it. You will design the most elegant concealment garments and I will wear them. We might even open a special department?'

He burst out into his harsh, coughing laugh.

'You plan for everything. Did you know they called you "The Bitch"? The staff?'

'Oh yes. So long as they do, I'm the boss. When you're very young you have to be like that.'

He put his arm round her, and she put her head on his shoulder. They were both shaken, desperate and in tears. She was pulling at the scraps of hope, as though she was

297

snatching chestnuts out of the fire. 'We must work as we have always worked, and keep our secrets, and we can have success even if we can't have happiness . . .'

The cab stopped in Juniper Place. The little house glowed, warm firelight behind the red rep kitchen curtains, gas-light behind the rosy satin of Florence's boudoir on the first floor. Ferdinand handed Margaret out. He never entered Juniper Place. Lady Normanby flatly refused to receive him.

Margaret went down the area steps and knocked. She heard Lecky's pattering feet along the stone flags within and bolts being drawn. The door opened a few inches on a sturdy chain and the little moon-face appeared about breast-level, topped with a white cap. After all these years her diminutive height still startled Margaret.

'Oh it's you Miss Maggy, love. I'd almost given you up. It's after eight. Come in . . . it's bitter cold.'

'Yes, I'm sorry. I was delayed.'

She went forward into the kitchen shaking the light snow from her grey fur coat, her scent filling the warm air with the perfume of flowers.

It was like stepping back into her childhood. The simple place where there was warmth, food, cleanliness, simplicity and orderliness – and Lecky. The bright coal fire burning in the polished cooking stove, the kettle singing on the hob. The rag rug. The table, covered with fringed red chenille, the rose-patterned tea-cups on the tray, waiting in the circle of yellow gas-light. Lecky's newspaper, the *Thornsby Evening Argus*, sent specially from Yorkshire each week. She never read anything else. She wore spectacles now, with steel rims, which slid on to the tip of her almost bridgeless nose.

Margaret undid her veil, took off her hat, and sat down on the low hassock near Lecky's wooden rocking-chair, peeling off her gloves, and extending her hands to the blaze.

'It's so lovely here, Lecky. It's so cosy. It's all I want.'

'Oh, aye,' said Lecky, heavily sarcastic. She put the simmering kettle nearer the flames, looking down at the richly-clad figure, the small strong hands with the brilliant jewels, held out to the blaze. '*I reckon!*'

'Well, all I want at the day's end. Quiet. No fuss, no responsibilities. You to look after me.'

'Don't talk so soft.'

She filled the teapot and put it on a tray. Brought a plate of treacle parkin and one of buttered tea-cakes out of the cupboard. Margaret stretched out, greedily biting into the fresh-buttered slice. Her hunger reminded her of her pregnancy.

'You're famished,' said Lecky. She cast her eyes up to the ceiling above where Lily Oglethorpe and Lady Normanby lived out their elaborate fantasies of high-toned social life. 'You've come to the wrong place for peace and quiet, I can tell you.'

'What's happened?'

'She's heard from your Papa again.'

'*No?*' Margaret was exasperated and amused. 'Does she want to send him more money?'

'Happen so. And she's heard from Miss Charmy too. Miss Flo was in a right state about that. Said she must give a party for her and Captain Chester – ask all her high-toned friends. Them nobody can see. Eh, it's nowt but nonsense. That Lily Oglethorpe – she encourages her.'

'But she's been more reasonable since Lily looked after her.'

'It seems that Captain Chester is still right poorly and they'll be going straight up North to his folk.'

Margaret had been longing to see her sister. 'You mean they won't be coming here?'

'So Lily tells me – I've not read t'letter.' Footsteps were heard descending the basement steps, and Lecky jerked her head. 'That'll be Lady Muck now.'

Lily sidled round the door with a refined little cough to warn them of her presence.

'Good evening, Madame Leon.'

'Hello, Lily.'

Lily looked the part of a lady's companion. Black bombazine but no apron. A lace-edged cap on her rigidly-braided hair. Her West Riding speech disciplined into an affected gentility. She looked at Margaret, leaning on Lecky's lap, with disapproval – Lecky, she thought, took advantage of the privileges of long service.

'Didn't Leck tell you, Ma'am, her ladyship wished to see you?'

'Yes. I'm having my tea. Have you the accounts here?'

'Yes. But Lady Normanby said . . .'

'Lily. You work for *me*. *I* pay you to look after my mother. And please call Lecky either by her name, or *Miss Leck*.'

'It'll not offend me. Sticks and stones, sticks and stones,' said Lecky sourly. 'Do you want a cup of tea, young Lil?'

'No thank you, Miss Leck,' Lily bridled. 'I've just had a cup with her ladyship. Her favourite orange pekoe.'

'Well, suit yersen'. It's like ant's piss to me.' Lecky put three lumps into her own cup and stirred it crossly while Margaret tried not to laugh.

'Well, let me see the books before I go up to Mama.' She sat at the table and Lily laid out the tradesmen's account books before her. They were all covered in gilt-embossed artificial leather, stamped with the tradesman's

300

name and mark. A fat lamb on the butcher's red book, a crab on the fishmonger's, a milch cow on the dairyman's.

When she had made out the cheques, she said, 'Lecky tells me there has been a letter from Sir Richard – does he want more money?'

'Your Papa wants help with his fare home.'

'But that was already sent – when Mama pledged my pearls.'

Lily had the grace to colour. But Margaret had forgiven her long ago.

'It's such a lovely letter, Madame. He's had such bad luck. I don't know how you can be so steely-hearted.' Lily was beginning to use the dramtic style of the novels she and Lady Normanby consumed so avidly. 'They've loved each other so long and faithfully, they deserve their reward even though youth has passed.'

'Well,' said Margaret drily, 'I'd better go upstairs and see what he has to say this time.'

In Florence's boudoir a bright fire burned, and the gas chandelier glowed on the rosy silk and satins and flowered carpet. Margaret lavished comfort on her mother. The portrait of Sir Richard as a boy dominated the room. He stood against a landscape of Danesfell Abbey, spaniels fawning round his feet. He wore hunting pink. His bold blue eyes smiled down upon them. Fresh flowers were arranged beneath the picture like an altar-piece. Lily's eyes moistened every time she looked at it.

'Good evening, Mama.' Margaret bent to kiss her mother's rouged cheek and caught the faint smell of spirits. She looked sharply at Lily who measured a minute space between her fingers, and whispered, 'Just a drop. She is so disappointed about Mrs Bellamy.'

'I was hoping,' said Florence, 'for a little gaiety. A small soirée for Charmy and her husband. To hear their

301

news. They have had such a splendid time in India, and she is considered a great beauty, she tells me.'

Margaret read Charmian's brief cable. It gave the time of their arrival at the docks and read:

'*One night at Royal Northern, leaving for Scotland next day. Bellamy very ill. Love, Charmian.*'

She sensed trouble. The lame ducks were flapping home to roost again. She said suddenly, 'Mama, I thought you should know. I am pregnant.'

She was unprepared for the expression of frozen disgust on Florence's face.

'I am having a baby, Mama. In the Summer.'

'I don't want to know. You have brought me nothing but shame and humiliation. If it is a boy no one will receive him. No good school. None of the best clubs. Do you imagine you can foist your shopkeeper's son on the family as heir to the Normanbys.'

'Heir to what?'

'To Danesfell Abbey. To the mines. To your Grandmother Normanby's fortune.'

'Danesfell belongs to Mr Hengrave. The mines to the American company with which he is connected. Grandmother Normanby has a bare eight hundred a year, which she will certainly leave to George. There is nothing now but what I earn.'

'Give me my drops, Oglethorpe,' cried Florence. Lily, bristling with reproach, ran to get them. 'I will not discuss it.'

'There is nothing to discuss, Mama,' Margaret said wearily. She took the brown laudanum bottle from Lily. 'Have you been taking much of this stuff?'

'She has not needed it. But today she's upset – please read Sir Richard's letter.'

It smelled of beer, as though it had been written on a bar table. It was the familiar tale of courage in the face of ill luck. A thousand pounds would see him out of his difficulties and bring him home to his dearest wife, but he could not ask her again. He would try to raise the money in California, even if he had to do low and menial work.

Margaret gave an uncontrollable little spurt of laughter. She looked at her mother helplessly. Did Florence really believe this rubbish, or was it just necessary to sustain her fantasies? How happy *had* she been? Had she ever been happy?'

'Mama,' she said, 'he won't come.'

Florence went rigid. Lily snatched the laudanum bottle from Margaret's hand and rushed to her side.

'Your ladyship. Madame . . . please . . . keep calm. He *will* come! Of course he'll come . . . Mrs Leon doesn't understand. She was only a little girl when he went. She can't remember him like you can. Please, your ladyship, don't be naughty . . . be good for Lily's sake. Please . . .'

Florence screamed, a loud, penetrating, harsh sound, like a machine that has seized up for lack of lubrication, and collapsed against Lily's shoulder. Very gently the girl raised her chin and administered the drops. Margaret was touched by her kindness.

'Now see what you've done, Madame.'

'Yes. I'm not always patient. I've lived with this all my life.'

'You think she's having us on? Just feel her pulse!' Lily said accusingly.

'Oh, I know all about that too.'

Between the clumsily-blackened lashes, Florence's pale eyes glittered with hatred. Margaret had no right to refuse the role of plain, unmarriageable, dutiful Maggy. Her practical, flinty authority was frightening. Her sophistication and superb clothes reduced Florence to infantile rage. She could not bear to think that Margaret had provided every comfort she had. Sometimes she felt like setting fire to it all. How could a mean-hearted tyrant like Margaret understand the beaut·ful devotion of her marriage to Richard?

'Put this stuff away. Mama, I will make out a cheque for one hundred pounds which you can send to my father. I will also deposit the money for his fare with a shipping agent which deals with San Francisco, so that if he really wishes to return he can apply for it. Will that satisfy you, Mama?'

'There now, my lady,' cooed Lily. 'That's a great deal of money to send. Sir Richard will be home with us here in no time now, think of that.'

Florence was frightened. So long as he was sent cash Richard would stay in California, safe in his role of dream lover-husband. Denied money he could be unpredictable. He had hit her when she did not want to give him the rose-diamonds, and then he had stolen them. She would not think of that.

'But he wants to settle all his debts,' she said loftily. 'What use would a paid passage be to him? He is a gentleman, not a tradesman. It would not be honourable for him to return without doing so.'

Margaret bent and kissed her pityingly. 'Don't *worry*, Mama. As I said, *he won't come*.' Florence jerked her head away, but she did not scream again. The blessed drowsiness was claiming her.

'I wish,' she said fretfully, 'that dear Charmy *would* come to see me. She was always so sweet to me.'

Margaret bade her mother goodnight. Down in the kitchen Lecky asked. 'What's to do then? I heard her hollering.'

Margaret sat on the hassock and bit into another piece of parkin. 'I told her about the baby.'

'What baby?'

'My baby – in the Summer.'

304

'Well, she'd *not* like that. She never could stand owt of that.'

'What do you mean?'

'Men. Going to bed wi' them. Babies! Like nasty little animals, she said. On her wedding night she screamed like that. Anyone would ha' thought he was murdering her. He was right mad at her. All t'house could hear – it made him feel a fool. She wouldn't let him touch her afterwards. She was lucky – or unlucky – for you and Charmy were in t'bag. His family wanted a boy, as all grand folk do, but nothing would make her go through with it again.'

'She *never* slept with him? After her wedding night? After we were born?'

'No. It was all balls and parties and suchlike, spending and dancing and gambling, and half the young fellows in London after her, she was so pretty – but nowt but a lot of hand-kissing and flattery. She liked that.'

'And what did he do?'

'Oh, he had women in plenty. It were all over London about him. She pretended not to know. She's allus been a great one for pretending.'

'How *terrible*! Oh Lecky! How *sad*!'

'It might have gone on forever if t'money hadn't run out. It were always money wi' him. It made him cruel to be without, and when hers had all gone, he couldn't be doing wi' her, pretty or not. He had to have the best. He couldn't give less than a guinea to a beggar. He couldn't bet in pounds, it had to be hundreds. They had to have their own carriage and riding horses. They spent so much on clothes, you'd never believe. And when there were nowt left he ran off to America and took all her jewellery.'

Margaret put her head down on the white, starched apron, and Lecky's calloused little hand stroked her hair. She relaxed with a sigh.

305

'When the baby comes, Lecky, you'll come and look after me, won't you?'

The stroking hand hesitated. Margaret lifted her head to catch the anxiety in the small bulging eyes. She seized Lecky's hands and shook them, fiercely pleading, 'Lecky, you've got to help me. What do I know about babies?'

'Happen you'll have one of them trained nurses.'

'Happen I *won't*! We had one. Do you remember? Before all the money went and there was no one left but you? I don't know what to do with a baby but I know what a baby wants. Someone like you to love it. You've got to come. Mama can manage.'

'Nay, then, nay, don't thee fret, love. I'll come. Until you're started off.'

'Why can't you stay? For always? There's Lily, and there's the housemaid, and there's a woman who comes in to clean, and the washing is sent out. I'll hire a cook. You can come to me.'

'Nay, nay,' Lecky shook her head. 'Tha knows it's not that. That Lily can't be trusted. She reckons to believe in all poor Miss Flo's uppity fancies, but if owt is wrong she'll give her the drink, and the laudanum . . . anything to keep her quiet. But I reckon for a baby they can do wi' out me for a while. And it's not so far. I'll come back here nights and keep an eye on them.'

'But you'll come to me? I'll *need* you with me. You're my mother really, Lecky. My real mother. I wish you were! I wish you were!'

'Don't be so soft,' said Lecky, but the rough little hand resumed its patting and stroking of the flaming silky hair on her lap and Margaret nuzzled into her like a kitten. The kitchen was warm and quiet. The old American clock on the mantlepiece ticked in the silence, still as the centre of a storm. If she could be like this for ever. There was the sound of wheels on the freezing snow outside, a knock at the door, and when the girl answered, they heard the coachman's hoarse voice asking for Mrs Leon. Margaret sat up with a long, reluctant sigh.

'That will be for me,' she said, rising. 'Tell the man I'm coming.'

Lecky went with her to the foot of the area steps.

'Do you want this bairn?'

'I – think – yes.'

'And Mr Ferdinand?'

'He has as little experience of children as I have.'

'Is it his'n?' Lecky jerked her head up towards the street where Ferdinand waited in the cab.

Margaret drew in a deep breath. 'No.' No use lying to Lecky.

'I thought as much.'

'You're not shocked, Lecky?'

Lecky gave the stiff little quiver of lips that was her nearest approach to a smile. 'Nay,' she said. 'Nay. You're not Charmian. Allus off like a bitch in season. You must have loved him whoever he was. Well, you'll manage. You always have. God knows what they'd have done wi'out you.'

Margaret bent and kissed her parchment-coloured cheek, smooth and unwrinkled like an old wax doll's, then hugging her furs about her, went up the steps to join her husband.

The pilot had come aboard at Gravesend and dark had fallen as the Indiaman crept up the river. Charmian, peering out of the porthole through the gathering dusk, saw the flat water meadows and little clapboard farms of Essex. She felt no joy or relief in being back in her native land. The voyage from India had been a nightmare as the tension between herself and Bellamy had increased, his jealous suspicions barely allowing her out of his sight,

307

and his nights were sleepless with guilt. He was drinking heavily. He could not forget, nor forgive her or himself for what had happened, and he could not begin to understand why she too did not suffer. When he spoke to her he railed at her accusingly. She was conscience-less, callous, shallow, promiscuous. She had made him a murderer.

Charmian was exhausted. She no longer had the energy even to try to please him. Other people gossipped and flirted, danced and played deck games and cards, got up concerts, and she, the prettiest woman on board, sat chained to this yellow-faced maniac who could not bear her out of his sight.

'Why must you keep on about it?' she had wept. 'It does *no* good. We *can't* do anything. Put it behind you. I really wish I was dead too, sometimes.'

'I wish we both were,' he replied.

During the last days at sea, as the steamer had rolled past the coast of Britanny, he had not been into the dining salon for meals, and only reluctantly allowed her to go. On the voyage she had been careful to wear her fresh, young-looking dresses and not paint her lips. When people paused at her table, and many of them did, she told them, trying to keep her lips from trembling and her eyes filling with tears, that Captain Bellamy was ill – malaria and nervous strain from working in the heat.

Poor little woman, the men murmured, and looked at the soft curve of her luscious breasts beneath the muslin, and the helpless, inviting sensuality of her mouth. Kenneth Allwood, only son of a tea importing family, going back to work in the London office, was so infatuated he could hardly speak to her and his young cheeks flushed scarlet when their eyes met across the tables.

Charmian rose to her feet and bent over Bellamy, sleeping the stunned sleep of drunkenness. She shook his shoulder. He did not move, his eyes opened and rolled unseeingly upwards, so that for one frantic, hopeful second she thought he might be dead. But they closed, his mouth dropped open emitting stertorous snores. Her mouth curled with distaste, she flung a tweed cloak about her, a fluffy white scarf over her hair, and left the cabin. On deck it was windy and bright, with a racing moon behind the clouds. And by the rail opposite the companionway young Allwood was waiting.

He turned as she came through the door, and she gave a little surprised cry, and held out her hands, felt his strong arms enfold her, and his lips against the curls on her forehead. It was working perfectly. She had guessed how he would react. It was her first and only kiss during the voyage and she was enjoying it.

'I slipped away,' she murmured. 'I had to get some air – it's stifling in the cabin. The smell of drink!'

'Drink?'

'Oh, I tell everyone he's ill. But he's not. He drinks. He abuses me, and calls me terrible names. I've had this for years. Kenneth, what *shall* I do?'

If the suggestive pressure of her body startled him it also excited him. 'How can I help you? Mrs Chester – Charmian, my poor lovely girl. How can I help you?'

'You can't. No one can. Or not here.'

'You mean in London? I can help you then? How can I help you? You have only to tell me.'

Charmian thought rapidly. They would spend one night in London before travelling to Bellamy's home in Scotland. If he got drunk again, and the chances were that he would, she might get away, and then she would not go back. Oh, she had promised not to leave him, but he had promised not to drink and had been totally unable to resist. She did not believe he would go to the police and

309

confess his crime – who would choose death when they could live?

She could, of course, seek sanctuary at Hanover Street with Maggy, or with her mother, but these were the first places that Bellamy would go when he discovered she was missing.

She had inherited all Florence's taste for drama together with her father's uncontrolled sensuality. She could feel through her thin muslin that the boy could scarcely control himself, and a guilty desire to drag her into the shadows of the boat deck was fighting with his chivalrous longing to protect her. She must not be too reckless.

With difficulty she began to withdraw from the situation. It was difficult, because after the long days of rejection and abstinence, the dull incarceration in the foetid, whisky-smelling cabin, an hour in the arms of this young, clean, virile youngster would have been a real pleasure. But she must be careful. The sweets always came after the nasty medicine.

'Forgive me!' She drew away, flushed, prettily confused. 'What *must* you think of me? I'm not a fast girl, really, Kenneth.'

'You are a sweet girl.'

'I shouldn't have let you kiss me. It was just that you're so kind and gentle.'

'Please, please, Charmian, let me help you in any way I can.'

'Well,' she faltered, 'I don't want to presume . . .'

'Please. Money – shelter – anything.'

'You've guessed I am going to leave him? I am going back to my mother, Lady Normanby. But I daren't go to her at once. He would follow me. I just want somewhere, a room, somewhere quite modest, where I can stay until I have seen our family lawyer, and managed to get some protection . . . Bell will go on to Scotland almost at once. His parents are expecting him. Then I can go to Mother. If you could help me to hide just for a few days . . .'

'Of course I will, of course. Anything.'

She made a hurried arrangement to meet him in the entrance foyer of the Langham Hotel. She would only bring a few things in a small travelling case. If Kenneth would book her a room, anywhere, so long as it was clean and quiet. He promised. She must not go back to her husband. He would protect her.

'If I'm not there within half-an-hour, please don't wait,' she said. 'It will mean that I cannot get away.'

'I will wait all night,' he swore.

The soft, dimpled smile, the inviting eyes, were caught in the light over the companionway door. Perhaps it was that, perhaps it was the startling passion of her rewarding kiss that triggered off an alarm in Allwood's bemused mind. But when he went into the bar, and a hardened Cavalry Major began to talk about pretty Mrs Chester in a derogatory way, instead of punching his face in, he listened miserably. A hot little piece, said the Major. Created no end of scandal in Simla. And worse in Bombay. Stopped moving with the Army crowd, and went into that rotter Abderhazy's set. Nasty business, that young fellow she was having an affair with, disappearing like that. Been mucking about with an Indian woman, people said. Whatever, little Mrs Chester was bad medicine for anyone . . . no wonder poor Chester was drinking himself to death. He always had been devoted to her, and she had made him look a fool with half the young fellows of the regiment.

Kenneth Allwood did not sleep that night. He was still insanely in love with her . . . but he was very young, and he had a reunion with his family the next day. His courage failed him, and when Charmian arrived at the Langham the following evening, he did not turn up.

She waited miserably, conspicuous as elegant Londoners passed her on the way to the dining-room. When he did turn up again, and she knew from experience that he would, she would make him pay for this.

Bellamy had been drunk and asleep when she had left. Once he had stretched out a shaking hand and drawn her down to him, quite tenderly. Almost as though he knew what was in her mind.

'Kiss me,' he had said.

She had bent and kissed him, disguising her disgust at his drunkard's breath.

'Poor child,' he had said thickly. 'Poor child. God help us both,' and had dropped back into sleep again.

She would have to go back – there was nowhere else to go. But Bellamy was not in their room at the Royal Northern Hotel. On the writing-desk were two envelopes. One addressed to his parents. One to the coroner.

The room was just as she had left it, the cases strapped ready for their departure to Scotland in the morning. The Royal Northern Hotel was newly-built and prided itself on the modern American-style steam-heating and toilet facilities. The bathroom door was open and a cold draught blew into the overheated room.

She went in fearfully, but the bathroom was empty too. The long, narrow window of patterned, dull glass immediately above the WC was wide open. She knelt on the closed seat and looked out onto a twenty foot square ventilation and drainage shaft down which the plumbing pipes went to the sewers. It was very dark, illuminated only by bathroom windows and a glass-panelled door opening on to the concrete yard six floors below. It was there that Bellamy lay, face downwards, blood seeping in a pool about his head.

In a trap Charmian thought fast with a feline instinct for self-preservation. She did not scream and she was not afraid. After all, *she* had not shot Angus. She went back to the bedroom and picked up the letters. The Royal Northern's hot water system did not let her down, and she managed to steam them open successfully.

The letter to his parents asked them to forgive him, saying he felt he could no longer serve in the Army and could not face any other life. He asked them not to blame his wife, who was no more responsible for her nature than for her great beauty. If she had made him unhappy it was not altogether her fault. He asked them to look after her, to continue her allowance, and make a home for her. She put it back in the envelope and resealed it, pressing it beneath a heavy hand-mirror.

The letter to the Coroner was a complete confession of the murder of Lieutenant Angus Black at Abderhazy's house on Malabar Hill. The young officer's affair with his wife had made life impossible. He named Baron Philippe Abderhazy as his accomplice in disposing of the body.

Charmian tore the letter and envelope into small bits and flushed them down the lavatory. She also destroyed the top sheet on the blotter where the letters had been written.

She went through the room, through Bellamy's cases, making sure there were no diaries or compromising papers. Then she rang the bell, threw open the door and ran screaming into the corridor.

If she had any feeling at all it was pride in her own clever quick-thinking.

When Margaret arrived at the hotel, having been summoned by an urgent messenger, she found the police and management in charge, and her sister now genuinely faint and shivering with nerves, distraught and weeping uncontrollably.

'I only went out,' she wept. 'I only went out for an hour . . . I hadn't been out all day . . . Bell wouldn't let me leave him. I thought I could slip out while he was asleep . . .' She looked at the officials like a lovely, terrified child. 'I only wanted just to look at the shops . . . we wouldn't have had time in the morning, and I've been longing to see them. He wouldn't even let me go and see my Mama . . . after years and years away . . .' She looked up and saw her twin, noting with astonishment her beautiful clothes, her cool distinction, sprang up and flung herself into Margaret's arms. 'Oh, Maggy, thank God you've come . . . I'm in terrible trouble . . . poor Bell is dead . . .'

And with that she fainted dead away.

Margaret took charge of her sister, and all the officials turned gratefully to her authority. A telegraph was sent to Captain Chester's parents in Scotland, his body was removed to the mortuary, and Charmian was taken back to Hanover Street and put to bed, after a glass of warm milk laced with brandy, one of Lecky's sovereign cures for shock.

Ferdinand came out of his studio as Margaret was helping her sister up the stairs. When she came down again he commented on Charmian's beauty.

'I suppose,' he said, 'we shall have to make her some mourning.'

'I hadn't thought that far,' said Margaret. She was distressed by the tragedy, although she scarcely knew Bellamy.

'With that skin,' Ferdinand kissed his finger-tips, 'she is going to look exquisite in black.'

Margaret went to the boudoir where a bed had been made up for Charmian. She lay sleeping peacefully, her dark golden curls spreading over the pillow. In sleep the sensual lines, the small puckers and slackening of self-indulgence were smoothed away. Her soft pink mouth was parted, and her extravagant lashes rested on satin-smooth, pale, tear-stained cheeks. She looked like a dreaming angel, tired with the sorrows of the world.

Margaret sat down by the bed, her chin propped on her hand, thoughtfully watching her sister. She stood up, smoothing her slender waist, knowing already there was a thickening heaviness. She did not like it, but she did not regard it with the horror that Charmian and her mother regarded pregnancy.

She had told Charmian about the baby, thinking to distract her. 'You must be mad, with all your money and the business. Bell was always on about children. I clicked once in India but there was a woman in the bazaar who did the trick for me. No fear, I saw all those memsahibs getting worn-out and yellow-skinned, no fun and parties, always with a brood of sickly children. Ever so many of them died. I said to Bell, "Perhaps when we get home . . ." and now, oh, my poor, darling Bell, it's too late.' She dissolved once more into tears.

It was all so familiar, as though the years of separation had never happened. The tearful evasions, the petulant denials, the martyred innocence with the lovely eyes sliding evasively away.

How jealous she had been of this pretty creature, and how she had loved her. How terrified she had always been that her sister would get into trouble and have to marry some besotted Thornsby boy. How relieved they had all been when she had married Bellamy Chester, an officer and a gentleman, of good family, comfortably off. A safe haven. And here she was, seven years later, back again, and poor Bellamy had thrown himself out of a

Chapter Twelve

The inquest raised barely a ripple of interest in the London press. The chambermaid was the only hotel employee to be called and she corroborated everything that Charmian had said, with one important addition. When Charmian had been down at lunch Captain Chester had ordered two bottles of whisky sent up to the room. Charmian, who genuinely did not know about this, was most convincingly distressed.

It was a cold December day, but she looked as beautiful as a white rose, tear-stained, fragile, and exquisitely chic in the new mourning Ferdinand had designed for her – the little jacket collared in black fox and a Mary Stewart bonnet with a flowing black veil framing her pretty face.

She gave her evidence with childlike directness. She had only slipped out to see the shop windows. She had never been in London in her life, having gone straight to India from Scotland after her wedding, and they were due to leave for Scotland early the next morning. She had thought it quite harmless. But she had been frightened in the London streets, there were so many rough people about, so she went back to the hotel immediately and discovered that her husband was dead. She broke down and wept. The coroner was sympathetic and allowed her to sit down.

'Not a word to me,' she cried, with another rush of tears. 'Only a note to his parents – his poor parents. But not a word to me.'

General Chester's solicitor handed up the letter which the Coroner read.

'These words – "*She cannot help her nature?*" Have you any idea what he means, Mrs Chester?'

There was a long silence. Then Charmian lifted her trembling chin, and looked bravely across the court, a child owning up to a petty naughtiness.

'Yes,' she said clearly. 'I suppose I *am* a flirt. I am sorry. Bitterly sorry, now. My poor Bell! Oh, *dear*, my poor Bell! I used to tease him. I never *dreamed* that he took it so seriously, and he didn't – not until he started this dreadful drinking. It made him quite different. He was always lovely to me. We were very happy. He was ill and didn't *know* what he was doing.' She pressed her handkerchief to her eyes. 'His *poor* parents. All because I am so silly and *thoughtless* . . .'

The reporters who had been scribbling idly, took notice. It would make a good headline. The Coroner was obviously impressed.

'Thank you, Mrs Chester, you may stand down.'

A little flush of triumph coloured Charmian's cheeks. It was going to be all right.

She leaned against Margaret's shoulder, and wiped her eyes. The court was with her, everyone deeply sorry for a young, pretty, thoughtless girl caught in such a trap.

She glimpsed Kenneth Allwood's agonized young face at the back of the court, and for a moment her heart raced fearfully. There was no need to panic. He knew nothing about anything, the silly, weak, young fool. No one knew anything except herself and Abderhazy, and Abderhazy was in China.

A verdict of death from misadventure was brought in. It was true that Captain Chester had been exceedingly drunk, and was also suffering from a sharp attack of malaria. Whether his death was deliberate or done in a burst of delirium while he was alone, it was difficult to say. The Coroner expressed sympathy with the young widow, who had been very courageous, but she must not put any blame on herself. She had not intended any harm, and a young and attractive woman naturally commanded admiration.

Charmian left the court between Margaret and Ferdinand, and drove back to Hanover Street. The evening paper carried a picture, and the caption '*Young Widow Declares – Yes, I am a Flirt!*'

'It's really a very pretty picture,' Ferdinand said drily.

She pleaded weariness – it had been so tiring and tomorrow she had to meet that awful solicitor man and travel up to Scotland to take Bell's body to his family. She would go to bed.

It was Margaret's evening for Juniper Place. Charmian did not wish to go. From what Margaret said it sounded like Hollingroyd Crescent over again. Everything that she wished to forget. A dull little house and a crazy mother who got drunk. Mama sounded worse than ever with her imaginary balls and routs, and noble friends. And she had not the slightest interest in seeing Jany Leck.

It was about eight o'clock when Margaret returned. She too was feeling tired. But she made her rounds of the business, visiting every department, before going upstairs.

'Did Mrs Langtry come in for her fitting?'

'Yes, Madame. Mr Leon saw her. He took the dress upstairs to make some adjustments. It is to be sent tomorrow.'

To have the custom of the famous Jersey Lily was a triumph for Ferdinand, who had met her in the smart theatrical set in which he moved.

Margaret went up the handsome curving stairs to the first floor, where she found the landing crowded with Charmian's luggage. The original destination – Glendhu House, Perthshire – had been crossed out and now read, '*care-of Mrs Leon, Maison Leon, Hanover Street*.' From Ferdinand's studio she heard Charmian's soft, excited laugh.

The door was half-open, and Ferdinand was leaning against his drawing-board. His eyes met Margaret's with cynical amusement. Charmian was standing on the turn-table on which he posed his models to drape and create the elaborate evening clothes for which he was famous. She was wearing the Langtry dress. He made a little gesture.

'What do you think? Is she not beautiful?'

'Beautiful,' agreed Margaret.

He had pinned the dress to fit her tiny waist, the long, seductive curve of hips and thighs. It was pale ivory satin, supported on the shoulders by fine strands of small pearls, a swirling design of which descended diagonally across the skirt and round the hem.

The colour of the satin was so near to Charmian's skin, and the support of the dress so cunningly designed, that her shoulders, arms and bosom rose from it with a naked mermaid quality. She stood with her beautiful arms high above her head, pinning up the red-gold curls to reveal her long, creamy, voluptous neck and throat, and laughing down at Ferdinand. His face was alight with pleasure. He lit a cigarette, and, as always when excited, lost the veneer of his Englishness and became very French.

'*Parfait – absolument! Parfait!* It is too large of course, because the Langtry is making weight, and you have the fine bones, which makes every dress look delicate on you.'

'How much will this cost?'

'One hundred pounds. The lace on the underskirt alone cost twenty . . . come down and move . . .'

Charmain stepped down from the turn-table and began to waltz so that the diagonally draped skirt swung open to disclose the chiffon, lace and rustling taffeta underskirt, a faint rose-cream, like the inside of a shell.

Charmian saw Margaret, stopped, and had the grace to colour.

'Don't be cross, Maggy-Waggy. I just had to let off steam. Ferdi was showing me the gown and I begged to try it on. Doesn't it suit me?'

'You look exquisite.'

'Better than Mrs Langtry?'

'Yes.'

'Ferdi says she won't pay for it.'

'If she wears it at the Devonshire ball, it will be enough. We shall have every rich little parvenu in London wanting something like it, whether it suits them or not.'

'Would you make me a dress like this, Ferdi?'

'If you were a King's mistress,' he smiled, and said to Margaret, 'I could build a collection round her which every woman in London would want to wear.'

'Especially if they saw her wearing it.' Their eyes met in the instant understanding they had about matters of business. 'I see you have had your luggage sent here, Charmian?'

'You must think I'm *awful*, Maggy. Poor Bell did. But everyone can't be sensible and good and hard-working and unselfish . . .' Her face clouded despairingly, and Ferdinand went over and kissed her very gently on the cheek.

'It is enough that some people are just beautiful,' he said. 'It makes our lives easier just to look at them.'

'Oh,' Charmian's eyes had tears of real gratitude. 'Isn't it funny, Maggy, that the men who simply don't want to sleep with you are nicer, kinder and so much more understanding than the ones that do . . .'

Margaret and Ferdinand began to laugh, but there was a touch of bitterness in their laughter.

'Look,' he said, 'take off those blacks, Maggy – wear your violet chiffon. You, too, Charmy, find something really pretty, and we'll go out to dinner . . . somewhere small and terribly discreet. The Langham, perhaps?'

'Oh, not the Langham,' Charmian cried. 'It is so stuffy. The sort of place where Bell's parents might go.' She broke off, realizing she should not know what the interior of the Langham was like, and added lamely, 'or so I've been told. I would love a smart restaurant. Just to cheer me up before that awful journey up to Scotland tomorrow.'

'You really have to go?' asked Ferdinand sympathetically. He too hated the sad and morbid things in life.

'Oh, I must,' Charmian took the shell-pink aigrette out of her hair despondently. 'Bell's parents will expect it. I must not offend them. And I must know my position financially – he did ask them to look after me, poor old darling.'

'Shall I travel with you?' asked Margaret.

'Oh no, thank you, Maggy,' Charmian said quickly. 'I'm travelling with Mr Crowther, the family solicitor. He was at the inquest. He said we would have a real chance to talk and to get to know each other.'

'I'll be bound he did,' said Margaret, and kissed Charmian affectionately. How clever she was to pretend to be such a fool.

The Langtry dress was unpinned and returned to its hanger and linen cover. Margaret changed into her violet dress and Charmian found a discreet brown velvet in her trunk, and Ferdinand took them to dine at Kettners.

The following day, again in her exquisite black, they took her to the station to meet the Bellamys' solicitor who was to travel up to Perth with her. The coffin and Bellamy's trunks were in a special van. The men removed their hats as the undertakers put the coffin on board.

There was one small cluster of white roses on it from Charmian. By the time the express had steamed out, Mr Crowther was solicitously holding her hand, and listening to her faltering anxieties.

Margaret and Ferdinand walked down the platform towards their carriage, both deep in thought. Ferdinand was thinking about Charmian, dressed by him exclusively, and attending various functions where she would be seen. That hair, not fiercely red like Margaret's, bronze-gold, curling and silken. That skin, like ivory silk; that long soft neck; those sweetly youthful arms, and pretty hands; that profile, wistful, childish, subtly sensual. She was a natural for a designer to work on.

Margaret was thinking too. Charmian had changed the labels on her trunks before they left left *Punjabi Queen*. She knew that Bellamy had asked his parents to look after her, although that part of the letter had not been read out in court. Therefore she must have read it and replaced it. And how could she have known what sort of place the Langham was?

'Do you think,' Ferdinand asked, 'we could use her professionally?'

'You said yourself modelling is no work for a lady.'

'I was not thinking of the showroom. But if we dressed her. Not too extravagantly, but exquisitely . . . I have friends who will be happy to take her to places. First nights. Race meetings . . . such things. She would be noticed.'

'Oh, yes. She *would* be noticed,' Margaret agreed.

'If, of course, she comes back to London.'

'She'll come back, my dear,' said Margaret. 'She has no intention of living in Perthshire at Glendhu House with the Chesters. She never had.'

Charmian was back within a week. She came to London accompanied by the attentive Mr Crowther, who should have returned to his office in Perth, but was full of a gentlemanly determination not to allow such a lovely young creature to journey back to London alone and unprotected. Men were obsessed with this desire to protect Charmian from their own sex because they were terrified that some other fellow might see her first.

Mr Crowther left her at Hanover Street, and as soon as he had gone Charmian told them indignantly what had happened. Bell's parents had actually demanded that she should live with them in Scotland.

'I wouldn't *consider* it!' she said furiously. 'Oh, they've had very bad reports of me from his friends in India. That beastly old Armstrong woman, the Colonel's wife. She was always jealous – those dried-up old mems are always such cats. Live in that great house with nothing but pine trees and not a neighbour in twenty miles! They must think I'm *déclassée*. I said I was going to live in London, as my dear Mama needs me.'

Ferdinand's face was a study.

'You mean you will live in Juniper Place?'

'Oh *no*! With Mama, who is quite mad now, and that silly old Jany Leck? I don't know why Maggy sets such store by her.'

'Do you want to live here, with Ferdi and me?'

'No, thank you, Maggy. You won't want me in any case when the baby comes, and honestly I can't stand babies – it's the one thing Mama and I agree about. No, that nice Mr Crowther says he can find me a little apartment just near Grosvenor Square, which will be near you, and the shops, and everything. It's a pity he works in Perth.'

'I am sure,' said Ferdinand, straight-faced, 'that Mr Crowther will often travel down to London to see you.'

'What are you going to do for money?' asked Margaret.

'Well, they will let me have a third of Bell's allowance,

unless I marry again. Bell had *no* money. He and his two
brothers have allowances from the estate. To keep the
capital intact, Mr Crowther says. Bell, of course, would
have inherited it all, and been the Laird, or whatever,
but now his next brother does that. I shan't have very
much money. Just one maid. But I won't have anyone
running my life for me.'

'The Merry Widow in reality,' quipped Ferdinand.

'Charmy, sit down,' said Margaret, and Charmian took
a chair opposite her on the other side of her large,
businesslike desk. 'Ferdi and I have a business proposition
to make to you.' The apprehension in her sister's eyes
made her burst out laughing. 'No, not *work*, love. Not
you! No. It will help you. We will dress you for nothing.'
Charmian's face lit up eagerly. 'But there are conditions.
You must not buy anything from another fashion house.
Ferdi has smart friends, who will be delighted to receive
you and to entertain you. They are not what is known as
the best society.'

'Not the *haute monde*,' explained Ferdinand, 'the *haute
bohème*. They will take you to theatres, race meetings,
restaurants, and perhaps to receptions and balls, because
the two worlds meet if they don't mix. You must be
discreet. You must not abandon your mourning too
quickly. You must not tell anyone of the relationship if it
can be avoided, but always tell them *where* you get your
clothes. Every time we get an order through you, you
will get a commission.'

Charmian clapped her hands like a delighted child.

'To wear lovely clothes, not to have to pay for them,
and get paid if anyone has them copied! You are angels.
Of *course* I accept.'

To have her own small place, free of Bellamy, be
dressed by the best house in London, to go to smart
places, where she would be admired, and to find a new

husband – and this time she would be careful. He must be rich, and he must be her slave. Heaven had suddenly opened its gates.

'You inspire me,' Ferdinand said simply. 'I've already made some sketches – a black velvet evening-dress, and one of black mousseline over deep lilac taffeta. You will have to come for fittings and, as Margaret says, you must not rush out of mourning. We have a big trade in elegant mourning. No bad impressions. But next year I shall really make you some ravishing clothes . . .'

The idea proved a success. Charmian behaved herself. The clothes Ferdinand designed for her were a sensation: deep, dramatic mourning into which he gradually introduced greys, muted violets, touches of pure white. She did not 'get into society' – but she became a rising star. A professional beauty. Photographers began to make her offers, and her lovely features could be seen smiling from postcard stands and magazines. She was at every first night. Men pursued the pretty widow, and women enquired about her clothes. The order-books were satisfactory, and Charmian seemed to love every minute of it.

In May, the week before they launched their Summer collection, Margaret received a telegram from Millicent Hengrave, typically unsentimental:

'*My dear Johnston died yesterday. Funeral in three days' time. Can you copy last tweed suit in black, and bring some patterns and sketches to Danesfell? I have to go to the United States shortly to see his family and the lawyers. Would you like to come personally, Maggy? Millicent Hengrave.*'

She knew how much that laconic final request concealed. Millicent without Johnston's dry humour and quiet, guiding hand was difficult to imagine.

Ferdinand chose a fine black bouclé and put it in hand that morning, fitting it on to Millicent's own dummy. It

326

would be ready for Margaret to take with her in the morning. She wired that of course she would come. She owed Millicent so much, from the first moment she had sailed into Madame Rosa's and asked personally for Miss Margaret. Henry would be at the funeral, so she would not go. Sometimes she ached for his beloved presence. Her increasing pregnancy was no comfort to her; she had no sentimental yearnings. With Ferdinand's help she concealed it in elegantly-draped clothes, and attended to her business as though nothing was happening.

On her morning inspection of the fashion salon she found Charmian had called in and was trying on a diaphanous tea-gown in pale rose-coloured chiffon, collared with a wreath of satin roses. On Margaret's entrance she slid hastily out of it and handed it back to the salewoman.

'Oh, hello, Maggy-Waggy,' she cried. 'I just came in to look at Ferdi's new things. I have a nice invitation coming up for Ascot week, and I want one or two special things.'

'But *not* a tea-gown, surely?' Margaret said drily. 'Will you come up to the office, and we'll talk about Ascot.'

Margaret turned on the smirking saleswoman.

'"The Bitch" I will tolerate,' she said icily, 'so long as it is behind my back, but if I hear "Maggy-Waggy" being bandied about by the staff you'll go without a reference, Miss Jenner.'

'I didn't hear, Madame.'

'No? We understand each other then?'

The paralyzed Miss Jenner, who valued her job, saw that the azure eyes were bright with suppressed laughter, and gave a relieved and sickly grin. Margaret burst out laughing.

'I mean it, though.'

'Yes, Madame, I will remember. Is it all right to send the tea-gown to Mrs Chester?'

'It is *not*. In future, Miss Jenner, nothing is to be delivered to Mrs Chester unless the order is signed and counter-signed by Mr Leon and myself.'

'Very good, Madame.'

Charmian who was listening to this exchange, flounced out like a reprimanded schoolgirl. She went ahead to the office, and began straightaway to fiddle through the fashion plates and patterns on Margaret's desk.

'Leave them alone,' snapped Margaret. 'I have just listed and sorted them to take up to Danesfell to Mrs Hengrave.'

'Someone dead?' asked Charmian indifferently, but her pretty, acquisitive hand did not put down the patterns.

'Johnston died yesterday.' Margaret took the patterns away, and sat down at her desk. Charmian had still the old talent for rubbing her up the wrong way.

'Really? I suppose the old boy has left her pretty well-heeled. Danesfell and all that. When I think of the pittance the Chesters allow me I could scream. If our parents hadn't been spendthrifts and idiots we might still have all that . . .'

Margaret did not bother to answer. This was her mother's territory of lost dreams. She had no time for it.

'I have told Miss Jenner not to send the tea-gown.'

'Oh Maggy . . .' Charmian wailed. 'You are *so* mean!'

'The arrangement was that we make clothes for you for occasions only. We have spent five hundred pounds on these, and we have had good orders from them, and you have had your commission. What is this invitation?'

'A friend of mine has taken a house for the Royal Week, and there will be a house-party. Young people. Very chic.'

'Do I know them?'

'Him.' Margaret raised her brows. 'He is called Kenneth Allwood.'

328

'Allwood the tea merchants?'

'The son. I met him on the *Punjabi Queen*, and he got me into a lot of trouble with Bell, always hanging around. I couldn't make him understand. After Bell's death he apologized, and sent flowers, and has been very kind and attentive.' She glanced at a small diamond-set watch pinned among her laces. There was a new expensive ring on her pretty hand. 'He's quite serious. I shall go to each day's racing.'

Margaret drew the order-book towards her.

'That will be three new outfits. I'll put them in hand at once. We're already fully booked. You'd better come in and see Ferdi about the patterns.'

'Evening-dresses too,' pleaded Charmian. 'It will be very chic. Dancing, cards, private theatricals. HRH may drop over. I might meet him.'

'You have sufficient evening-dresses.'

Charmian sulked for a moment, then said, 'Oh, and can I borrow the carriage sometimes to drive in the Park? You and Ferdi never use it during the day. I cannot drive there in a hired cab.'

'*Charmian!* Only rich tarts and kept women drive alone in the Park. It's where they display themselves.'

'Oh, how stuffy you are!'

'You could take Mama.'

'Oh heavens, *no*! I've seen her there with that woman of hers, Lily. What a fright! Those old-fashioned clothes and false curls. No, thanks . . .' She glanced again at the small diamond-framed watch. 'Well, I've got an appointment with my hairdresser . . .'

Both sisters rose. 'Don't forget I need the dark violet satin next week.' Ever since the Prince Consort's death at least twelve months' mourning was still conventional for widows, but Charmian, encouraged by Ferdinand, was already moving into the pearl-greys and muted violets

329

tentatively allowed for half-mourning. 'I'm so *sick* of black!'

'Charmian, everything delivered to you from now on has to be signed by both Ferdinand and myself.'

'Oh Maggy – don't you trust me? Your own little sister?'

'No,' Margaret said good-naturedly.

'Well, of course, I'll never get a decent husband without clothes.'

'You have the best in London.'

'I didn't think Ferdi would be so stuffy. I could tell people a few things about him, if I had half a mind!' She met Margaret's abrasive glance, and realized she had gone too far.

She was perfectly aware of what Ferdinand was and was quite sure the coming baby was not his, but she had not the nerve to question her sister outright. Things were going well, and the clothes and commission from Maison Leon were important to her. With Mr Crowther's practical help in finding her a small but delightful flat on the North side of Mayfair, and that silly boy Kenneth Allwood arriving in tears, bearing roses, and going on his knees for forgiveness at ever doubting her, and the rich and amusing people she had met through Ferdinand, life was all right. She must not put her foot in it when she was having such fun, and old Maggy-Waggy looked really frosty this morning.

The following day Margaret left for Yorkshire, Millicent's new black bouclé *tailleur*, perfect in every detail, packed in a black dress-box, with gold and purple lettering. She felt excited. She had not been back to Thornsby since she had joined Ferdinand in Hanover Street, five years ago, and she was curious to see it again.

Leeds seemed smaller, grubbier, darker than she

330

remembered. As though the city had shrunk while she was away. There was an hour before the train to Thornsby left, and she walked through the Arcade. Madame Rosa's was no longer a gown shop. It was a milliner's. The window was crowded with cheap hats and bonnets on an unimaginative arrangement of long brass stands, like flowering lamp-posts.

Supposing Millicent Hengrave had not recommended her to Ferdinand? Would she really have married that oaf Willy for the sake of the business? And would she have made a worthwhile thing of it? Or would she now be the harrassed landlady of a public house. She shuddered at the thought.

At Thornsby the carriage from Danesfell was waiting for her. She drove past the long stretch of mills along the Bradford Road, still proclaiming in gold letters, four feet high, GRIMSHAW & SONS (THORNSBY) LTD. FINE WOOLLENS.

Unlike Leeds, Danesfell Abbey had not shrunk. As the carriage went up the drive it appeared from the undulating parkland, grey and enormous, every one of the fifty rooms of the South front shuttered with mourning.

She got out and looked round, almost expecting Henry to appear, remembering the day he had first kissed her in Grandmother Normanby's little parlour, and she had been as eager and recklessly responsive as only an eighteen-year-old can be. Once, holding her in his arms, in the water-lapping darkness of the riverside inn, he had said, 'That day I could have taken you, there and then. I touched you and I was wild with desire.'

'What?' she had mocked. 'With your sister, your future bride and mother-in-law staring through the window!'

'They saved you that day, Maggy Normanby.' He had never used her married name.

'You went red as beet with anger at being caught,' she

331

accused him. 'I thought it quite funny. Those six astounded eyes. Then I felt humiliated. As though you'd been caught kissing the housemaid.'

'And I felt ashamed because you were such a child.'

She had sighed, and laughed against his breast in the darkness, secure in his love for her.

Had it really only been last year? One of those periods of her life when time had shifted so fast, taking her out of girlhood into love. Into maturity. Into loneliness and pregnancy. For the first time she wondered about being a mother. She could not believe it in spite of the strongly moving child within her womb.

Across the fields there were lights in Danesfell Church, dwarfed by the ruins, cosily clad in the thick Spring green of the surrounding trees.

A woman wrapped in a black shawl came through the cattle gate from the park and walked towards her across the enormous sweep of the forecourt. She would know that graceful stride anywhere – Millicent Hengrave always walked as though her long legs were never impeded by petticoats. She looked pale, but calm, as she took Margaret's hands, looking at the betraying bulge beneath the beautifully cut and draped mantle.

'You didn't tell me?'

'I didn't tell anyone except my mother and she did not want to know and has not mentioned it since. She shudders and looks away when I go to see her. The draper's child! Unmentionable!'

'You didn't *want* anyone to know?'

'No,' Margaret said firmly. 'A pregnant woman is a slight embarrassment in a fashionable dressmaker's – although Ferdi has made a profitable feature out of maternity clothes.'

They turned towards the house from which a man-servant had emerged to help the coachman with the luggage.

'It is a big and very active baby. I shall have to work behind the scenes now until he has arrived.'

'You seem very sure it will be a boy. When are you expecting?'

'In August.'

They went up the wide steps through the great entrance door. Through the pilastered ballroom door on the right was a glimmer of candles, and a smell of flowers. Millicent took Margaret's arm and went to the entrance. The coffin stood on a raised velvet-covered bier, and two village women had just put down a basket of white violets. Millicent spoke to them, shook hands and thanked them.

'Where did you get so many?'

'T'young uns went into Deep Woods before school this morning. He were a good Squire, Mr Hengrave, though he weren't from Yorkshire.'

When they had gone, Millicent told the manservants to take the dress-box and Margaret's case upstairs and to serve tea in Lady Margaret's parlour. 'People have been coming all day, bringing flowers – the village people, and the mining folk over from North Fell. It's nice. He was a good man. I've been over to the church – to see everything is ready, and to say a little prayer.'

'I didn't know you were a believer.'

'No. I'm not. But Johnstone was . . . and if any prayer of mine will do my old darling any good, God is welcome to it.'

'Millicent – you look happy.'

'Yes. I'm glad he's at rest. He struggled so hard for my sake. And – these last years, since his illness, have been so extraordinarily happy. We really did live for each other. I can't explain. He wanted to die here, and to be buried here. He was very proud of Danesfell . . . Ah, here is the tea. Sit down, and take your mantle and hat off.'

A log fire was burning in the open hearth. The evening outside was beautiful with Spring blossom and loud with bird calls. 'You'll stay with me, Maggy, for a day or so? I've never had a real woman friend. You're the nearest. Angela is so obsessed with her coming child. The local doctor calls every day. The specialist travels once a month from London. A new wing has been built at Cliffs Edge. A day and night nursery, bedrooms for the nurse and nursery girl, a special little kitchen. It's a baby palace. She can think and talk of nothing else.'

'She is keeping well?'

'Physically she is very well. She had some mild infection about two months ago. There was a minor epidemic – some form of measles. Nothing serious, but there was the devil of a fuss.'

Margaret gazed silently into the fire.

'Since her pregnancy she has become possessive and has learned what a weapon ill-health can be against a considerate man, even if he does not love her.'

'It was his choice,' said Margaret coldly.

The flickering firelight lit up her pretty, stubborn face, etching shadows under the cheekbones, and the slanting, thick-lashed eyelids. Millicent wondered what sort of child would come from the mating of two such self-willed egotists.

'It is Mrs Torrance, the mother, I cannot stand,' she said. 'I am sorry for Angela – a nice enough girl who has tried to do her duty by too many people. Mrs Torrance is worried about who will inherit Danesfell.' She refilled Margaret's cup. 'She is one of those women who take soup and blankets to her tenants instead of mending their roofs, or putting in piped water and damp courses. Johnston could not stand her. I don't want her sympathy or her company. I need you here, Maggy. Poor Angela is even jealous of me. I cannot ask Henry to be with me, although we are very close. It would upset her. Please stay.'

'I might meet him,' said Margaret. 'I mustn't meet him.'

'It is his baby, of course?'

Margaret's clear eyes lifted. 'Yes. Of course.'

'And he doesn't know?'

'No.'

'And you're not going to tell him. Why?'

'Why should I? He didn't know when he left me. It's my baby. I can afford to look after it. I am respectably married. I'm not going to wail on Henry's neck as though I was the only woman in the world who had got herself into trouble – it was my doing too.'

'What does your husband say?'

'Ferdinand?' Margaret smiled, not without affection. 'He is very understanding. He is loyal in his own, curious way. We are extremely fond of each other, you know.'

'Yes, I can understand. You learn to understand such things in the theatre. You want to get back to London because you don't want Henry to know. And if he sees you, he will know?'

'Of course. He will know at once. That is why I cannot stay.'

'Oh, you needn't worry. This is a big house. You can stay out of sight. Stay with me a while Maggy.'

'I will stay tonight and tomorrow night. Then I must go.'

The long windows of her bedroom overlooked the park, with the lights of Thornsby town in the distance on the rising side of the far valley. They stood looking out together. Millicent put her hand through Margaret's arm.

'Maggy, Johnston left me Danesfell and the income from the mines. Outright. I will not marry again, and I

335

am too old to have children. I shall leave my property to Henry's children. Legitimate or illegitimate.'

Margaret said nothing.

'One day he will find out about your baby, and when he does he will want that child too, however many Angela has.'

'He can't have it. It is my child. What you do with your money is your business, Millicent. But this baby is mine. I can provide for it. I can look after my own. For God's sake, haven't I looked after them all – Mama, Charmian, Lecky – ever since I was old enough to work? What's a baby in comparison?'

'I might have known you'd say that. I never wanted a child until it was too late. I know how you feel. Goodnight, Maggy, love.'

Margaret looked across the moors to the valley. The town where she had grown up, Hollingroyd Crescent, Henry's mills strung along the Bradford Road, Cliffs Edge, where he lived, where he was now, was barely a mile away. She could walk there in half-an-hour. The longing to see him was so great that she actually rose to her feet, and then, hugging her swollen body, as though in pain, she began to weep agonizing tears of loss for the first time since he had left her.

She woke to the tolling of a bell, and remembered it was the day Johnston Hengrave was to be buried. A maid came in, raked together the embers of the fire, and laid dry tinder and coals so that in a moment it was leaping and cheerful, and a few minutes later brought in a breakfast tray.

Millicent, already dressed, came in a few minutes later. The black costume, trimmed elaborately with Russian braid, fitted her like a glove, but she wore no hat. Instead she had tied a small square of fine black lace over her hair, a point above her forehead, and she wore not the

336

prescribed jet jewellery, but a pair of long and very beautiful diamond earrings that Johnston had given her when they were married. She looked the picture of what an exiled queen should look like but rarely did – the touch of theatre that lifted her out of the ordinary and made it so rewarding to dress her.

'Don't get up until you feel you want to,' she said, 'and do what you like . . . the crows will be gathering soon, then people will come back here for the wake.' She smiled, or her lips smiled; her dark eyes were haunted still with loss. 'I hate this business. I hate all the mourning and the dear departed thing that the Queen has introduced.' She looked at Margaret, lying back on her pillows, glowing and rested. Yesterday, after travelling from London, she had looked like a starved white kitten. 'I suppose you've seen a doctor?'

'Only to confirm the pregnancy.'

'Have you booked a nurse, or ordered a nappy? Or thought where you would have this baby? Or where, when it comes, you will put it, in a fashionable gown establishment?'

Margaret shrugged. Her unbound hair, tumbling about her shoulders, was fiery in the morning sunlight. She looked as resilient as a coiled spring, radiant with vitality. 'Oh, there's plenty of time,' she said. 'I'm as strong as a horse, and Jany Leck, my old nurse who looks after Mama, is knitting and sewing for me.'

'Babies sometimes don't wait until the last minute. You'd better see your doctor when you get back, and make some plans.'

'We've plenty of room at Hanover Street – there's the attic floor quite empty . . . for a nursery.'

The bell tolled again.

'I must go,' said Millicent. 'I'll have you some lunch served up here. Everyone should be away by midday, and then I shall be lunching the family – just Henry and the Torrances – in my little parlour. Then we should have the afternoon and evening to ourselves.'

'Millicent. Is Henry happy?'

'No, of course not. How can he be, tied to a complaining, suspicious woman? No. He is bored. He works like ten men. He expands the business, endlessly rebuilding and modernizing his factories.'

'And the foreign ladies?'

'No foreign ladies. He has promised!'

'His political career?'

'He works at that – but it is a game. He is too cynical to be a good politician. The meetings, and the dinners and the conferences keep him away from Cliffs Edge and the eternal concern and attention that Angela demands. The perpetual reassurance that he will never leave her. To me, even as a girl, he was a solid as a rock. I had no one else. Mother was dead, father was a brute. Henry was everything. But now, there's a brittleness about him. I feel he might explode – like a volcano. Blowing everything sky-high.'

Margaret went to the window. The bedroom was on the main front and she could see the plumed black hearse and horses standing at the main entrance. Along the drive the coaches were arriving and a long, winding procession of foot mourners was coming across the fields. Villagers, farm labourers, tradesfolk, rural craftsmen with their wives and children, and the miners from the North Fell seam, their pale underground faces washed, wearing their Sunday blacks and the uniform white scarves about their necks. Johnston had made a better job of being Squire than all the Normanbys before him.

Millicent came down to the steps on Henry's arm. He looked thinner in the black mourning suit.

The brother and sister, fair and dark, slim and square-set, handsome and successful, stood talking earnestly, Henry holding her hand. A woman's head, black-bonnetted, came out of the window of the following carriage. Margaret guessed it was Angela.

She could hear nothing but Angela must have called. Henry's head switched round irritably, and she could see his brows meet in the familiar intolerant scowl. He said something sharply, and the black bonnet was withdrawn, with a flutter of a white handkerchief.

He kissed Millicent tenderly, turned and strode back to the carriage. There was impatience in the way he banged the door closed behind him, not waiting for the footman to close it. The cortège moved off along the private road to the church, half-a-mile away across the fields.

Margaret dressed and went out, over the moors and down to the town on a nostalgic tour of Thornsby. Past the elaborate gates of Cliffs Edge, past Henry's great factories along the Bradford Road, past the Britannia Mill which her grandfather had once owned. Her only memory of Thomas Jagger was an empurpled face and frothing mouth, and swollen, shaking hands stretched out in pleading to her mother for a glance of love or a word of thanks before death claimed him.

Then she went to Hollingroyd Crescent – it looked impeccably neat. Hart's-tongue fern and aspidistra dominated the windows before the stiff, Nottingham lace curtains. In the semi-basements the kitchen ranges glowed with good local coal to prepare the dinners. Soon the mistresses would be back from shopping in the town, and at twelve the men in their shops and offices would glance at their watches, take their hats, go to the saloon of the Station Hotel, or to the bar at the Conservative or Constitutional Clubs, to have a drink, a midday meeting with competitors, before taking the horse-tram up the hill to dinner. Dinner was at midday in those North Country houses. At six o'clock high tea was served.

She thought, amused, what an odd household the Normanbys must have been in this conventional milieu, with their mad, drunken mother, no servants apart from Lecky, always owing money. Charmian a boarder at a school for young ladies, and herself apprenticed and out to work at fifteen like any workman's child.

She went on into the town, not expecting to be recognized. But she was mistaken. A burly, pink-faced man of about thirty, standing aproned on the doorstep of a large provision store, stared at her, and raised his bowler.

'Excuse me, Miss . . . Ma'am, but aren't you Miss Margaret Normanby?'

'I was.' She stopped. 'I am Mrs Leon now.'

'I thought I recognized the hair.'

'Oh yes, indeed,' she smiled. 'It's still very red.'

'You are visiting?'

'I brought Mrs Hengrave's mourning from London.'

'Oh, aye. I heard you were in the dress line. Everyone was sorry to hear about Mr Hengrave.' A pause, a covert glance back into the clean, spacious, spice-smelling shop, where a woman at the raised cash-desk was busy with figures. His wife. 'I was right sorry to hear about Captain Chester. It was in the local paper. How is your sister?'

'Charmian?' She suddenly recognized him: Charmian's passionate admirer, Billy Heaton, the hero of stolen kisses behind the lilac bushes in the park. 'Oh, she is well. She lives in London.'

The round pink face seemed to quiver.

'Is she still as bonny?'

'Oh yes, Mr Heaton, more so, I think.'

'Aye,' he sighed, and seemed to contemplate his own bulky, already middle-aged figure. Then he asked, in a hoarse whisper, 'She's all right? He left her quite well-off then?'

Margaret was touched.

'Oh yes, quite adequately, thank you.' Was this another knight errant ready to rush to Charmian's aid?

'Aye. Well, I'm glad. I wouldn't have liked to think of her wanting for owt. She wasn't meant for that, if you know what I mean.'

'I do indeed,' said Margaret drily.

'And I hope all goes well wi' you, Ma'am.' He glanced tactfully at the bulge which her beautiful quilted taffeta mantle did not quite conceal.

'Thank you, Mr Heaton. I'll remember you to my sister.'

He watched her walk away with her light, springy walk, the small head with its crown of red hair balanced on the fine column of her slender neck. They'd been a couple of rare 'uns, those Normanby girls. She'd always looked an aristocrat, that Margaret, but no airs and graces. But it was Charmian who still troubled his dreams.

The Town Hall clock stood at one, so she took a cab from the rank. The funeral would be over. Millicent would have her lunch served in her room. She told the driver to go round by the stable entrance, and did not realize until she came out from the yard archway that she was in full view from the back of the house.

She was tired and hungry. She could see no one at the windows. It was scarcely a hundred feet across the gravel to a rear entrance. She took a chance and went quickly across the open space and had reached the door when she saw Angela standing in the window of the small parlour, a handkerchief pressed over her mouth, her eyes red and swollen, staring down at her with horror and recognition.

341

'Oh, heck!' Margaret thought angrily and bolted into the house.

The luncheon had been a nightmare to Millicent, with Angela's parents trying to keep the conversation on a suitably funereal level. To both Mr Torrance and his wife this meant respectful memories of the dear departed. Neither of them knew anything about Johnston's shrewd, worldly humour, or his easy tolerance of human frailties. She could not recognize the man they spoke of. Their other subject was property, Mrs Torrance endeavoured to hide her greed with piety but the fact that Millicent was childless, and Henry, her only relation, would soon be a father, was never far from her mind.

That Danesfell Abbey, with its wide acres of which their own two hundred at Abbey Farm were only a small part, and the profits from the coal mines at North Fell seam which Johnston's American finance company had re-opened and modernized, might now belong to Millicent, and therefore come one day into the possession of their family, was very much on the cards.

Henry and Millicent were perfectly well aware of this. They were locked into a mischievous mood, determined not to give the Torrances any information about how Johnston's money had been left.

Johnston was dead, and they had both loved and valued him, the cool, clean, witty American gentleman. They talked of past good times, the three of them together, Johnston, Millicent and Henry . . . meeting up together in the great pleasure cities of the world. They made Angela feel provincial and inadequate. She was shocked that they should laugh and speak like this of one so lately dead. She was jealous of the closeness of their friendship.

They had been speaking of a weekend at Baden-Baden, when royalty had been present, and Johnston had boldly flirted and outrageously monopolized the royal favourite.

Angela burst out suddenly, furiously, 'I don't know *how* you can talk like this, with Johnston barely in his grave! It's indecent! Must you turn everything to laughter?'

Millicent and Henry turned astounded faces towards her.

Henry said quietly, 'Johnston always preferred laughter.'

She sprang to her feet, and went to the window, a tall woman, heavily pregnant, moving awkwardly in her unbecoming black. She had given up attempts at beauty. Love and anxiety had made her lose her way. Her handkerchief came out once again, crying, as she so often did, not for Johnston, but for herself.

'Sometimes I think you and Henry live in a world of your own,' she accused. 'It is a pity you did not invent your own language, then no one need even pretend to understand you.'

Henry exchanged an exasperated glance with his sister. The months of his wife's pregnancy had taught him every opening gambit of Angela's hysteria. She seemed driven by some inward demon to make trouble. As though she could not bear to share even a glance of his attention. Her coming child was everything in her world, for she was sure it was only that which kept him by her side.

She looked out of the window and saw the thin, graceful young woman with the brilliant hair, and time shuttled back to that day before Henry had proposed to her. The girl with the bright blue eyes. The young manageress from the shop in Leeds where, on Milly's advice, her trousseau had been made. The girl she had glimpsed, momentarily, in Henry's arms. The girl who had looked at him so hungrily, unable to hide her infatuation. Her tears vanished, and her voice became accusatory and harsh.

343

'What on earth is that woman doing here? The dress-maker girl from Leeds who made my wedding dress? The one who came to the church to arrange the train?'

The silence was solid. Like fog. She felt her tension rising to breaking point. Her voice rose shrilly. 'The one with the red hair.'

'She is still my dressmaker,' Millicent said calmly. Beneath the tablecloth her hand pressed Henry's knee warningly. The colour had drained from his face, and she saw the thin silver coffee-spoon bend in his fingers. 'She has a fine establishment in London now. She was Miss Normanby, you remember, before her marriage. She has kindly hurried through my mourning and travelled up from London with it. She is a very good friend of mine.'

'Now, Angela,' her mother said reprovingly, 'don't let's have any fuss. Come back and finish your lunch like a sensible girl.'

Angela flashed her a look of pure hate. Margaret had vanished out of sight into the side door of the house.

'But she is expecting,' she said. 'She is with child too.' Her accusing eyes went from Henry to his sister. Millicent's were blandly surprised. The furrows deepened in Henry's forehead, and his mouth set like a trap.

'Oh, Christ,' he thought. 'Oh, dear Christ. *Maggy is here!*'

As he had once nearly walked out of his wedding and taken Margaret Normanby with him, now he wanted to walk out of this room and go to her. If she was with child, it was his. Not just a child to reap the reward of his labours, his property, money and position, but Maggy's child, the child of their love. Millicent's voice brought him back, calm and amused, handling everything with her superb competence.

'Well, for heaven's sake! She *is* married! She *is* Madame Leon, wife of the most brilliant couturier in London. She

344

has as much right as the next woman to have a child. It was kind of her to travel up in her condition, and she only did so because we *are* such old friends.'

The gentle hand on Henry's knee pinched viciously, making him start and meet her eyes, reading the message there. '*You* started the game. Now you must play it out until the end.' He rose, went to the sideboard, poured himself a glass of brandy.

'If she is a friend of yours,' demanded Angela, 'why didn't she take lunch with us?'

'Oh, come now, Angy, be sensible,' said her father uneasily. 'This is a family meal for a sad occasion. One does not ask that kind of person. Did we invite the undertaker?'

Henry's face suddenly flamed.

'Millicent,' he said, 'would you be so kind as to ask Madame Leon to honour us with her presence. Perhaps she would take coffee with us.'

'Oh, please,' Angela said frantically, her colour rising, and her heart racing, '*do* ask her up.'

'Angela, this is *most* improper,' said Mrs Torrance.

'It may be . . . it may well be.' Her anguished eyes shot a reproachful glance at Henry. 'But we shall see.'

'Angela,' said Henry gently, 'try to control yourself. It does you no good – or the child!'

'That child . . .' she said furiously, 'is all you think about! What about *me*? Oh, God, what about *me*?'

Millicent went out into the hall. She was exasperated – she loathed scenes and women who made them. Margaret had just reached the first bend in the carved oak stairway.

'I'm afraid you've been seen, love. He knows you're here. It's that damned hair of yours – like a beacon. Will you come down? Have coffee? Face it out? Or just ignore them? It's your choice.'

Margaret gave a small smile, undid her mantle, drew her gloves from steady hands.

'I'd like coffee,' she said.

In the little parlour the atmosphere was like the presage before a storm when the glass drops and the air hangs still and heavy as lead.

Margaret paused and took a deep breath, then advanced into the centre of the room, a slim queenly figure, superlatively dressed, bearing her pregnancy lightly, like a skimming full-sailed yacht, and looked straight across at Henry.

He could not conceal his feelings. His iron front crumpled, his face lit with the welcome of love and the memory of happiness. It was naked and undisguised. It set her alight too, remembering. The colour leaped to her pale cheeks like a flag of triumph, but she turned courteously to Angela, and bowed.

'Mrs Grimshaw, I hope I find you well?'

'Thank you,' Angela gushed, quite out of character. 'We were talking of that lovely wedding dress you made for me. It caused a sensation. Everyone congratulated me.'

Margaret looked into the sallow face and frantic eyes, and recognized hysteria. She had known women make scenes in the showroom because a hem had been out by a fraction of an inch – not because the hem was too long but because of the indifference of the man for whom the gown had been created.

'Thank you,' she said gravely.

'Your husband is not here with you?'

'Great heavens, no,' Margaret laughed and so did Millicent. 'Ferdinand is not in the least a country person. Mrs Hengrave asked me to bring her suit, and some patterns and sketches. This morning I made a nostalgic tour of the town. Also, I still own a house at Hollingroyd Crescent. I wanted to see it.'

'You have found many changes?'

'None at all. The town seems to have shrunk. Everything seems smaller. I have changed a great deal. I could not live here now. But, of course, Danesfell is still very beautiful.'

'I can remember an incident,' said Angela dangerously, 'just before Henry and I were engaged. Mother and myself, and Mrs Hengrave walked past this window, and I saw him kissing you.'

There was an appalled silence. Mrs Torrance's imposing face turned puce. Mr Torrance was struck into helpless silence. Angela laughed with a pitiful, brittle gaiety. 'I nearly refused him. But Mama persuaded me to let the whole thing pass. She explained to me, and I was very ignorant about such matters, that gentlemen were weak where certain women were concerned.'

'Certain *women*?' Margaret glittered, keeping her temper. 'Certain silly girls, I think you mean. I had an adolescent passion for Mr Grimshaw. He had been kind in recommending Mrs Hengrave to patronize Madame Rosa's shop in Leeds, and she brought my first really big commission.' She began to laugh. 'It was really very funny. I literally threw myself at him. When I saw your three faces at the window I thought I would die of shame, but one doesn't. One doesn't even die of love. One grows up. Poor Mr Grimshaw, I never knew how he explained the matter to you.' Her bright blue eyes were alight with mischievous laughter. 'I *hope* you were not too severe.'

Her glance went from face to face. The Torrances' rigid horror, Millicent's appreciative amusement. She dare not look at Henry. She went on, rather too volubly. Chattering. She did not chatter. 'I was a giddy girl of eighteen, unschooled, and unpredictable.' She smiled ingenuously at Mrs Torrance. 'But my sister Charmian and I were unfortunate; our mother, Lady Normanby, was always ill and unable to chaperone us. Why, only today in the town, that nice Mr Heaton . . .'

'The grocer?' exclaimed Mr Torrance, shocked out of his silence.

'Yes. He reminded me how much in love he was with Charmian, and how he kissed her one day in the Park. Behind the lilacs. And asked her to marry him.' She met Henry's eyes, and her own fell. She went on blindly, babbling out her smoke-screen of nonsense, 'Just think, she might be behind the counter of that perfectly splendid shop today if Grandmother Normanby hadn't whisked her away to Edinburgh.'

'And why were you not sent to Edinburgh?'

'I wouldn't go. I had apprenticed myself in Leeds. I was always the work-a-day girl, hell-bent on independence. My own trade. My own business. I thought I'd find my own husband too. Which I have. And now,' she patted the bulge beneath the black silk mantle, 'my own baby soon.'

The blue eyes smiled farewell, inscrutable as a cat's blinking in the sunshine. 'Now perhaps you will excuse me. I have not taken lunch yet, and I want to catch the early evening train back to London. There is a great deal to do if Mrs Hengrave's clothes are to be ready for her to sail in a few weeks' time.' She gave a small nod, turned and went out. Millicent just managed to restrain a round of applause.

She went up to her room, and sat down. The cold lunch on a tray was appetizing but she could not touch it. She drank a glass of wine and had packed her bag, when Millicent came in.

'I'm sorry, Maggy, I apologize. They were insufferable.'

'They were afraid. Especially Angela. And she has

reason.' She thoughtfully pressed on the fine black gloves, easing the fingers one by one. 'I shouldn't have come back. Call me a carriage, Millicent, and I'll get into Leeds . . . there is a train about seven I believe. I'll telegraph to Ferdi, and he'll meet me. It's better so. I hope she believed me. I don't think she did.'

'Perhaps not. But you were splendid. I am sorry you will not stay. But you know your own mind.'

Henry drove Angela back to Cliffs Edge in silence. He had thought the open carriage would be good for her on such a fine May day. In the birch plantations that Johnston had planted the bluebells were breaking into azure rivers beneath the breaking green.

'Was she your mistress?' she asked.

She had expected a denial, an exasperated evasion, but her bitter game of provoking his attention had turned ugly. Under the scowling brows his gaze was rivetted on the little cob he was driving so skilfully. He said, 'Yes.'

'Still is?'

'No.'

'Why not?'

He turned and looked at her then, and she shrank back.

'You know why not. You extracted promises from me for your reassurance, and for the safety of our child. I have kept those promises. In return you have tormented yourself and me with unwarranted suspicions und jealousies. If it has brought you some kind of satisfaction, I simply don't understand. Do you enjoy it? It is time you knew the truth and stopped imagining my infidelities.'

They turned into the drive at Cliffs Edge, and he pulled up the gig before the steps, sprand down, and handed the reins to the groom who came running out from the stable quarters. He handed Angela down, took her arm, and walked her fiercely away from the house into the rose-garden. It was overlooked by the new nursery wing which Angela had had built at great expense for the coming child. There were stone seats about a central lily pond.

He said, 'You'd better sit down.'

'Is it your child she is carrying?'

'Yes.'

'How can you know?' she said harshly – 'A woman like that . . .'

'Because she was twenty-five and still a virgin when we fell in love. That story – about throwing herself at me – ' he laughed, his eyes clearing momentarily, 'how well she did it. It wasn't true, of course. She was five when I met her. She was eighteen when we met again, and I wanted her from the moment I saw her. I was in love with her mother when we were boy and girl, here in Thornsby. Florence Jagger. I was besotted with her beauty; she was spoiled, weak-minded, dishonest and vain . . . poor creature. She spoiled women for me – all women – until I met Maggy, and she taught me differently.'

'You should have married her.'

'I should have married her. But eighteen and forty-three? A difference of over twenty years? She was so free, and bold, and quick to learn. She was not afraid of work, or responsibility. She was so everything her mother never was. So much ambition. She wasn't meant to be any man's domestic shadow. It would have been like caging a bright bird. I couldn't do it.'

She had never heard him speak like this of anyone. She had never dreamed that he had poetry in him. She had only seen the down-to-earth, powerful Yorkshire-man. She had thought of his women as sexual escapes.

'Were you going to leave me?'

'It had not arisen. We were happy as we were.'

'Why did she come here?'

350

'I think – I think she must have needed to be near me –
even if I did not know. I remember once in London . . . I
got in early. We had arranged to meet that evening . . .
but I walked to Hanover Street and just stood outside the
place. I had to feel near her . . . it was like that between
us. We neither of us, ever, intended that you should be
deprived of anything.'

'Except your love.'

'You never had that, Angela. I did you a great wrong,
and I am desperately sorry for it.'

He raised his head sharply, listening. Far away up the
moors in the silent air there was the sound of a carriage
on the road.

His hand rested on her shoulder momentarily, then he
went quickly, springing over the low wall into the steep
grazing-field, plunging down over the fell, jumping from
crag to crag, his strong, sturdy body running easily until
he was out of sight.

She sat alone for a long while, then rose heavily and
walked round the back of the house to the stables.

Henry waited by the roadside until the carriage from
Danesfell rounded the corner of the lower moorland
road. He shouted to the coachman to stop.

He saw Margaret's white face and red hair glimmering
through the glass, and wrenched the door open.

'Maggy, get out. Walk over the moor with me. We can
tell him to meet us on the main road, outside the town.'

She sprang lightly down. The carriage went on down
the incline, the pair sliding a little on the rough road. He
had not released her hand. He led her across the sheep-
cropped grass, where the path wound steeply towards the
town. Thornsby spread before them, ceilinged in its murk
of smoke, its mill stacks sprouting like towers from the
blue-grey curves and horizontals of the endless rows of

slate-roofed houses. You could smell the town, even from the fresh moors.

They walked together down the dipping lanes.

'You weren't going to see me?'

'No.'

'Or tell me about the baby?'

'No.'

'Never?'

'Perhaps one day, when he is grown and we are old.'

'You're so certain you're carrying a boy!'

She gave him a strange look. 'Oh yes. Of course.'

He pulled her roughly against him, and held her close, kissing her lips and face and eyes, trying to rouse desire in her, but she was quiet in his arms. The fire was there, the vitality, but tensely controlled.

'Why did you come back? You could have sent one of your women with Millicent's clothes. To see me? *You came to see me?*'

'I came to see it all. Even if Angela did not exist and we could marry, what should *I* do here? It holds nothing for me. You've got that great business – I'd have nothing. I'd rather have a corner shop in London than come back here.' She shook off his restraining hands and began to hurry down the hillside. 'I must go and catch my train.'

'There are plenty of trains,' he said furiously. 'The London train does not leave until the early evening.'

'I want to go. I don't belong here any more. I – I can't stand this situation. It's not just humiliating. It's stifling.'

She went quickly past him with swift, deliberate steps, almost running. He caught her again and swung her round to face him; she did not struggle, but she was indomitable and unconquered. The small heart-shaped face was set, the blue eyes adamant.

'You can't keep me, Henry. It's impossible!' She

stamped. 'Why must you be so *stupid*! Just thank God for what we had and let it go!'

'Maggy, I gave Angela my promise and I am keeping it until her child is born. Then it will be different. We can see each other again. It can be as it was.'

Below they could see the junction of the road, with the horses cropping the grass, the coachman pacing to and fro waiting for her.

He caught her arm, and held her with a grip like a vice, glaring at her. There was no tenderness between them. He was beside himself – he could not bear that she should go. There was no need.

'Maggy, you shall have anything you want,' he cried. 'You shall live like a queen. I want you – I want your child too. I want to care for you both, and I can. I told Angela today – I will keep my promise to her, but then she must let me go.'

'Don't hurt me!' she cried angrily, and bending, bit his hand, her eyes blazing. Red tiger-cub – now red tiger-cat. His hand opened and he let her go, looked at the half-circle of small red indentations on the back of his hand, and the anger went out of him.

'This child is mine!' she said fiercely. 'No one has any right to it but me. I could have killed it and you would never have known. You have another child coming, be content with that. You think you can make life do what you want – you think you can make everyone do what you want? You can't. It was you who made the break, not me. Remember that. Now let me go.'

She lifted her skirts from her slim feet, and in spite of her bulk went down the hillside with sure, light footsteps to the carriage. The coachman opened the door, and in a moment she was inside and had driven away.

It was utterly final. He watched until the carriage was

out of sight, and then he turned and walked up over the moors.

He did not know how long he walked or in which direction. It came on to rain. He found himself at Blackmoor and went in to the inn and took a glass of brandy, hired a chaise and drove home. When he arrived the doctor's gig was in the drive and the house in a turmoil. Angela's labour, nearly a month before time, had begun.

His head groom, white-faced, screwing his cap between his hands, was waiting in the hall. Botham, the butler stood nervously beside him. 'Will's been waiting to see you, Sir . . .'

'It worn't no fault o' mine, Sir,' the man burst out. 'The Missus had saddled up Merlin and was mounted and off before I knew. I couldn't stop her. She didn't fall, or nowt like that. She brought t'horse back, quiet as a lamb. It worn't my fault.'

'You mean you let her go out on the horse?'

'Mr Grimshaw, I was having a cup o' tea, and I heard a horse in the yard, and looked out, and there she was . . . in her dress. Not a habit, boots, nor nothing . . . saddled up. Went to the mounting stone, and up and off before I could be out after her . . .'

'You damned idiot, get out of here and out of my house!' roared Henry.

'It's a little boy, Sir,' said Botham tentatively.

'You mean – it's *over*? The baby's here?'

'Oh yes, Sir. Two hours ago. A little boy, the nurse said . . .'

'Mr Grimshaw, sir . . .' The doctor stood at the top of the stairs, putting on his jacket. 'Would you come up?'

Henry raced up, two at a time.

'My wife?'

'Mrs Grimshaw is asleep. She is quite well.'

'The baby . . ?'

354

'A boy.'

'Something's wrong?'

'I – I regret to say so, yes.'

'Was it the ride?'

'No. No. The birth was very easy. No, whatever caused the harm it was in the very early stages of pregnancy.'

'He will live?'

'Yes. I think he might.' His pink, round face was filled with pity. 'Perhaps it would be as well if he did not.'

'What the devil do you mean?'

'There is considerable weakness – abnormality in the back and the lower limbs. The child's heart and lungs seem normal. I have seen several such cases in the valley this year. It is a mystery. It has been a good healthy year, only the mildest of childish epidemics. No smallpox, no scarlet fever, no typhoid or cholera. But this type of thing in births – some very severe.'

'What does it mean?'

'It means he will be a late walker . . .'

'You mean he may never walk?' Henry asked.

'There is that possibility. It is a condition we know very little about. Your son will, of course, be able to have the best care and medical attention . . . but – there is that possibility.'

'Does Mrs Grimshaw know?'

'Not yet.'

'Can I see him?'

'Of course.'

He followed the doctor through into the luxurious nursery wing, and looked down at the baby, robed and capped in silk, in the elaborate trimmed and ruffled cot. The small face looked skeletal, sunken blue-shadowed eyes, hollow cheekbones. Like a child of famine. Not like Henry Grimshaw's son.

'He looks terrible.'

355

'That is because he was premature. That will pass, as soon as he puts on weight.'

'Can I hold him?'

'Better not, Mr Grimshaw, not yet. Leave it to the nurse. He will need very careful handling.'

'And – the ride had nothing to do with it?'

'I'm not saying that – it may have brought on the premature birth. But if this baby has gone full term, he would still be disabled.'

'I see.' He looked down at the pitiful scrap that was his longed-for son, and his heart was torn with pity, and his mind filled with rejection. He could love this child, but could he ever be proud of him? He had never dreamed of such a thing. That he and Angela might never have children he had been prepared for, but that he, Henry Grimshaw, with his broad, bullock shoulders and tireless energy, could sire a cripple had never entered his mind.

He accompanied the doctor downstairs, and bade him goodnight. Will was standing in the hall, practically in tears. He paused, put a hand on his shoulder.

'All right, man. It wasn't your fault. Get back home.'

He went back upstairs and sat by Angela's bedside, waiting until she woke. She looked pale and tired, but younger with the lines of watchful jealousy smoothed by sleep. When she opened her eyes he was holding her hand – her face lit up, and then she remembered.

'He's all right?' she asked.

He took her in his arms and told her.

'You mean he will never walk?'

'He will, of course. But late. He will need a lot of care.'

She gave a cry of pain.

'It's not your fault,' he said. 'It wasn't the ride. It is something they don't understand.'

356

'I thought that everything would be all right when the baby came. But it's worse, isn't it?'

'We have a son. We will move heaven and earth to make him strong and well. I know he will be all right one day.'

He could hear Margaret saying, 'You think you can make life do what you want. You think you can make everyone do what you want. You can't.' He added, helplessly, 'We are young, Angela. There will be other babies.'

She turned her tired face away from him. The very thought was odious to her. She only wanted to forget everything, particularly her crippled child. When the London specialist travelled up to see the boy he said that in view of her nervous condition and age, it would be better not to consider another pregnancy.

They called him Stephen Dyson Grimshaw. He lived like a little Prince in his purpose-built palace, nursed, waited on, surrounded by every comfort and medical care, while his parents hovered and watched and hoped – every hint of progress greeted with joy, every set-back a terrible defeat. For Henry it was a dogged battle to make the boy strong and well. For Angela it became, as time passed, a concentrated and possessive love, as though she wanted this fragile creature to love no one but herself, and could keep him a child she could possess for ever.

Chapter Thirteen

It was a day which threatened storm. Margaret was past her time, the baby already six days overdue. For the past two months she had kept her aggressively pregnant figure in the background of the business and out of Ferdinand's way, for however affectionately he regarded her he could not disguise the fact that her swollen body was an offence to him. He did not like to be seen with her and longed for the return of his slender, elegant partner and wife. He was going to Paris to buy for the Spring and Autumn, as he did every year – as he had last year, when they had travelled together on their strange, disastrous honeymoon. It seemed so much longer. So much had happened. But she was glad he was going. She did not want him near when the baby came.

Business was slack – it had not been good even in full season. They had not made a loss, but they had not held the sustained success of the previous year. The extra hands in the workroom were laid off.

She was as restless as a queen cat before her time. She longed to be free of her pregnancy and back watching the front of the house, trying to find the cause for this small, disquieting recession. Business, her competitors assured here, was very good. Why then should Maison Leon find things a little slow?

She sought endlessly for a reason, going over the books and stock, checking the orders and the buying, poring over Ferdinand's sketches for the coming season. The falling-off was among the customers Ferdinand called the 'top brass'. Impeccable lineage and inherited riches. And there was an infiltration of an undesirable type of customer. Women with money to spend, expensive, kept women, the mistresses, not the wives. She did not want that kind of reputation for Maison Leon. The strong child kicked and moved, keeping her awake, as though it, too, was bored by its inactivity and longed to escape into the world. She wished Millicent were not away – Millicent always had her ear to the ground in the social scene. If there was a reason for the change, she would know.

She was eating alone in her boudoir, when Ferdinand knocked and came in, a graceful, thin figure, distinguished in his beautiful evening clothes, carrying his shining topper, the cloak about his shoulders showing a lining of ivory satin.

'Will you be wanting the landaulette, my dear?'

'No. I am not going out tonight.'

'You don't mind if I take it then?' He rang for Judson and told him that he would like the carriage right away.

'Do sit down and wait,' Margaret said. 'Can I offer you something? A Madeira? A hock and seltzer?'

As she rose to serve him from the sideboard, she saw the faint, quickly controlled look of disgust on his face. She saw also on the fine skin, beginning to wrinkle about his eyes, a faint touch of rouge. She passed him the glass and returned to her meal; it was set out on her desk, where she had had the clerk bring the ledgers for her go go through.

She sat down, took a sip of wine, then said, 'It was not a good Summer season. We just about broke even.'

He shrugged. 'It happens. It will return.'

'There is a clique of ladies, and important ones – not the greatest spenders, but by far the greatest names – who are not giving us their custom this year.'

'Do not worry, Margaret.' He glanced at his watch. 'I

just came in to ask about my trip tomorrow. I leave early. You have given me all the lists?'

'Yes. But – be careful. We must buy cautiously. The tailoring department particularly. It started so well. We are already down on the orders for the Autumn. Roy Brinkley tells me that Willis & Harrington have had an excellent season.'

'W & H are a store. Not in our class,' said Ferdinand loftily.

'Have you eaten?'

'I am dining out.'

'This sole *Dieppoise* is delicious. I eat so much nowadays.' She saw the curl of his lip, and said suddenly, 'Are you losing interest, Ferdi?'

He looked up sharply, sipping his cold spritzer.

'What do you mean?'

'Ferdi – don't be evasive. You *are* the centre of this business. I have to know.'

He smiled, but the clever, lazy eyes did not meet hers. 'For some time, Margaret, I have thought myself a fool to work in London. The South of France is opening up with a Winter season of great elegance. Nice, Monte Carlo, Cannes . . . and the smaller resorts of Beaulieu and Villefranche. Royalty and the rich, especially the rich Russians, are building there. The King of the Belgians has a huge villa at Cap Ferrat. Why don't we open up there in a small, exclusive way? I am beginning to feel the pressure here and the climate is mostly detestable. I could make pretty clothes for the sunshine, smart clothes for the casino? And no boot-licking, like these boring *grandes dames* demand. On the Riviera there are the great whores, the actresses, the Princesses, it is all sunshine and gambling, and flirting and pleasure-seeking. I think it would suit me.'

'And leave Hanover Street?'

'Oh, no. You could run this place alone – with perhaps a good, young designer. I would run the new place in France.' He selected a grape from a large purple bunch and ate it delicately.

'Capital?' she asked. 'You are not proposing to take capital out of Maison Leon for this new adventure – we cannot afford it now.'

'I would have to, although I have a friend who has just inherited a large fortune, and who would be prepared to back me.'

'Raoul de Montesque?'

He coloured a little. 'You remember? Of course. His father died. He is now very rich.'

'I understand. You want to leave me?'

'Margaret,' he took her hand. 'At first, it was fine. I did not begrudge you your love affair – or any love affair. But domesticity does not suit me. As we were – partners, and friends, yes. The child, as you said, will make us respectable – but I cannot live in a nursery atmosphere. Babies howl, and are ill and messy. They need attention – they dominate their surroundings. It is not for me.'

She felt heavy and resentful towards the child. She could not let Ferdinand go . . . not yet. He was becoming increasingly idle and extravagant, but when he got down to his drawing-board he was still the best designer in London.

'I promise you that the child will make no difference to you. By the time you come back from Paris it will be here. It will not be necessary for you even to see it. This isn't a little corner sweetshop, Ferdi. It has taken fifteen years of your life, and seven of mine. Last year we were the most respected and successful and sought-after business in London. We can't throw it away.' She picked up some drawings he had made of evening-dresses for the Winter season, the sleeves flared, enormous, diaphanous,

361

like butterfly wings. 'There is no one to touch you, and you know it. I have a feeling the next year will be crucial. Stay with me. We have been friends. I hope we still are. If you wish, in a few months' time, we can separate discreetly. I can find somewhere else to live. But stay until I'm in running order again, and until we find out why we are suffering these set-backs.'

He patted her hand reassuringly. 'Margaret, you are always so sensible. Be sure, I will make no plans until this business of yours is over.'

'Do you think it is Charmy?' she asked suddenly. 'Do you know what she is up to? You see her more than I do. Is she encouraging the wrong kind of customer? She has no sense of proportion – or propriety. All she thinks of is what she wants at any given minute – whether it is a dress or a man.'

His charming smile gave nothing away.

'You must not be censorious. Charmian has had a hard time. She deserves some fun. She is very young.'

'She is ten minutes younger than me.'

'It is difficult to believe. I must go. Don't think I am not grateful, Margaret. I admire you . . . I love you. I could not have done it without you. But I am older now, and would like to relax a little . . . I would like to do less work. I would like to live in the sunshine. I am nearing sixty, Margaret. Think it over.' He kissed her hand. 'I shall see you before I go in the morning.'

At nine o'clock Jany Leck came, stumping up the back stairs on her short legs, wrapped like a cocoon in her grey shawl, her old-fashioned bonnet perched up above her moony little face. She came every day. Margaret was too tired and too heavy to go round to Juniper Place now, so Lecky came to her. Besides, Florence, like Ferdinand, could not endure the sight of her heavy figure. Lecky brought the accounts and made her report.

362

'There's summat going on,' she declared, 'and I don't know what. She and that Lily have got their heads together. She keeps on about Charmy getting married. Seems she's got two strings to her bow. A Mr Allwood, and a millionaire she met out East. It's maybe nowt but a tale. And she and Lily are getting it from somewhere – the brandy. It's my opinion that Lily's getting to like a drop hersen.'

'Hah! You'd better send her round here. I'll stop that. I just couldn't stand scenes now.'

'I brought this. I thought you would want to know.'

She took out an old copy of the *Thornsby Evening Argus*, dated in May: '*To Mr and Mrs Henry Grimshaw, a son, Stephen Dyson.*'

So – Henry had his first son. As though in protest her own baby moved violently within her.

'I've heard it's none so good.'

'What do you mean?'

'That Amy that used to work at Hollingroyd Crescent. She writes sometimes. The baby's got summat wrong wi' its back. Doubtful if they'll rear it. Of course, there's nowt about that in t'papers.'

'Oh *Lecky*!' Margaret's face crumpled with pity. She could fly at Henry in anger, but she could not bear the world to hit him. 'To want a child so much for so long – it would have been better if it had not lived.'

'Now don't tek on,' Lecky said crossly. 'You've your own trouble to face and from t'look on you, it won't be long now.'

She was right – the labour started the following day, about midday, as though the baby, in obedience to Margaret's wishes, had waited until Ferdinand left.

She ordered the landaulette and collected Lecky from Juniper Place and drove round to the new smart lying-in home near Welbeck Street which had been started by a group of eminent gynaecologists.

The idea of a lady having her confinement away from home was a startling innovation. On being told of it, Margaret had seized on the chance – determined that neither the business nor Ferdinand should be embarrassed by her confinement. It was luxurious, and spotless, and in her pretty room she was attended by two rustlingly starched young nurses. Her specialist called to see her, and removed his frock coat and put on a white overall (like a grocer, weighing cheese, Lecky said) for the examination, and pronounced there was some time yet. The labour was long and protracted. The nurses, who had not taken to the short little Yorkshire woman being in constant attendance, were glad of her stubborn imperturbability as the time wore on and Margaret's spirit and endurance reached a low and despairing edge.

'The damned child has shoulders like a bull,' the sweating doctor muttered, and Margaret laughed in the midst of her agony, seeing a miniature Henry Grimshaw butting his way regardless into the world. The laughter seemed to release him because he came out with a slithering rush, purple, bruised, blubber-faced and howling; a baby weighing ten pounds; a boy.

'Yon's a big 'un,' Lecky said as she put him, clean and be-shawled, and now healthily pink, into Margaret's arms.

'Oh, God, how ugly he is!' she exclaimed. 'He looks like a prize fighter.'

'He's had a reight old fight getting here.'

But as the days passed, beauty emerged like blossom from the bud. The silvery-blond hair. The two vertical lines between the invisibly fair brows when he cried. The firm little nose. The ears flat and shell-like against his delicate skull. He was, or so the specialist said, the strongest, biggest and healthiest baby he had ever delivered. Margaret, who had had no particular feelings about him, was astounded at the helpless tenderness he aroused. The slatey-coloured eyes of birth began to turn a dark blue, and glared at her indignantly as he clutched at her breasts. She felt the power of him in her arms, as once she had felt the power of Henry within her body. She knew nothing about small babies – their primitive anarchy, their fierce demands, their uncontrollable protests. He was called Thomas Wykeham after his two grandfathers. She loved him with terror and with pride.

'Thomas Wykeham Leon doesn't sound right. Too foreign. Normanby or Jagger would have been better.'

'Or mebbe Grimshaw,' said Lecky with a prim little smile. 'I wornt born yesterday, Miss Maggy!'

Margaret felt her stomach beneath the blankets. Apart from a little tenderness it was reassuringly concave. Her small breasts had filled up quite alluringly.

She did not feel tired or languid; she felt light and free without the burden of Thomas's ten pounds. So she paid her bill and took him home to Hanover Street.

The alterations were finished on the nursery, including a cork-lined door to protect Ferdinand and the business premises from infantile yells. Tom had lungs of brass. He had two nurseries, a bathroom, a small kitchen and a bedroom for Lecky and a young girl from Thornsby Moors, a farmer's daughter, Bertha Lister, as nursery-maid. A cook-housekeeper was engaged at Juniper Place to look after Lady Normanby and Lily.

Lecky was in her element with a baby in her arms again. He was taken down the back stairs into the mews for his airings in the Park in his light, high-wheeled perambulator. Lecky was his slave, but Margaret was his mother, the source of life. The violet-blue Normanby eyes followed her about the room, the pink mouth opened to roar when she departed, and when she buttoned her bodice over her breast, and put him back in his cot, even the cork-lined door could not contain his yells.

Ferdinand, after a politely brief appearance at the christening at St George's, receiving congratulations on his fine son with a detached amusement, never went near the nursery. 'When it is a boy, my dear Margaret,' he said, 'I shall no doubt be delighted with him. But that squalling little monster is so far only a young animal.'

Margaret knew that Thomas would need a stronger hand than hers. Every week he grew bonnier, rosier, demanding more attention than she could possibly give him. He needed a father to control and guide him. He was so much Henry's son that it was almost laughable if it had not been so tragic that Henry, who had dreamed of such a boy, should be saddled with a fragile cripple to care for.

As the Autumn progressed towards Christmas and into the Spring of the New Year, the pattern of business continued. Ferdinand had bought beautiful materials in Paris, and produced some ravishing designs, and yet steadily, the good trade declined. Still she held out against accepting the custom of the high-class *demi-monde*. She looked at the blanks in the orderbook, and could not understand why this should happen. Ferdinand, to her surprise, did not seem unduly concerned.

She knew that if he took his capital out, if business continued to slack off, and she had to continue on her own, she would not be able to do so at their present standard. She did not want a small, second-rate business. She was proud of their establishment. She had got to the top and was going to stay there.

And then – Lady Lucaster cancelled her order. Such a thing had never happened, that a customer should do so without a word of explanation, when half the order had

366

already been cut out and was on the workroom tables being made.

'She will have to take or pay for the work we have started,' Ferdinand said.

'We want her back. We don't want to quarrel,' said Margaret. 'I'll go and see her.'

She dressed herself very carefully, wearing a new Autumn costume of dark cherry-red, a muff and toque of smooth dark sable, and took the carriage. When she presented her card, she had a moment of dread. What could she do if Lady Lucaster refused to see her? Nothing. But, they had liked and respected each other in the distant relationship of saleswoman and customer.

When the butler came down and said that Lady Lucaster could spare her a short while, she breathed a sigh of relief, and followed him up into the drawing-room overlooking the plane trees of Cavendish Square.

Lady Lucaster was sitting at her escritoire near the window. She had never been a fashionable customer. She was a rather old-fashioned country woman, more in the Queen's circle than the Prince of Wales', but she had daughters to launch and marry and it was on them she spent her money. For three successive seasons Ferdinand had created an illusion that her geese were swans, and three marriages had been the result. She swore by Maison Leon. What had shaken her faith in them?

She raised her lorgnette and regarded Margaret's slender figure in the dark red cloth, with the sleek black cap, *à la Russe*, on her bright hair. She did not rise, offer her hand or a seat, and Margaret stood inwardly simmering, outwardly calm, and waited.

'Ah, Mrs Leon – you have no doubt come about the cost of the garments ordered for my daughter, Lady Clare, that have already been put in hand. I quite see that, if work had already been started upon these, you will be out of pocket. I did not intend this to happen. If you will let me know the cost, you will of course be paid for what has been done, but I do not wish you to continue the order, or deliver any garments.'

'The work has been started upon a suit, a ball-dress, and an afternoon-dress. If you are displeased with them we shall not go ahead with the order. However, from a customer as valued as yourself, my lady, we did not expect such brusque discourtesy.'

'Indeed?'

'We will not accept payment. But we should like to know the reason for the cancellation.'

Lady Lucaster was silent.

'I will tell your ladyship, frankly, that we have noticed a falling-off in our better-class customers, and had many enquiries from people whom we cannot possibly accept. As though some – some whispering campaign is working against us.'

'Are you suggesting that I would be party to such a campaign?'

'No. But you must have a reason for cancelling. And if it is not the quality of the clothes or our workmanship, then what is it? We are fighting an invisible enemy.'

Lady Lucaster looked at the clear young face, the frank blue eyes, and relented. She had always liked young Madame Leon . . . she had liked the way she had not used her aristocratic connections in her trade. She had approved of the courteous manner which held no touch of servility. Like many impulsive people, after losing her temper she capitulated.

'Please sit down, Madame Leon,' she said.

'I would rather stand.'

'No. Please. Perhaps I have been over-hasty. But with girls to bring into society and my connection with Her

Majesty one cannot be too careful. But please to sit down.'

Margaret sat down on the edge of a chair and waited.

'My dear Madame Leon, I am sorry.' Her ladyship was calmly sympathetic. 'I know you have worked very hard, and have recently been confined. But I am afraid your invisible enemy is your sister, the notorious Mrs Chester.'

Margaret's eyes blazed.

'My sister is certainly Mrs Chester. She is the widow of Captain Bellamy Chester. I would be glad to know why you use such an offensive term when referring to her?'

'You have not hear the wild rumours that are circulating about her?'

'I have not.'

'Perhaps they are only rumours. But it is being said that your business is a place for immoral assignations.'

Margaret shot to her feet, her face deathly white. Lady Lucaster said quickly, 'Please . . . please sit down.' Margaret did not move. 'Very well. I must say I did not believe this, but rumour grows unpleasantly. It is being said that your sister is a courtesan and will accommodate any man who cares to pay. These reports are too absurd. People are malicious. But I know one thing – I am friendly with Lady Louisa Allwood – she was Lady Louisa Saville, and married Mr Allwood of the tea importing family. In *spite* of this we are still friends. She tells me that her eldest son met your sister on board the *Punjabi Queen* when he was returning from India, and that since then he has spent a small fortune upon her. He has provided her with a carriage and pair, a horse to ride in the Park, jewels, clothes, paid her gambling debts and for her entertaining – and according to my poor friend she entertains a great deal and the people at her gatherings are not the kind one could ever know.'

Margaret felt a fool. A carriage and pair? A riding

369

horse? Clothes other than those provided freely from Maison Leon? She had seen no signs of this extravagance. But she had been away, occupied with Tom, and she had not been round to see Charmian.

But Ferdinand must have known, and he had said nothing.

'At her last visit,' she said stiffly, 'Mrs Chester told my mother that Mr Allwood had made her an honourable proposal of marriage, and that this month she had been invited to stay with his parents at their country house.'

She was frozen with humiliation.

'I am afraid, my dear Madame Leon, your confidence has been misplaced. This is *not* true. Neither Lady Louisa nor Mr Allwood would allow your sister in their house, and if Kenneth should be mad enough to marry her, his father, a religious man whom my poor friend has so far kept in ignorance of the affair, would disinherit him, and never see him again. He is being trained to take over the very rich and important firm of Allwoods, and a woman like your sister has no part in Mr Allwood's plans.'

Margaret listened to the calm, measured tones. Lady Lucaster had no doubt plenty of experiences in dealing with pregnant or dishonest housemaids, and that was how she made her feel.

She drew in a deep breath.

'I will see my sister at once,' she said. 'I should be obliged if your ladyship will contradict any rumours referring to my business, these at least I can deny with complete confidence. With regard to the half-made gowns you have ordered, I will consider the order cancelled, and will not accept payment. Thank you for your frankness. Good day to you, Madame.'

She walked out quickly, terrified of her own feeling of outrage and fury and despair. If this were true – only partially true – Charmian had undermined all her hopes,

370

all her work over the past seven years. She told her coachman to drive to Charmian's apartment near Grosvenor Square, and the man hesitated, puzzled.

'Spencer Mansions, Madame? Don't you mean Mrs Chester's new address at Number Twelve, Park Street?'

For a moment Margaret could not recover herself. Park Street contained the most elegant new small mansions in London; she had no idea that Charmian had moved. Then she gave a little laugh, putting a kid gloved hand to her forehead. 'How silly of me. Of course . . . I am so used to the old address.'

'Yes, Ma'am.'

From the drawing-room windows Lady Lucaster watched her go, shaking her head. She remembered Richard and Florence Normanby when they had come to town from Yorkshire in the first glorious years of their marriage. The small house in Suffolk Street, the parties at Marlborough House. How beautiful they had been, how popular the two of them. Now Florence was that crazy scarecrow one saw driving in the Park, and God knows what had happened to Richard Normanby. A scoundrel. But how good-looking. And these two girls, one a dressmaker and one a whore. She sighed and shook her head and went back to her desk.

Charmian's pretty carriage drew up before Romano's at about three o'clock and the group of six young people came tumbling out of the restaurant, loud-voiced, laughing, flushed with champagne. It had all started when Charmian had met Captain Ralph Coleherne when she was riding that morning. She had known him briefly in Bombay, and he had been attentive and great fun. They had greeted each other like long-lost friends, and he had implored her to lunch with him.

'Not *tête-a-tête*, Ralph,' she protested. 'After all I *am* still in mourning.'

He had looked at her beautiful figure, tailored to perfection in her expensive riding habit, the bowler pulled down and veiled over her red-gold curls.

'You must be the prettiest widow in England,' he said. 'All right. I'll invite another two fellows and a couple of girls. There's safety in numbers.'

He had called for her at midday, and she had worn a velvet dress of such a dark purple it was almost black, but there was a flash of magenta in the rustling taffeta petticoats when she lifted her skirts to step into the carriage, and in the lining of her black fox muff. Diamonds, not jet, sparkled at her ears and wrists.

The other two men, whom they met at Romano's, proved to be two fellow officers, whom she did not know. The girls rather startled her. They were both ballet girls from the Empire Theatre, very young, radiantly beautiful, extremely well-dressed, and very common.

'Stone the crows, Mrs Chester,' said one of the girls, 'you mustn't half be rich to own a shay like this. Different to the Old Kent Road, eh!'

A remark which sent them all into fits of laughter. They dropped the girls at the Empire stage door where there was a late rehearsal call.

'Don't come to the show tonight, love,' the other cried. 'I'll fall orf me points after all that bubbly.'

The other two young men also left them at Leicester Square and Ralph and Charmian drove on to her new house in Park Street. The drive through the crisp Autumn air sobered Charmian up, and she knew she had again been very indiscreet.

This luncheon was not her worst indiscretion. Abderhazy had been across from Paris where he had opened up a branch of the family banking house. He had sought her out immediately.

He described the mansion on the Avenue Henri-Martin he had bought from an American railway millionaire. It had a ballroom and electric lifts, and a conservatory full of orchids, and humming birds, and in the basement an oriental pool, where the water was always warm and scented, and there were interesting mosaics copied from those in Pompeii.

'We have such delightful parties there,' he said. 'I really think it is time you came to live with me, Charmian.'

'But Philippe, I am *only* in the *marriage* market,' she said disingenuously. 'Are you proposing to me?'

He laughed, finding her enchanting, child and siren in one.

'Why not? I need a European hostess and in Europe one's hostess must be one's wife.'

'But Madame de Marcos told me once you had four wives.'

'Yes, in the eyes of God. The mothers of my children. Our religion does not permit them to bare their faces and entertain other men. In Moslem law the infidelity of a wife is punishable by death. But this would not apply to you, Charmian, you are a woman of pleasure, and I would not wish to curb your talents.'

She felt her cheeks go hot, for he had taught her many subtle sophistications, had shocked and excited her in the few days in which he had been in London. He was clever in the use of drugs that roused her to a fever pitch of abandonment.

'A French legal marriage – I am quite willing. You would never want, Charmian. I have so many sons I have no need for more children. You would have every possible luxury.'

'Why do you really want me?'

373

'We know so much about each other, Charmian. Too much.' His heavy, sleepy black eyes held a vague threat. He always roused a shiver of fear in her that was mysteriously close to pleasure. 'It is safer for both of us to have interests in common. The English law in India could still be tiresome, even though poor Bellamy is dead. We are both what is known as accessories after the fact. We did conceal a murder.'

'I don't know what you are talking about.'

'Ah, Charmian, you lie so delightfully. A Great asset. When I first met you, I knew that one day you would give me great pleasure. I think that day has arrived. I will not persecute you with jealousy. We can both be very useful to each other. No need to make up your mind, or worry your pretty head. I am settled in Paris now. Just come if you wish.'

Her recklessness was increasing – like a drug addiction. She should never have allowed Abderhazy to be her lover. She should never have had lunch today with Captain Coleherne and those common girls. Sometimes she wondered if she was a little mad. The streak of Normanby madness that could risk everything on the turn of a card, or a lifetime's reputation in a casual embrace.

The carriage stopped before the smart new house which Kenneth had taken for her. Ralph Coleherne handed her down and prepared to follow her into the house. She regarded him with wide-eyed indignation.

'Well, aren't you going to ask me in?'

'Captain Coleherne,' she exclaimed. 'It was a luncheon invitation. I *was* surprised at the company, but we are old friends and I did not want to embarrass you by leaving. There is no reason for you to presume so offensively.'

He burst out laughing.

'Well, you beat cock-fighting, Charmy. You can't pull

374

that one on me. Don't come the innocent, Charmy, everyone knows you're on the game.'

To her alarm she saw Margaret's landaulette turn the corner and drive up to the house. Her violet eyes filled with tears.

'I say, all right,' he protested. 'If I've made a mistake I'll grovel. But you seemed such a sport today with those little bits from the Empire, I thought . . .'

'Captain Coleherne, you have grievously wounded me. I cannot see you again.' She turned away in a rustle of taffeta and a breath of French scent. 'Oh, there is my sister, come to call. I beg of you to go. Good day.'

Coleherne strode off, red-faced, and Charmian approached Margaret with a tentative smile, at a loss what to say. Margaret did not give her a chance.

'Don't start lying and crying, Charmy. We had better go into this new house of yours which you so conveniently forgot to tell me about.'

She followed her sister upstairs into a charming boudoir. She saw the careless pile of bills in the escritoire, spilling on to the floor. She picked one up. A hundred pounds from a wine merchant in St James's.

'Who pays for all this?'

'Kenneth, of course,' Charmian said innocently. 'Who else?'

'Are you his mistress?'

'Oh, Maggy-Waggy, how could you *think* such a thing!'

'Very easily.'

'We are getting married shortly,' Charmian said, 'that is why he took the house and furnished it – he thought I might just as well move in as stay in that potty little apartment.'

'A somewhat unusual arrangement. You have no chaperone?'

'Maggy, I am – or was – a married woman.' Charmian

was indignant. 'Kenneth is very naughty about paying up. He leaves everything until the end of the month when he receives his allowance. He is coming tonight, and I am to dine with his parents, and then visit them in the country.'

'Lady Louisa Allwood has invited you?'

Charmian's eyes strayed away evasively.

'Of course!'

'Oh, don't lie, Charmy. I have been told by Lady Lucaster today that the Allwoods will not receive you and will never give their consent. That if he marries you his father will not have him in the firm.'

Charmian burst into tears. 'That horrid Lucaster woman is mad because she wanted Kenneth to marry one of her plain girls.'

'That may be so. That is your affair. Mine is that you have brought my business into bad repute. It is said that you have used it as a place of assignation, and you have certainly sent people to Hanover Street whom I could never serve as customers. Well, do what you like with your own life – but don't touch mine. We shall make no more clothes for you.' Charmian's mouth dropped open. She had forgotten the clothes. The beautiful, free clothes, designed especially for her. 'Whatever mischief you get into, I won't of course, abandon you,' Margaret said more gently, 'but your life in London threatens my business, my son and my husband.'

'Oh, don't talk to me about that Ferdi,' Charmian exclaimed pettishly. 'I know enough about that gentleman to put him in gaol at any time. That would teach you not to boss me about.'

Margaret had turned away, but the threat set off a spark. Her temper surged like a volcano, bursting, murderous, damped down for too many years. She strode over to Charmian, who quailed in terror, and took hold of her by her bronze-gold curls, and shook her until she screamed with fear.

'You stupid, selfish, brainless, little trollop!' she yelled.

'You've killed me,' Charmian cried. 'You've killed me!'

'I wish I could! Sometimes I really wish I could!'

Charmian picked up an expensive crystal vase and threw it; it fell into the hearth where it shattered into prismatic slivers. Her face was distorted, her eyes slits of hatred like those of a child in a tantrum.

'You think you're so clever, but you're still the same frigid little spinster. What do you know about life? One lover, who has left you with a child he doesn't want. Don't think that silly Kenneth Allwood is the only man who is crazy about me. There's a man in Paris, a rich merchant banker, a millionaire. A Baron. He wants to marry me too.'

'Well, you'd better marry him then,' said Margaret. 'You can drag yourself up and down the Haymarket at a shilling a time, for all I care. But you're not dragging me down with you. And don't you dare to show your face at Hanover Street again. I'm going back now, and I'm going to tell the staff that on *no* account are they to serve you with anything, nor any of the precious friends you send to me.'

Without another word she stormed out of the room, and out of the house.

Charmian dried her eyes. Sulked a little, cried a little, sent for a bottle of champagne and with a glass on the dressing-table began the evening ritual of dressing. The gown she chose was by Maison Leon, of diaphanous black lace, discreetly veiling her beautiful arms and shoulders; no diamonds, a small posy of white violets and *muguet* – suitable for meeting Lady Louisa Allwood.

But Kenneth did not come. Broke, threatened, bullied by his family, he once again ran away. Charmian waited until after ten, getting a little drunk, and then unable to face the evening alone, sent out the manservant to a nearby restaurant to buy a cold supper – oysters, pheasant, chicken *chaud-froid*, salads – and a girl scuttling round to Ralph Coleherne's with a note. Perhaps she had been a little short with him today. She did not want to quarrel with an old friend. Would he like to bring a few friends round for supper, and cards, and a little music? The answer came by return. He would be delighted.

He left her bed in the early hours and dressed, admiring her beautiful body relaxed in sleep, her hair tumbled among the silken cushions. He took five pounds out of his wallet and left it on the bedside table, before he went out into the cold Mayfair morning.

When Charmian found the money she was furious and humiliated. Did he think she was a tart? But she was afraid, too, prophesies whispering in her mind. 'You can drag yourself up and down Haymarket for a shilling a time, for all I care.' 'You will end up in the gutter unless someone cares for you,' Bellamy had often said. And Abderhazy, softly, 'You are a daughter of pleasure, Charmian, and will need protection to keep afloat – I should be delighted to be your – protector.'

'Protector' – it was what the street women called their pimps. But Charmian did not think of that – Abderhazy was so rich and had promised she would never want. She sent a wire to him in Paris, packed her clothes and jewels, made a quick deal on the carriage and pair for ready money, and left for Paris, leaving Kenneth Allwood, in whose name everything had been acquired, to face the debts. His family settled gratefully.

The following month, in an obscure surburban *Mairie*, Charmian became Baroness Philippe Abderhazy.

Margaret read the announcement in the *Morning Telegraph*. There was a paragraph about Abderhazy, the

378

distinguished Persian merchant banker with branches in Bombay and Shanghai and now in Paris. The title was Hungarian; the Baron had often advised the Imperial family about finances. He was planning to settle in France and had bought a mansion on the Avenue Henri-Martin. He had a fine string of race-horses training at Chantilly. He kept a superb ocean-going yacht in Nice.

Margaret did not know whether to laugh or cry. She would have to break the news to her mother, who, with Lily's help, would build it into a triumphant fantasy.

She felt bereft, as though her lovely wayward twin had died and she would never see her again, for despite everything, she had a deep affection for Charmian. But she also felt relieved as at the vanquishing of an enemy.

Chapter Fourteen

Charmian's departure from London and much-publicized marriage had quelled the rumours, but it had been hard going to repair the harm. But the eighteen-nineties, the *fin de siècle*, had produced a brilliantly gay society of which the Prince of Wales was the leader, the old Queen being virtually retired from public life, and under his influence acceptance broadened to include the wealthy middle class, the arts and the theatre. Society was invaded by a new generation of women, with ideas of their own and appreciation of originality and taste, and no dressmaker in London could compete with Maison Leon in this respect. Business came back, slowly at first, and then with a rush so unprecedented that Margaret and Ferdinand thought of moving so that the whole of Hanover Street could be used for the business.

It was Thomas Wykeham Leon's third birthday, and he was not the sort of child to bring up on business premises – unless, perhaps the business was that of a blacksmith or a livery stable. Lecky brought him to Margaret's bedroom first thing in the morning as she sat up in her pale blue satin jacket, drinking her tea, and her heart filled with pride and apprehension as she looked at him. Her beloved, her joy, her burden and her tyrant, broad and sturdy, straddled confidently on his solid little legs, his head a mop of pale yellow silken curls. A picture-book baby, whom sentimental ladies in the Park cooed over, delicious in his cream silk smock. But a pugnacious, strong-willed boy was already emerging from the charming rosiness of babyhood.

Margaret adored and feared him. But he looked so lovely standing there, bathed and powdered, brushed and combed to shining perfection by Lecky, that she held out her arms and he dropped Lecky's hand and hurled himself on to the bed, sending her cup flying out of her hands on to the floor.

'Careful!' she cried. 'Be careful Tom!' Lecky removed the tray and collected the debris, and Margaret drew him into her arms, where for a moment he lay content, nestling into her, before wriggling down and running about the room.

He was beginning to talk fluently, learning new words every day. He could charm if he wanted to and storm to get his own way, and was rapidly learning his power in the world of women. He called Ferdinand 'Papa' but there was no filial or paternal feeling between them. Tom had no doubt who had authority over him, and it was not Ferdinand.

Bertha Lister, the strong young nursery-maid who had been engaged to help Lecky, could manage him. He seemed to regard her as a much-loved gaoler when she picked him up and strapped him into his perambulator or locked the gate leading from his attic kingdom down into the scented business premises below.

'Sit still, sit still!' implored Margaret, 'Heavens, it's like having a large puppy on the bed.'

'Tom want egg.'

'Well, Tom sit still then.'

The two-line track cut into the smooth white forehead as he scowled with the effort to keep still, watching while Margaret cut strips of buttered toast, and dipped them in her breakfast egg, and fed them to him. He opened his mouth obediently and ate all her egg.

'Well?'

'Thank you, Mama.'

She drew him against her again, and at once his strong arms went round her neck, and he smothered her with kisses. She held him away.

'Happy birthday Thomas, my darling.'

'Birf-day?' he said uncomprehendingly. 'What's birf-day?'

'It's when you have presents. The day you were born.'

'Present for Tom?' he said eagerly.

'Yes, come . . .' She sprang out of bed, put on her slippers and gown, and took him back up the stairs to the nursery floor. He stumped up reluctantly. He was always trying to get down into the offices and show rooms, where he could create mayhem, his eager little hands reaching for every brightly-coloured object. Once, in the stock-room, he had tipped out the trays of silk bobbins and sent them rolling across the floor. Since then a sturdy gate kept him in his own premises. But he hated it. He hated being tied, shut-in, restricted.

Margaret led him through into the day nursery where the presents had been brought in while he was downstairs. A big rocking-horse from her, and from the staff a large stuffed fluffy dog on wheels.

Lecky and Bertha stood smiling.

'Well, do you like Mama's present?'

'For Tom?'

'Of course, my darling, they're for you.'

He went forward slowly, and pushed the fluffy dog, which ran along on its wheels, his eyes big and wondering, then he touched the painted horse which dipped on its rockers, hit it with his open hand so that it rocked back, then suddenly he turned and went over to Lecky and buried his head in her apron.

'Not doggy,' he said miserably. 'Not horsey.'

The three women looked at each other helplessly.

'Folk in the park have dogs and he plays with them.

382

He needs a real dog,' said young Bertha, red with the effrontery of speaking up.

'We can't have a dog *here*, barking, and getting down into the salon.'

'Martin gives him rides on t'carriage pair down in t'mews,' Bertha went on stoutly, 'and says he sits as firm as a man.'

'He is too young to have a pony.'

Bertha's honest round face went poppy-red, and she burst out, 'It's no life for a real lad like him. Mrs Leon. Not here. He needs other children, and real animals. He's nearly out of being a baby . . . he's a real spunky little lad.'

'That's enough. Bertha,' Margaret said sharply. But she knew the girl was right.

She had invited six small children that afternoon and there would be a nursery tea, with jellies and cakes and crackers, and a Punch and Judy man. It would be his first birthday party, although he had attended other children's recently, and they had invariably ended in fights and tears. The children were all too young to understand the adult politeness that forbids the snatching of attractive things from their owners, and Tom snatched quicker, hung on more doggedly, and pushed harder than all the others of his age. He could be gentle and affectionate with the little babies, but he met aggression with aggression, and he was so strong. If older children or adults intervened he would kick and scream with rage, and bite like a terrier.

Margaret went downstairs to dress for the salon. Ferdinand was not yet up – he had not returned until the early hours of the morning, and she knew he would not put in an appearance until the afternoon. There was an important customer coming, an American lady of vast wealth, who had brought her beautiful daughter over for the season. The beautiful daughter was in pursuit of a titled husband, and a small fortune was to be spent on her clothes. Margaret rang for Ferdinand's valet:

'Would you remind Mr Leon that Mrs and Miss Van Hagen will be here this morning, and that he has not yet finished the sketches to show them.'

He would be down in about an hour, a little pale and irritable. He was a night-bird, hating the early light of day.

Ferdinand went out just as much, and stayed out later, and he was drinking more. His work was suffering. He took so little interest in the actual running of the business these days, that she might be the sole proprietor. He was too talented to do bad work, but what he did was not comparable with his brilliant creations of three years ago.

She made her tour of the showrooms and workrooms, and then went up to the office. It was a day when travellers called and she saw them all herself now. She took the finished and half-finished sketches for Miss Van Hagen, and the colour charts from Ferdinand's desk, to see if they had the necessary materials in stock or whether she would have to order them from the salesmen.

She had a clerk of her own now, a Mr Callow. Middle-aged and balding he was certainly no temptation to Ferdinand.

Ferdinand came in shortly afterwards, wearing the pale grey velvet jacket he wore for showroom interviews, with a pink carnation in the buttonhole. He looked as he always did, charming, world-weary, debonair.

Callow knocked, and put his head round the door.

'Mrs and Miss Van Hagen are here,' he said, 'and have you read your *Morning Post* today, Madame?'

'Not yet.'

'The engagement has been announced between Miss Van Hagen and Viscount Malvern.'

'Has it by Jove!' Ferdinand and Margaret's eyes met with complete understanding. Such a wedding would be the fashion event of the year. A triumph to the house which secured the order. 'In that case I think we had better see the Van Hagens together, Margaret. And, Callow, send round to Florestan's for some flowers for Miss Van Hagen. Nothing enormous – they know what I like – a few very choice, perfect blooms. Bring them back here immediately.' He held out his arm to his wife and the old rapport, positive as an electric current, flowed between them. 'Come, my dear, let's see about this wedding.'

They spent the whole morning with the Van Hagens, ate a hurried luncheon together, and then he went to the City to look for brocade for the wedding dress. Before he left he gave her a small parcel – a present for Tom. 'For your little barbarian,' he said. 'Something charming for him to break to pieces.'

'It is kind of you, Ferdi, to remember.'

She worked until three o'clock, when the manservant came in to say the first of the party guests had arrived. She rose hastily, her mind full of the new Van Hagen wedding. It would not end there. Once it was known who was making the trousseau, a flock of lady guests would want gowns.

A children's party was the last thing she needed. But she went up to the apartment to greet Tom's guests who were coming up the private stairway to the apartment.

The guests were the children of smart young mothers, the West End shop wives, a little over-refined, none of them forgetting that whatever Margaret was now, she had been a Miss Normanby. It went quite well – chiefly because it was Tom's birthday, and the gifts were for him, and as usual when given something he examined it very carefully, and if he liked it refused to be parted from it, and if he did not handed it immediately to another child, saying imperiously, 'You have, Tom not like,' which was generous, if not tactful. Tea went without too many squalls, the Punch and Judy man was an enormous success, although Tom insisted on having Dog Toby, a shivering little terrier, in his arms during the whole performance. Now he lay on the floor, his arms round the seedy little terrier, his face flushed as he talked to it, his white silk smock stained with the strawberry jelly with which he had insisted on feeding it. 'Not like,' he said reproachfully to Lecky, 'Lecky. Doggy not like.'

'Nay, love. Dogs don't like jelly.'

'What dogs like?'

'Happen he'd like some water.'

'Water!' ordered Tom, pulling the dog along by his red-and-white frill in thedirection of the nursery stairs and the bathroom, to be forestalled by Bertha, who hurriedly fetched a bowl of water, which the over-heated little animal lapped noisily.

'Dog like!' said Tom triumphantly. 'Tom have dog?'

It was no use explaining that Toby was a trained show dog, and therefore not for sale. When the Punch and Judy man carted him off with his set-up, Tom howled dismally. The party broke up, the children were ushered away, and Tom, still giving vent to his frustration was carried off upstairs.

Margaret went to say goodnight to him and took up Ferdinand's gift. It was a charming little golden brooch with his name, Thomas, set in pearls and tiny rose-diamonds. Tom took it in hs strong, co-ordinated little fingers.

'It's from Papa,' said Margaret.

'What for?' asked Tom.

'To pin your bib,' she said. He looked at it scowling, and threw it on the floor. 'Tom wants real dog,' he said.

She put the pin back in its expensive case.

Bertha was clearing away the baby bath from before the nursery fire.

'Bertha, you live on a farm?'

'Yes, Ma'am, up in the moors beyond Danesfell. Dad's one o' Mrs Hengrave's tenants.'

'And you've got small brothers?'

'Aye, aye, a pack on 'em. The littlest is just about Master Tom's age.'

'And there are animals about – dogs, cats? What do you farm?'

'Sheep, mostly, Ma'am, on t'moors, though we have some dairy cows and chickens, and down the vale Dad has wheat and Winter feed and suchlike.'

'Bertha, do you think your mother would let you take Master Tom home, say for a month, soon, before the bad weather sets in? It would give Lecky a rest, and I'm going to be very busy. I think he'd like it.'

The girl's fresh face lit with pleasure.

'I reckon he'd love it, Ma'am, and I'll be bound Mother would love to have him.'

'Well, write and ask her . . . ask her how much she will charge . . .'

'Oh, she won't bother wi' that . . .'

'Nonsense. I shall insist. Please write immediately, will you?'

She went downstairs. Ferdinand had brought back patterns from the City wholesalers, a chalk-white brocade for the wedding gown, woven with lilies and roses, with a silver thread that caught the light. He was full of ideas for his Winter bride – the whole order would bring in at least a thousand pounds, perhaps more. It would put them right back where they deserved to be. At the top. They needed time, time to confer and plan, with no distractions to break their concentration. She hardened her heart and dispatched Tom to Yorkshire in the care of Bertha Lister, with instructions to appeal to Mrs Hengrave at Danesfell if any problems arose.

She felt as though her heart would break when the train went out, but she could not deny the overwhelming feeling of freedom as she drove back to Hanover Street. The little barbarian was no longer in command. All her attention and energy was released for her work. It was exciting.

That night, eating a sent-in meal from Verrey's, in the office, with the chief cutter, the embroideress, the master tailor and Ferdinand, planning their campaign, she met her husband's eyes and they burst out laughing. It was like it had been in the beginning when they had been close friends and workmates. Her tiredness had left her. She was no longer split in two. She was doing her real work which she loved, which she had trained for, and knew from bottom up; she was not eating her heart out feeling her inadequacy to deal with an adored three-year-old tyrant.

The months flew past, the wedding attracted so many customers they had to close their books until it was over. The day was fixed late in November so the young couple could go to New York for the Christmas season. Margaret and Ferdinand, in their element, worked like the brilliant team they could be at best.

Bertha's letters from Thornsby Moor were enthusiastic. Tom had cried a little while when the train went out, but had been so fascinated by it that he soon forgot. At the Listers' farm he was really happy, had taken to her brothers and sisters, loved the animals, and Mrs Hengrave dropped in every day to see him. Madame was not to worry.

* * *

It was ten o'clock one night in late October, Ferdinand had gone out and Margaret was still in the office when there was a ring at the doorbell, and the young housemaid from Juniper Place was shown in, breathless and in tears. Margaret rose apprehensively.

'Oh, Madame,' she gasped, 'Miss Lily says will you please come round. And vould Miss Leck come too. There's been terrible scenes, Ma'am, and her ladyship is dying . . .'

'*Dying!*' Margaret repeated incredulously. Florence had been 'dying' as long as she could remember. 'Is my mother really ill?'

'It's her heart the doctor says. The shock was too great.'

'*Shock?*'

'Oh, yes, Madame . . . her husband came – this evening. Sir Richard, from America. We didn't rightly believe in him, Ma'am, you know how my lady makes up stories, but he's here – about an hour ago, and ran straight up to see her.'

'Why didn't you send for me at once?'

'It is *almost* at once, Ma'am,' the girl sobbed. 'With her ladyship taking ill, and running round to Portman Square for the doctor, I'm nearly dead myself.'

'Is he still there?'

'The doctor? Oh yes, Ma'am.'

'No – Sir Richard?'

'Yes, Ma'am.'

'Right,' said Margaret. She rang the bell and ordered the carriage round. 'Go upstairs and tell Lecky, tell her to put on her bonnet and shawl and to bring a bottle of brandy. We'll come right away. Take a cab back.'

In the carriage on the way to Juniper Place she put out her hand, and Lecky took it between her two hard little paws.

389

'Lecky, I never dreamed he would come. I never really believed in him.' She began to laugh, shakily. 'Do you think he's found gold at last?'

'If he's found it, he'll keep it for hissen,' Lecky said tersely. 'And whatever he's come for, it'll be no good. He's a bad penny, that one, though he's your Pa.'

She remembered the broken wreck of her beautiful young lady on the bridal night, and the debts and duns, the lies and the ladies.

But Florence was really dying. Her heart and lungs, weakened by emphysema, were failing under the shock when reality had walked in upon her that evening after twenty-three years, a reality that neither hysterics nor brandy nor laudanum nor fantasy nor romantic fiction could dissolve. When Margaret arrived she was lying white and motionless, her breath coming with difficulty, her eyes sunk into dark hollows, her lips blue. The doctor had sent for a professional nurse. He told Margaret to be prepared, as he did not think her mother would last the night.

'But – she's not old – she's only fifty.'

'She is old,' he said. 'She has made herself old. No air, no exercise, lying here on the sofa, hardly eating, and, let us be frank, Mrs Leon, an addiction to both brandy and laudanum since girlhood. Oh, don't blame yourself . . .' he said quickly, seeing the distress in her eyes. 'She is lucky to have had a daughter who protected her and surrounded her with every comfort and luxury. Without you she would have been in the madhouse years ago. Poor woman.' He looked at the thin shell of worn-out beauty lying among the lacy frills of her pillows, the thin grey hair, still with a suspicion of its once luxuriant curl, spread out on the pillow. 'I will call in the morning, or come back during the night if I am sent for. I bid you goodnight.'

390

Margaret and Lecky stood on each side of the bed, looking down helplessly. Lily, broken with horror, was in the kitchen, weeping. The uniformed nurse, professionally calm, witness of so many death-beds, sat knitting by the fire.

Florence stirred, opened her eyes, looked about her in terror, saw Lecky's familiar moon-face looking down, and lifted her arms, relief flooding her ravaged face.

'Lecky, oh Lecky, don't let that man come near me. Don't, Lecky, I can't bear it . . . I can't bear it. I don't know him. It's not Richard. He's pretending to be Richard.'

Lecky took off her bonnet and sat down by the bed, drawing the fragile grey head down against her breast.

'There, love, it's all right. You've had a dream. Lecky will stay here. You go back to sleep.'

'That awful old man. Saying he was my Richard. He said dreadful things to me. He said . . .'

'All right, all right . . . rest, my love.'

'Lecky, stay with me. Give me my drops?' Lecky glanced towards the nurse who shrugged, and nodded. 'You stay with me, Lecky. I don't want anyone else . . .'

Lecky measured out the pain-killer and gave it to her as she had done for over thirty years. She settled Florence on her pillows, took a low seat and sat holding her hand. She looked up at Margaret and said, 'It's all right, love. I won't leave her.'

So Jany Leck sat there until the small hours, holding the worn-out shell of the petted, indulged, spoiled young mistress whom she had so devotedly served. She remembered nights long ago, keeping the lamp burning, the satin quilted bed warmed, the fire bright in the grate, the fine be-ribboned nightdress and lacy nightcap laid out, the clean brushes for the nightly ritual of grooming her golden hair, waiting and listening until the small hours for the sound of the carriage toiling up the moorland road bringing Florence Jagger home from the party or dance in her velvet cloak lined with white fur, her golden curls shining, her huge blue eyes the colour of sapphires, the most beautiful face she had ever seen; and she remembered how she had loved her.

Margaret went downstairs to the kitchen. The household was in the flutter of the anxiety serious illness brings. The housekeeper still up and awake, and the two young housemaids dropping with sleep.

Lily sat huddled and weeping in a chair by the fire. When she saw Margaret, she ran across to her, no longer the prissy, over-genteel lady's companion, but the raw ignorant girl Margaret had brought from Thornsby.

'Oh, Madame, oh Miss Margaret, I never thought it could be like this. All she had told me about him, I thought it was all true.'

'Lily, don't cry. You are very silly, but you are very kind. You have made my mother happy these past years in a way I never could. Don't worry. I'll look after you – now go to bed . . . *and* you two girls. Just a word with you, Mrs Smithers, and then no doubt you too will be glad to get to your bed.'

'I will, indeed, Mrs Leon.'

'Well first just tell me what happened?'

'It was all so unexpected, Madame. About nine there was a knock on the door. Her ladyship had had her meal, and Lily had got her ready for bed, and was reading to her in the boudoir, as she always did. The girl went to the door, and there was this gentleman.' She spread bewildered hands, confused. 'He was shabby, but when he spoke you could tell he *was* a gentleman. Said he was Sir Richard Normanby and he wanted to see his wife. Then he pushed past the girl and went up the stairs calling, "Flo, I'm here! I'm back . . ." He went straight in to her room and she just stared at him, and he stared back as though neither of them could believe what they saw. I think he was drunk because he was unsteady. He went to kiss her and she started on to scream as though she was being murdered. He said, "Christ, Flo, you can still make a bloody scene, worse than any woman I ever knew." Then he said, "What in God's name did you expect? We're both older." But she wouldn't stop and he got angry and called her names – old, scrawny, mad – I told him to leave, but then she fell down with her lips going blue, and I think that frightened him, because he went downstairs, and we sent for the doctor, and then for you, Mrs Leon.'

'Thank you, Mrs Smithers. And where is this gentleman?'

'In the parlour, Ma'm. I didn't know what to do. I didn't like to call a constable in case of more trouble. I just let him stay.'

'All right, Mrs Smithers. You may go to bed. Miss Leck and I will watch with the nurse. He must not be here when my mother awakens.'

She went into the parlour and regarded her father. Sir Richard Normanby, Bart. Asleep, breathing stertorously, his mouth open, ageing, shabby, there was barely a shadow of his once superlative good looks. His teeth were beginning to discolour with tobacco, the once profuse chestnut curls grizzled, dyed and sparse about his balding head.

She noted the rubbed cuff edges, the pathetic patches on the soles of his upturned shoes, the grubby, dashing wideawake hat of the American Westerner, with a greasy sweat-stain round the ribbon-band.

There was a decanter and a glass beside him, and the smell of brandy. He had obviously been helping himself.

'Sir Richard Normanby,' she said loudly, and he woke,

bewildered, bleary-eyed, recollected where he was, struggled to his feet, and bowed, the old charm switching on automatically because there was a woman to deal with. A tall, slim young woman, quietly and beautifully dressed, with direct blue eyes, and the brilliant red-gold hair that ran in his mother's family. She said coolly, 'Forgive me. I am Mrs Leon, who was Margaret Normanby. We have not met for many years. I presume you are my father. Have you anything to prove this?'

He had thought to deal with a young woman distraught with grief, disconcerted with shock. He brought out a passport and some documents from the shipping company. Margaret glanced through them, and handed them back.

'Well, these seem in order. Why are you here?'

'You're a damned cool little customer for such a pretty girl,' he said, and held out his arms. 'Margaret. Let's be friends . . . I am your father.'

She moved adroitly away, wanting to laugh at his effrontery, wanting also to cry.

'My mother is ill, perhaps dying. The shock has been too much for her. My carriage is at the door.' She opened her bag, and took out some money. 'Will you ask the driver to take you to a hotel for the night. And tomorrow come and see me at Maison Leon, Hanover Street. Ask for me personally.'

His eyes narrowed with an edgy defiance.

'I came back because your mother asked me to come.'

'My mother has lived in dreams. She did not really think that you would come. Now will you please leave, and I will see you tomorrow.'

He looked at her belligerently, then at the money in his hand. Ten golden guineas. His spirits rose; he picked up his hat and at the door turned and looked at Margaret, and drawled, '*Now* I remember. You run a shop. Your mother wrote that you'd married a dress maker.'

He swaggered out of the room. She thought of the wreckage this man had caused. The death of her grandfather, the breaking of Henry Grimshaw's young heart, the burden on her own aspiring young life, the shiftless, conscience-lessness of Charmian's selfishness, the thankless life service Lecky had given to his deserted wife. This old clown, this old trickster, with his worn-out shoes, and insolent manner. This was the reality behind the legend of the beautiful, wicked, dashing, irresisitible Sir Richard Normanby. This was the dream her mother had nurtured through all these wasted years.

It was three o'clock. Margaret, stretched out in her mother's boudoir, had dropped into an exhausted sleep when the nurse shook her awake. She sprang up, her heart beating in alarm.

'She's gone, Mrs Leon. I think you'd better take Miss Leck back with you. She's very tired.'

'Of course.'

She went into the bedroom and the nurse covered Florence with a fine linen sheet, edged with monogrammed lace, a relic of the once-grand days in Suffolk Street.

The tears streamed down Lecky's little apple-face, unwrinkled, and rosy like that of a stuffed doll. Margaret could not bear to see her cry. Everyone else had cried on her shoulder and in her lap, but Lecky herself had not cried. Like a sturdy little tree in the midst of them, she was the one they had all leaned upon for support.

'Don't,' implored Margaret. 'Don't cry. Let her go. You cannot help her any more.'

'When I first came to work for her at Cliffs Edge, she were sixteen, and as far as I knew, I were fifteen. Never

395

knew my age or my real name. It were my first job. Kitchen-maid – then she made me *her* maid, because I could sew and iron and wash . . .'

On the bedside table was an exquisite old-fashioned night-cap of muslin and lace, threaded with lavender ribbon. 'I got this up for her only yesterday.'

'Come, Lecky. Let's go home. I need you, and Tom needs you now.'

Lecky went on as though she had not heard.

'They sent for me from the kitchen at Cliffs Edge, up to her room. She was just home from school. I'd never seen nowt like it. All satin and white furniture, and scent-bottles, and pillows with lace. After the Institute it were like heaven – then when I saw her there with her golden curls, and blue eyes, as lovely as an angel, and she asked me to be her own maid, and look after her, I thought I was in heaven.' She wiped her eyes. 'She worn't an angel, though. She was just a girl and silly at that, spoiled and selfish. We were all so mad on her, Tom Jagger and his Missus, and me, and your Henry Grimshaw, who was but a lad then – we all forgot everyone has to grow up. She never did . . . that was what it was all about. She never grew up. Fairy stories. It were all fairy stories.'

Margaret helped her to her feet, tied on her bonnet, wrapped her in her big grey shawl.

'Come along, Lecky, let's go home.'

'He finished her – Sir Richard. She'd no more idea of what it was to have a man than a baby, and he took her at last like a street girl. She was never right again. Always pretending. He spent all her money, ruined her father, gambled everything away, and then left her. And now he's killed her. Like he'd shoot a partridge.'

'Lecky, come home . . . come home to us . . . it's all over now. We tried, you and I, God knows, but we can't do any more.'

The carriage had returned. The gentleman, the coachman said, had asked to be put down in Piccadilly. He said he would find himself a hotel. On the way home, Lecky asked suddenly, 'Where'll you put her? Where will she be buried?'

'I thought I would ask Mrs Hengrave if she could be buried at Danesfell Abbey. After all, she set great store in being Lady Normanby.'

'Aye,' said Lecky. 'Aye. She'd have liked that.'

Sir Richard arrived at Hanover Street next morning. He was shaved and barbered and had acquired fresh linen and a new hat. He strolled into Margaret's office, where she sat at her big desk. She was wearing a simply-cut dress of black velvet with a high Alexandra collar, edged with white. She indicated a chair opposite, and he sat down.

'You would like some coffee, Sir Richard?'

'So you are not going to call me Papa?'

'I see no reason,' she said evenly. 'Coffee?'

'Something a little stronger, perhaps.'

'Whisky? Scotch or Irish. Bourbon?'

'Bourbon, please.'

She rang and gave the manservant the order.

Sir Richard leaned back and looked around at the large, light, efficient room with its files and ledgers, the big desk, and the five-foot-high iron safe. Sketches of gowns and suits lined the walls, and signed photographs of distinguished customers.

'Gad,' he said admiringly, 'I'd no idea women's frills and fancies were such a business. You have certainly done very well for yourself, Maggy.'

The uniformed manservant entered bearing a tray with a decanter of whisky and coffee. Sir Richard poured himself a glass.

'Of course, my father would have turned in his grave to think of his grand-daughter in trade, and married to a frock-maker. How does *my* mother take it?'

'My Grandmother Normanby died last year. She was always kind and helpful to both my sister and myself. You didn't know?'

'No.' A fleeting sadness touched him and vanished. The sensible proud Scottish mother was a figment of the past. 'And Charmian? The little, pretty one? I have read she married well.'

'Her second husband is very rich. She does not live in England.'

'Ah, disappointing.' Then he brightened and spoke with smiling condescension, 'I'm glad you've both done well. I learned to appreciate the power of commerce in America. I don't despise it. Not at all. Industry deserves to be rewarded.'

'Thank you.'

The direct blue eyes that reminded him of his dead and despised father-in-law, old Thomas Jagger, regarded him calmly. He sought a way to penetrate her armour, one could always get round a woman in the end.

'Margaret, please believe me, I would never have dreamed of visiting your mother had I known how ill and deranged she was. Her letters were perfectly sensible.'

'You thought so? When she wrote as though you were both still in your twenties?'

'How was I to know she had altered?'

'Had she?' Margaret said drily. 'I cannot remember her being any different. She had lost her grip on reality when you left. Perhaps before that.'

'Still, I blame myself, Margaret.' He made a little gesture, his smile was frank and appealing, she guessed it had once broken many hearts. 'You behold your old father. A failure in everything. They gave me a rough time in the States – fleeced me of everything. Then I remembered you had guaranteed my passage, and came away – ran away, if you like – penniless, to throw myself on your mother's charity and forgiveness.'

Margaret said nothing.

The bloodshot eyes glanced at her in the same evasive way in which Charmian glanced when she was being particularly devious.

'Your mother left a Will?' he asked.

'No.'

'Then I shall at least have whatever small property she possessed.'

'She had no property.'

'The house?' he said indignantly. 'The old woman, her mother, left some sort of pittance and a house in Thornsby.'

'She left them to *me*,' said Margaret. 'The house in Juniper Place is my property. Your mother left what little she had left to your brother George who is now serving abroad.'

'Personal possessions?' he insisted. 'Jewellery?'

'She had jewels – from her father, from the Normanby family, and I believe you, although there is no record of you ever paying for them. Unfortunately, you either stole, sold or pawned them before you left for America. She has had no jewels since. There are her clothes – quite exquisite. Twenty to twenty-five years out of date. We would like to keep them here, as – well, a sort of reference. A museum. But these were her personal property, so you are welcome to them. A dealer might give you two pounds for the lot.'

'But I have rights, surely – *legal* rights? You cannot leave me to starve?'

'I have not earned my living, run this business and supported my mother and sister without being very careful of *my* legal rights,' Margaret said smoothly. 'I have had the best advice in everything I have touched. My property and investments have all been secured to me. When I married, my husband agreed to waive all legal rights save that of his fair share in the business and the profits. You see, I had no father to protect my interests, so I had to protect myself. But if you wish to take action, do so by all means.'

Richard's face went an angry red. He had never been spoken to like this by a woman in his life.

'A daughter,' he almost yelled, 'has a duty to her parents.'

For the first time, Margaret smiled.

'There, I agree. A parent, also, has a duty towards his – or her – children, which neither you, nor my poor mother seemed to recognize. However, they say blood is thicker than water – although water is at least cold, clean and honest. I have decided I will allow you two hundred pounds a year.'

'It's a pittance!' he said furiously.

'I assure you many of my people here would think themselves fortunate to command such a salary. And would keep themselves very respectably on it.'

'It is an income for a counter-jumper, not a gentleman.'

'Well, that I cannot judge. I have worked in the counter-jumping trade all my life.' Her hands were steady, her eyes cold. She moved some papers on the desk. 'I have drafted a letter to my bank. The money will be paid into an account for you in twelve monthly instalments, so that you can collect it.' She waited, looking at his now almost empurpled visage. 'You are at liberty to refuse. It is all I am prepared to give you. You are not yet sixty. Presumably, in the United States, you found some means of subsistence during the past twenty years? Until Mother misguidedly sent you money? There

400

is no reason why you should not procure some employment. If I allow you this, you can live in simple comfort. It is entirely up to you. I am *not* going to make a home for you. Neither will I ever settle your debts. If you gamble this money away instead of using it as an income for your comfort, that is your business. I shall not come to your rescue. Take it or leave it.' She passed the documents across the desk. Richard glared into her imperturbable face, then angrily signed, shoved it rudely back to her.

'Have you no feelings?' he demanded.

'Not for you.'

She drew the paper across to her, and put a beautiful heavy glass paperweight, full of spirals of azure, crimson and blue, on top of it, her small, clever hands resting on the glass globe.

'There is one request I have to make,' she said. 'Not for myself, but for my mother. I was going to make this income conditional on your agreeing to my request, but I decided that would be ungenerous. The income is yours, whatever you do. But I would be grateful if you would come to my mother's funeral. She told so many people so many romantic lies about you. If you were there it would make her foolish illusions credible and uphold her dignity.'

'Where is this funeral?'

'In three days time at the Parish Church on the Danesfell Abbey estate; Mrs Hengrave has telegraphed her permission.'

'Damn her impudence,' he roared. 'What right has she to give or withhold her permission?'

'The right of ownership,' said Margaret. 'Mr Hengrave left her the entire estate.'

He put his face into his hands and groaned. The great house of Danesfell Abbey, the hundreds of acres of land, the farms and cottages and villages, the mines at North Fell, falling derelict in his time, now with new pit-heads, newly-opened seams, working full-time. It could have been his. He looked up, and met his daughter's eyes, as calm and impassive as any opponent he had ever met across a poker table.

'I cannot *make* you come,' she said. 'I hope you will do this one last kindness to her. I will give you the money for your journey to Danesfell, and twenty pounds to buy mourning.'

'Yes. Very well.' He rose to his feet, snatching up his new hat, with a frantic grab after dignity.

'Thank you. I have your promise?'

'My word of honour.'

'Let us not rely on that,' she said calmly. 'Twenty-five pounds.'

She rang the bell, and when Callow appeared handed him the keys. Like a fascinated rabbit Richard Normanby watched the man unlock the big safe, bring out a cash-box, count out twenty-five golden sovereigns, put them into a small leather bag, hand them to Margaret, replace the cash-box, relock the safe and hand back the keys to her. She passed the bag over to him, and rose, signifying the interview was over. He thrust the bag of coins into his inner pocket. At the door he turned, and looked at the slender, erect figure.

'You cold-hearted unwomanly little bitch,' he said, and went out.

On a chill but sunny October day, Florence was laid to rest at Danesfell Parish Church. It was a good turn-out. Not so many people who knew her, but many older people who had known and respected her father and mother and the Normanby family. The wreaths were thick on the grass. One, an enormous, elaborate piece of lilies, orchids and roses, everything expensive and out of season. The card read, *'From Baron and Baroness Philippe Abderhazy. For Mama, with love, Charmy.'* But Charmian did not come.

Jany Leck sat in the front pew between Margaret and Millicent Hengrave. Margaret thought it was strange how she and Millicent sustained each other in times of loss. They each held one of Lecky's little black-gloved hands. Margaret had taken a hand off the great Van Hagen wedding for a whole day to make Lecky her mourning. A black dress and mantle such as she had never worn before. Fit to sit among the gentry. Lily Oglethorpe was there sobbing copiously, but Lecky was quite silent, except for joining fervently in the old hymns she knew so well.

The Vicar's voice droned on in the sunshine, the clouds scudded across the moors against a bright blue sky, the red and yellow leaves fluttered in the wind. The earth was cast into the grave. Lecky gave a long, shuddering sigh.

There was a shaking of hands and a murmuring of condolences. A local woman spoke to Margaret.

'I hear your father has returned. It was in the local newspaper. How sad he should return to this.' She glanced round. 'Is he here?'

'Apparently not,' Margaret said. 'No doubt he could not make the journey.'

'Well, we are all getting on. What a beautiful wreath from your sister. I am glad she has done so well for herself. But she was always a beauty.'

'Come, Lecky,' Margaret said. 'Let us drive you back to Danesfell and we'll put you to bed with a hot-water bottle and a drop of whisky. You must not cry any more.'

Lecky shook her head stubbornly. 'Nay, I'll be all right. Happen I'll go over to Listers' farm to see young

Tom. Bertha says he's growing out of all his clothes. If Mrs Hengrave'll get someone to drive me I'll go after my dinner. I reckon I'm too stiff to walk over the moors nowadays.' She set off along the path towards the carriage, Millicent and Margaret walking behind.

'My father did not come,' said Margaret. 'I gave him the money and he said he would come – on his word of honour.'

Millicent gave her scornful, snorting little laugh.

'Richard Normanby's word of honour! Attend a funeral with money in his pockets? He will have put it on a horse.'

'I – I had hoped he would do this for her. I will never speak to him or see him again.' Her voice broke a little. 'It was so awful that there was no one there except dear Lecky who truly loved her.'

'How about the devoted Lily?'

'Nay, she was just part of the illusion.'

'And you?'

'No, I couldn't. When I was little I longed for her to love me. She never did. I pitied her, but as I grew up I could never love her.'

'Here is one who loved her to distraction – a long time ago.'

Margaret followed her glance and saw Henry Grimshaw, swinging down from his horse, tethering it to the gate, and striding across to the heaped flowers, where no mourners stood now. He carried a spray of some pink-and-white flowers and stood there, booted and spurred, then dropped the frail blossoms into the open grave.

'Wait for me,' said Margaret. 'I must speak to him.'

She met him as he turned from the grave. 'Thank you for coming,' she said.

He stretched out a hand, and took hers. 'I had to. She was so lovely, and so silly, and once I loved her to

404

insanity. She stole my youth away. Well, poor child, perhaps she is at peace now.'

'But thank you, anyway. I must go. Millicent is waiting to drive me to Danesfell.'

'How long are you staying?'

'Until tomorrow. I just came up for the funeral. We have been busy on this great wedding order – the Van Hagen-Malvern wedding. I daresay you've read about it in the papers.'

'Yes.' He hesitated. 'I have been told your boy is up here – staying at Listers' farm with his nurse girl.' She glanced at him with quick alarm, and he said, 'I haven't been to see him. I wouldn't, Maggy, without your permission. How is he?'

'He's grand. He loves it on the farm. I am dreading taking him home. He's not an easy child for a woman to manage, and Hanover Street is not the right place for him. He needs a stronger hand and more time than I can give him.' She stopped abruptly, realizing she had betrayed her fears to him.

'Maggy,' he said desperately. '*May* I see him? I've longed to see him. I've heard he's a grand little boy.'

She looked at him doubtfully. Tom was so like him it was laughable. Surely no one, seeing them together, would doubt whose child he was.

'Your interest could cause a scandal,' she said. 'Neither of us wants that.'

'What do I care about wagging tongues!'

'It's not just you, Henry.'

She became physically aware of his presence, like a burning flush sweeping up over her beneath the sober black mourning.

'Millicent is waiting for me,' she said quickly. 'I must go. Yes. Go and see him if you wish. I'm very proud of him. Thank you again for coming. Goodbye.'

She did not offer him her hand. He watched her go, light as a bird with her skimming, graceful walk. Then he mounted his horse and rode to the Listers' farm, a long, two-storeyed building of quarried stone, with big barns and cow-sheds, built in a sheltered fold of the moors.

Bertha Lister came to the door, drying her hands, a big rosy girl. 'Master Tom? He's in the barn wi' the lads, Sir. I'm just going to get them in for their tea . . .'

He walked across to the big black-timbered barn, hearing the shouts of the children inside, and slipped quietly into the shadows between the bales of hay. There was the Listers' brood of boys ranging from fifteen to three, and a sturdy baby with wheat-blond hair, stumping about among them, hanging on to the corduroys of the eldest Lister boy shouting, 'Me. Me, now. *Me!* Bert. My turn!'

Bert Lister picked Tom up and went up the ladder to the loft. Henry felt his blood run cold. They were playing a dangerous game as farm children will; they had rigged up a seat on a pulley-and-tackle for lowering sacks, and while two big boys hung on to the rope, they were riding the smaller ones dizzily down from the high loft to the ground. When he saw them fastening Tom into the seat he started forward, terrified, but before he could speak, Tom was launched, with a shriek of joy, out into the air, and down on to the hay bales below. He staggered up, covered with straw like a hatched chick, rosy with delight, hardly able to stand for laughing. One of the biggest boys released him, and he was running back towards the ladder again, shouting imperiously, 'Me. Me. More, Bert! My turn!'

'Nay, you tek your turn, young Tom,' shouted a five-year-old Lister, shoving him back. Tom, enraged, started to kick, but the Lister boys, used to babies and tempers, just tipped him off his feet, and went on with their game.

He got up, his temper subsiding into a big, smiling grin, and took his place among the shouting boys. Henry stood motionless – watching.

This was *his* boy, imprinted with his features, with his character. Tom was a little Emperor among these children. He wanted this child, to love and rear, to work for, to teach to control his inheritance.

Stephen was Angela's baby. Henry loved him with a guilty tenderness, cossetting his weakness, terrified at his fragility. But this boy's every feature and expression were his own. He wanted to tell the boys not to play at the dangerous game with his son but he could not. He knew Tom would be playing dangerous games all his young life, and would not want him otherwise than he was, bold and fearless, handsome and determined. He thought of him among the silks and satins of Hanover Street, bearing Leon's name, and could not stand it. This was *his* boy. He had a right to see him. Margaret must be made to understand.

Margaret and Millicent were sitting at tea when the note came for Mrs Leon. She read it through and changed colour.

'It's from Angela Grimshaw. She asks me to take Tom over to Cliffs Edge to tea tomorrow. To meet Stephen.'

Millicent poured the tea. She guessed Henry had insisted upon this invitation.

'I advise you to accept. They *are* half-brothers. There are the mills, which I cannot imagine poor Stephen running, and there is Danesfell Abbey. All my property. Including the mines. They will be rich and powerful men in the valley one day. It is better that they should know each other as boys, and learn to be brothers and friends.'

'Tom is *my* boy,' said Margaret stubbornly, 'and Henry is not taking him away.'

'He can't of course,' Millicent said wryly. 'Tom's your

property now, and like all your property you will keep control over him.'

Margaret went to Millicent's escritoire and scribbled a note of refusal, and gave it to the man. 'Give this to the messenger from Cliffs Edge. And send someone over to Listers' Farm. Tell Lecky and Bertha to have Tom here in the morning. First thing. We are going back to London.'

At Newmarket Sir Richard Normanby watched the horse carrying his money sail past the post, a winner by six lengths. He had had an excellent day. He had even met a few old acquaintances, who had been pleased to see him. Birds of a feather. They had told him of clubs where there were good pickings to be had for a skilful player. Not the exclusive clubs he had belonged to once, but nowadays he was not so fussy.

To have a hand or two at cards would be pleasant. Thanks to Margaret he had money in his pocket. He scarcely remembered the purpose for which the money had been given to him.

Chapter Fifteen

The month of the Van Hagen-Malvern wedding was the most difficult month of Margaret's life. Years later she would look back and wonder how she had managed to survive.

The great wedding was dominated by the conflicting egos of the two mother-in-law, Mrs Van Hagen who had secured an earl's son for her beautiful daughter, and the Countess of Wynyates who had secured a great American fortune for her son.

The postponements, the crises, the boggling changes of plan were unpredictable. Margaret felt like the defending general on a battlefield. Defending her business, defending Ferdinand's designs, taste and choice, driving on her staff, always there, always available to soothe, calm and restore the contending parties to good humour, firm as an operating theatre sister in the midst of the temperaments and the tears. Ferdinand opted out – he did the designs, he watched the dresses being made, but the rest he left to his wife. She was working from dawn until well after midnight.

She had little time for Tom and he was driving her insane. It was a battle of wills. With gifts and spoiling and treats she was trying to get him to accept her environment, but he had now had a taste of freedom and an exciting masculine world. The two deep lines ate into his forehead.

'Tom go in train and play with boys?' he demanded.

'Not today, darling.'

'A-morrow?' he insisted, twisting her heart.

'Soon, darling, soon. When Mama isn't working.'

The tram-line scowl deepened.

'Mama always working,' he said desolately. Scolding and pleading made no difference. Imperiously used to getting her own way she could not believe that a baby could defy her. She had a premonition of an adolescent Tom, completely uncontrollable – at any rate by his mother. It was too cold for the parks and gardens, drives in the closed landaulette bored him, the polite local children brought the devil out in him. Then, to her horror, he began to pine. Her marvellous, strong, little boy sat thumb in mouth, in his high chair, pushing aside his food, turning away from her, cuddling into Bertha, inconsolable.

She could have sent him back to Listers' farm, but if she did she knew that Henry would be unable to keep away from him. He had steeled himself to make no further approach to her, but with the boy only a few miles away from Cliffs Edge, the temptation to get to know his son would be irresistible. Millicent had written:

'Henry is completely besotted with your handsome son. He has only spoken to me about it – but whether you choose to give him access to the boy or not, I can tell you he is already consulting his solicitors so that Tom will one day come into his share of the Grimshaw inheritance.'

She was afraid of giving way. Henry could do so much for Tom. It would make her life easier. Try as she would, love him as she did, she was not a maternal woman. Henry had no legal right to Tom, but he could steal his heart away. He could give him all the freedom, all the exciting masculine things that he would long for as he grew into boyhood. But she would have no share in that world. Her world was here, in Mayfair, and at this moment it was claiming her every waking hour.

It was no use promising a three-year-old that he would

have another country holiday. He had not reached that point of reasoning. After the Van Hagen wedding? That meant nothing to Tom. At her promises he only scowled like a blond baby eagle, and said, 'When? Now? Mama take Tom in a train today? See boys? See the horsies? Now?'

'Soon, my darling, soon . . .'

His lips would stick out, something would go flying, and he would glare defiantly, and yell until he could be heard downstairs in the showrooms. In desperation she bought him a puppy, which proved a success, but made things noisier than ever, as boy and dog careered about the top storey, with a rush of feet, barking and laughing, the tumbling of furniture and the banging of balls. Once the puppy escaped through the nursery gate and down into the showroom, with Bertha and Tom in hot pursuit, leaving a wreckage of frills, satins, flowers and overturned stands in their trail, and sending the staff into fits of nervous laughter. A higher, stronger gate with a lock was installed on the nursery floor, but Tom shook it like a small caged gorilla, with the puppy yapping enthusiastically by his side. So on fine days they were taken out in the Park, on wet days driven in the carriage, and every day he grew more morose and stubborn.

At last the order was finished. The day before the wedding, the two delivery vans with their bowler-hatted, grey-uniformed drivers spent the morning taking the gowns to the customers, finished in every exquisite detail, packed in tissue within long lavender-and-gold boxes. The following morning early, Margaret would go round to the house the Van Hagens rented in Grosvenor Square to supervise the dressing of the bride, drive with her to the church for any last-minute adjustments, inspect the ten aristocratic bridesmaids, and wait until after the

411

reception to help the bride change to go away on her honeymoon.

Ferdinand would not be there. His work had finished some days ago, and as always after a major creative effort, he was restless and bored.

He came into her boudoir that evening. Wearing a loose tea-gown she was stretched out on the cretonne-covered sofa, dozing, too tired to sleep. Ferdinand bent over her, and lifted her hand to kiss, and she looked up and smiled. The wedding had been an exciting challenge, they had secured the order in the face of high competition, and had enjoyed working together. He poured them both a glass of Madeira and sat by her feet.

He was not in evening dress. But in his beautifully-tailored grey suit with a rose in his buttonhole, he looked a great dandy.

'Margaret,' he said, 'I feel like celebrating. Get dressed and let's go out together – a lovely London night out. Marie Lloyd is at the Tivoli, and then over to Gatti's for a bite.'

'Ferdi, honestly, I'm worn out. I still have to go to Grosvenor Square at ten tomorrow to dress the bride. I'd love to come – make it tomorrow evening. And Ferdi, I thought we could steal a week away somewhere – Le Touquet, or Deauville. Tom has never seen the sea.'

An expression of amused irritation came into his eyes.

'Don't include me in a domestic holiday with your little barbarian, Margaret. I couldn't stand it. You take him with Lecky and Bertha. I'll go to Paris. But tonight I feel like some fun. Fifty gowns. How many hundred fittings? How many arguments between the two Mamas? How many faintings and vapourings by the bride? How many yards of lace and silk? Thank God tomorrow will see the end of it.'

'You will see the end of it. Not me.'

'Well, you don't mind if I go out alone?'

'Of course not.'

'Don't wait up for me.'

She never did – they never questioned each other's actions outside the business. He put on his grey bowler at a jaunty angle and went out. Margaret had some consommé and a sandwich and went to bed.

She was awakened by a hammering at the street door and sat up, her heart beating in alarm. It was four o'clock in the morning. The thunderous knocking came again, and she sprang up and turned up the small lamp that stood near the bed, put on a gown and ran out on to the landing. Judson the butler, a greatcoat pulled on over his nightshirt, was pulling down the chain on the large gas chandelier, filling the hall with light. Then he went unhurriedly to the main door. She heard him speaking in a low voice to someone on the step and called to him:

'What is it, Judson?'

'It's a messenger, Madame, for you.'

'Well, let him in, and bring it up.'

A shabby, furtive youth, with ill-cut hair, sidled into the hall. Judson took the note between his finger-tips, dropped it on to a salver and brought it up to her. It was from Ferdinand, and very brief:

'Margaret, I am being detained at Bow Street Police Station. For God's sake get Davis Pelham and bring him here at once to get me out. I need bail arranged. For God's sake be quick or I am ruined.'

She went slowly down into the hall. The scruffy boy eyed her doubtfully.

'Did you see the gentleman?'

'No, Mum. A rozzer brought it out. The gent must 'ave slipped him summat.'

She guessed the nature of what had happened. She put her hand to her aching forehead. Why the devil had not she pulled herself together and gone out with him? He was her partner and friend. It had been a direct appeal for the comfort and protection of her company. Ferdinand might be ruined – and so might she.

'Give the boy a florin and tell him to go, Judson,' she said. 'I have to go out. See if you can get a night hansom and keep it waiting. It would cause too much noise and disturbance to wake up Marley and get the carriage out.'

'Yes, Madame.'

'I have to meet Mr Leon. He is in a little difficulty.'

'Yes, Madame,' Judson said impassively, and she knew then that he knew about Ferdinand and always had.

She ran back to her room and dressed, reached for a hat, and stopped, went upstairs to the nursery floor where Bertha met her, white and scared, clasping Tom, still fast asleep in her arms.

'What is it, Ma'am? Is the house afire?'

'No, Bertha. Put Master Tom back to bed, and go back yourself. I have to go out.'

'At this hour, Ma'am?'

'Mr Leon has sent for me . . .' she smiled. 'He seems to be in a little trouble, as gentlemen sometimes are.'

The girl from Thornsby Moor was not so sophisticated as Judson, but she understood that gentlemen, like other men, were apt to get the worse for wear at times.

'Can I borrow a shawl, Bertha?' Margaret asked. 'It's my hair – I don't want to be recognized.'

'Of course, Ma'am.'

She put Tom back to bed, and found a big grey shawl, and Margaret wrapped it over her tell-tale hair. She stopped by Tom's cot where he lay, asleep, sprawled, sweet-limbed, beautiful – she bent and kissed him, covered a small relaxed hand. Judson was waiting when she went downstairs.

'There is a cab outside, Mrs Leon.'

'Thank you. Will you tell him to drive to Gray's Inn. To Mr Davis Pelham's house.'

'Very good, Madame. Would you like me to accompany you?'

'No, but thank you, Judson. I shall be all right. I shall be back as soon as I can. I have to be at Grosvenor Square by ten o'clock to help Miss Van Hagen dress for her wedding. Just look after everything here.'

The city was Winter-cold, dark and empty at this hour. Manholes steamed, and in the doorways and round the garbage bins the night creatures had gathered. Theatres and restaurants were all closed An occasional night hansom, like her own, passed. She prayed that no news had leaked out, imagining the field-day the papers would have if this happened on the day of the Van Hagen-Malvern wedding. Ferdinand's Winter bride, all white brocade and diamonds. *'Ferdinand Leon, dressmaker to Queens, who created Miss Van Hagen's trousseau, was this morning charged with obscene behaviour concerning minors.'*

What was she imagining? It might not be that. He might have just got drunk. But that note had been written by a desperate, not a drunken man.

Mr Davis Pelham, a spare, middle-aged man, was not at all happy at being roused in the early hours of the morning. It was the sort of thing that happened to criminal solicitors, not a quiet, respectable firm which dealt with partnerships and property. It was he who had drawn up the partnership agreement between Ferdinand and Margaret, which protected her interests after her marriage.

Margaret showed him the letter. He stroked his long lawyer's jaw, and asked her if she had any idea of the nature of the charge.

'I can guess,' she said.

415

'I suppose he got drunk and made a nuisance of himself in public?'

'No.' She met his questioning eyes unwaveringly. 'I think it will be quite a serious charge. I don't know what the police jargon will be. Gross obscenity, perhaps? Unlawful sexual practices with a person of the same sex? Procuring a minor for immoral and unnatural purposes? Something of that nature.'

'Mrs Leon!' Pelham was frozen with horrified disbelief. 'What are you trying to tell me?'

'I am trying to tell you, very badly, that Ferdinand is one of those unfortunate men who are attracted by young members of their own sex, and I believe the charge and detention will be concerned with this.'

'Oh my God!' said Mr Pelham. 'He surely doesn't expect *me* to handle such a case? We are not criminal lawyers.'

'No. But you are our solicitors, and I would be glad of your support,' she said firmly. 'My purpose is to get Ferdinand out of jail tonight.'

'You will stand surety for bail?'

'Of course.'

He realized how tired she was. He made a helpless gesture, and turned to the stairs. 'I'll get dressed,' he said.

Ten minutes later they were bowling through the empty streets towards Covent Garden.

'He's in his sixties,' he said suddenly. 'Funny how so many men drop their guard at that age.'

'You've had to deal with it in court?'

'No. But I've known it happen.'

'It could ruin him – and our business.'

'Very likely. If he gets bail it might be better for him to leave the country.'

'He's been wanting to do that for some time. To live in

416

France.' The cab stopped outside the police court. The opera-house loomed dark and enormous opposite. Carts parked with vegetables were lumbering into the market behind. 'I'll wait in the cab, Mr Pelham. Please try and get his release tonight.'

'I'll do my best.'

She sat in the darkness waiting, and time crept past. Policemen came and went . . . a roaring drunk, bellowing obscenities, was hauled up the steps, followed by two women, painted and showily-dressed, blood running down their faces, screaming hatred at each other. The riff-raff of the London night.

Then she saw Ferdinand come down the steps, leaning on Pelham's arm. She could not believe it was the same man who had left their home, so elegant in his pale grey suit, with the rose in his buttonhole, such a short while ago. He looked thin and old, the beautiful suit was soiled with mud, and there was a bruise across his cheek-bone. The discreet make-up he wore showed starkly against the livid pallor of his face. He looked part of the ugly night-scene, like the drunk and the painted women. She felt a shiver of revulsion – not for him, but for what he had become. She pushed the door open and helped him in.

'Margaret,' he said. 'Margaret, help me . . . it is all up with me.'

'You are hurt?' She touched the bruise.

'It's nothing. I fell . . . I found a back way out of the house and ran for it, but they caught me and pulled me down . . . Margaret . . . take me home . . .'

Mr Pelham stood by the door.

'Better to get him home, and get some rest. He has to be in court in the morning. I will meet you there.'

Tomorrow she had to be at Grosvenor Square at ten to dress the bride.

'In view of the nature of the charges,' Mr Pelham said

stiffly, 'I feel obliged to tell you I do not feel I should take the case. I have acted – and am pleased to act – for you, in business matters, but I feel this is out of my province.'

'I quite understand, thank you,' Margaret said stiffly. He hesitated. He had always admired her. What had shocked him so appallingly was that she had known of this. He wondered whether she *really* understood.

'Mrs Leon,' he ignored Ferdinand, 'I hope for your sake the newspapers will not get hold of this. If they do there will be many men who would not permit their wives to cross your doorstep. I should feel that way myself.'

'Then they will be denying themselves the services of the finest dressmaker in London,' she said proudly.

But she knew he was right. The cab turned towards the West End down Long Acre. It passed a tall house, the front door open, a small crowd of shabby nighthawks hanging about, a policeman on duty at the door. A tall, grim, sordid-looking house with secretly drawn blinds.

'Was that the place?' she asked.

He glanced up. 'Yes.'

'Oh, Ferdi,' she burst out. 'Why, in God's name?'

'You know why.'

'No, why did you take such a risk? Why did you jeopardize everything we've built together?'

For the first time she saw enmity in his eyes.

'Jesus, how should I know? The comfort of being among one's own kind. Of not having to pretend.'

They drove on through the empty city, past the workers and inhabitants of the night. Street women, road-sweepers, night-soil carts with their overpowering stench, the creeping homeless shivering in alleys and doorways. The dark shop windows. The pacing police in their shining black capes. She remembered the time before when they had driven back through the night-bound city together, and he had told her bitterly and honestly about himself. Neither of them had spoken of it since.

He said, suddenly petulant, 'You don't know how much I've missed you. Ever since we were married. Before, we were such good friends. Then Grimshaw came, and then it was that damned baby – it has spoiled everything between us. You're a different woman.'

'Ferdi, we should never have married. You should have told me, before we married.'

'I was afraid you'd leave me and the business. It worked with us so well. I'd never have done it without you. I couldn't do without you. Then I thought it *might* work . . . we understood each other, we were such friends, and good partners. So close. You had such style, and I admired you. I just thought it might work.'

She patted his hand as though he were a child and not a man almost thirty years her senior.

'What do you want me to do now?'

'I must get away. I am not going to court, or risk trial. I must go at once. Davis Pelham told me as much. There will be a public scandal.' To her horror he broke down. 'Help me, Margaret. Tell me what to do.'

'Ever since I can remember,' she said wearily, 'people have been asking me to help them, to look after them, to tell them what to do. Now I just don't know. This time, Ferdi, you will have to tell me.'

'Bail was fixed at two hundred pounds. You will have to pay that if I don't appear. If I go to court I shall be sent for trial. I haven't a chance. The boy and I were naked when the police broke in . . .'

'How old was he?'

'Fourteen.'

'Oh, heavens, Ferdi . . !'

'I wasn't the first,' Ferdinand said defensively. 'He was

419

a boy of the streets. I would not have been the only one tonight.'

He was always so fastidious. She could not believe this of him.

'Don't tell me. I don't want to know.'

The cab had drawn up in Hanover Street before the two tall houses so beautifully clean and freshly-painted, window-boxes bright with evergreens and Autumn flowers, pots with bay trees on the spotless stone steps, the cold dawn light creeping down the street, illuminating the gilt letters on windows and doors: *Maison Leon*.

Margaret looked up at it with pride and agony.

'It's such a fine business. We've worked so hard together. After this wedding tomorrow, we could have taken it a little easier. Tonight, after you left, I was thinking about your going to France, thinking you could, and still design for me . . .'

'Well, it's the end now. From tomorrow no one will come. Not a customer. Not a salesman. Not even the staff. They will be afraid.'

'We got over that business with Charmian,' she said stubbornly.

'It's not the same. Besides, I shall need my capital. I have to live in France. We will wind up the partnership, sell the leases and the stock. We shall be all right, Margaret. Quite comfortable in our old age.'

'I'm not thirty yet,' she said fiercely. 'And I'm not giving up my business. I don't want to be – just comfortable! If that's what I'd wanted Henry Grimshaw would have given it to me. A house, comfort, money . . . doing *what*? I am going on. Supposing I bought you out?'

'Could you raise the money?'

'I don't know.' They sat in the carriage together. 'I could try.'

420

'It wouldn't be any use, Margaret. when the papers come out this evening Maison Leon will be dead.'

'Not if I can keep it alive. We can't decide tonight. Tonight you must go. You must change and pack and get an early train to the coast. We must hurry. Come now.'

Judson opened the door as though nothing untoward had happened, and went to pack for Ferdinand. Margaret took three hundred pounds out of the safe and gave it to him.

'This will keep you going for the time being. You must write to your bank and give them instructions to send you what you want. Then we must decide what to do about the business.' She stood thoughtfully, looking round the office, then closed and locked the safe. 'I'll get the money. I'll buy you out, Ferdi. I would like to be on my own. Then, if mistakes are made, they will be mine alone.'

They had kept the cab waiting and she drove with him to Victoria. The early train to Dover was waiting at the platform. The station was dank and cold, hissing with steam.

'We may never meet again, Margaret.'

'Nonsense,' she said determinedly. 'Next year I shall come to Paris to buy for the Spring. I shall have to do it myself now. And you don't *have* to be in Hanover Street to design clothes.'

'Oh, Margaret,' he said, and smiled with so much affection that she could scarcely bear it. She felt furious – with him, with Fate. Why could not he have been different when they had so much together? Talent and hard work, ambition and friendship. Everything finished because of a pretty street urchin, willing to sell himself to any toff who would pay. 'Margaret, you are indomitable. But this time you will find you cannot fight. Tell me, now, after what I have done, do you regret it all? That I came up to Leeds and persuaded you to join me here in London all that time ago?'

The colour flared up in her face. 'Oh *no*, Ferdi! No. It's been wonderful. You've taught me so much . . . you've taught me to want the best. Material, workmanship, customers – everything. It's been a wonderful seven years.' She reached out and embraced him, and they were both in tears, overwhelmed by their affection, by the wasted friendship and the ruin of their high endeavour.

'Goodbye, goodbye,' they cried to each other. 'Good luck . . .'

The train slid away smoothly, disappearing round the bend and under the iron road-bridge. She felt incredibly lonely. Not torn and heart-broken as she had felt when Henry had left her, but lonely for her partner and friend.

When she got back to Hanover Street, the cleaners were at work in the showrooms and the porter was polishing the brass on the front doors. She went upstairs to the apartment, bathed and dressed very carefully. Today she must look her best. She was still in mourning for her mother, and black suited her white skin and the brilliance of her hair. She wore her new jacket of shining mink, and a small toque of bunched black ribbons and fronds of ostrich which floated as she moved her head. She felt deadly tired. She took some black coffee and some toast, went up to kiss Tom, who was being tiresomely naughty, spilling his porridge and throwing his bread and butter down to the puppy. She could not kiss him for fear of getting milk and butter over her clothes.

The carriage came round at exactly half-past nine to take her to the Van Hagen house in Grosvenor Square.

The wedding was sheer perfection. The couturier's dream. Ferdinand's London swansong was his masterpiece. The bride, a statuesque vision in silvery white. The ten aristocratic and/or plutocratic bridesmaids in chalk-white tulle, with clusters of Christmas roses and scarlet berries. The two pages in eighteenth-century suits of white velvet, with curled perukes, and red heels on their little shoes. The bride's formidable Mama in emerald green velvet, the bridegroom's imperious and intimidating parent in sapphire satin, wearing the Wynyates diamonds. The church decorated with holly and tall white lilies.

Margaret dressed the bride, and drove to the church, adjusted the train, cast her critical eye over the fluttering bridesmaids, twitching a curl here, a flounce there, until Mr Elmer Van Hagen took his daughter up the aisle. A cab waited at the rear of the church to drive her to Grosvenor Square to wait for the bride's return. She stood by the bedroom window waiting. Her heart jumped every time a newsboy ran up the street, but it was never about Ferdinand. The winner of the big race, the divorce of a famous actress, more trouble in Ireland. But nothing about Ferdinand – not yet. She felt a stir of hope. Perhaps nothing would happen. Perhaps it would all pass unnoticed.

She waited in the bedroom. The trunks had already left for Liverpool with the clothes for the wedding trip. A different evening-dress for each night of the crossing, dresses for morning, and for afternoon, furs for when the bride arrived in New York, and twenty-seven evening-gowns for the Winter season there. Each one a different colour, each one with its matching accessories. The bill was over two thousand pounds.

Mrs Van Hagen was effusive in her thanks and con-gratulations. She introduced Margaret to a royal personage who expressed her congratulations and assured her that she would be in touch with her about her clothes for a foreign tour. Mrs Van Hagen pressed a cheque for two hundred pounds into her hand for distribution among the staff, and asked her to express her personal gratitude. She was planning a series of balls and receptions in New York and Long Island in the Spring, would it be possible for Monsieur and Madame Leon to come over to make some clothes for her daughter and herself?

Margaret said she would consult Mr Leon. She bowed herself out. Marley was waiting with the carriage. He put the rug over her knees and she leaned back, dead with weariness, wondering if Ferdinand had really got away. Even in the church she had been listening for the raucous shouts of the newsboys.

The carriage turned into Conduit Street and past St George's where she herself had been married, into Hanover Square, across into Hanover Street, and stopped outside the two big houses that contained Maison Leon. Everything seemed calm. Across the road Mr Stepney, the wine merchant, stood on his step, his left hand under his coat-tails, his right holding a cigar. A red-faced rather coarse man whose wife boasted that she knew Madame Leon and that her children went to little Thomas Leon's parties.

A newsboy came racing down from Regent Street – Margaret caught the words, 'Warrant for arrest . . .' saw the placard, Ferdinand's name in black letters. She saw Mr Stepney drop his cigar, and buy a copy, his red face switching upwards to gaze at the two immaculate façades opposite, his mouth dropped open in horrified surprise.

Well, here it was. The avalanche. She had not rested and scarcely eaten since she had driven down to Bow Street before dawn. She felt weak as though all her strength had drained out of her. She knew in that small space of time what it would feel like to be very old. And then, she thought of Tom. These newspapers, these placards and shouts were damning Tom's acknowledged father as a pervert, an obscene and unnatural seducer of youth, a slur that could cling to him all his life.

Marley had opened the door and lowered the step and stood waiting for her to descend.

'Marley,' she said, 'I want you to buy me fifty copies of the *Evening Star*.'

'Fifty copies, Ma'am?'

'Yes. When you return, rest the horses, but don't put the landaulette away. I believe there is an evening train about seven – I am taking Master Tom up to Yorkshire tonight. Would you go to the local office and book a first-class compartment for me and Bertha. Oh, and bring the newspapers to Briggs – he will be waiting for them in the hall.'

'Yes, Madame.'

With a silent, graceful movement, she turned her head, saw Mr Stepney's goggling stare from across the street. His wife had joined him on the step. Behind them the heads of his assistants bobbed and stared. At other shops and other windows faces appeared – white blobs of curiosity. People, holding the evening paper, were turning down from Oxford Street, stopping and staring up at the business.

Margaret smiled graciously at the Stepneys, bowed, and sailed into the hall.

Briggs, the hall-porter, resplendent in his pale grey uniform with dark purple facings, was waiting for her. His broad Cockney face was expressionless.

'Good afternoon, Briggs. Are there any messages?'

'Afternoon, Madame. The coppers have been. This morning, just after you and Mr Leon left. We wasn't open.'

'What did you tell them?'

'I told 'em Mr Leon was off to France early this morning. They asked for you, and I ses you was at

425

Viscount Malvern's wedding, looking after his lady's dress, and they said there was no need for them to go there. I said that Mr Leon was French anyway.' She gazed at him, surprised. 'He is, isn't he, Ma'am?'

'Why, yes. Of course he is.'

'Well, then they can't bring 'im back, can they? As long as he stays over the other side.'

Ridiculously she had not even thought about it. Ferdinand had never taken out papers for British nationality.

'Not that they'd bother, anyway,' said Briggs. 'It ain't as though he'd robbed a bank.'

'You knew?'

'Well, I worn't born yesterday, Madame.'

First Judson, now Briggs. He too had worked for Ferdinand ever since the first salon had been opened. Like Judson he must have known about Ferdinand and said nothing. As though guessing her thoughts, he said kindly, 'A very good boss, Ma'm, Mr Ferdi. Wery thoughtful. Wery kind.'

'Thank you, Briggs, Are there any customers in the showrooms or fitting-rooms?'

'No, Madame.'

'Well, close up. Marley will be back in a moment with the evening newspapers. I want you to distribute them among the staff. I want them to read all about it before I speak to them. Ask them all to go into the big workroom. I'll be down in a moment.'

There was quite a crowd in the street below. They were mostly women, many of them street-walkers who only ventured into the main thoroughfares after dusk. She heard shrieks of laughter and abuse, and someone flung a stone which cracked against one of the salon windows. Briggs had turned out the showroom lights. A couple of policemen began to move people away. Newspaper men arrived and hung about the step and occasionally rang the bell; neither Briggs nor Judson answered. She took off her hat, smoothed her hair, and went down to the workroom, with no plan, not knowing what she would say to them, only knowing that she must keep this wonderful team of saleswomen and craftswomen together if she was going to keep the business afloat; and she was going to do it if she had to beg, borrow or steal to do so.

The staff were all there, clustered in groups, waiting, scared. The hum of their voices died. She was no longer Madame, "The Bitch", the Power, the one who created their jobs, who paid them, who could sack them. She was a woman who had been married to a monster of depravity and vice. It said so in the glaring headlines of the rustling newspapers they held.

The salon staff clustered around Miss Jenner. The workroom girls, already wearing their hats and coats ready to go, hung together round the chief gown-hand, Mrs Smythe, a prim woman with scraped-back hair, a widow and a Methodist. She would be bitterly shocked, and she was not afraid of being unemployed – she was too good a craftswoman. She would easily find another place.

For a moment Margaret was near to cracking, facing this barrage of prurient curiosity, disapproval, mockery. The workroom girls were not refined young women, however delicate their craft. She knew what they were thinking, whispering to each other. ''Ere, fancy "The Bitch" being taken in? She must be a right fool! Anyone could see old Ferdi was a queer one.' They had worked hard with her. She had trained many of them and moulded them into the best dressmaking team in London. They needed their jobs and she needed them.

They had not seen her yet; their voices hummed like bees as they read the newspapers. She stood looking down into the room with its long tables covered with brown paper, lit by unshaded gas-mantles. There were rows of treadle machines. There were dummies, each made to the measurement of particular customers, some with half-finished dresses pinned to them, some with holland patterns. The floor was covered with the day's debris of small cuttings, bright as confetti, waiting to be swept up and bagged for the ragman. Scraps of sewing-silk, curling with grey dust, hundreds of fine steel pins waiting for the apprentices to collect with magnets for cleaning and re-use. The strange smell of it all. Of new materials with the dressing still in them, of hot flat-irons, of girls, perfume and sweat. It was as heady to her as the smell of size and greasepaint to an actor.

It was her life she was fighting for, not just a money-making trade. It was something she and Ferdinand had created; special, splendid, first-class. She stepped forward and the fifty heads switched upwards, rows of faces like white patches in the gas-light. She found her voice – that clear, high, authoritative Normanby voice.

'I wanted to thank you for the work you have put in on the wedding, and to tell you that it was the most beautiful and successful we have ever done. Mrs Van Hagen asked me to thank you all personally, and she has given me a cheque for two hundred pounds as a token of her appreciation, so that there will be two pounds each extra in your wage-packet this week.'

There was a small murmur of pleasure, a glance from eye to eye, a smile. Behind the drawn blinds they could hear the voices of the crowd, and another spiteful crack of a thrown stone, then the sound of police horse, the authoritative shout of the police clearing the street. Margaret did not glance round. Her eyes glinted and her chin went up.

'You have read that Mr Leon has left the country. I

have decided to carry on with the business alone. Under my own name. To enable me to do this I shall have to seek financial support and I shall need a full staff. You are the best in all London. Tomorrow I have to go up North – I am going to take Mr Tom up there to – to relatives. I shall be back on Friday. I would like you all to come in while I am away and finish the orders in hand, and continue as usual. Miss Jenner will be in charge. This nonsense . . .' her lips curled scornfully, 'will be forgotten in a day or so. But on Friday I shall need to know how many of you will stay with me, and how many will give in their notice.'

Mrs Smythe rose. 'I'm giving in my notice now, Madame. I don't want to be associated with this firm.' Her cold glance went round the listening faces. 'It's scarcely the place for a young girl to earn her living. It's disgusting.'

'You must do as you please. Having been trained here, you will find no difficulty in obtaining other employment. Your second hand, Rose Briggs will take charge.' Young Rose, Brigg's daughter, flushed and squared her shoulders. 'You must all do as you please. I shall continue, either here in Hanover Street or at new premises.' She picked up one of the papers. 'I understand no more of this dreadful business than you do. To me Mr Leon was always a kind employer, and a good husband and friend. He was a most brilliant designer. I can find and train a new staff, I can find other premises. But whether I can replace him, that I don't know. However, I shall be here on Friday to learn your decision. It's not going to be easy . . . but *I* am not at fault, and *I* am *not* giving up. So off you go to your homes, and think it over – as I shall be doing. You will be quite safe leaving by the back entrance as usual – Briggs, Marley and Judson will stand by the gate until you have gone and will call the police if anyone

429

should attempt to molest you. Thank you for your loyalty and the beautiful work you have done in the past to make this the finest fashion house in London. And my thanks to the showroom staff for their patience, politeness to customers, and their efficiency. Goodnight to you.'

As she turned one of the young apprentices, a rough girl from Bermondsey, with bright, dark eyes and clever little hands, shouted, 'Good old Maggy, never say die! That's "The Bitch" for you!'

There was a burst of laughter, and a ragged cheer, then they began to clap, fitfully at first, then whole-heartedly. Her red head switched round, her bright smile flashed, and her eyes were full of tears. She shook her head, fighting for control, and then went quickly out of the workroom.

They covered their work with the big white dust-sheets, and filed out. She heard the sudden buzz of their excited voices as they put on their outdoor clothes and straggled out of the staff entrance through the mews at the back. She turned out the lights. Outside, the crowd, denied blood and excitement, was filtering away. Margaret went slowly upstairs to her office. Briggs brought her the keys as usual and reported everything locked before he went.

The house was utterly silent. She sat at the big desk, unable to think or plan. Soon she must pull herself together, soon she must decide what to do, for herself and for Tom. It was not as though she would be without means. The business was sound. The house in Juniper Crescent belonged to her, and the house at Hollingroyd Crescent. Her Grandmother Jagger's money, invested in Britannia Mills, had increased in value. If Maison Leon had to close, a third of everything would be hers. She might, as Ferdinand had suggested, be very comfortable. Her temper flashed at the thought, like powder to tinder. She did not want to be comfortable – she wanted to *live*.

She was not prepared to give up her business – but was she prepared to give up Tom?

She knew that the tentative invitation from Angela to bring Tom to see his half-brother at Cliffs Edge had all Henry's imperious longing for the boy behind it. She knew that Henry's business, and Millicent's inheritance, would one day be shared between the two boys.

How could she prepare him for such a life? What could she offer him in exchange? Suppose she changed their name, lived obscurely as a quiet widow with one treasured boy to rear? How would Tom react to that? How would she?

If she stayed in business, overcame this scandal, sent him away to school when he was old enough, spending his holidays with her, would he be happy? She went upstairs to the nursery floor and found him standing on a chair by the window, flushed and excited, quite disappointed that the angry crowd had gone.

'Horsies come and policemen and send bad men off,' he said delightedly. 'Tom get big stick and hit 'em on the head.'

She smiled. 'Like Mr Punch?'

'Yes. Killum dead.'

She laughed and kissed him. Her little barbarian.

Bertha and Lecky looked anxious, relieved that everything was quiet.

'Wasn't it terrible, Ma'am? Do you think they'll come back?'

'I don't think so. I have sent a wire to Mrs Hengrave asking if I can take him up to Danesfell. We can catch the late express. Marley will have the carriage ready and the horses rested and fed within the hour. Will you pack for Tom and yourself, Bertha? Quite a long stay. I'll send your supper up to you. Lecky, come down with me and help me pack. Just for two nights. I'm returning on Friday.'

Tom's sharp ears caught the word Danesfell, and his head came up from his supper broth.

'Tom not come back? he asked. 'Tom stay and play with boys?'

'Yes.' She felt the first razor-edge of parting. 'Yes, my love. This time I think you will *have* to stay.'

Judson brought her a bouillon, some cold chicken and a glass of wine, and Lecky packed a small valise. 'You're going to let his Dad have him then?' she said bluntly.

'If he really wants him.'

'He wants him all right – but will his Missus want him too?'

'That's what I have to find out. I could send him to Mrs Hengrave, but she is not young, she travels a great deal, and is not used to children. She cannot give him what I want for him any more than I can. A home and a family, and his father. That's what he needs and what I want for him.' Her voice failed. 'I know now,' she said, 'why it's better to part with a child at birth if you have to part with it at all. When they cut the cord and separate you, that's the time. Never see it again.'

'Don't talk so soft,' said Lecky crossly. 'You're just sorry for yourself.'

Margaret laughed. 'Oh, Lecky, if everyone was like you. Of course I am. With reason. It's been a heck of a day!'

They caught the train up North. Bertha wrapped in rugs with Tom tucked up in a big white shawl. It took him some time to settle down – the excitement of catching a train instead of going to bed kept him awake and lively until after nine. At last the lights were put out, and Tom went to sleep with his head on Bertha's lap.

It was a cold night of full moonlight. Margaret drew up the blind, unable to sleep, wrapped in her furs, watching the countryside stream by, silvering with frost as they travelled North. The moonlight fell on Tom's face, turning him into a marble cherub, smooth, colourless, lifeless.

A down express rattled past and he woke with a start, like Henry, instantly awake and aware. He had travelled by train before. When it had passed, a sweetly-rounded arm was raised out of the shawl and a little dimpled hand patted Bertha's face demandingly. 'Bert, I'se awake. Bert, I'se frightened . . . Bert . . . Tom wants you . . .'

The girl opened her eyes, kissed the small hand, and tucked it away, and drew him higher on her breast. In seconds they were both asleep again. Margaret experienced a stab of painful jealousy. This farm girl was closer to Tom than she had ever been.

Chapter Sixteen

It was midnight when the train ran into Leeds, where the carriage from Danesfell was waiting for them. Tom did not stir in Bertha's arms, and Margaret was stupefied from weariness. When they arrived Millicent sent them all straight to bed, and Margaret slept the night through. Waking late, she dressed hurriedly and went down to Millicent who was breakfasting in her boudoir. She was as handsome as ever, her dark cloud of hair winged with grey. She stretched out both hands in a warm welcome.

'Come and sit down, Maggy. I'll ring for some breakfast for you.'

'I can't eat.'

'Nonsense. Some toast and honey? You must have coffee. You look half-dead.'

'I feel it. Was it in all the newspapers? About poor Ferdi?'

'No. Only in the London dailies, and not so many people take them here. You've brought Tom away from it all?'

'I can't have him in London.'

'Maggy, I'm moving into a smaller house, Fellside House, one of the little manors on the estate, and I'm letting Danesfell to Lord Wellsdale. He is a young man with a large family who can use it. His lease will terminate the year the boys are twenty-one so they can decide what they want to do then. I shall keep my Chelsea house, and travel a lot. I will willingly keep Tom with me now, but not permanently. I'm too old to manage such a boy. In twenty years' time, perhaps, if I am still around.' She laughed. 'A man, yes. But small boys are different cattle.'

'What am I going to do with him?'

'Why did you bring him to Yorkshire? To ask Henry to have him?'

'Yes, if he will.'

Millicent gave her short, expressive laugh.

'He'd give his eyes to have him. He has talked to me of nothing else since he saw him at Listers' farm, the day of your mother's funeral.'

'But what about his wife?'

'She will have him if Henry says so.'

'On sufferance? I want a family life for him. Living above the business he has been bribed to be good, petted and spoiled by a lot of women. He's turning into a baby tyrant. He needs a strong father and a kind mother.'

'Well, he would have both. Henry needs him, Maggy.'

'Yes. More than I do. Henry has a future for him. I have Maison Leon. What future is that for a boy like Tom? And now – with this disgrace of Ferdi's. It means I must give everything up if I keep Tom with me. I don't think I can. I've weathered the business over Charmy, and I'll get over this. It's like being the Captain of a ship, Millicent. Not just me. The premises, the organization, the staff I have trained, who trust and depend upon me. It's not just a job. It's my life. But I can't have Tom pointed at as Ferdi Leon's son.'

'What else could you do?'

Margaret's face was scornful. 'Sell up. Invest the capital. Take a small house in the provinces with Lecky and Bertha, change our name and pretend to be a respectable widow. Send him to a good school. Occupy myself with the things women do. Terrified someone would recognize us, and give the game away. The wife and son of the notorious Ferdinand Leon.'

435

'You'd go mad,' said Millicent. 'You'd make your life and Tom's a misery. Imagine all your energy and drive concentrated on one unfortunate child!' She was relieved to see amusement glimmer in Margaret's eyes, and went on, 'D'you suppose Henry would give up the business of Grimshaw & Sons if Angela went off the rails?'

The idea was so ridiculous that Margaret burst out laughing.

'But Millicent, you were not there. The crowds in Hanover Street threw stones, the scum of Piccadilly was outside, street women, and their pimps, shouting abuse. As though Ferdi's exposure was some kind of triumph for them. I don't care for myself. The staff are loyal. I'll get over it. But I can't stand Tom being smeared with this muck. Pointed out at school, avoided by the friends he has made. Their outraged Mamas snatching them away from him. It could follow him through his whole life.'

'So you'll ask Henry to take him?'

'If Angela will agree – yes.'

'Oh, Maggy,' Millicent took her hand, 'Angela will have him if Henry tells her she must, and he will.' She knew that inwardly Margaret was being torn apart. 'I can't advise you. Knowing that Tom is every inch Henry's son, I think you are right. Will you go over to Cliffs Edge?'

'I'll see Henry alone first.'

She wrote a brief note and sent it down to the Britannia Mill by a groom, and within an hour the man was back with an answer. Mr Grimshaw was sending his carriage for her. She kept the carriage waiting while she changed. She deliberately wore the fine blue tweed suit of their last meeting, a small hat trimmed with iridescent cock-feathers. She must put on a brave front even if she was more undecided, more anxious than she had ever been in her life. Previous decisions had been for herself – this was for Tom. She wanted the world and more for her handsome baby, and she was not quite sure how to get it.

She drove along the Bradford Road, with its procession of stone-built mills, the smell of wool, and dye, of stable straw, horse-flesh, and machine-oil. The hum and clatter of machinery. She alighted outside the square stone-built Master's House which now housed Henry's offices and counting-house.

A clerk took her into his private office. There was a bright coal fire, a good Turkish rug, furniture in leather and mahogany. A portrait of her grandfather, Thomas Jagger, looking down at her with her own bright blue eyes. The founder of the firm, a well-set man in his thirties, wearing a blue velvet coat, and an air of inimitable self-confidence. She thought of the stammering purple-faced hulk dying at her mother's feet.

The door opened and Henry came in. He looked older. His thick hair was quite white now, although his eyebrows, flanking the central scowl, were still dark. His figure was trim and young, the strong hands that had once taught her love, the same; well-shaped, long-fingered, smooth, well-cared for. He stood motionless, his heart in his eyes and she knew then that the past three years had been worse for him than for her. After the first humiliation and loss she had plunged into hard work, and then Tom had come, bringing responsibility and an exasperated love. For Henry the physical loss had been wellnigh unbearable. She went to him and he put his arms about her. He did not kiss her. He just held her against him, his eyes closed, and then said, foolishly, 'Take off your hat, Maggy love, and let me see your bonny hair.'

She blushed as though he had asked her to unbutton her blouse – it brought memories back like a flood. He had always, before touching her in love, unpinned her cloud of bronze-red hair. She was shaking and her body

437

burning with longing for him. She took off her smart little hat and put it on the desk.

He touched her hair. 'It's still like fire when the sun's on it.' Then with a sound like a groan, moving his head as though he would shake off some unbearable yoke, 'Oh, Maggy. My love, there's not been a day I haven't wanted you . . .' He sat down in his big mahogany armchair, drew her down on his knee, and buried his face against her breast. 'I've starved for you, Maggy,' he said.

She lifted his head, and kissed him, touching his lips with her hand, and rose, drawing herself away.

'No. I have to think, Henry, and I cannot think when you touch me. The only time I have ever gone into anything without knowing exactly what I was doing, was when I fell in love with you.' Her smile was shaky, her eyes clouded. 'Look where it landed me! I have come for your help, and I must think clearly. Stay there while we talk.'

She put the big desk between them. The London newspapers were spread across it. They were the provincial editions and Ferdinand's arrest and flight did not dominate the headlines as they had in London. What interest had the West Riding in a London dressmaker?

'It's a bad business for you, love.'

'Yes. I got Ferdi away. They can't touch him now.'

'He won't come back?'

'He can't.'

'What will you do?'

'I'll carry on. I've come to you because there is no one else I can come to.'

'About the boy?'

'What else? I'm not frightened for myself.'

The window overlooked the whole of the central loading yards, with its cranes for lifting and lowering bales, enclosed within a square made by the Britannia and

438

Water Meadow Mills. The big dray horses were kept there and the long drays with the Grimshaw name lettered on their sides. Behind the main manufacturing buildings were the boiler-houses with the towering chimneystacks like giant smoke-scarred monoliths against the sky.

'It's so big,' she said. She was chattering. Trying to collect her thoughts. 'Thornsby-born, and I've never been inside a mill before. I had no idea. How many people work here?'

'Six hundred. Another three hundred up at Calder Beck.'

'It makes Hanover Street small beer.'

'Without business like Hanover Street we could not exist.'

'Big fleas need little fleas,' she said unsteadily.

'Maggy, love, what can I do. Tell me. That's all. Tell me.'

The clean-smelling warmth of his big body was so near, so achingly familiar. She longed to put her head down on his shoulder and weep. To play the little woman, to stop struggling . . . she knew if she did he would look after her and Tom forever. 'I've brought him to you, if you'll have him. If you really want him.'

He went white.

'I cannot leave him indefinitely at the Listers'. They are good folk, but he must be educated. He cannot stay with me at Hanover Street, and I cannot give up Hanover Street. I've put too much of myself into it.' Her blue eyes, red with weariness and the hidden tears she had shed, still shone with the old flame-like determination. 'Henry, I will not go under and give it up because of Ferdi. I should never have married him, or I should have broken away as soon as I realized what he was. But until Tom came there was no need. I have to think what is best for Tom. You said you wanted him. Do you still?

Will you have him and bring him up in your home as your boy?'

'My God, Maggy, you *know* I will.'

'He won't always be three. What are your hopes for him? You must have thought about it – tell me, Henry?'

'He will be my son, legally adopted, equal to Stephen in every way. There is plenty for both of them.'

'People will know he is your boy – you've only to look at him. They will talk. It will make a scandal.'

'What the hell do I care for scandal? I'm not making frocks for society ladies. That sort of malice cannot touch me.'

'But – your wife? Angela? Her parents? They are straightlaced people of good family.'

'They haven't a penny that they don't owe me. Do you think I care for the Torrance family with their soldiers and clergymen? If you leave Tom here he will be my son and Angela will do as I ask. How about Leon – will he consent? He is, I suppose, the boy's legal father?'

Margaret gave the vestige of a smile.

'Don't think too hardly of him, poor Ferdi. We had the finest fashion house in London, and he has put it all in jeopardy. I can't forgive him – but I'm sorry for him. He has so much talent. But I am not going to close up and run off into hiding with Tom, change my name, pretend to be a respectable widow. And I can't have Tom stuck with Ferdi's name, like a sort of brand. "The pervert's son." Well, you have given me my answer, Henry, and thank you – but you must speak to Angela first. She already has a son she loves.'

'Who is also my son,' he said proudly. 'Angela will do as I wish.'

'Yes, I'm sure!' There was a frosty glint of amusement in her eyes. 'But will she hate Tom? Will she think of him as an interloper? If she does, then I must think

440

again. You must speak to her, and when you have both decided then send for me. I will be at Danesfell with Millicent until Friday.'

'You shall hear tonight. I want him more than anything I have ever wanted. He is a splendid child. He is my son. And he is yours too, Maggy, and that means more to me than anything else.'

A messenger brought a note from Angela that evening formally inviting Margaret to bring Tom over to see Stephen the following afternoon.

That afternoon Bertha washed the smell of the farm-yard off Tom and put him into a white silk smock. She brushed his blond curls until they stood up in a fluffy golden halo. She dressed him in the pale blue coat with the fur lining, the little cossack cap of brown mink, the white kid gloves, and white kid boots. He looked so beautiful and so bad-tempered that Millicent burst out laughing. The carriage was ordered and they drove out to Cliffs Edge. Ordinarily he would have played hell in protest at having to leave the farm and go visiting in these horrible clothes, but something in his mother's face kept him quiet. He was aware, like a loving little animal, of her deep unhappiness.

When they were shown into the large, opulent drawing-room Henry was standing near Angela who was seated near the blazing fire. She had a small fair child, still in petticoats, seated upon her knee. They looked stiff and unnatural. Like a family posing for a photograph.

For three years old Stephen Grimshaw was pale and undersized. His high forehead was bony, his grey eyes shadowed, his cheeks thin. But the same thick fair curls sprang over his head, the same two lines were drawn between his fair baby brows and he had the same stubborn

Grimshaw jaw-line as the sturdy little boy who marched into the room and stood looking at them.

Stephen was three months the elder, but Tom towered over him. They were as alike as two little bull-calves. Handsome, tenacious, tyrants if handled weakly, and Stephen had been coddled and indulged since his birth.

The grown-ups exchanged meaningless civilities, their eyes on Tom, who stood staring suspiciously at his half-brother – he had been told he was going to see a boy. This little thing in petticoats did not look like a boy. But Stephen stared back with equal aggression.

'Now, Master Tom,' Henry said authoritatively, 'don't you take off your cap before ladies?'

Tom was well aware he should have done this, but knew at once that the man was not cross, that he was pleading with him to behave and be at his best. He turned to his mother and saw the same look in her eyes.

'Who's you?' he demanded of Henry.

'I'm Mr Grimshaw. Your – Uncle Henry.'

Tom snatched off his little fur•cap, tossed it up in the air, and shouted, 'There! Hip-hip-hurrah!'

Stephen curled up with laughter, and Tom went over to him and bent until their eyes were level. Stephen had Henry's luminous grey eyes, the iris ringed in black, but Tom's held the authentic Normanby violet-blue. Stephen, despite Henry's protests, was still kept in skirts to conceal his weak legs.

'You girl?' asked Tom.

Stephen flushed furiously. 'I'm damn well not,' he said in his high treble. 'I'm a boy like you.' He was much more articulate than Tom, and he sounded so like Henry that involuntarily the three adults exchanged amused glances.

Tom favoured Angela with a smile of dazzling sweetness.

442

'Who's you?' he asked.

There was a long silence. Henry and Margaret waiting, holding their breaths.

'I'm your Aunt Angela.'

'Like Angel?'

'I suppose so.'

'Aunty Angel,' Tom said, and called her that for the rest of his life. 'What's your name?' he demanded of Stephen.

'Stephen. What's yours?'

'I'm Tom.'

Tom began to tug at the buttonholes of his coat. Margaret quickly helped him and drew off his warm gloves. In the centre of the floor there was a thick rug, with toys scattered on it. 'Stephen play with me?' he demanded.

'Play?' repeated Stephen – he had never been allowed to play with another child. 'How?'

'With the toys,' Tom tugged impatiently at his arm so that Angela clutched him to her, pushing Tom's hands away.

'Don't hurt him!' she cried. 'He nearly fell. He can't walk yet.'

'*Can't walk?*' Tom was astounded. 'Is he still a baby?'

'I'm not a baby!' Stephen yelled furiously, flushing crimson up to his fair curls, and hitting furiously at Angela. 'Let me go! Mama – put me down!'

'Shut up!' ordered Tom in commendable imitation of big Bert Lister. 'Only babies cry, and no one hits ladies.' Stephen stopped at once, equally astounded. Tantrums usually brought him kisses and sweetmeats. 'Come with me,' Tom said cockily. 'Me – Tom – *I* will show you *how* to walk.' And with that he seized Stephen round his middle and hauled him off Angela's knee before she could cry out in protest. Henry said sharply, 'Let them be.'

Tom staggered slowly across to the rug where the toys were scattered, swinging his light little brother with each solid step, so that Stephen's helpless feet swung in the air with weightless steps. They began to giggle, and as they reached the rug, rolled over together, shrieking with laughter.

'You see,' Margaret said, 'he *will* be careful with him. He hates being dressed up like this. He's a boy's boy. He likes to run and shout. He likes to be with men. The groom, Marley, lets him help with the carriage horses. He loves Farmer Lister and the boys. He's very kind to small creatures and children. He fights with the big boys, but he's good with the small ones . . . He . . .' she suddenly buried her face in her hands. Henry stood in agony, longing to comfort her.

'I'm sorry – I have had a difficult week,' said Margaret. 'I will be glad if you will let me know what you have decided.'

Henry had told Angela what she must do. Never since their marriage had she ever attempted to oppose his wishes. Never since her breakdown had she fought him. For the past three years the care of Stephen's fragile life had been her sole concern. She did not want Tom – she wanted only the weak little tyrant rolling so ecstatically on the rug.

'If you refuse,' Henry had said, 'I shall understand. I will ask nothing against your will. But I must make a good life for Tom and I shall do so even if it means moving away from you. I would leave Stephen with you, and Cliffs Edge, and everything you need. But I want Tom to come to me, and I hope you will accept him.'

Tom was substance while Stephen was the shadow. If she refused he would carry out his threat – with courtesy and every consideration, but her marriage would be at an end. And she knew also that in these first few minutes Tom had captured Stephen too. That when he had hauled her baby from her lap he had broken Stephen's dependence. She resented it bitterly. If Margaret was suffering it was what she deserved. She saw Henry watching her, rubbing his chin with his thumbnail, and gave a little start. She said, 'If Henry wishes him to come to us, and it will help you, of course I agree.' On the rug Tom was pretending to be a bear and eat Stephen, who was almost hysterical with joy. 'It is obvious that Stephen will be delighted. Let us hope Tom won't be too much for him.'

'It's what he needs,' Henry said brusquely. 'Another lad around. He's been made a baby and an invalid too long.'

'You will let Bertha Lister stay with him?' said Margaret. 'He loves her. While he's little, anyway.'

'Of course,' said Henry. 'Will you come to see him often?'

She did not dare look up into his eyes.

'I want him to settle. I think it best to give him time. I want him to feel he belongs here.'

'He belongs to you too,' said Henry gently, 'and I don't want him to forget you are his mother.'

Angela rose sharply, controlling a gesture of protest. Margaret smiled gratefully, but shook her head.

'I will come – I want him to remember me too. But not too often – perhaps, two or three times a year.'

'It will be an eternity for him,' said Henry but his eyes said, 'and to me.'

There was a long, painful silence. She must go quickly, or she would never leave her baby. She called Tom to her, and knelt, her arms about him. 'Mama's going back to London, darling.'

'Tom come too?'

'Not this time. You are staying here.'

'At the farm? With the boys?' His face lit eagerly.

'No, Bertha will stay and look after you, but not at the farm. You'll stay with Stephen, here at Cliffs Edge.'

His lower lip began to tremble ominously.

'Don't want to.' Stubbornly.

'You'll like it.'

'Can I have Toby?'

Margaret looked up at Henry. 'It's his dog. A puppy. It's at Danesfell.'

'Of course,' said Henry, 'I'll send over for it at once.'

Margaret held Tom closely in her arms and he covered her face with fierce, damp kisses before struggling away. 'You come back soon?' he insisted. 'A-morrow?'

'Very soon, my darling,' she lied, and rose, pulling her veil across her face. She did not want him to see her cry and she knew that soon she would be crying for a long while.

'Thank you. Thank you both.' She half-turned towards Angela. 'Thank you especially – I know it isn't easy for you, and I know he isn't really an easy boy. He's lovable . . . but self-willed. But – his father must deal with that . . .' She stood, swaying a little, then went quickly out of the room. Tom stood silent with his thumb in his mouth and Stephen, flushed and bright-eyed with excitement, crawled across to him, shouting for him to go on being a bear.

'Don't want to,' said Tom sulkily. Stephen's face creased up with disappointment, and Tom said grumpily, 'Oh, all right . . .' and got down on his hands and knees.

It was as though Tom was a magnet drawing Stephen towards him.

'You had better go to Margaret, Henry, and tell her I will do my very best,' Angela said stiffly.

He lifted her hand and kissed it gratefully.

'Thank you, my dear, I promise you will never regret this.'

But when he ran through the hall to the entrance the carriage had already moved away and Margaret was gone.

Margaret returned to London feeling as though she had left half herself behind in Yorkshire. No noisy boy – no noisy puppy. The big elegant apartment, Ferdinand's empty rooms, she had Lecky and the Judsons – so quiet at night one could hear every footfall in the street outside.

The first thing to be done was to wind up the partnership. She sold Juniper Place and Hollingroyd Crescent, and Millicent put up the collateral for a loan. She put a notice in the London newspapers to say that Mr Ferdinand Leon had now no connections with the firm in Hanover Street, which would continue to trade under the name of MARGARET NORMANBY. Although business was not so good, and the upper-crust of Court patronage had been withdrawn, she could not help feeling a thrill of pride when she saw, for the first time, her name in gilt letters, three feet high, across the double frontage. MARGARET NORMANBY. And this time every stick and penny of it was hers. *Her* business. *Her* responsibility – to succeed or fail. She managed to persuade Roy Brinkley to leave Willis & Harrington and join her as general manager. She engaged a young graduate from the Royal College, and set him to studying Ferdi's work.

'I don't want you to imitate him,' she said, 'I want your own ideas. But I want the same distinction and elegance. Every customer must feel a queen when we make her a dress.'

She was nervous when the Spring collection was launched, but it was a success. She worked as she had always worked, with every nerve in her body, and every

447

thought in her head. And it was only at night, alone in her bed, sleepless among the soft, down pillows that she thought of Tom's smacking kisses when she had gone to say goodnight. Upstairs the nursery floor was heartbreakingly silent.

But Henry sent her regular reports and there was no doubt, after the first wrench of parting, Tom was happy. The memory of his restricted life in Hanover Street faded: there were paddocks and orchards, stables and gardens at Cliffs Edge where he was free to roam with Stephen, gaining strength and now promoted to breeches and crutches. It was a touching sight to see the two little brothers together. Tom very solicitious and bossy, Stephen mischievous and defiant. Both of them now had their own ponies with a special saddle for Stephen. There were friends in the district. But the whole life of the house revolved round the two boys.

Henry would drive them proudly about the town, and take them into the mill with him, carrying Stephen, and holding Tom's hand, showing them every department, explaining every part of manufacture and introducing them to the staff from his chief clerk to the rough workmen in the sheds, with whom Tom became a great favourite, and who referred to him openly as 'Grimshaw's grand little bastard'. Henry did not mind – he was in love with his two fair-haired boys and with Tom beyond everything. They were the heirs apparent and well aware of it.

Only Angela and her parents suffered embarrassment over Tom. As the years passed she became more like her mother, religious in a stiff, conformist way, widening the gap between herself and Henry. Margaret's visits were painful with constraint, although Tom was always excited at seeing his 'pretty Mama'. When finally the boys were sent to school, Margaret ceased to go to Cliffs Edge and took him out for the day by herself. They enjoyed themselves. She was good at finding interesting things to do. But Angela would not allow Stephen to accompany them, and the two boys had grown close together – Tom resented not sharing his treats with Stephen and Stephen equally resented being left out. Margaret knew Angela regarded her as a bad influence, but would not cause dissention by telling Henry. So gradually she limited her visits to one a year on Tom's birthday, leaving him to adapt into his new world, and burying herself in her own.

The boys were turned seven years old when Tom's legal adoption was made final.

Henry wrote to Margaret asking her to meet him in London for lunch to talk about it. The settlement of Tom's position as his son and co-heir with Stephen gave him an overwhelming sense of relief. But also a feeling of guilt. He needed to see her. To reassure her – and in doing so to reassure himself.

He was waiting in the entrance foyer of the Savoy when he saw her come in from the street, and at once felt the old excitement and delight at her presence. She was different to any woman he had ever known.

She was so complete, so shapely and assured, bearing the elegance of her clothes with such careless grace. She was in brown velvet, wearing a wide-brimmed hat trimmed with one enormous apricot-shaded rose. From the top of her head to the tip of her ivory-handled umbrella she proclaimed the height of fashion and the height of good taste, and everyone watched her as she walked towards him. Which was what she wanted, and why she dressed as she did.

He stepped forward, and said, 'Maggy . . .' She gave a little exclamation of surprise and pleasure and gave him her hand.

'Henry. I was miles away.' She was very calm, then said, with a tentative little smile, 'And how's my Tom?'

'He's grand, Maggy. He's a wonderful boy. Now it's all settled I had to see you. To tell you how grateful I am – we all are. What a help he has been to Stephen – how happy he has made our lives.'

'I'm glad.' She glanced round at the fashionable crowd moving towards the restaurant, and said, 'I'm so *hungry*. Shall we go in?' Just as though it was quite an ordinary meeting and Tom did not exist. He sensed an edginess, defensive, keeping him at a distance.

'Of course – I forget my manners.' He beckoned to the *mâtre d'hotel*, who led them to their table. It was curious to be with her in this exclusive and expensive hotel. When they had been lovers they had done such simple things – country places, simple food, wanting no distractions but each other.

'I have been in Paris staying with Ferdinand. He had a very pleasant apartment there.'

'You saw Leon?' He was surprised.

'I always do when I go to France. He helps me buy, he designs special orders for me, and tells me all the gossip. I have two young designers, but Ferdi is still our inspiration. I pay him well. No one knows – and now, if they knew, who would care? The old dowagers round the Court, perhaps?'

'Do they matter?'

'Not so much – but I'd like to see them back. I always want to win.'

He laughed. 'You don't change. I was in France too – in Paris – recently. I did not know you were there.'

'Perhaps it was just as well,' she said mischievously, and there it was again between them – the old, powerful attraction – so that his breath quickened, and he said, 'Maggy . . .' but she moved her hand before he could

450

take it, and lifted the large menu which had been set before her.

'Why did you so particularly want to see me?'

'I thought you might be distressed.'

She frowned a little, concentrating on the menu. He saw a nerve tick at the corner of the firm red mouth.

'I could not bear that you should lose anything because of me. You gave me the only real happiness I have known. And now you've given me Tom.'

'I'll have some cold consommé and the salmon poché. Tom belongs to no one but himself. You can give him the life he needs – I couldn't. But he'll fight you as he fought me if he wants something else. You must be prepared for that, Henry.'

'That is years ahead.'

'I knew from the day he was born that my sort of life and my sort of woman could never rear the kind of man he would be. Don't think that because he is so like you you will always agree.'

'I'll make him a son you'll be proud of.'

'He's that already. Don't worry about me, Henry. I don't cry over spilt milk. I didn't when Mama rejected me. When my father deserted us. When Charmy went to the bad. When you decided that a son was more important than me. Nor when Ferdi nearly wrecked our years of hard work. I don't stay broken-hearted. I wanted a different life for Tom, and now he has it. It is what I wanted. I'm not crying.'

He had ordered champagne. She drank, savouring it, putting it down without coquetry. No meaningful glances over the lip of the glass. But the composed face under the dipping brim of the big hat was alluring. The neat, small, capable hands. The white throat dipping into a V of ecru lace, like a dart between her small velvet-covered

451

breasts. He wanted her with the same instant compulsion with which he had wanted her from the beginning.

'I had no maternal yearnings when he was born. I'd never even *held* a baby. And then ther he was, so big, hamdsome, demanding and *awful*. Oh, God, I'll never forget the day he and the puppy ran through the gown showroom, knocking over the display stands and setting the girls and customers shrieking – they talk of it to this day!'

'You are extraordinary, Maggy. Isn't there anyone you really need?'

For a minute she did not answer, then the big rose lifted, and azure eyes were looking at him beneath the brim and he was shattered by their unabashed desire.

'Yes. *You*. Is that what you want to hear? My lover and companion? I never had a companion or close friend until you came. I have never wanted anyone else.' The hat-brim slowly lowered until he was looking into the flame-coloured heart of the big rose. He could not see her face. 'I miss you, Henry. Sometimes it is more than I can bear.' She looked up and he took her hand.

'I know,' he said. 'It's like losing a limb that still throbs after the amputation. At first I thought I could not stand it. Then Stephen needed me so much – we did not think he would live . . . or if he lived, his life might be worthless. But he's fine now. And there is Tom too – I don't look back so much now.'

'No, of course,' she said.

'I feel I know everything about you, Maggy. Every flash of temper, ever quirk of humour, the feel of your body and your lips . . .'

She smiled, but did not change colour as she had in his office when he had asked her to take off her hat so he could touch her hair.

'Yet how long did we know each other? Those few

452

days in France? An occasional snatched weekend that Autumn? Added together it would scarcely be a single month. We were always saying goodbye.'

'Maggy – time is going for me. I am over fifty. I want you – and I want you now. Shall we say goodbye again?'

She looked around the sunny room with its swags of gilded flowers round the mirrors and panels of brocade, and smiled mockingly.

'Here?'

'I am staying here. Come up to my room?'

'There are people I know here – customers.'

'We will finish our lunch. I will see you to the door and I will go up. Walk round the corner into the side entrance. It is on the first floor – number fifty.'

She laughed, the bright clear sound bringing back so many memories.

'A planned campaign, *mon général*. For how long have you planned it?'

'Since you walked through that door today.'

They made a pretence of finishing their lunch. They did exactly as he had said. She walked up to the first floor and no one saw her. He opened the door, and as it shut behind her she took off the big hat and skyed it across the room, and pulled the pins out of her burning mass of hair.

They did not lower the blinds – the early Autumn sun was part of their delight – an enflaming visual delight to him. She was older now, more deliberately abandoned, the sunlit hours stretched to sunset, and they were still there in each other's arms, naked, satiated but not content as the blue twilight crept through the trees of the Embankment gardens, and the starlings chattered home to roost.

'I must go,' she said, 'I must get back before they close.'

'Maggy, I shall be in London for the night. Stay with me.'

'I cannot stay here. This afternoon has been risk enough.'

'Meet me at Waterloo – like we used to. We'll go down to the inn on the river again. We could stay all tomorrow. Maggy, please . . .'

'At what time?'

'There are trains every hour. Meet me at eight.'

'Very well.' She rose and dressed quickly. Bent over him, kissed him once, and was gone.

It was the hour between tea and dinner and few people about. She went out and the doorman hailed a cab for her.

She leaned back and closed her eyes, her hands moving over her breasts as though she would quell their renewed urgency. She would always love him – but they could not snatch recklessly at love as they had eight years ago. They both needed a real life, the lasting happiness which for them had been impossible from the start. She had deceived herself to think otherwise. Neither she nor Henry were capable of the self-effacement and sacrifices that a life together would have demanded. One of them would have to submit, and for neither of them was it possible, although neither of them would ever be satisfied with anyone else.

The cab stopped outside Hanover Street. The large gilded letters across the frontage bravely proclaimed her name. MARGARET NORMANBY. As she crossed the threshold Roy Brinkley came running down to meet her, a look of excitement in his eyes. He had changed a great deal in the past years, sloughing off his Cockney brashness, becoming shrewd and handsome, well-dressed. He wanted to marry her. She had been able to keep his

454

devotion at arm's length – but he was young and ambitious. Sooner or later he would demand an answer or he would grow tired of the pursuit.

'Madame – Lady Lucaster is here.'

'Ah,' said Margaret, expelling a small triumphant sigh. Seven years since Lady Lucaster had cancelled her order and kept her standing like a housemaid while she had explained that Charmian was a whore. Margaret grinned to herself. Her ladyship had been right about that – poor Charmy. And since then Ferdi had added his scandalous tomfoolery. But Margaret Normanby had survived. This was surrender. But then Lady Lucaster had that unlikely last daughter to marry off. Gossip said that a match was pending with Kenneth Allwood, now a sober director of the family firm.

'Did she ask for me, Roy?'

'Not yet, Madame.'

The blue eyss glinted. 'I'll go and take off my hat. And Roy – don't *tell* her I'm in. But let it be known I am.'

'Yes, Madame,' he said appreciatively.

'And don't fetch me down unless she asks for me personally.'

'Yes, Madame. I understand.'

He went down into the main gown showroom where Lady Lucaster and her undoubtedly unattractive daughter were studying fashion plates with Miss Jenner in attendance.

Lady Lucaster turned to Roy and said in her high, fluting, aristocratic voice, 'Mr Brinkley. Would you be so kind as to ask Madame Normanby if she could spare me a few minutes? I do *so* need her advice.'

'With pleasure, your ladyship.'

He went upstairs three at a time and flung open the office door. 'It's a cinch, Madame. She says will you spare her a minute. She's the first of the big nobs to come back.'

'Yes,' said Margaret. 'Now they'll all come.' She smiled into his devoted, spaniel eyes, and said, 'Run along, Roy. Three minutes.'

She rang for Mr Callow.

'Would you send this note to Mr Grimshaw at the Savoy – by special messenger, please.'

When the door closed behind him she rose, patted her hair, straightened her bodice, lifted her chin, and went unhurriedly down into the showroom to welcome Lady Lucaster back to the fold.

Henry was writing a telegram to send to the inn on the river, and as he addressed it remembered the Autumn days he and Margaret had spent there together. The flaming colours of the trees at Cookham, and Margaret, so young in a blue cloak, and her red hair loose about her shoulders.

He had kept his promise of fidelity to Angela far beyond the date of Stephen's birth, and the first anxious three years of the boy's life had seemed to sap all her physical energy. If she had been tense and unresponsive before, now she was passive and exhausted.

He had learned late in his life that making love to a woman with whom one was passionately in love made the sexual act a transcendent experience, unforgettable. Now he knew it was only repeatable with the beloved. He now was a-dream again, planning like a young man how he would come often to London, how he and Margaret would be together whenever it was possible, that perhaps now Angela would give him his freedom. Life was running by – he had just turned fifty. He wanted the rest of his life with Margaret and all his driving will began to plan towards this.

There was a discreet knock at the door, and the room valet brought him a note. He opened it quickly.

My Darling,

It won't do. It cannot work. It did not before and it will not now. Only when I was young I did not understand. If we go on Angela will know sooner or later, because in her own way she loves you, and people always know when someone close to them is in love with someone else.

Your mother died when you were a small boy and your father had been cruel to her as he was cruel to you and Milly. My mother was a drunken dreamer and my father a vain, selfish gambler and rake. I don't want Tom to have the sort of life we had. Nor your Stephen. I want their childhood and youth to be secure and not broken by family partings and passions. Later on, when they are grown, they will decide what they want to do with their lives – but neither you nor I must do anything to hurt them now. But it was a lovely goodbye, my darling, and I shall always love you.

Margaret

He went down into the bar and got drunk, not like a young man, riotously and defiantly, but with steady dignity, getting up to his feet at midnight and going unswervingly to his room, where he fell on the bed fully-clothed and into instant blackness of drunken oblivion.

In the morning he rose, and sat for a long while with the heels of his palms pressed against his eyes to prevent the tears from falling. Then he bathed, shaved and dressed, and drove to the station to catch his train back to Thornsby.

At Thornsby the station was full of people. It was the last day of the races and the crowds were streaming back from the course. He wanted to get home. He needed the familiar house and he needed his boys. He had wanted sons more than anything in the world. By the time he was sixty they would inherit what he had built. But what guarantee had he that they would want it?

His carriage with the coachman in attendance was waiting for him. The traffic descending from the race-track on the moors was solid as far as he could see, and the sun was about to set as the carriage finally approached Cliffs Edge. Through the orchard trees he could see the lights, and knew the boys would be waiting for him and for the presents he always brought back. For the first time he had not remembered. He should have remembered. Tomorrow he would take them into Leeds and let them choose something for themselves.

The traffic was at a standstill again, and he jumped out impatiently to walk the remaining distance to the house, and was at once accosted by a tall, elderly man, extremely well-dressed and wearing the kind of wideawake hat which Henry's mind associated with the novels of Mark Twain and with Mississippi gamblers. A breath of whisky emanted from him. He wore no overcoat, although the late afternoon was chill. He seemed a little short of breath. The yellowing whites of his bloodshot eyes framed irises which still showed a touch of violet-blue.

'May I presume upon you, Sir . . .' the old man began, and Henry began to feel in his pocket, recognizing a touch which he saw one, 'to assist me with a small loan. If you will give me your address, Sir, it will be returned – my honour as a gentleman!'

Recognition flashed upon Henry. It was Sir Richard Normanby! He looked at the trembling hands, and the drink-bleared face. He thought of the beautiful young man who had swept Florence away from him at the ball at Danesfell all those years ago. He could remember her pink dress with its huge skirt like an upturned rose and the wild excitement in her eyes.

'You've had a bad day, Sir?' he said.

'Yes indeed. Lady Luck – Lady Luck! A fickle jade,' Richard sounded like an old huckster. 'I must get back to

458

London where I have money awaiting me. I confess to a slight embarrassment. Just a matter of a bite before the train goes, and my fare.'

'I understand,' said Henry. He tried to remember his murderous jealousy, and could not. How absurd and violent one was when young. How different happiness was to anything he had imagined then.

He counted out five sovereigns and Normanby's jaw dropped in surprise. He had expected a crown piece at the most. His hands shook as he took the money.

'I am exceedingly obliged to you, Sir. I assure you it will be returned.'

'Please – think nothing of it. And, oh, may I give you this?'

Henry took out a pocket knife and prised the golden half-sovereign from his watch-chain and handed it to the astonished old man. 'It is pierced but I think negotiable.' His cool eyes searched for a glimmer of recognition. 'I believe you come from these parts. Sir Richard Normanby? Yes. You gave me this once many years ago but you will not remember. May I return it to you now for luck. It has brought me a great deal. Please take my carriage to the station. Goodnight to you, sir.'

Richard stared at the broad-shouldered, well-dressed stranger, tried to place him, but could not, shrugged, thanked Henry again and climbed into the carriage, leaning back negligently and lighting a cigar to the manner born. The coachman turned the horses and drove back towards the station.

Henry laughed out loud as he walked towards the house, waving up at the schoolroom windows as he drew near, hearing four fists hammering on the panes to attract his attention, and, as he went into the house, the boys came down, Tom leaping, Stephen limping, to throw themselves into his arms.

459

Chapter Seventeen

There was a stir in the entrance foyer of the Salon Privé at the Casino at Monte Carlo, as an extremely beautiful woman entered with a small entourage of young men in evening clothes. Swarthy, dark-eyed young men, impeccably groomed and dressed. Not Frenchmen but speaking good French. The lady was in her early thirties, with red-gold hair, her bare arms and shoulders of a glowing whiteness, her eyes of a melting violet-blue. She was exquisitely dressed and jewelled, but a close observer would have noticed beneath the beautifully-applied cosmetics there was a weariness and pallor, and that she moved quickly, nervously, like a darting tropical bird, as though searching desperately for something that would not bore her.

She could have been a great lady or a great courtesan, and she was in fact both. She was the Baroness Philippe Abderhazy. The Baron was staying on his yacht in the harbour. The Baron did not gamble at casinos. He played for higher stakes.

Charmian looked round the gaming tables and saw her quarry playing baccarat on the far side of the room. A smooth, brown Armenian, with hooked nostrils and restless black eyes. She had no idea what Philippe wanted from him. Shares, oil, coal, steel? Railways, slaves, gold, ivory, brothels? Secrets, information about the intentions and interests of Governments? For in spite of French nationality, and Persian birth, Philippe belonged nowhere.

But she was not required to know such things. She was

required to attract, enslave and to compromise . . . to get the quarry into the position of non-refusal. It was the same old game the women played in the cobbled streets behind the harbour – the badger game. But Charmian and Philippe played for millions.

She knew, because now she knew all there was to know about every sort of man, that the Armenian would not want to be disturbed yet. He was a gambler and would not leave the tables until well past midnight. But she must stay, and hold her little court, and be very gay and attractive – because Philippe would be angry if she did not bring the Armenian back to supper, and she was very frightened of his anger. She felt deadly tired. She was tired because she was bored. She now had all the things she had once longed for and felt she had nothing.

She took her place at the roulette table and began to play. Hussein, one of Philippe's mysterious 'nephews', who rumour said, were really his sons, brought her the chips and stood beside her, occasionally bending to whisper advice in her ear. He was her lover. Philippe permitted it as he would permit a pair of handsome tame animals to couple if it amused them and did not interfere with his plans. He had long since ceased to desire her for himself.

The Armenian finally threw down his cards, and came across to kiss her hand. Hussein discreetly faded into the group of attendant gentlemen behind her chair, leaving the field clear for Abderhazy's prey. The Armenian owned oil wells.

'Shall we go, M'sieur?' she smiled. 'Philippe is looking forward to seeing you for supper – and luck seems to be running against us both tonight.'

The carriage was waiting to take them down to the harbour. She regarded the night before her with unutterable weariness. Would this man, whom she did not know,

461

or even find attractive, come to her state-room? If he did not, perhaps Hussein would come. She did not love Hussein but at least he was young, handsome and infatuated with her. That he reported her every action to his 'uncle' had long ceased to matter. She never slept until dawn, and then she would take some of the small white pills that a famous German specialist had prescribed for her to make her sleep.

It was extraordinary, but at these times, she would find herself longing for Thornsby, and the cosy kitchen at Hollingroyd Crescent, with Maggy and Lecky and old, red-faced Grandma Jagger dozing before the fire. And her poor mother, up in her boudoir, weaving her fantasies of past grandeur and riches. How proud she would have been to see her now. A real Baroness. Mama would never have suspected the hidden undercurrents of her life, and if she had she would have pretended they were not there – as she tried to herself, sometimes managing to forget that she was, at best, an expensive whore, and that Philippe Abderhazy was the whoremaster.

Sometimes she remembered the boy – whose name she had long forgotten – who had kissed her behind the lilac bushes in Thornsby Park and asked her to tea with his mother. She had been so young then, so fresh, but never innocent – a born woman of pleasure, Philippe said. What was pleasure? Something that grew stale the moment you grasped it?

The Thornsby lad had been a big fair-skinned North Country boy, rather like Angus Black. But she tried not to think of Angus, or of Bellamy. When she looked back, Thornsby seemed like a world full of light. She wished she had gone to tea with the big, fair boy and his mother. She might have married him, and then perhaps she would not feel so old, although she was still so young.

She took the Armenian's arm and sent Hussein for her

cloak, and another of Philippe's young men for the carriage. People stared at her as she floated out into the warm Riviera night, thinking how wonderful to be a famous beauty, married to a rich man, and not one of them dreaming that this exquisite, self-assured, smiling lady was little Charmian Normanby, still out of her depth, always frightened and nearly always looking for a way of escape.

But there was no escape back to innocence. And if there were she would not take it, for luxury and admiration had become drugs which she could never do without. And Philippe would never let her go while she was useful to him. But one day he would discard her.

She would never want. She would have a comfortable income, her jewels and expensive clothes. He would buy her silence with security. But she did not think about the future, or about herself and whether there was any meaning in her life, in case she should have a real glimpse of the silly, devious, selfish, brainless, little girl who, like her mother, only clung to sanity by pushing all frightening realities away.

She *was* the Baroness Philippe Abderhazy, beautiful, famous and greatly admired. She tried not to look at the haggard, older women sitting night after night, evening after interminable evening, watching the wheel spin, hearing the splattering flip of baccarat cards, clinging to the shallow, bought young men who attended them, in case she saw a reflection of the future.

And sometimes she took too many of the little white pills, and slept all day. And sometimes she thought of the black, moonlit water through which the yacht steamed on their endless voyages, the music from the orchestra drifting through the night, and it seemed to her that faces looked up and called to her from the waves. The white and ruddy Angus, the dark tormented face of Bellamy,

463

almost as though they were calling her to join them, and she would turn away terrified, yet tempted by the thought of silence and peace.

Margaret was in her forty-fourth year. She did not feel it and she certainly did not look it, with her smooth, fresh skin and clear eyes, and her back as straight as ever. But sometimes she felt a sort of chillness, a heralding of age, as the wind along the river, blowing East, was a herald of the Winter to come.

She no longer lived in the apartment above the premises in Hanover Street. That too had been absorbed into the business. She lived in a new apartment building in Chelsea, which had big rooms overlooking the curve round the green trees of Battersea to the Whistleresque towers of Lots Road power station. Millicent, when she was in London, lived near, as did many people she knew in the arts and theatre world.

The start of the century had been full of pressure – the flood of mourning when the old Queen had died. People had talked of the end of an era, and perhaps it was, but to Maggy it had been mountains of black – silk, lace, cloth – all black, and the streets of London gloomy, without a flash of the blues, the jade greens or delicate pinks and yellows which she loved. She had agreed with Rose Briggs who had said, 'Fair gives me the 'ump it does. She was a nice old cow but I'll be glad when Teddy gets 'isself coronated and we can 'ave a bit of a knees-up again.'

Edward had been King for six years now, and the firm of Margaret Normanby had prospered. It was August. Soon she would be making her annual trip up North for Tom's birthday. He and Stephen had finished school in July, and were due to go to University this Autumn. She knew they were to go to Oxford but no further details.

After she came back she would go to Paris to buy, to meet Ferdinand and discuss the Spring collection. She did not quite know where she wanted to go then. Certainly not to stay with Ferdinand, who was turning into a faddy, frail, old gossip, perpetually scandalizing about his friends. And Milly was away in the United States.

Her father had died five years ago – she had neither seen nor spoken to him since her mother's death. When his long-suffering landlady had reported his serious illness, she had, without letting him know, provided him with every medical care and comfort. Typically he had not even enquired where the help was coming from. She arranged for his burial at Danesfell but did not go. And she had not heard from Charmian for many years.

Jany Leck came in with letters and newspaper. In her sixties she looked little different to when Margaret had first known her. Her sparse hair still as sparse, but not grey. Her round, moon-face unwrinkled. She rustled in in her blue bombazine and large white apron. There was a second cup on the tray and a chair drawn up, but she waited as she did every day, for Margaret to say, 'Sit down, Lecky,' which she did at once, while Margaret went through her diary for the day.

Margaret poured two cups of tea, and stretched out her hand for the paper, surprised when Lecky held it fast.

'What has happened? Why don't you give it to me?'

'It's young Charmy.'

'Oh, *Lecky*!' Margaret relaxed. Unknown fears had gripped her. Henry? Tom? 'You gave me a turn. What's Charmy been up to now?'

'Nowt,' said Lecky, handing over the newspaper. 'Poor lass. She's dead.'

'What?' Margaret went white.

On the front page there was a photograph of the

beautiful Baroness Abderhazy – Charmian – taken some years ago, at her most alluring, and a short paragraph. The Baroness had been found dead in her apartment. She had been suffering from insomnia and it was believed had taken an overdose of sleeping tablets. It was thought to be an accident.

Margaret stared at the picture through a rush of tears. Her sense of loss was indescribable. *Charmian! Dead?* That silly, lovely little sister! She said, helplessly, 'I had only just thought I would write to her. Perhaps go and see her. Oh, Lecky . . . I *should* have written.'

'No use getting in a state,' said Lecky. 'You did all you could for her. And for your father.'

But had she really? She had done a great deal for them and had asked for nothing in return – but had she loved them? Whom had she loved? Henry? Tom and Lecky? Three people. Not very many for forty-four years.

Poor, pretty Charmy, so vain and so silly, she had loved her when they were children. She hoped her death had been an accident. She did not like to think of Charmian in despair. But there was nothing she could do now.

A cab came for her at nine o'clock. Roy Brinkley would be in at eight-thirty. He was her general manager and devoted to her but had married about a year ago, ambitiously, the daughter of Mr Willis, the senior partner in Willis & Harrington, his late employees. She guessed he had ambitions for a partnership with her. But not yet. She was not prepared to give up yet.

When she arrived at Hanover Street, Roy came forward to meet her.

'Good morning, Roy.'

'Good morning, Madame. Er, Madame . . .'

'Yes, Roy?'

'Master Tom is here.'

466

'My Tom?' she exclaimed, dumbfounded.

'Yes, Madame. In your office. He travelled down overnight so I took it upon myself to send out for some breakfast for him.'

'Thank you, Roy. That was thoughtful of you. I will go up.'

It was twelve months since she had seen him and he took her breath away. Nearly six foot tall, fair-skinned, fair-haired like his father, broad of chest and shoulder, but with a grace that Henry had never possessed. He was standing by the pigeon-holes where the cloth patterns were kept, turning over the swags of tweed, feeling the quality with a highly professional air. He heard her, looked up and smiled, and she felt her heart explode with love.

He had been a beautiful child, and he was now a splendid boy. He was all his father – apart from the grace, the winning smile, the assured manner of privilege and the eyes of the true Normanby violet-blue. But his eyes were not greedy like Sir Richard's nor emptily seductive like poor Charmy's. He looked at her with such appreciation that she felt at once like an attractive woman and not merely a mother. She was glad she had put on her smartest suit and her sables, and was wearing a breath of grey tulle and massed velvet gentians that called itself a hat.

He came forward eagerly and kissed her, and her eyes filled with tears.

'You're glad to see me?' he asked anxiously.

'Oh, Tom, of course. But what are you doing in London? I was coming up next week for your birthday before I go to Paris.'

'I thought, for a change, I might have my birthday down here with you.'

She took off her hat, sat down at the desk, and perched

a *pince-nez* on her small, charming nose. She only needed glasses for close work, but she hoped they made her look staid and motherly. Tom burst out laughing.

'You look like a little girl playing school-marm, but please don't try to. I've had enough lectures from the Angel recently to last a chap a lifetime.'

'You don't get on?'

'No. So yesterday I decided to leave.'

She took off the *pince-nez* and her shrewd glance was neither girlish nor motherly. He straightened up, the cajoling smile went from his face, then, unexpectedly, he smiled again.

'You're just like Dad,' he said. 'Do you remember that day when you and he both turned up at school to see me – in my first year, before Steve came?'

The two boys had been sent to separate schools, much against Henry's wishes. In middle-age Angela had turned back to the traditions of her family, and had sent Steve to an ancient foundation with a strong ecclesiastical influence, where the Bishop, her grandfather, her two uncles and a brother, all clergymen, had been pupils. Tom was sent to the Master Weavers Guild College, founded in the eighteenth century by the rich woollen merchants for their sons. A school for men of commercial ambitions, with a fine scientific reputation. Stephen had made himself such a nuisance in his determination to join Tom that Angela had had to give way, and let him do so.

Margaret remembered that blissful day – just one in the fifteen years since she had left Tom with Henry at Cliffs Edge. Coincidentally they had both arrived to take him out and for one long summer Saturday the three of them had been a family together.

'I remember,' she said.

'D'you remember that Spanish boy I was friendly with? Gomez? We took him out to tea and on the river?

Afterwards he said you and Dad were two halves of an orange. It's a Spanish saying – like we say chalk and cheese for being different. It means exactly alike. Fitting. The Angel and Dad are chalk and cheese – you and Dad are two halves of an orange. I always remembered.'

'Did you tell him we were not married?'

'No.'

'Because you were ashamed?'

'No,' he said, 'so far as I'm concerned you *are* married.'

She was filled with gratitude and could find no words to express it. He came round the desk and hugged her with the old impetuous affection.

She held his hand.

'You're in a row?'

'Yes.'

'With Henry? Your uncle?'

'Oh, Mama, you don't have to go on pretending. Everyone in Thornsby knows I'm his son. The workmen call me Grimshaw's bastard.'

'And do you mind?'

'I told you – no.' He scowled, the two grave lines between the handsome winged brows making memory twist, bitter-sweet, within her. 'No. Who wouldn't be proud of being Henry Grimshaw's son? It is the Angel. She's taken against me – since I grew up. She says I'm unmanageable.'

'Can she manage Steve?'

He hooted derisively. 'No one can manage Steve. But that's different. He's her son. He's great, but he's a devil. And looks like a choirboy. He's going to Oxford because he says it might be fun, and it's near enough to London to come down to see me and have a night on the town. Dad and I will lay any odds he won't end up a clergyman. No, he'll come into the business with me. We'll be the Grimshaw Sons.'

469

'You've decided to do that?'

'We never wanted anything else. I've decided not to go to Oxford. I'm going to take an engineering degree at London. We've got it all worked out. Dad's good at selling and organization. Steve's good at figures and finance, and I like machines. England's not going to be the only country with advanced technology. Germany and America are racing ahead. We'll have to keep modernizing, ploughing back capital to re-tool. It's always been Dad's policy, and it's important. You can go on patching and repairing plant until it's as out of date as the Dodo . . .' he stopped, and the attractive quick colour flushed up beneath his fair skin. 'Am I boring you?'

'No,' said Margaret, 'no *indeed!* Go on.'

'Machine engineering. And electrics. I want to know as much as I can. When we've got our degrees, both Steve and I will take a course at Leeds to learn about the wool trade – then we'll be ready to be useful to Dad.'

'And was all this his idea?'

'Well, he's always said that when we were old enough we were to chose to do exactly what we wanted to do. "It's your life," he said, "take your time." But being his sons, and seeing the mills, and knowing all about them since we were babies, of course that's what we wanted. It's difficult to explain.'

'Not to me,' she said. 'I suppose it's what I'd hoped to hear. I'm glad you value your father – he deserves it.'

'There is just one thing,' he said ingenuously, suddenly, in spite of his manly confidence, looking very young. 'While I'm studying in London, may I live with you? I swear I wouldn't be a nuisance, or get into scrapes.'

'Did you think of this?'

'Yes. I – I thought it was time we got to know each other.'

470

'I know you,' she thought. 'Oh my beauty. I know you like my own heart beats.'

'Of course,' she said.

He gave a little sigh of relief.

'Well, I'd better let them know where I am. I walked out last night and caught a late train.'

Her eyes were hard and bright. She slapped the desk so that he jumped like the schoolboy he had been only a short while since.

'I'm sorry,' he said, 'I just lost my temper. Dad won't worry. He knows I'm not a fool.'

'That's as maybe. But his wife will worry. I can't stand unreliability. That's one of the reasons I fell in love with your father. He's like a rock. He sees his duty always, clearly. Too clearly sometimes for me.' She looked at him, her blue eyes fierce, 'Don't forget you are a Normanby. Not because they are aristocrats – but because most of them were rotten. Remember I won't be played around with. Don't ever lie to me. Don't ever keep me in the dark . . . and don't think of me as a – well, the sort of delicate woman who can't be told the truth. Come to me. I'm your mother – I'll help you every way I can – but don't expect me to make excuses for you, or to let you off the hook just because you're my son.' The temper fizzed out of her, leaving the small face a little sad. 'You'd better get on to your father and tell him where you are. Tell my secretary to get you a trunk call to his office.'

He did so eagerly and was told the call would take about half-an-hour. They settled down to wait.

She looked at her neat desk, picked a letter off the intray and dropped it. 'I can't work this morning,' she said helplessly. 'Why don't I take the morning off?'

'Well, why don't you?'

'I've never done such a thing in my life.'

'Never?' he said incredulously. 'Not even when you and Dad . . .' he stopped, the colour flooding up his cheeks. She tried to remember what it was like – being eighteen. Swinging from confidence to tongue-tied shyness. From sophistication to untried innocence. Was it the same for a boy?'

'No, not even then. We had so little time. That must make us seem a couple of cold fish.'

'Ah, no,' he said eagerly. 'No, not you – nor Dad.'

'We had about ten days together in France – then one or two weekends – perhaps three. You see, we were both workers.' She gave a shaky little smile, then said determinedly, 'But today I *will* take a day off. In fact, I'll take a holiday. When do you start at College?'

'In about three weeks.'

'That's a long time. Shall we have a holiday together? Where would you like to go?'

'To Paris,' he said at once. 'For my birthday.'

It seemed a long while before the call came through. Almost as though they were waiting for Henry's permission to begin life together. When it finally rang they both started, glanced at each other, and Margaret said, 'You speak to him, Tom. You're the one who ran away . . .'

He knew that she would never make excuses for him or try to cover up his mistakes – that her unswerving honesty would be as hard to live up to as Angela's hypocrisy. But he was glad. He knew where he was with her.

He lifted the receiver and said cautiously, 'It's Tom,' and Margaret heard the angry crackle over the wire and smiled.

'Yes, I know,' Tom said ruefully, 'Mama's already had a go at me. I'm sorry. I thought if anyone knew they wouldn't let me go, and there would be more scenes. Oh, yes, Steve knew, but swore to keep quiet. Dad, Mama says I can stay with her in London. If it's all right with you.' He paused, 'She'd like to speak with you.' He passed the telephone across the desk.

'Hello?' she said cautiously.

'Margaret?'

'Yes.'

'How are you?'

'I'm very well.'

How long since that last farewell? Eleven years. She had not seen him since.

'And you?'

'Yes. Very well. So you're having Tom while he's in London?'

'If you don't mind.'

'I'm glad.'

They sounded like two polite strangers. She thought, rebelliously, that she had been obeying the rules too long. Angela's rules – to protect Stephen. But it seemed that neither Stephen nor Tom required protection – or not that kind of protection.

'I'm going to Paris,' she said, 'buying for the Spring – then I'll take a holiday. May Tom come with me? We might go to Switzerland – and the Italian lakes. I'll have him back by the time his term begins.'

'I'd be delighted – it's time he widened his horizons. He's lucky to be going with you.'

'In Paris,' she said softly, 'we shall be staying at the Hotel Ventura Royale. I always stay there. They give me the same suite.'

Memories raced along a silence.

'Why don't you come over? For Tom's birthday?'

He burst out laughing as he always had at her effrontery.

'You are a bitch, Maggy Normanby,' he said, 'but I may very well do that.'

She put down the receiver and rose, twinkling, brilliant-eyed, put on her hat, adjusting it to an exact and perfect angle on her red hair. Slid the rich silken furs about her shoulders, smoothed pale grey gloves on to her hands. Tom watched with delight. She was more than just his mother – she was the quintessence of London, of fashion, of sophistication, of fun. She was like a blue, sparkling sea after the repressive backwater of Cliffs Edge.

'Come along,' she said. 'Shall we go shopping? You'll need some clothes. Have you evening clothes? We'll get you a suit for Paris . . .'

She would have him for a few precious years before that great smoke-blackened business in Thornsby claimed him for ever. They would get to know each other and enjoy each other, talk about Henry together and recreate the missing years.

He offered his arm and they went down into Hanover Street where her carriage was waiting. Marley smiled and touched his hat. Tom handed her in.

'You ought to get one of these motor cars, Mama,' he said. 'I've told Dad he ought to get one. Be in the swim.'

'A motor car?' she said, startled. 'Could you drive one of those things?'

'I don't see why not. I'd soon learn anyhow. You too.'

'Me? Will you teach me?'

'Of course. Just think – we could motor through Europe together.'

Margaret burst out laughing. She could almost smell the long, straight roads of France, with the poplars marching into the distance and the white dust blowing up behind the tyres, and she and Tom, gloved and goggled, driving adventurously together.

'What a *lark*!' she cried. 'What a great idea, Tom. We'll go and order one of these contraptions today.'

Marley shook up the reins and they moved off into the traffic delighted with each other and their gay holiday mood, and that after the years of separation they had found each other again.

Outstanding women's fiction in paperback from
Grafton Books

Mary E Pearce

The Land Endures	£1.95 ☐
Apple Tree Saga	£2.50 ☐
Polsinney Harbour	£1.95 ☐

Kathleen Winsor

Wanderers Eastward, Wanderers West (omnibus)	£3.95 ☐

Margaret Thomson Davis

The Breadmakers Saga	£2.95 ☐
A Baby Might Be Crying	£1.50 ☐
A Sort of Peace	£1.50 ☐

Helena Leigh

The Vintage Years 1: The Grapes of Paradise	£1.95 ☐
The Vintage Years 2: Wild Vines	£2.50 ☐
The Vintage Years 3: Kingdoms of the Vine	£1.95 ☐

Rebecca Brandewyne

Love, Cherish Me	£2.95 ☐
Rose of Rapture	£2.95 ☐
And Gold was Ours	£2.95 ☐

Pamela Jekel

Sea Star	£2.50 ☐

Chloe Gartner

Still Falls the Rain	£2.50 ☐

Nora Roberts

Promise Me Tomorrow	£2.50 ☐

Gloria Keverne

A Man Cannot Cry	£3.50 ☐

Josephine Edgar

Margaret Normanby	£2.95 ☐

To order direct from the publisher just tick the titles you want
and fill in the order form.

Outstanding fiction in paperback from Grafton Books

Nicola Thorne

A Woman Like Us	£1.25 ☐
The Perfect Wife and Mother	£1.50 ☐
The Daughters of the House	£2.50 ☐
Where the Rivers Meet	£2.50 ☐
Affairs of Love	£2.50 ☐
The Enchantress Saga	£3.95 ☐
Never Such Innocence	£2.95 ☐

Jacqueline Briskin

Paloverde	£2.50 ☐
Rich Friends	£2.50 ☐
Decade	£2.50 ☐
The Onyx	£3.50 ☐
Everything and More	£2.50 ☐

Barbara Taylor Bradford

A Woman of Substance	£3.50 ☐
Voice of the Heart	£3.50 ☐
Hold the Dream	£2.95 ☐

Alan Ebert and Janice Rotchstein

Traditions	£2.50 ☐

Marcelle Bernstein

Sadie	£2.50 ☐

To order direct from the publisher just tick the titles you want
and fill in the order form.   **GF1481**

Outstanding fiction in paperback from Grafton Books

Raymond Giles

Sabrehill	£2.50 ☐
Slaves of Sabrehill	£2.50 ☐
Rebels of Sabrehill	£2.50 ☐
Storm over Sabrehill	£2.50 ☐
Hellcat of Sabrehill	£2.50 ☐
Dark Master	£1.95 ☐
Rogue Black	£2.50 ☐

Edgar Mittelholzer

Children of Kaywana	£2.50 ☐
Kaywana Heritage	£2.50 ☐
Kaywana Stock	£2.50 ☐

To order direct from the publisher just tick the titles you want
and fill in the order form.

All these books are available at your local bookshop or newsagent, or can be ordered direct from the publisher.

To order direct from the publishers just tick the titles you want and fill in the form below.

Name _____

Address _____

_____

Send to:
Grafton Cash Sales
PO Box 11, Falmouth, Cornwall TR10 9EN.

Please enclose remittance to the value of the cover price plus:

UK 55p for the first book, 22p for the second book plus 14p per copy for each additional book ordered to a maximum charge of £1.75.

BFPO and Eire 55p for the first book, 22p for the second book plus 14p per copy for the next 7 books, thereafter 8p per book.

Overseas £1.25 for the first book and 31p for each additional book.